ƆNG OF SWORDS

OF THE DRACULA BROTHERS

BOOK THREE

ES

SONG OF SWORDS

SOUTH EASTERN
EUROPE
C. 1464
POLAND
HUNGARY
Transylvania
R. Danube
Posonium
Strigonium
Buda
R. Drave
Slavonia
R. Save
Agram
Adrian
Trieste
Venice
Pola
CROATIA
DALMATIA
Zara
Ravenna
R. Tiber
ROME
Naples
Benevento
Bari
Tarentum
Palermo
Messina
Catania
Syracuse
BOSNIA
SERVIA
Belgrade
Jaicza
Banialuka
Naissus
D. of St Saba
Trebinie
Ragusa
Cattaro
Budua
Duklea
Zenta
Scutari
Ochrida
Duraz
Kastoria
Butrinto
Ioannina
Thessaly
Nikopoli
D. Leukas
Arta
Rogos
Corinth
Megara
Athens
Modon
Coron
Misithra
Napoli
Monembasia
Candia
Crete
Rhodes
BULGARIA
ROUMELIA
Sardica
Phillippolis
Serrhae
Thessalonica
Hermanstadt
Segedin
Orsova
WALLACHIA
R. Danube
Silistria
Varna
Mesembria
Anchialos
Skopia
Vidin
St Vissend
Aidos
CONSTANTINOPLE
Hadrianople
Nikomedia
Aidia
Broussa
Angora
Smyrna
Maander R.
Ikonion
Tarsos
Antioch
BESSARABIA
MOLDAVIA
Jassy
R. Dniester
R. Dnieper
R. Don
R. Volga
Kaffa
Cherson
Sinopé
Amastris
Herakleia
Samsoun
Trebizond
Halys R.
Kars
Edessa
R. Tigris
R. Euphrates
Bagdad
Nikosia
Famagusta
K. CYPRUS
50
45
40
35
10
15
20
25
30
35
40
45
Greek
Latin Powers
Venetian
Knights of St John
Genoese
Independent Slaves
Magyar
Albania
Ottomans

CHAPTER 1

ELBISTAN, WINTER 1448

Sitting almost four thousand feet high between Anatolia's mountains, the Beylik of Dulkadir is no stranger to cold winters. Neither are its people, but the winter of 1448 holds the whole of Elbistan in a tight grip.

This is the coldest winter Sittişah has seen in her fourteen years. She skips from stone to stone on the path from the sarayi to the hammam under the red morning sky, watching her breath turn into steam as it hits the cold air. She laughs, and blows out loops of steam like she's smoking. White with frost, the dry grass crunches under her feet.

Winters are harder in Rumelia, they say. And longer. They have snow and ice, unlike here in Anatolia. But, snow or no snow, Sittişah loves winter in the Elbistan sarayi. The hot braziers glow with embers and soften the chill, the silver cups with sweet hot tea warm her fingers, and the fur-trimmed velvet kaftan brings out her lovely complexion. And then there's the hammam.

Since today is such a special day, Sittişah plans to spend her morning here, making herself extra pretty. Her sisters will do the same, of course, but they can't compare. Unless the sultan's messenger is blind — and she shouldn't be — they can't but notice Sittişah's sparkling green eyes and her splendid red curls. Everybody says she looks just like her mother did, fifteen years ago, when she caught Father's eye and became his favorite.

Not like her sisters are ugly — they are all Dulkadir princesses, born from the most beautiful women that Süleyman Bey's men could find him — but none of them has Sittişah's exuberant light. She's been her father's favorite since before she could walk, so he encouraged her antics and her attitude. He held her on his knees to play with her, his belly shaking with laughter, like he did with her brothers, but not with her sisters. Never.

Yesterday, he called her to his rooms.

Laying on his side on the green brocade pillows with his head in his hand, he measured her with his shrewd, narrow eyes as she kneeled to kiss his hand. "I have a suitor for you."

"For me?"

"For one of my daughters. And I can't think about anyone more worthy."

She fell on her knees to thank him. "Thank you, Father. I take it he's a suitor you approve of?"

Her father laughed so hard his belly shook like it had a life of its own. "Do I approve? There is none better. This is the best husband any girl could hope for. He's a catch like no other, and I hope you'll get him."

Sittişah bowed deeply, touching her forehead to the marble floor. "Thank you, Father. May I ask who that is?"

Her father looked left and right, then spoke so low she could barely hear him. "He's the future sultan of the Ottoman Empire. He's young and handsome and has an amazing future ahead of him. His name is Mehmed."

Sittişah bowed again. "Thank you, Father. I am not worthy."

"I hope you are. But of course, it's not up to you. Not up to me, either. His envoy arrives tomorrow to check my daughters and she'll choose one."

"She? He won't be coming?"

Father choked with laughter. "Are you out of your mind? What business would another man have inside my sarayi? Of course not. The wife of Hizar Paşa, the Governor of Anatolia, will choose one of you."

"Did he send her?"

Father laughed again. "No way. The sultan did. I don't think anyone told Mehmed he's getting married. Not yet. He'll be told when necessary, like I should have done with you. But I can't help having a weakness for you, since you remind me so much of your mother, Allah in Heaven keep her safe. Make yourself as pretty and gentle as you can. Men like pretty women, but even more, they want them soft and docile. And no matter how you wrap me around your pretty little finger, we both know you're anything but that. You're a hellcat, just like your mother, but it would serve you well to hide that tomorrow. Be soft and meek if you want to become validé."

Sittişah bowed deeply. "Thank you, Father. I can't wait to obey you as always. May I ask a question?"

"Go ahead."

"Is the... is Mehmed impaired in some way?"

Father laughed so hard he had to hold on to his belly, then wiped his eyes. "He's strong and handsome. He received the Sword of Osman when he was twelve and has already been a sultan for two years. He's the handsomest husband a girl could hope for."

"One more question, Father, if you'd allow. Does he have wives?"

Her father looked at her in sadness. "Nobody is perfect, are they? He's seventeen. He's got one wife, some Albanian slave who bore him a son. And a bunch of concubines, of course. One or two of them heavy with child. But what does that have to do with anything?"

"I understand. Thank you, Father."

"Good. Remember that people die. Even in the enlightened Ottoman Empire, less than half of all kids live to be five. You can be validé, with Allah's blessing, as long as you give Mehmed a son. But first, Hizar Paşa's wife has to choose you instead of your sisters."

Sittişah kissed her father's hand and left, deciding to become the prettiest, softest, and most humble girl in the sarayi for the sultan's ambassador.

That was yesterday. Last night she was too excited to sleep, so this morning she got up early and headed to the hammam at the first light of dawn, expecting to be first. Nope. Three of her sisters are already there, chatting and laughing and splashing each other, but they fall quiet as soon as they see her.

She sighs and lies on the warm marble slab, wondering who tipped them.

"Good to see you all."

They nod, then ignore her to chat with each other. They don't like her much, since she's been Father's favorite ever since her mother died at birth, and Sittişah pays them in kind. They're all dark and stupid, and bow to their mothers and their brothers. But Sittişah is a princess, and she was brought up by slaves, who are inferior and deserve to be treated as such.

But today is different. She needs to remember to be meek and kind. What bull. But it is what it is.

She glances left at Atiye, her elder half-sister, who looks away. She doesn't want to talk to Sittişah, but that doesn't bother her one bit. "How lovely to see you here so early. How come?"

"I had trouble sleeping. How about you?"

Sittişah smiles. "Somebody spilled the news. Have you heard about Mehmed?"

Atiye shrugs. "Who hasn't?"

"Apparently, he's looking for a wife. The sultan thinks he needs a strong, outspoken girl to help him out of his shell. He's terribly shy, they say. And he doesn't like pretty girls."

"Why not?"

"They intimidate him. That's why they're looking for a plain, strong-willed girl who'll let him shine." Sittişah rests her head against the marble and closes her eyes.

"Really? How do you know this?"

Sittişah smiles. "Father told me. 'Look plain but determined,' he said. 'The sultan's envoy is looking for the perfect bride, and she's neither too pretty nor shy. If you want him, you'd better look the part.'"

Atiye nods and closes her eyes, and Sittişah turns to her younger sister, Bensu.

"Lovely to see you here so early. How come?"

Bensu is only eleven, and she hasn't yet had her first blood. She looks up at Sittişah as a role model. They've never been rivals till now — and she doesn't even know it.

"Mother sent me. She said I need to get pretty and look good, since there's a suitor for one of us today. I didn't think I was ready for a suitor, but Mother knows best."

"Sure she does. You'll have to look young and innocent. That's what they're looking for. A very young virgin. You'll look the part better than any of us."

"But... Don't you want him for yourself?"

Sittişah laughs. "Are you crazy? Why would I want a husband? To tell me what to do and how and when? I'm happy here. I can do whatever I want, and Father is always kind to me. I don't want to go away. I want to stay here forever."

Bensu nods, and Sittişah sighs and closes her eyes. This silly little girl doesn't know there's no other purpose for a woman than to get married and have sons. For a woman, that's the only path to success. And if you give birth to a şehzade, then you've done it right. The only thing better than being a sultan's wife is being a sultan's mother. That will take many years and lots of work, but she'll do it. She'll get Mehmed. She'll marry him and have his son, whether or not he likes it.

CHAPTER 2
THE CHOSEN ONE

The banquet room of the Elbistan sarayi is so quiet you'd think it's deserted, but you'd be mistaken. The largest room in the sarayi is packed with Süleyman Bey's daughters, their mothers, their grandmother, and any servant who found an excuse to squeeze in.

The girls sit quietly on brightly colored pillows, waiting for Hizir Paşa's wife. She's late, as befits a woman of her stature carrying out a monumental task. Choosing the wife of the Ottoman Empire's future sultan and a mother for the next şehzade is a responsibility few can brag about.

This is not the first time an Ottoman sultan looked at the Dulkadir dynasty to find a wife. Dulkadir may be small compared to the Ottoman Empire, but they are a noble family, rich in horses and horsemen, and they've always been Sultan Murad the Second's strongest allies against the Karamanids, may Allah strike them all like the unfaithful dogs they are. Sultan Murad's own mother, Emine Validé, was a Dulkadir princess, Nasreddin Mehmed Bey's daughter. But that was fifty years ago, and it doesn't make today's event any less memorable.

Sittişah rolls her shoulders and shifts her weight to relieve the numbness of her bottom, hoping the sultan's envoy arrives soon. She glances at the women in the packed room, astonished at how they sit unmoving like they're dead. But even more amazing is the silence. Usually, the sarayi is a cacophony of song, laughter, and screaming fights between the kids. Sometimes even the women. But today they're all like mutes.

Her eyelids get droopy when heavy steps outside startle her. These can't be the envoy's steps — a woman's little silk shoes don't make that much noise. This must be Father, she thinks, just as he enters with a short woman in tow. Her fluttering veils make her look like a sailing ship.

"Thank you for honoring our humble home," Father says, pointing at the luxurious display of rich velvets, brocades, and Chinese silks, at the sparkling jewels embellishing the women's necks and ears, and at the women themselves, all beautiful, all his: wives, concubines, daughters, slaves. He's proud of us, Sittişah thinks, struggling not to laugh when Father winks at her.

"These are my daughters, all faithful girls, and lovers of Allah's word. They all can read the Quran, sew, draw and sing. Their mothers taught them to be humble and respectful toward their husband like they are to their father and to Allah, may his name forever frighten the infidels. Nowhere on earth will you find a better wife for our future sultan."

The sultan's envoy bows, as expected, and Father leaves to let the women talk. The woman takes off her hijab, uncovering jet-black hair richly braided with gold, emeralds, and rubies that make her full-moon face even plainer. She's not pretty or young, the messenger, but she's powerful. Her choice will forever change someone's life, and Sittişah hopes it will be her.

"Sit, please. You must be tired, hungry and thirsty after your long trip. I trust you traveled well?" Grandmother, the mistress of Sittişah's father's sarayi, claps her hands, and servants carrying heavy silver trays loaded with deliciousness appear out of thin air. Luscious dark olives shining like black pearls cuddle to squares of sweet white cheese and crusty golden bread and red pomegranates and sweet cataifs and baklava dripping with golden honey.

The platters get set in the middle for everyone to share, and Sittişah's mouth waters. With all the preparations, she's been too excited to eat, but this is not the time to look greedy. With the corner of her eye, she watches Atiye grab an olive without waiting for the guest to start. She's trying to show she's determined and independent, Sittişah thinks, keeping her hands crossed in her lap and her eyes cast down.

Grandma glares at Atiye, but the girl ignores her and leans to grab a baklava. Sittişah bites her lip so not to laugh. Grandma shrugs and helps herself, opening the way for everyone to do the same.

The guest sips on her chilled lemon sherbet, studying the girls over the rim of her cup. It shouldn't be hard, Sittişah thinks. Atiye has already made a blunder. She also made herself as plain as can be, with her unadorned olive skin and her hair pulled in a plain braid. Even her clothes are drab and ill-suiting, an off-white chemise topped with a kaftan the color of burned earth that doesn't help her complexion.

Her eyes so wide the white shows all around them and her mouth half open, little Bensu looks even younger than she is, staring at the visitor like she expects her to produce a rabbit out of her ear. Only Devlet, her oldest sister, is a real competition. But she's old, almost eighteen, and she's more interested in the Quran than she is in marriage. Devlet refused both men who asked for her, and Father agreed, since he had higher hopes for her. But there's nothing higher than the future sultan — unless it's the present sultan, and that one's old and very married. Devlet is delicate and beautiful, with a smooth skin like golden honey, eyes like the night sky and a voice like the soft murmur of water. Sittişah wishes she was ugly and mean, but she's not. Oh well. It's up to Allah.

Finally sated, the visitor thanks Grandma, then turns to Bensu. "What's your name?"

Bensu's cheeks catch fire as she stutters to answer.

"Bensu," Atiya says. "She's eleven."

The visitor glances at her without smiling. "Thank you. I was asking her. Would you like to get married, Bensu?"

Bensu's eyes grow even wider. She sobs, and fat tears run down her childish cheeks. Sittişah puts her arm around her, then wipes her tears with her own embroidered handkerchief.

One down. Two to go.

"What's your name, pretty girl?"

Sittişah hides her smile. This morning's work paid off. Her flame-red curls fall over her shoulders to her waist and her green eyes darkened with kohl sparkle like emeralds. The beet juice she stained her lips and cheeks with didn't hurt, either.

"I'm Sittişah, my lady."

"How old are you?"

"I'm fourteen."

"Would you like to get married?"

Sittişah struggles to blush. "I'd like to do whatever Father says. And the sultan."

The visitor smiles, then turns to Devlet, who seems deep in thought. "And you? What is your name?"

"I'm Devlet. I'm seventeen."

"Seventeen? How come you aren't married yet?"

"The men who asked for me weren't suitable, Father said. And there was no hurry."

"Would you like to get married?"

"Maybe. It depends."

"On what?"

"On the man."

"What are you looking for in a husband, Devlet?"

"I'd like him to be a man of faith. Kind, wise, and patient."

"We'd all like that in our husbands. But it's Allah's choice, since we don't get to know our husbands before our marriage."

"Is Prince Mehmed like that?"

The visitor stops to think. "I've never met Prince Mehmed, but I know he's handsome and brave. And he's had the best education the Ottoman Empire could provide."

"Does he have other wives?" Atiye asks.

The visitor studies her. "What's your name, young lady?"

"Atiye. I'm fifteen."

"The answer is yes. He has a wife, Gülbahar, and a son, Bayezid. And plenty of concubines. His wife will have to fit in his harem and get along with the others. A wife's job is to keep peace in her husband's home. The men are busy with more important things, so the women must get along."

Her hands demurely crossed in her lap, Sittişah nods. *I'll take care of that. I'll teach them to get along.*

"What are your special talents, young ladies? What are the things you most enjoy doing?"

"I love nothing better than reading the Quran," Devlet answers. "I'd be happy to do that day and night."

"I love playing ball," Bensu says. "I'm good at it, too. I'm the best, even though I'm the smallest."

"I enjoy running the house. I like ordering the servants and planning the meals and making things happen," Atiye said.

"How about you, Sittişah?"

"There's nothing I love more than spending time with Father to bring him solace, show him love, and help him rest after a rough day. Whenever I can make him laugh, I'm happy."

The visitor smiles. "Lovely ladies you have here," she tells Grandmother. "All beautiful and wise beyond their age. I wish I could take them all."

"You'd leave us poor. They are the treasures of my son's sarayi, and we can't part with all of them. So, which one will it be?"

"I'll choose the one I know Mehmed will love. She'll bring light to his home and solace to his nights."

From the deep folds of her kaftan, she takes out a ring with an emerald as big as an egg, like none of them has ever seen. In the silence of frozen breaths, she kisses Sittişah's eyes and slips the ring on her finger.

"Congratulations, Sittişah. You'll be the wife of our future sultan."

EDIRNE, SPRING 1449

Edirne Palace is all dressed up for spring. A profusion of green buds brought new life to the old plane tree. The soft evening is fragrant with the scent of daffodils and pink hyacinths, and throbs with the thrills of turtle-doves. A couple of woodpeckers keep the rhythm, and Ali can't help but smile.

As the sun goes down, the palace towers, the old trees, and the delicate fountains throw long shadows across the inner courtyard. Right in its middle, two twisted shadows lick the ground, dueling as fiercely as their owners.

Their shiny curved blades, wide at the tip, sparkle and sing as they clash. They clatter, clang, and bang as they cross and re-cross while the two men look for each other's soft spots but meet only hard steel. The song of swords reverberates against the stone walls, and one by one, people gather to watch: a servant carrying a tower of platters to the kitchens; a stable boy walking the sultan's horse; a red-clad janissary returning from the dungeons; a young eunuch carrying a silver tray loaded with delicacies. They gawk but keep away from the scuffle, watching the two sweaty men try to kill each other. They hadn't see a fight like this here since Sultan Mehmed used to train in the courtyard.

But he's been gone to Manisa for years, and none of the fighters look like him.

The blond one lunges and slips. The dark one twists and thrusts his kilij towards his adversary's unprotected belly, but the first one recovers and counters with a cut from below, meeting the other blade with his own and forcing it away. The dark fighter stumbles and the blond one's sword reaches for his throat. But the dark man kicks the blond's feet from under him, and they crash to the ground. The blond fighter rolls, but the dark one's even faster. He twists like a snake and touches the other one's chest with the tip of his kilij.

"You give up?"

"I do."

They help each other up and leave together as the crowd watches.

"Who are they?" the janissary asks.

He's got to be new, Ali thinks. He must be coming from Anatolia if he doesn't know the men of the day. "The Wallachian princes. The Dracula brothers," Ali says. "Vlad and Radu."

"They sure know how to fight. I thought they'd kill each other a hundred times."

"Someday they will," Ali says, heading back to the sarayi where she belongs.

She sets down the tray in front of Mara's door and knocks their special knock.

"Come in."

The deep, accented voice melts Ali's insides. She slips in and bolts the door.

Mara smiles. Between the ivory silk sheets, her golden skin shines like sun-warmed honey, and her curvy body warms Ali's heart. "Come," Mara says.

Ali unties the string holding up her blue shalwars and crawls under the sheets. Her hungry hands can't get enough of Mara's golden curves, and her mouth hungers for her taste. She inhales her scent of sandalwood, lavender, and spice, happier to be here than anywhere else on earth. She suffers the beautiful pain of Mara's mouth turning her inside out as her skilled tongue explores parts of Ali no one else has ever touched. She never knew they could bring such pleasure — not before Mara.

She tried to resist as long as she could. She pretended she didn't care, and ignored the voice inside her that told her that Mara is joy, Mara is beauty, Mara is love.

Until the day she failed.

She fell into Mara's bed and exposed herself for the fraud that she was: a eunuch that's not even a eunuch. Just a girl with a secret.

Mara explored her like a navigator cruising unknown seas for new land. She inspected every spot, felt every curve, kissed every crease. She touched her everywhere and tasted things Ali never knew should be tasted. She brought Ali to a joy she didn't know existed. And, after she turned her inside out, she smiled.

"Why?" she asked.

Ali fumbled. "I'm not a eunuch."

"Of course not. You're a girl. I knew that. I'm not interested in eunuchs. But why? Why pretend to be a eunuch?"

"I... my mother sold me. I wasn't that pretty, so she thought she'd get more for me if people thought I was a eunuch. She had a friend help her with the... modification. And she sold me as such."

Mara looked at her, her golden-brown eyes melting with pity.

"That's even worse than my father. Serbia's despot sold me as a woman, for whatever good that did him. I don't think he got what he bargained for — nor do I care. I hope he rots in hell someday, that bastard. To keep Serbia's throne, he sold me. Now I'm locked in Murad's harem, the man who blinded my brothers for plotting against him, and my father struggles for his throne. He still expects me to help him after screwing me up. But that's life, isn't it?"

But that was long ago. At first, Ali worried that Mara would betray her, but she didn't. She even covered for her, as her growing body became harder to hide. She helped her through many tough spots and gave her more love and trust than Ali deserved.

Because Ali lied, of course. Her mother didn't make her a eunuch.

Her mother knows nothing about this, since Ali ran away long ago. She came to the Ottoman court with her friends Ion and Codru to spy for Hunyadi, Transylvania's voivode, and send home information.

But when Codru's werewolf curse caught up with him, he had no choice but to run. Then Ion's brilliance caught the sultan's eye, and Murad sent him to Wallachia to help Vlad Dracula take his father's throne from Vladislav the Second, the usurper.

That's how Ali was left all alone, a Transylvanian spy at the Ottoman court. Nobody here knows her mission, and that's good, because if anyone finds out, Ali's life is worth less than last winter's snow.

CHAPTER 4
THE DRACULA BROTHERS

Vlad's new quarters at the Edirne castle are worthy of his rank in the Ottoman army. Just like his brother Radu, he gets an officer's salary and special accommodations: large rooms, rich carpets, beautiful weapons. Nothing changed since October, when he went home to take Wallachia's throne. And still, everything did.

He looks around and shakes his head. "I can't believe I'm back to this," he says, pouring wine into two cups and handing one to Radu, who sits cross-legged on a pillow. "After just a few months. It all went smooth as butter when I left. The Royal Court of Târgoviște was all but deserted when I got there. They opened the gates, and I just walked in and sat on the throne. Nobody even tried to stop me. It was like walking into an empty house. And now I'm back here, a beggar again. How can that be?"

Radu takes a sip. It's good wine, a Wallachian red from Dealu Mare, near home. He seldom drinks, since he eats with the troops, and they serve no wine, since Allah doesn't approve of it. But he remembers it from back home. That's what they drank ever since he was old enough to hold a cup.

"Where did you get this wine?" he asks.

"I brought it from Târgoviște. I grabbed a few barrels from Father's cellar, since I couldn't bring myself to let it go to waste."

"So you weren't in that much of a hurry?"

"Not at all. The vice-governor of Transylvania sent me a letter inviting me there to talk. He told me that Vladislav was returning with whatever he had left of his army after Kosovo Polje, so I had plenty of time to get ready."

"Ready for what?"

Vlad shrugs. "For whatever. To fight or to flee."

"Did you fight?"

Vlad shakes his head. "I didn't."

"Why not?"

Vlad sighs. "I didn't have my own army. I only had the sultan's men, who didn't care what happened. And the Wallachians didn't either. That's what hurt the most: our people didn't bother to welcome me. It's like they said to themselves 'Oh, boy. Another voivode. How long will this one last?' They didn't give a hoot. I'd hoped they'd welcome me with open arms, like the savior I planned to be. But they didn't care, so I didn't see the point of fighting."

"What did you do?"

"I loaded my carts with whatever looked valuable and headed south. Even then, I still hoped our people would beg me to stay, but they didn't. They didn't even bother to watch me leave. It was like Father never reigned. Nobody cared."

"But you're not Father. And you've been gone from there forever. They probably didn't even know who you were."

"Oh, they knew it all right. 'That's Vlad Dracul's son,' one said. 'Really? I heard they blinded him and buried him alive,' a woman answered. 'Not that one. That was Mircea, his older brother.' The woman glanced at me and said, 'Well, I hope they don't do the same to this one. He's just a kid.'" Vlad drains his cup.

"And you know what, Radu? That woman's words chilled me to the bone. Of course, I knew I could end up dead, but that? Blinded and buried alive? I can't do that. I don't know how anyone can do that. Our brother Mircea was a better soldier than me, and brave and strong, but I don't know how he could take that. Just the thought of it turns my stomach."

"Mine too."

"So why stay here and wait for Vladislav to torment me when our people don't even care, I thought? Vladislav tortured Mircea and killed father, and he'd do it again. He and those two-faced boyars. I was alone but for the janissaries who didn't care if I lived or died, so I fled. I was so terrified I almost shat my pants."

"Of course you were. Anyone would have been."

"I shouldn't have been. Now I'm so ashamed I can barely live with myself. I should have fought, but I didn't. I didn't even try. Now I'm drowning in sorrow and shame. I swore to avenge Father and Mircea, but I ran away like a coward instead. I didn't even look for their bodies to have them blessed and buried in our Orthodox faith."

Vlad's sunken eyes burn, and his voice breaks. He's so distraught that Radu can't help but feel sorry for him. Vlad has never doubted himself before.

"You did better than I would have, brother. I couldn't have done as much as you did."

Vlad shakes his head in dismissal. "But it's not over. It's never over till it's over. I'll return to avenge our father and our brother. I swear to God I'll kill Vladislav with my own two hands, and I'll make those boyars feel sorry they were ever born. Mark my words: I will keep my oath and avenge our kin. And free our people, God willing."

That's the Vlad Radu knows, bursting with hate, rage, and fire. Good. He's back to normal. Thank God. He lifts his cup: "To victory."

"To victory."

"What will you do?"

"I'll find a way to go back. Sooner or later, Vladislav will fumble. With a smidgen of luck, old Hunyadi will perish under the Serbian's sword. You know Đurađ Branković locked him in Smederevo?"

"I've heard. But won't he buy his way out?"

"Maybe. But this time the old despot has got him by the short hairs. He demands that Hunyadi's son marries his granddaughter, and he wants back every corner of Serbia he's ever occupied. Also a monstrous ransom and some things that aren't Hunyadi's to give. If Hungary's diet doesn't come through, he'll hand Hunyadi to the sultan. They'll end up cutting a deal, but that won't look good for Hunyadi. He's past his prime, while the sultan is on the rise."

He refills the cups and looks at Radu. "But enough about me. How are you, brother?"

"I'm hanging on."

"You've grown so much! And I can't believe your fighting skills. You almost got me a couple of times. I remember when you couldn't even hold a sword, and look at you now all grown up."

Radu shrugs. "I'm almost fifteen, and I'm an officer, like you. Prince or not, they wouldn't have me unless I was worthy. Sword fight, archery practice, strategy lessons — you know the drill. I do my best, but it's not my thing. I'd much rather sing or write poetry."

"What for?"

Radu glances at Vlad to see if he's kidding, but he's not. Not being snarky either. He just doesn't get it.

"Poetry is about beautiful things. And feelings. It brings beauty to the world."

"And what's the point of that?"

Radu laughs. "Don't you care for beauty?"

Vlad smiles. "I like well-endowed women."

"How about sunsets and flowers and birds?"

"I like a chicken, if it's well cooked."

Radu laughs, and Vlad does too. They empty their cups again, glad they can finally talk to each other like brothers, even though they're so different. They're all that's left of the House of Dracula. Wallachia's blood flows through them, and their father's legacy weighs on them both as they live in this country not their own.

Radu cherishes it, but he knows Vlad hates it. He'd rather be back in Wallachia, riding his horse and bloodying his sword. Sooner or later, he will, Radu thinks, glad it won't be him.

"How's your friend Ali?" Vlad asks.

"He's... he's OK. He gets along well with Mara. He seems happy."

"Tell him I want to see him to tell him about his friend Isa."

"What happened to Isa?"

"He left."

"Where?"

"He didn't want to return to Edirne. He said he's been a slave for too long. He sailed to Constantinople instead."

CHAPTER 5

CONSTANTINOPLE, SPRING 1449

Spring has come to the Polis, and the thousand year old cradle of the Orthodox Christian faith bursts with new life. Some say it's the richest city in the world. Some say it's the most beautiful. And they're right, Ion thinks.

His eager eyes take in Hagia Sophia, the gilded cathedral that has sheltered the Crown of Thorns and the True Cross, then turn to the magnificent Imperial Palace and the University of Constantinople, whose library of over ten thousand tomes include everything that was left from the legendary Library of Alexandria.

Still, the city's most famous monuments are its Theodosian Walls: four miles of double walls separated by a killing field and surrounded by a sixty foot wide, thirty foot deep moat. For a millennium, these walls have protected Constantinople through twenty-three assaults without ever breaking down. The Theodosian Walls are the shield of Eastern Christianity.

But no one cares about them now, since they're safe, and busy having fun. Children scream, women laugh, and countless street merchants sing praises to their offerings: silver fish straight from the Bosporus, so fresh they're trying to jump back; long-grained white rice;

fat sheep dressed in thick wool; cheap wine by the barrel; fragrant pink hyacinth and lacy honeysuckle. Heavy carts thunder downhill, their wooden wheels rattling over the uneven cobblestones. The warm breeze is heavy with smells, from mouthwatering hot bread to holy incense and donkey dung. The place is so alive it makes Ion feel livelier too, more than he did in Edirne, and even back home in Transylvania.

He rechecks the scrap of paper with the map. It's got to be the second street on the left. The yellow house.

The armed guards watching the gate glance at him with bored eyes, then look away. No wonder. His clothes have seen better days, and they aren't even his. He didn't think a janissary uniform would serve him well in Constantinople; that's why, as soon as he disembarked the ship from Braila, he went to the bazar and traded it for some paper-pusher's musky garb. The merchant smirked, thinking he'd conned him, but Ion was delighted to exchange his flashy red turban for some nondescript rags nobody would notice. He looks just like any of the harried Romans scurrying along the crowded streets, except he's not walking. He stands in front of the yellow house looking like a palace, and the guards don't like it one bit. Oh well.

He bows politely and asks in Greek: "Mr. Notaras, will he see me?"

The men glance at each other and burst into laughter. "Who are you?"

"I'm Isa from Edirne. I came to see the megas doux with business from Vlad Dracula, the Voivode of Wallachia."

The guards laugh even harder. "Really? You're the best one he could send?"

Ion takes out the sealed firman Vlad gave him. It looks official, and it is — it's sealed with the red wax Wallachian Eagle carrying the cross in his beak. The seal is untouched, just like Vlad gave it to him months ago.

"There you go," Vlad had said. "I don't know if it will help you, but that's the best I can do. It says inside that you are my trusted advisor, and I urge them to respect and trust you. I hope it helps you. Still, are you sure you don't want to return to Edirne with me? The sultan said that you had a great future in his administration. And Ali must miss you."

"I'm sure. I've been enslaved for too long. I need to spread my wings and find my way. God knows if I make it or not, but I must take my chances. Thank you, my voivode."

Vlad had looked upon him with kindness, which didn't come easy to him. But over the months they had spent together untangling the troublesome politics of two greedy empires, and wondering how Wallachia's meager treasury could fund her freedom, they had grown to respect each other. Vlad came to recognize Ion's quiet competence. Ion realized Vlad was a force of nature, like earthquakes, blizzards, and floods, and learned to respect his strength. Being with Vlad taught him a lot about princes. Worthy lesson, though seldom fun.

But that was then, and this is now.

Ion watches the soldiers study the seal. They touch it with their dirty fingers to make sure it's real, then shrug. One heads inside to ask for instructions.

"My firman, please?"

The other guard hands it back. Ion replaces it inside his sleeve, wondering what to do if this doesn't work out.

He's been in Constantinople for months, struggling to make ends meet. He unloaded ships, laid bricks, and made bread. All good things and worthy, but he knows he can do better. Unlike most workers, he can speak, read and write in Romanian, Greek, Ottoman language, and Latin; he can read maps and use a bow and a sword. But more than anything, he can play with numbers like it's nobody's business. Numbers speak to him; he can add, subtract and multiply like he breathes. Just like Vlad shoots arrows, Ali reads people's minds, and Codru fights. It's a gift he shouldn't waste.

The other day, his boss tried to calculate how many bricks to order for a complicated building. Ion told him the number. The man laughed at him and kept at it. Half an hour later, he stared at Ion like he'd fallen out of the sky.

"You're right. How did you know?"

"I calculated."

"How?"

"I don't know. It just comes to me."

The man stared at him with newfound respect. "If so, your future is not in laying bricks, my man. You must make the most of your talent, and bricklaying isn't it. Why don't you go see Lukas Notaras? The megas doux is the head of the treasury and one of the emperor's most important men. That Greek is smarter than a fox and meaner than a pit viper, but he could use someone with your talents to look after the empire's treasury. It's said to be in terrible shape, despite all the taxes that we, the humble people, pay. The emperor, the patriarch, and Notaras must have some way to cover their expenses. Go find him and see if he'll take you."

That's why Ion is here this morning, amusing the guards, instead of on his knees, laying bricks. Being dressed better would help, but laying bricks doesn't pay much, and he'd rather eat than look good.

The guard returns and opens the gate. He leads him down a narrow stone path winding through the well-kept garden to the palatial yellow house. This isn't the gilded Edirne Palace, but it looks more luxurious than Târgoviște's Royal Court, which is nothing but cold gray stone.

The guard opens the door to a large room crammed with icons and candles. But for the long dark table, you'd think it's a church. A hoard of dark skinny saints, their golden auras stuck to their heads in improbable angles, point their fingers to the sky. They remind Ion of his village church, and his heart cries with longing for his family. For a moment, he wishes he went home instead of coming to Constantinople. But he remembers his oath, his mission, and his friends. It's not over yet. There's work to be done before he can rest; that's why he's here.

The man perusing a heavy leather-bound tome full of numbers at the head of the table is dressed like a king. He glimmers in silk, brocade, and gold, and his mantle is trimmed with white fox. But he's neither smiling nor handsome. A lock of greasy hair falls over his narrow, shrewd eyes that measure Ion from head to toes and find him falling short.

"Who are you?"

"The Ottomans call me Isa, but my birth name is Ion. I worked in Sultan Murad's tax office in Edirne, then I was Wallachia's voivode's special advisor."

"Which one? There's more of them than stray cats."

"Vlad the Third. Vlad Dracul's son."

"Didn't he die with his father?"

"That was his older brother, Mircea."

"But the voivode is Vladislav. Hunyadi put him there."

"Indeed. That's why Vlad the Third left and returned to Edirne."

"Sure he did. He's the sultan's pawn. So why aren't you in Edirne with him?"

"I got tired of being a slave, so I asked his permission to leave. He agreed."

For the first time, the megas doux's eyes sparkle with interest. "Really? So what can you do for me?"

"I'm good with numbers. I can look after your treasury and ensure that your expenses match your income. I can tell you what you're missing out on and where you should trim your expenses to do well. I can tell you if anything is amiss and how to fix it."

Notaras laughs. "Is that so? Then tell me what's wrong here." He shoves the heavy book to the end of the table where Ion stands, leans back in his chair, and crosses his arms across his chest.

Ion leans over the book, checking the long columns of numbers headed in Greek: Household expenses, kitchens, weapons, emperor's retinue, stables. He takes them in one by one, calculating as he goes down to the totals, then slides the book back to Notaras. "You missed the unmarked ten thousand ducats for the emperor's retinue. Maybe an expense he didn't want made public. A mistress? Or a spy?"

Lukas Notaras' face darkens. He goes back to checking number after number, counting on his fingers and taking notes. When he's done, he lifts his eyes to Ion. "How did you do this?"

"I don't know. Numbers speak to me. I just look at them and I know."

The megas doux measures him, then glances back at his records. "How do I know I can trust you?"

"You've seen my firman."

"But that's from an Ottoman pawn. How do I know you're not a spy they want to plant in the heart of Constantinople?"

"Didn't the Ottomans help Emperor Constantine get the throne against his brothers? Do you also have doubts about him?"

"Constantine is the Byzantine emperor. You're just a... someone looking for a job."

"True. On the other hand, how do I know that those ten thousand ducats were really used by the emperor instead of going into someone else's coffers?"

Notaras gasps.

"We both have to take risks. You, with my allegiance. Me, with your honesty. I don't want a master I can't trust. The last thing I need is to be someone's scapegoat. But I don't know you, and you don't know me. We both have to take chances."

The megas doux measures him again. His narrow eyes are shrouded, and his mouth narrowed to a line. "When can you start?"

CHAPTER 6

TRANSYLVANIA, JULY 1449

Hidden in the shadow of the mountains, the quiet Bran monastery is a place of faith and prayer for the nuns. Few travelers ever stop by, even though the monastery isn't far from the major way that joins Transylvania and Wallachia, and the road from Brasov to Târgoviște is always busy. Heavy carts loaded with grains, salt, and fish screech their wheels, heading up north. They return hauling timber, sheep skins, cheese, and honey. Lone messengers spur their dusty horses from Hungary to Wallachia and back. Units of tired soldiers cross the border back and forth, bringing havoc, tears, and destruction, and sometimes bringing help.

But the tiny monastery with its roof so sharp it sheds the snow, thick stone walls, and wooden gates reinforced with steel is out of the way, so the twenty-two nuns living here seldom see any of that. They live a modest life of prayer and contemplation where silence is a virtue. Busy mouths make for idle hands, Mother Superior says. That's why the only things breaking the silence are the wind, the rain, and the bell calling for prayer.

The shadows grow long, then blend into darkness. The sisters recite their evening prayers, then shuffle to their white-washed cells with narrow cots and rugs they weaved themselves to spend the night. Nights here are short, since the bell rings before dawn to call them to pray and serve the Lord and Mother Mary, the patron of their humble church.

Lena sheds her wooden clogs to climb into her bed, then remembers she forgot the laundry. The evening sky was heavy, hinting of rain, so she'd better go get it now that it's dry.

She grabs a wicker basket and heads to the yard. The white linens, whipped by the wind, flutter like flags. She's almost done when she hears the horses. There's got to be a dozen of them, she thinks, feeling the earth shudder under their hooves.

An impatient hand rings the bell by the gate. The sharp sound sends an icy shiver down Lena's spine. Whoever's at the gate has no time and no patience.

The knocks start as she heads to tell the Mother Superior. And they're not just someone's fingers rapping; it's someone knocking with the hilt of their sword or the heels of their boots.

A flickering candle, and Mother Superior emerges from the darkness, invisible but for the white trim of her black garb and the tired face lit by the candle. "Who is it?"

"Messengers from Vladislav, the Voivode of Wallachia. Let us in."

"What for?"

"We need to talk."

"Talk then."

"Not through the gate?"

"Then come back tomorrow."

"We were sent by the Voivode of Wallachia. He donated hundreds of ducats to your coffers, remember?"

"He was most generous, and our poor are most grateful. Now, if there's nothing else, I'll see you tomorrow."

"Open the gate."

Mother Superior laughs. In the entire year she's spent here, Lena hasn't yet heard her laugh, and she's not sorry. She shudders and hugs herself, hiding in the shadow of the eaves.

"Not in a hundred years. I don't know who you are or what you want. For all that I know, you're a bunch of Ottoman marauders coming to steal the monastery's treasure and take us all into slavery. It wouldn't be the first time a bunch of outlaws pillaged a Holy Monastery. If you're even thinking about breaking down the gates, don't. They're reinforced with steel plates and unbreakable. And if I ring the church bell in the middle of the night, every man, woman, and child in seven villages will rush to our help."

"Listen, woman. We have no business with you, your treasure, or your sisters. The Voivode of Wallachia sent us to get the child you have in your care. Give him to us and we'll be on our way."

The Mother Superior goes quiet, and Lena's heart stops beating.

"What child?"

"Come on! We know he's been there for almost a year. Voivode Vladislav is trying to help you. He'll care for him much better than you can."

"Supposing we had a child here — though I can't imagine who could have told you so — what does Vladislav want him for?"

"He's... he's the son of his friend. He wants to help care for him."

Mother Superior laughs again. "He's most generous, Vladislav. But we can't help him. We have no child."

"You're lying. A nun like you shouldn't be lying. God won't like that."

"God won't like your lies, either. Nor your plan to harm an innocent child. I have no child for you. Go in peace and don't come back."

"Listen, woman. Don't forget how generous the voivode has been to you. Very generous. He'll change his mind if you don't help us."

"I wouldn't expect any less from a man of his stature. Go now, or I'll ring the bell to round the villagers. Now, I said."

A string of curses, and a clatter of hooves as the men ride away. Mother Superior waits for the noise to die down, then turns to Lena. Her face is whiter than the moon peeking through the clouds. "They're gone. Come with me."

Lena follows the flickering candle into the empty church.

"You'll have to go. They're off now, but they'll be back tomorrow, and, sooner or later, they'll find a way to get in. Your best bet is to hide him elsewhere."

"But where?"

"Let me think. Go gather your things. Take this," Mother says, handing her the handful of coins from the collection box. "You'll need it. I'll go saddle Joseph and meet you at the stables. You'd better be gone before daybreak."

Lena's heart pounds as she rushes back to her cell. For a year, this has been her sanctuary.

No more.

CHAPTER 7
AN HEIR FOR WALLACHIA

When Lena came to the monastery last year, the thing that shocked her the most was the silence. Other than the bells, all you ever heard was the wind whispering through the old pines.

But not that night. That night, someone's screams shook the walls, and their pain shattered the earth. Lena stared at the wooden cross above the door, wondering who that was. Another scream split the air. Lena gasped and realized it was her.

Her screams carried through the smoke of holy incense, rattling the monastery and the nuns' souls. Soft steps and choked whispers told her that no one was sleeping. Outside her tiny white cell, the sisters walked the hallways, praying for her and the child who refused to be born.

Another searing wave of pain cut through Lena's innards like a hot knife, and she wailed like she was torn apart. Because she was. She struggled to stand, but soft hands stronger than steel held her down. So, she yelled even louder.

"Now, now, Lena," a soft voice said, and somebody wiped her forehead. Their hands smelled like lavender, verbena, and mint, and

Lena recognized Smaranda. She's been here since the ordeal's beginning whenever that was. Yesterday? Last week? Last year?

Another stab of pain took her breath away and choked her brain in a fog of hurt and fear.

"Here, drink this," Smaranda said, bringing a cup to her lips.

Lena turned her head to avoid it, but she couldn't. The bitter liquid puckered her mouth and trickled down her throat, making her gag.

"Good girl. That will help you feel better."

Lena wanted to tell her that nothing will make her feel better, but the brain fog thickened. She couldn't remember who she was, where she was, or what she was doing there. She faded away.

When she returned, the fog had vanished, and she heard the women talk.

"How is she?"

A hand touched her chest and counted her heartbeats. "She's all right, just exhausted after three days of struggling to give birth," Smaranda said.

"Should we call the priest?" Mother Superior's voice was soft, like she was praying.

"No. She's not dying. Yet."

"But the baby? He may be dead inside her already. Christening him would save him from eternal damnation."

"The baby isn't dead. And it won't be, unless you make a fuss and people find out about him. Then, he might die. She might too."

"But why? Who'd want to harm a newborn baby?"

"The Voivode of Wallachia, for one. Maybe even the pretenders to the throne. Vladislav would kill him in a heartbeat. Vlad too. Maybe even Radu. If it's a boy, he's an heir to the throne, therefore their rival. They'll want to get rid of him before he grows up to cause trouble. Letting them know Lena's here, about to give birth, is risking having them come to kill her baby."

"I'll wait then. But how about getting her a doctor? Or at least a midwife? She's been in labor for three days already."

"No need. She's doing all right. She's a tough, strong girl. She'll do better on her own than with some filthy barber pawing all over her."

Lena's brain drowned in darkness again. When she returned, she drifted on a cloud, weightless and pain free.

"She opened her eyes!"

"Lena?"

Her throat was so raw, she barely moaned.

A cup touched her lips. She emptied it and asked for more. That was the best water she'd ever tasted. She smiled, and Smaranda's hand touched her cheek. Her old eyes were full of light, and her smile was love.

"You gave birth to a son, Lena. A strong, handsome boy. Here he is."

She laid a white bundle on Lena's chest. Somewhere inside it, there was a baby. Pink, with rose lips and a puff of dark hair. His wide-open eyes, the color of far-away mountains, stared at her like he tried to figure out who she was.

Lena's heart melted with a tenderness she didn't know existed. She kissed his cheek and marveled at his tiny, perfect fingers. She was in love.

"I'm proud of you, Lena. What would you like your son's name to be?"

Lena thinks about Mircea. "Call him Vlad, after my father," he'd said.

"Then you'd better be there for the christening," she had said.

He'd laughed, but he wouldn't be there for the christening. He died in the forests of Târgoviște, and she didn't even get to see his body. May God curse the killers and never give them sons.

"Mircea. We'll call him Mircea, like his father."

That was almost a year ago, Lena thinks, and her heart melts as she watches her baby sleep in her bed. With his dark hair and firm chin, he's the spitting image of his father and the light of her life. She'll do whatever it takes to keep him safe.

She bundles their few belongings, picks him up, grateful he's still asleep, and heads to the stables.

Joseph, their mule, grazes placidly on a patch of grass, unconcerned by the strangeness of being out in the dark. Lena ties little Mircea across her chest, grabs the reins and mounts.

"Where will you go?" Mother Superior asks.

"Back home to Moldova, I think. But I'll first try to get to Smaranda's and wait for them to lose my trail."

"Don't stay there long. It's too close and they'll find you."

"I'm good, as long as they don't find him."

CHAPTER 8

A MOTHER'S LOVE

I t's dark as can be, and a wild wind whips the spruce into a frenzy, threatening rain. It's July, and the night air is warm even here up in the mountains, but Lena can't stop shivering, so she clenches her teeth to keep from biting her tongue.

It's not far from the monastery to Smaranda's — just six hours on foot across the mountain. But the climb through the woods is steep and uneven, over tree roots and around deep ravines, and the descent is abrupt and treacherous even in daylight, let alone in the dark.

Fortunately, little Mircea's still asleep. He's such a good baby, he seldom wakes her up at night. He hardly cried, even when he was teething last winter. Which is good, because how on earth can you hide a crying baby? Their lives may depend on him sleeping through tonight, Lena thinks, and that sends another shiver down her spine. How woefully perishable humans are!

Placid like the old mule he is, Joseph follows the trail in the dark. His short legs are steady and his hooves silenced by the thick pine needles that give the ancient forest an otherworldly quietness. Once in a while, the full moon comes out of the clouds, throwing deep shadows sliding quietly like ghosts. It's beautiful but scary, since the full moon is the mistress of werewolves, striga, and other otherworldly creatures. Here, in Transylvania, nobody would brave it unless they had to. But Lena knows better.

She thinks about Mircea as they chug along up the trail to the top. His smell of man and horse and leather. His soft lips and fiery embraces. The love in his eyes and the promises he didn't live to fulfill. Their time together was so short, she'd think it a dream if not for the baby in her arms. They met, they fell in love, they shared a few passionate nights, then he left and died. And all that's left of him is this. She glances at the baby lying on her breast. His face glows like a pearl in the moonlight and his rosebud mouth sucks in his sleep. I hadn't known such love could exist, Lena thinks, pushing Joseph further.

They're almost at the top. Straight ahead, there's a short flat trail, then the descent, which is dangerous, even more so in the dark. But, thank God, they're halfway. A few more hours and they'll reach Smaranda's hut, where they'll be safe, even though she has no soldiers and no weapons. But she's got magic, Smaranda, and she'll find a way to protect the baby. And she's got Negru.

What would Mircea do? Lena wonders. Then she smiles. He'd fight, of course. What else? That's what he always did, no matter how many, no matter how hard. But what he would do doesn't matter now, does it? He's not here. She is.

As they reach the top of the mountain, the unchained wind bursts into a frenzy. With a horrible creak, an old pine breaks somewhere close, bringing down others in its fall. Another tortured tree screams far away. The entire forest is crying, Lena thinks, watching a long burst of lightning split the sky from one end to the other. In the otherworldly brightness, the shaking trees look like black skeletons wringing their hands in fear. Four heartbeats later, the thunder follows. Not too close, Lena thinks, just as the rain starts.

The sky breaks. A wall of water crashes over her, so much that it's hard to breathe. She leans forward to protect little Mircea with her body, but seconds later she's soaked, and he must be too. But there's nothing to do but go on, so she tightens her arm around the baby and pushes Joseph further. Her heavy, wet braid slaps her back with every step.

Another shot of lightning, followed by a thunder so loud it startles her. This one's right here, she thinks. A hundred feet away, a tall pine catches fire, scorching the air and blistering the surrounding trees. Fire rains over Lena, and she clutches the baby even closer, glad that her hair is too soaked to catch fire.

But the raging inferno is not Lena's problem. Her job is to take Mircea to safety, no matter what, so she tightens her knees to push Joseph, but he's had it. The old mule stuck with her through the climb, the rain and even the thunder, but the fire is too much. He won't go any further. Oh well. Lena dismounts and pulls him behind her, following the path despite the rain, the darkness, and the fire.

Slow but steady, Joseph follows. They leave the fire behind and start the descent, whipped hard by the wind and raging rain. Another lightning strikes, followed by rolling thunder not two heartbeats later. The earth shakes under Lena's tired feet. She leans again to cover Mircea with her body, but this time it's too much.

The baby starts screaming like he's getting flayed. His sharp cries cover the whistle of the wind and the rain's rumble. Lena hopes for another thunder, but no such luck. The dark sky went silent. She tries to soothe the baby with her breast, but he spits it out. He's wet and angry, and he wants the world to know it.

There's nothing to do but go on. Lena shuffles forward carefully, holding Mircea, dragging Joseph, and trying to keep on the path. She's wet, cold, and tired, but none of those matters. All that matters is saving her son.

Another lightning bolt shatters the darkness. It's not close, but it's the scariest, because it reveals two riders waiting just a hundred feet ahead, listening for Mircea's cry. The lightning fades, leaving the darkness behind even deeper, and a long rolling thunder follows.

Lena sighs. This is it. Those men are here for Mircea. There can be no other reason for them to be out at night in this foul weather on a hidden path nobody ever takes. Vladislav's men must have divided to look for them, and these two found them, and they'll kill him. In the lightning's short brightness, Lena glimpsed the eagle with the cross on their coats of arms and she saw their swords. They're Vladislav's soldiers, armed to the teeth, and Lena's just a woman. She can't outrun them, she can't defeat them, and she can't even hide with a screaming baby in her arms.

There's just one thing left to do.

In the deep darkness, she ties Joseph to a branch. She grabs the bundle with their meager belongings and steps off the path. She unties a screaming Mircea from her chest, kisses his cheek one last time, then sets him under a bush where he's easy to hear, but impossible to see.

"I love you. If we never meet again, make your father proud."

Wet, cold, and abandoned, the baby screams even louder.

Lena steps away and hides behind a tree. They won't be long now.

Another strike of lightning. The men have gotten closer. They're just feet away as they dismount and step off the path to look for the baby, and the treacherous moon shows her face to help them.

"Here. He's there, under that bush."

"What the hell? Why would she leave her baby here?"

"She ran to save her life. Smart girl," the first man says, kneeling to pick Mircea.

His hands reach for the baby, and he dies as Lena's axe sinks deep into his skull. Blood spurts, hot and salty, splashing them. He crumbles over Mircea under his partner's horrified eyes.

"What the hell?" the man says.

Lena struggles to pull her axe out of the dead man's skull, but it's not easy. Just like when splitting wet wood, the bone gripped the axe and holds on to it.

Lena puts her foot on his neck and pries the axe out as his gaping partner stares at her.

"What ..."

That's all he gets to say before the axe splits his forehead, widening the space between his eyes. He gasps and crumbles over his partner.

Lena pulls the axe out again. You never know. There may be more.

She drags them off Mircea and picks him up. He's sticky with blood and covered with leaves, but there's no time to clean him now. The rain will do the job, she thinks, tying him back to her chest and offering him her breast. His hungry mouth closes around it, and he goes quiet.

She unties Joseph, who's munching on a patch of grass, and gets back in the saddle.

"Time to go. We're running late."

As she rides down the path to Smaranda's, Lena spares a prayer for the old soldier who taught her how to kill with an axe, long ago, when she was just a child, and saved her from a terrible ordeal. Since then, she loves to split logs, and never leaves home without her axe. It served her well.

CHAPTER 9

ANATOLIA, JULY 1449

It's a glorious summer day in Anatolia as Mehmed rides Rüzgar in the old woods around Manisa. He loves feeling the wind in his hair, the great stallion dancing under him as he races across fields, and his peregrine falcon gripping his glove with her talons as her hungry yellow eyes search for prey. Güzel is strong and well-trained. Gone are the days when some cunning old hare could trick her. She'd catch a fox if one was stupid enough to get in her way. As for Rüzgar, he knows Mehmed so well he can read his thoughts from the touch of his knees on his flanks. It's like they are one being, he and the horse. A centaur.

All in all, Mehmed has never been happier. Being governor of Manisa beats being sultan any day of the week. When he was a sultan, he felt like a slave. He had to always be available to whoever wanted him for anything. No matter how he tried to hide, the grand vizier ambushed him to talk about the janissaries and the taxes; the ambassadors chased him to discuss boring treaties; and every paper-pusher in the administration needed him to sign something or other. But now he's free to do whatever he wishes, and what he wants to do is hunt and gallop over the green hills on his stallion. He no longer needs to ply himself to anyone's whims.

With one exception. The dusty rider galloping to intercept him must be Mother's messenger. She's the only one with no respect for his wishes, his time, or his choices. Mother still treats him like he's a toddler, not an Ottoman sultan. Sort of.

"What is it this time?"

The man jumps to the ground and takes a deep bow. "Your mother requests your presence, my sultan."

"What for?"

"She didn't say, but... there's a messenger from Edirne."

Edirne? That's got to be from Father, and that's always important.

"I'm coming."

With gentle, loving moves, he covers the falcon's eyes with the soft leather mask the falcon master made for her to keep her calm and grounded. He ties the strings, then takes off at full speed with the messenger in tow. Güzel sinks her claws into his glove and complains bitterly, holding on for dear life.

"I'm sorry, sweetheart. Mother wants us back, and Father sent a messenger. There's no way around this. We'll be back tomorrow."

He's lying, of course. Whatever's important enough to interrupt his hunt won't go away overnight. But the falcon doesn't know politics, and neither does the horse, so he'd rather break it to them slowly.

Back at the palace, he drops the reins with a stable hand and eases the falcon to her cage, then heads toward Mother's quarters, all dusty and sweaty. He'd love a bath, but he's got to deal with this, whatever this is, before he can relax and enjoy it.

Mother's Manisa quarters are nothing like she had in Edirne. As the validé and the mistress of the harem, she only had the best of the best. Here, she's just the governor's mother, so she has to contend with smaller rooms, plainer gardens, and fewer servants. But she still lives like a sultan's wife, and she has nobody to vie with or tell her what to do. Mehmed wishes that would make her happy, but her narrowed eyes tell him that happy isn't on the schedule today.

"Good evening, Mother."

He bows and kisses her hand, then crosses his legs to sit. Mother's on fire, as usual. Her red hair is streaked with white, and the skin around her eyes has softened, but her burning cheeks brighten the untamed green fire of her eyes. She looks frail though, and Mehmed wonders if she's well.

"How are you, Mother? As lovely as ever, I see. What can I do for you?"

Mother narrows her eyes and looks at him down her nose, just like she used to whenever he soiled his diapers. "Didn't you read your father's message?"

"Not yet. I came to see you first."

"He's got great news. You're getting married."

"Married? But I'm married already. I have Gülbahar, and a boatload of concubines. I'm all set, thanks."

"Come on, Mehmed, you know better than that. The sultan arranged your marriage to a Dulkadir princess. Her name is Sittişah, and she's beautiful."

"Why?"

"You're seventeen. It's high time you got a wife worthy of the Osman dynasty. Your father needs the Dulkadir to crush the Karamanids in Anatolia, once and for all. And you need more wives to give you sons. You must secure the succession."

"I'm perfectly happy with Gülbahar. I thought you were too. She gave me a healthy son, and there's no sweeter girl. I need no more wives."

"That's nonsense. I agree with your father. As lovely as she is, Gülbahar is just a slave; she came with no connections, no dowry, and no alliance. But whatever you and I think doesn't matter, since there's nothing we can do. The marriage contract is already signed. And the Ottomans need something to celebrate. They've had nothing but unrest, war, and fear, for years. They need something to rejoice about and give them hope, and there's nothing people love more than a beautiful wedding. Unless it's a circumcision, of course, but Bayezid is too young."

"But Mother, what if I don't like her?"

"Then don't spend time with her. Many political marriages never get consummated. Once the wedding is over, you can send her somewhere and never see her again. But I suggest you wait until you see her. Hizir Paşa's wife chose her, and she says the princess is wonderful. And the Dulkadir are an old dynasty. Your own grandmother comes from there, and she'll want you to give Sittişah a fair chance."

"What will Gülbahar think about it?"

"What will Gülbahar think? Who cares? Mehmed, Gülbahar already gave you a son. As long as Bayezid lives, you have no business bedding her again. The Prophet's teachings say that you can have up to four wives. That's four heirs to the Ottoman throne. That should keep you plenty busy."

"But I love Gülbahar."

"And so you should, since she's the mother of your first-born son. But that has nothing to do with your marriage. Get over it."

"That's not fair, Mother. How would you feel if you were in her shoes?"

Mother laughs so hard her eyes tear. "How would I feel? Really? Do you remember when your father married Mara and sent me away? I know exactly how it feels, since I've been there. I never complained. I took care of you and did my best to teach you and make you the best next sultan you could be. And I prayed Mara wouldn't have a son. A woman's feelings don't mean squat. Gülbahar is a sensible girl, and she'll do the best she can for her son. She will do her duty, and so should you. You are the future sultan of the Ottoman Empire. Sultan Murad, your father, told you to get married, so you'll get married. That's all there is to it. Get over yourself."

There's nothing left to say. Mehmed has no choice but to obey the sultan whether or not he likes it. Şehzade or not, he's just as trapped in the empire's rules and traditions as the lowest janissary.

"When am I going back?"

"Tomorrow."

CHAPTER 10

EDIRNE, JULY 1449

My dear Cousin Vlad,

I hope my letter finds you in good health. It's been a long time since we last broke bread together at the Royal Court of Târgoviște, and many sad things have happened since.
I would like to present you and your brother Radu with my most sincere condolences and tell you both how much I share in your grief. Your father, Vlad Dracul, God rest his brave soul, was like a father to me for many years. He taught me most of what I know about politics and strategy, and I will never forget his kindness in taking me in when I direly needed shelter. Both he and your lovely mother will forever be in my heart.
As for your brother Mircea, he was like my brother, and he taught me most of what I know about fighting and bravery. He died like a hero to save your father's life and mine. I just hope that someday I'll get to be half the soldier he was. He fought valiantly for his kin and his country, and no battle was ever too hard. The world was better because he lived in it.

That's why I hold you and Radu in my heart, not like my cousins, but like my true brothers.

The reason I'm writing to you today is to tell you that the tide has finally turned in my father's favor. After years of exile and hiding in Hungary, Poland, and who knows where else, fighting wars that weren't his and courting every foreign power to support his vision for Moldova, Father has finally gained a mighty supporter.

As I'm sure you know, Moldova's voivode, little Alexăndrel, is only nine. That child is nothing but a pawn for the boyars who rule in his stead, and for his cousin, Cazimir the Fourth, the King of Poland. And since Poland's relationship with Hungary turned sour, Father caught the ear of the mighty Hunyadi, who agreed to support his quest for the Moldavian throne. They are looking to start a campaign in the fall. In the meantime, Father works on connecting with the Moldovan boyars who are unhappy with Alexander's rule to build a Moldavian opposition he can rely on if he recovers the throne.

So, we're getting ready to fight. Would you like to join us?

I know this is not your fight, and I can understand if that's of no interest to you. But I thought I'd tell you about it and let you make up your mind.

I also know that Hunyadi played a role in your father losing his throne. But I was with Vlad Dracul when he died, and I can tell you that Hunyadi was nowhere near there. I'll also remind you of a lesson your father taught me: Neither Moldova nor Wallachia is strong enough to hold the great powers at bay. That's why we must play dangerous games and keep switching partners. Today's enemies are tomorrow's allies, and vice versa. Hunyadi is the counterweight to the Ottoman power, who'd swallow us whole if it wasn't for Hungary, and the other way round. We can't let the wounds of our past get in the way of our future.

Whether or not you join us, I'll forever be your loving brother and I wish you all the good in the world.

*Trust the messenger I sent you. He'll bring you to our camp should
you choose to come, or bring us your letter if you don't.
Wishing you only the best. See you in better times.
Your loving cousin/brother,
Ștefan*

Sitting on his bed, Vlad drains his cup, waiting for Radu to be done with the letter. Their eyes finally meet.

"What do you think?" Vlad asks.

"They're in a world of hurt. Bogdan, Ștefan's father, has been struggling to get Moldova's throne since before we were born. This is likely to be another wild goose chase. And even if he takes it, he won't last long. Why on earth would you go there?"

"Because Ștefan is our cousin. More than a cousin, he's a brother, and needs help. If he succeeds, he'll be a powerful ally, and may help me get Wallachia's throne someday. And, above all, we'd get to fight in a real battle! We could be fighting in the field! How exciting is that?"

"Not much, if you ask me. I'm not mad about fighting, especially for no good reason. And I can't see a good enough reason to go there."

Vlad shakes his head. "I really don't get you, brother. I can't wait to join them and fight. I'm glad to help him, of course. But, more importantly, I can't wait to get my sword bloodied."

"In Moldavian blood? They are our brothers, remember? Not our enemies."

"The enemies of our friends are our enemies. They are my enemies now. Until our uncle takes that throne."

"When are you leaving?"

"Tomorrow."

"Did you tell the sultan?"

"Yes."

"What did he say?"

"I told him I'll be fighting alongside Hunyadi. He didn't like that much. But when I told him I'll dethrone the Polish King's nephew, he said: 'OK. If you can dethrone the Polish King too, I'll give you a promotion. Good luck.'"

"Well, brother, I have little more to say. I wish you lots of luck and can't wait to hear your stories. Give Cousin Ștefan my best wishes." Radu stands to leave.

As he's at the door, Vlad calls on him. "You didn't forget what I asked you? Just in case I don't make it back?"

"Of course. I'll do my best to avenge Father, Mircea, and you, if things go bad."

"Thank you, brother. How about Sophia?"

"Sophia?"

"Gülbahar. Remember?"

"I do. How I could forget?"

CHAPTER II

EDIRNE CASTLE, AUGUST 1449

The clamor outside is so loud Radu can't hear himself think, so he closes the door to get some peace. As an Ottoman officer, he has two entire rooms for himself and Sari. His belongings he used to feel cramped his little bedroom are now scattered over four times the space, so the place looks almost empty, but Radu likes it this way. He needs room to think. That's why he usually does his best thinking outside, but not today. The whole Edirne Castle is in such a turmoil that he's better off staying in.

The Ottoman Empire is getting ready for the wedding of the century. Mehmed's nuptials are supposed to last for three whole months. There'll be enough food to feed an army, and dancers, singers, jugglers, and countless other entertainment. And, to have everyone share the joy, no less than five hundred poor children will get circumcised at the sultan's expense. Their families will forever brag about their son's magnificent circumcision party they couldn't otherwise afford.

The bride is coming an awful long way. She's a Dulkadir princess from Elbistan, and her caravan took more than a month to reach Bursa, where the Ottoman dignitaries waited for her. After she rested and recovered, they escorted her to Edirne, another month away. Her caravan is still on its way, so Mehmed hasn't met her, of course. He won't get to see her before the wedding, but they say she's beautiful and fiery and very much like Hüma Hatun, Mehmed's mother.

That should be fun, Radu thinks. He wonders what Mehmed will say about having a wife just like his mother, but he has trouble wrapping his mind around that. He can't imagine having any wife, in fact. Radu has no interest in girls — not that there's any hanging around here at the palace school. But Mehmed has been with plenty of girls, and he seems to like Gülbahar, Vlad's Sophia. Thank God he's gone, Radu thinks. But Mehmed won't bring Gülbahar to his wedding to another woman — or will he? After all his years here, Radu still finds some of the Ottoman customs weird. Who knows? Maybe the old wife hands the man to the new one like a baton? Wouldn't that be fun?

But no matter what, Radu looks forward to seeing Mehmed again. He missed him terribly since he left for Manisa, more than a year ago. And he's been working on Mehmed's wedding present for weeks: a poem Radu wrote just for him. He'd better get it done, since Mehmed should arrive at any moment. The wedding starts in three days.

Radu leans over the piece of paper where he wrote the graceful Ottoman characters with his best calligraphy and endeavors to turn the poem into a work of art. He illuminates the letters in a rainbow of colors to create splendid arabesques whose beauty goes way beyond the words:

> It's been too long since you left,
> The nights too dark,
> The days too long,
> Oh, dear one, how I long
> For the love in your eyes,
> The touch of your hand,
> The taste of your kiss

Where the hell did that last line come from? Radu wonders, staring at the piece of paper like somebody else wrote it when someone knocks on the door.

Radu turns the paper face down. "Come in."

Mehmed bursts in.

"Radu!"

Radu's breath freezes. He's waited for this moment for months, but he never imagined it like this. Mehmed is no longer the boy he knew. His friend is all grown up. His wide chest is covered in chain mail, his hair is a mess of red curls, and his beard is unkempt. He's all man, and all that's left unchanged are the warm green eyes that smile at Radu just like they used to.

"Look at you! You've grown so much!" Mehmed says, measuring him from head to toes, and Radu wishes he'd gone to the hammam and prettified himself. But what difference does it make? A friend is a friend, no matter how they look. Not like Mehmed cares.

"I'm so glad to be back, my friend."

Mehmed's hug is like a bear's. He's hard all over and strong. He smells like horse, sweat and dust, and Radu melts into his embrace, hoping he'll never let go.

"Me too," he says. "You can't imagine how much."

Mehmed lets him go, but Radu holds him close a moment longer to breathe in the scent of his skin. They sit to talk, but the easy banter they used to share is gone. There's something in the air, like the heaviness before a storm. Still, they chat, trying to ignore it.

"How was your trip?" Radu asks.

"Uneventful but fast. I had to delay my trip because Mother fell ill. She was supposed to come too, but she didn't feel well enough. Too bad, really. She looked forward to meeting Sittişah."

"I've heard your new wife is very much like your mother."

"I hope not. One woman like that is enough in any man's harem. Most certainly in mine. I can't think about anyone who could handle two. Even Father could barely deal with Mother. But tell me about you. How are you? What's new?"

Radu nods. "I'm well. I've been looking forward to your return. I'm so glad you're back."

"Me too."

Radu struggles for something to say. "Are you glad to get married?"

"Hell, no. I'd much rather go to war, but I don't have a choice. You know, Radu, people think a sultan is free to do whatever he wants, and spends his days eating baklava and watching naked women dance. Nothing could be further from the truth. I wish I could let them be sultans for a day. It's nothing but work since the morning prayer wakes you up. Everyone keeps harassing you: read this, decide that, talk to those emissaries, make judgements, start over. None of it is any fun. And then at night they send you women, and they're not the ones you want. I want Gülbahar, but I can't have her. Mother says there's no point bedding her, since she already has a son. Excuse me? I want her. That's the point. But what I want doesn't matter. Not to Mother, at least. I'm almost glad she's not here. That makes one less person to tell me what to do. Father and the grand vizier are plenty, thank you. And now a new wife that looks like Mother. Are you kidding me?"

Radu laughs. Mehmed laughs too, but he's not kidding. Their eyes meet, and the tension is back. Radu can't help but feel overwhelmed by Mehmed's presence, his force, his closeness. He looks for something to say, but nothing comes to mind.

Mehmed stands to pace around the room, looking at Radu's things: his books, his weapons, his prayer carpet. He picks up the paper sitting face down on the table. "This is beautiful! Did you write it?"

Radu nods, and Mehmed reads it aloud.

> "...The warmth of your hand,
> The taste of your kiss..."

He drops the paper like it's hot, then glances at Radu, whose cheeks are burning. "You... you met someone?"

Radu stares at him. "Met someone?"

Mehmed points at the paper. "That you wrote that for."

"I wrote that for you. That poem is your wedding gift. I just need to finish illuminating it and..."

"For me? You wrote that for me?"

"Of course. Who else?"

"Oh, Radu!"

Mehmed touches Radu's cheek. His rough hand, calloused by the reins and the hilt of the sword, feels rose-petal soft. He runs his fingers through Radu's hair, then traces his neck down to his chemise. He hesitates, waiting for permission.

Radu takes off his shirt, then kisses Mehmed's hand and sets it on his booming heart. His eyes meet Mehmed's. "Please."

"You... you want this?"

"I want you."

Mehmed gasps and pulls him close. His mouth covers Radu's.

Radu's knees soften, and they fall on the bed.

The taste of your kiss, Radu thinks. Then a whirlwind of rainbows pulls him in, and he thinks no more.

CHAPTER 12

TRANSYLVANIA, SEPTEMBER 1449

Locked right in Transylvania's icy heart, the fortified city of Sighișoara is a hard nut to crack. Many tried to conquer it and failed. The houses, square and sturdy, stick together like sheep huddled around the white church, and the square towers holding up the walls of the fortress stand guard, with their small windows like narrow eyes always watching.

The nine foot thick walls and the dark cobblestones, slippery with rain, haven't changed one bit since Vlad left them ten years ago. He was seven, and Radu only three, when Vlad Dracul conquered Wallachia's throne, and their mother packed the house to move them to Târgoviște. Vlad still remembers playing with the Saxon merchants' kids, and riding bareback along the narrow streets to race them to the ice-cold waterhole.

The big yellow house is still in the corner, its sharp roof sheltering half the crossing to the house across the street where Vlad went to play with his friend Dieter, the ropemaker's son when Father was just Transylvania's military governor, waiting for the Wallachian throne to come within reach. It feels like forever ago.

The kid he was is long gone. So much happened since: years in

Târgoviște, then Father sending them to Edirne, his imprisonment in Tokat, then Eğrigöz. Then Father's death and his own brief turn on Wallachia's throne that ended so poorly.

Vlad should feel sad, but he doesn't. He feels nothing but numbness, but for one thing: Sophia. He hasn't seen her in years, and she's now Mehmed's wife and the mother of his son, but Vlad's heart still aches for her.

Her memory hurts, but that's good, because it makes him feel alive. Without her, it's like he's dead inside, and that's not a good feeling; he'd rather hurt. But what keeps him going is the hate.

He hates them all: Hunyadi, the Ottomans, the boyars who killed Father and Mircea, Mehmed, and Murad. But the list is too long to go through, because the messenger stops. They arrived.

The small gray house looks just like the others — a square old house on a narrow, cobbled street. Nobody would think it shelters Moldova's future, should things go as planned.

The messenger raps a code on the low wooden door opening to a dark room. After his time in Eğrigöz, Vlad doesn't like dark rooms, but he has no choice but to follow, hoping it's not a trap. But why would it be? They could have killed him a hundred of times since leaving Edirne. And who'd bother to trap him? Quite a few, as a matter of fact. Hunyadi. Vladislav. The boyars he swore to kill. And others.

But there's no trap. It's just Ștefan, his cousin, who pulls him into a bear hug and won't let go. "Look at you! You're all grown up!"

"You too," Vlad says, looking up. Ștefan is tall, blond, and handsome, making Vlad feel even shorter and darker. He looks like Radu's brother more than Vlad does.

"Father, this is Vlad."

Bogdan Mușat, soon to be Bogdan the Second if God listens to their prayers, hugs him, too. He's tall and plain, with scant brown hair framing a rare clean-shaved face. "So glad you joined us, Vlad. Last time I saw you, you were just a little boy. Now you look like a grown man. Have you seen battle yet?"

Vlad shakes his head. His heart aches remembering how he left

Târgoviște with his carts loaded with wine, icons, and carpets, instead of staying to fight, defend the country, and make Father proud.

"Don't worry, you will. Ștefan has already seen plenty. Not thanks to me, but thanks to your father and your brother. I'll do my best to train you both, and I'm glad to gain another son."

But where did Bogdan see battle, Vlad wonders? He's never been a voivode.

Bogdan laughs like he's heard Vlad's thoughts. "All those years when Ștefan was in Wallachia with your folks, I fought in Hungary, Serbia, and Poland. And plenty of other places. Don't worry, I have more experience as a fighter than I have as a voivode. And there's more fight coming. In a few days, we'll join Hunyadi's troops, then cross into Moldova at Békás. That's where we meet the boyars who want to overthrow Alexăndrel, so they'll support us. We'll head north towards Suceava, but we won't get that far. Alexăndrel's men are heading south already, so we'll fight somewhere along the way."

Vlad hopes Bogdan knows what he's talking about. He wants to trust him, but it's hard. Trust doesn't come easy to Vlad, and Bogdan feels it.

"Feel free to ask me anything. I may not answer, but I'll never lie to you."

"When you tried to get the throne years ago, Hunyadi chose your brother instead. Why would he help you now?"

"Things changed for Hunyadi. He's been through some rough spots. His reputation faded after he lost at Varna, then again at Kosovo, and shattered when Đurađ Branković, that nobody thinks much of, captured him and asked for an exorbitant ransom to let him go. Hungary's diet coughed up the money, but they got so obnoxious that Hunyadi decided to play his own game. He got old, and he's no longer Hungary's regent, but he's just as ambitious as he's always been, and he needs to prove he still matters. Now that Hungary and Poland are at odds, and Poland supports Alexăndrel, Hunyadi will help me take Moldova to strengthen his own borders. Bottom line is, he only helps me to help himself."

Vlad nodded. That he understood. "But don't you feel bad about dethroning Alexǎndrel? He's your nephew, and he's only nine."

"Not at all. I'm doing him a favor. That kid is just a pawn in this ugly game. His uncle, the King of Poland, and the power-hungry boyars only use him to get what they want. Could you lead a country when you were nine?"

Vlad shakes his head.

"There. *Quot eras demonstrandum.* That's all I needed to prove. Anything else?"

Vlad looks him in the eye. "What will you do if you lose?"

Bogdan laughs. "I won't."

"But what if you do?"

"If I do, then I didn't deserve to win. And I deserve whatever I get. Anything else?"

Vlad shakes his head.

"Vlad, sometimes we win, sometimes we lose. Sometimes we deserve it, but sometimes we don't, and we fall victims to our bad luck. But we always do the best we can. Being the best you can be may not be enough to win, but it's enough to give you peace of mind. If you've done your best, you've done enough, no matter if you win or lose."

That's gibberish to Vlad. You either win or you lose. And losing is for losers.

CHAPTER 13

EDIRNE, FALL 1449

Today's the day they've all been waiting for. The Dulkadir princess with her retinue and the Ottoman escort that accompanied her from Bursa are arriving, and the Edirne Palace is on fire. People hang out everywhere — at the gates, on the walls, and clustered in the courtyard — spreading rumors and getting in Ali's way.

"Did you know she rides an elephant?" a kitchen boy whispers to another.

"No way! I've heard she rides a dragon," the second one answers.

"They say she's beautiful as the sunrise and more than six feet tall," a janissary tells a stable boy who stole a moment from work, hoping to at least see the horses.

"Really? Six feet tall? What will Sultan Mehmed do with her, then?" the pimply kid snickers.

"Whatever he wants, baby. Whatever he wants."

The janissary chokes at his own joke, and Ali shakes her head and rushes back to the sarayi where the preparations have reached a frenzy.

The parties — since men and women party separately, of course —

are about to start. The kitchen stoves are red hot, and so are the men minding them. Hundreds of chefs and their apprentices have sweated for days, slaughtering goats, sheep, and chickens, cooking soups, stews, and roasts, and baking mountains of breads — round *pide*, sesame-sprinkled *simits*, *yufka* and *lavas*, not to mention the sweets — *cataifs* and *baklavas* and every kind of confection known to men that will soon vanish inside the thousands of hungry mouths.

In a shady corner of the inner courtyard, the musicians are getting started. Their legs crossed, they sit on the grass to strum their stringed *laoutos* and *kaba kemençe* and check their *davuls*, the large drums covered with goat skin on one side and sheep on the other to produce distinct tones. Next to them, a dozen young *köçek*, boys decked up in women's garb, their eyes dark with kohl and their lips way too red, stretch their long legs and skinny arms and click their clickety *çarpare*, ready to dance.

But the soul of the party is in the sarayi, where the sultan's women are getting ready to welcome someone they'll share their lives with. The harem is its own world. The women live with each other more than they do with their husband, even though the sultan has power over all their lives. Their master is Murad, but he's on his way down. When Sultan Murad dies, his wives will become Mehmed's property to deal with. He can send them away, marry them off, or let them rot in the harem forever.

But Ali has better things to do than worry about that now. She needs to make sure the banquet room is ready. The musicians are already hidden in a corner with their instruments, closed from the room by a paper-covered wooden partition. They're men, so they're not allowed to see the women, even though they're here to entertain them.

The rich Isfahan carpet in muted shades of pink and green hides the white marble floor. Priceless Chinese vases a grown man could hide in sit in every corner, overwhelmed by the profusion of greenery and roses. A dozen scattered pillows invite the women to settle, but they're not ready.

They all crowd against the windows, eying the gates. They can't wait, even though they know they'll get to see her, touch her, and tell their friends. Unlike the men, who have their own party, but they'll never see her face. They'll just try to imagine her from the flutter of her veils, the grace of her walk, and the color of her skirts. But they'll never get to see her eyes, let alone her body. Those belong to Mehmed, whether or not he likes them.

"How's it going?" a soft voice asks.

Emine Validé, the sarayi's mistress and Mehmed's grandmother, came to check on things.

"It's all good. The kitchens are ready, the musicians are waiting. All we need is the bride," Ali says.

The validé nods. "Good. Thank you, Ali. Over the years you've been here, I've never seen you go wrong. If this wedding is a success, I'll have a special present for you."

Ali bows, wishing she was elsewhere. The validé's praise makes her uneasy, since she betrayed this lovely woman in more ways than she can count. But there's no time to worry about that.

The drums outside beat faster and faster, matching Ali's heart, and the musicians in the corner start playing like something's happening. But is it? Ali glances through the window.

"She's here. The caravan arrived."

Sadly, there's no dragon. Not even elephants. Just riders, horses, and carts.

The gilded carriage surrounded by dusty eunuchs stops at the gate. The dark curtains open, and four women step out, covered from their head to their toes. They line up by the gate, waiting for the bride. She's veiled too, of course. She hops out, her veils fluttering, then stops to look at the castle.

The crowd cheers. Thousands of men shout and stomp their feet in welcome. The princess nods and sails in, her steps fast, her movements smooth, her walk a dance like that of leaves under the rain. She prances in like she's about to conquer the castle, and Ali's heart skips a beat.

"Isn't that funny," a low voice whispers behind Ali's ear, and Mara's soft bejeweled hand touches her arm. "I miss you. Tonight?"

Ali's heart aches to turn and hold her, but she knows better. "I hope so," she says. She turns to see Zambak watching them. Her lips are tight, her eyes daggers. The girl's mouth softens into a smile when she meets Ali's eyes, but Ali's heart knows better. Zambak hates her, and she can't wait to hurt her. Ali doesn't need her magic cross to tell her the girl is trouble and danger is looming — she feels it in her bones. She'll have to deal with her, but not now. Now, she has a wedding party to run, and this is just the beginning. The ceremonies will go on for months. But one way or another, she'll have to make time for Zambak.

Ali scans the room, making sure the silver trays in the middle of the carpet are loaded with drinks and appetizers. The musicians are ready. She glances at the servants bringing loaded trays from the kitchens, making sure they're ready to bring the dishes as the night evolves. The fat white candles flicker in the breeze and the fountains murmur softly. The air is heavy with the scent of roses, and the mouthwatering aroma of roasted lamb with rosemary. To the best Ali can tell, the Edirne Palace is ready for its new princess.

She bows deeply, leading the ladies to their places: Mara, her eyes warm, her lovely mouth smiling. The validé, her soft white face lighting the room. Halime Hatice Hatun, heavier than ever, sitting by the tray of baklavas. The beautiful young consorts elbowing each other out of the way while pretending to know their place. They're as ready as they can be.

The door opens, and a handful of veiled women walk in. The first one struts in like she means business, and the others shuffle quietly behind her.

The princess lifts her veils. "I'm Sittişah, your next sultan's wife."

The room freezes. That's the harshest introduction they've seen over many years. Nobody else barged in like a conqueror. Until now.

Mara recovers first, like she always does. "Welcome Sittişah. Lovely to meet you. I believe you're Mehmed's new wife, the Dulkadir princess?"

"I am. You?"

"I'm Mara Branković, Sultan Murad's third wife and Serbia's despot's daughter. Let me introduce you to our ladies. This" — she points to the validé, sitting quietly on her pillow — "is Emine Validé, our sultan's mother, Mehmed's grandmother and the mistress of our harem. This" — she points to Halime Hatice, who's already munching on a baklava — "is Halime Hatice Hatun, Sultan Murad's first wife and the mother of his favorite son, Aladdin, who unfortunately is no longer with us. These lovely ladies are Sultan Murad's concubines. You'll get to know everyone, but they're too many to remember today. We are delighted to see you, and hope that you'll be a great addition to Şehzade Mehmed's harem."

Sittişah bows. "Thank you. How about my husband's mother? Hüma Hatun?"

"Sadly, Hüma hasn't been well enough to join us. But I'm sure she looks forward to meeting you in Manisa, where your husband is deployed."

"I can't wait to meet her. And everybody else. I'm so glad to see you all."

The princess spreads out the charm, but it's too late. She walked in like a victor instead of the new girl trying to find her place. It took her only minutes to put off the entire sarayi.

The fact that she's Hüma's living picture doesn't help either. With her red hair and sharp green eyes, she could be Hüma's little sister, and nobody here wants Hüma back.

Least of all Halime Hatice, who struggles to stand despite her bulk fighting her. "Good to see you all. I'll go rest now." With heavy steps, she waddles out in deep silence.

"Why does she walk like that?" Sittişah asks. "Is it because she's so fat?"

The women's laughter fills the room.

"Not quite," Mara says. "Sultan Hatun is heavy with child. Insha'Allah, our new şehzade, Sultan Murad's new heir, should be born soon."

CHAPTER 14

EDIRNE, OCTOBER 1449

Tonight's the night, Sittişah thinks.

It's been week after week of celebrations, talking, meeting people, and finding out who's who at the Edirne Palace. She smiled and never complained, doing her darnedest to look pretty and meek. Sometimes she's been more successful than others. But this crap is finally over. The wedding is over tonight, and she'll finally meet Mehmed, the father of her son who will make her the Ottoman Empire's validé.

She breathes in the aromas of eucalypts and jasmine, letting the heavenly heat seep into her bones and soften her shoulders, willing it to take away her pain and her longing. She misses home and Father. Here, she's not at home and nobody likes her. Well, nobody liked her at home either, other than Father, but here she tried really hard to be nice.

But it's finally over. Tonight's her wedding night. She'll spend it in Mehmed's bed, and she'll get him so hooked he'll never want another woman. She must be the most beautiful girl he's ever seen, and she'll do her best to be softer, kinder, and more appealing than any other, Allah willing.

"Hello, Sittişah." The woman sighs with pleasure as she lies on the marble slab next to her. Her skin glows like gold, and her dark hair flows to her thighs.

Sittişah tries to remember her name, but they've been so many it's hard to keep track. "Hello."

"How are you doing? Tonight's the great night, isn't it?"

Sittişah glances at her through the steam. "That's what they say."

"Are you ready for it?"

Ready? Of course, she's ready. She's been ready since she was ten. That was the first time her father considered marrying her to a warlord of questionable descent, but with oodles of horses and sheep, and a taste for very young wives, the marriage fell through, but the teaching didn't.

"You'll have to spread your legs and let your husband do whatever he wants," her aunt had said.

"Like what?"

"Like whatever he wants. Anything." Her father's sister frowned, struggling to get the message through.

"Like what?"

"He may want to… He may want to put his thing inside you."

"What thing?"

Her aunt blushed and ran to call her grandmother.

"Men and women make children together. That's how sons are born. Your husband should want to plant his seed inside you. If your womb is fertile, you'll grow a baby inside. If you're lucky and Allah blesses you, the baby will be a boy. That's what all husbands want."

"What if it's a girl?"

"It is whatever Allah wishes, but a girl won't endear you to your husband. He'd probably prefer a falcon. Or a horse. Even a hunting dog. Nobody wants girls."

"Why not?"

Grandma shrugged. "Girls are useless. They're worse than useless, they're a pain. You must watch them like a hawk so they don't get in trouble, then you need a dowry to get rid of them. You'd better focus on giving your husband a boy."

That's why Sittişah will focus on giving her husband a boy. The heir to the Ottoman Empire, God willing.

She smiles at the woman. "I'm ready."

"Good."

The woman looks like she feels sorry for her, and that's not something Sittişah is used to. Inspiring pity does not befit a princess.

"Good luck," the woman says, as the bath attendant wraps her in warm towels. She walks away without looking back.

"Who was that?" Sittisah asks.

The bath attendant looks at her like she's feeble minded. "Mara Branković. The sultan's wife."

Oh well. The servants wrap her in perfumed towels, then start scrubbing her skin with rough sponges. They untangle her hair with olive oil and, with shells sharp enough to draw blood, they remove every errant hair. It hurts, but that's all par for the course, Sittişah thinks, waiting for the ordeal to be over.

When the grooming is over, they smooth her hair, darken her eyes with kohl and dye her lips with beet juice. They make her prettier than her prettiest self and perfume her with jasmine and roses.

Her ivory silk chemise is softer than a saint's whisper, and so are the gold-embroidered blue shalwars. The servants wrap her in a pearl-embroidered golden kaftan trimmed with black fox, more magnificent than any other Sittişah has ever seen, and she's ready.

They take her to Mehmed's bedroom, which is empty but for the bed, a worn-out prayer rug, and a few thick white candles. They lay her between the blue silk sheets and tell her to wait.

She waits and waits, but nothing happens.

She wonders if something went amiss. Did they take her to the wrong room? Did something happen to Mehmed to keep him away from his wedding bed?

She's almost asleep when heavy steps startle her. He's coming! She smiles her best smile and spreads her hair over the silk pillow, then opens her legs just enough to entice him while keeping her modesty.

"Sittişah?"

Like who else?

"Yes, my sultan."

The narrow door opens and Mehmed steps in. He's tall, strong and handsome, more so than any man she's ever seen. Well, truth be told, other than her young brothers, the only man she's ever seen is her father. She loves him dearly, but as for handsome... But there's no comparison. With his broad shoulders, dark red hair, and fierce green eyes, Mehmed is a sight to behold.

Sittişah moistens her lips.

Mehmed's eyes narrow, and Sittişah's heart skips a beat. She knows she's as pretty as Allah's will and the hammam people could make her, but her new husband doesn't seem pleased.

"Are you all right?"

"Yes, my master." She puts all the sweetness she can muster in her smile, enticing him to come closer.

But he doesn't. He just nods. "Good. Let me know if you need anything. See you soon." He turns around, and, just like that, he's gone.

Sittişah's stomach twists and her throat tightens. What the heck was that? Where did he go? And why? She's never been lonelier than now, abandoned on her wedding night. Where did she go wrong?

She cries through the night, but she's smiling in the morning when the guards take her back to her quarters. She messed up Mehmed's bed and turned over the wet pillow to hide her tears. More importantly, she scratched herself bloody and stained the sheets to bear witness to a consummated marriage.

Her eyes downcast, she shuffles out like she hurts down below.

"How was it?" someone whispers.

"Wonderful," she whispers back.

One way or another, she'll get these bastards. Mehmed too.

CHAPTER 15
MEHMED'S WEDDING NIGHT

A hundred feet away, in the officers' quarters, Radu rests in his bed, reading by the flickering light of a candle. The book is an ancient Chinese treatise on the art of war translated into Latin. Hard to believe, but the old tome feels as fresh and relevant as if it was written yesterday, not a thousand years ago.

Radu struggles to understand Sun Tzu's theory of excellence in war.

To fight and conquer in our battles is not supreme excellence; supreme excellence consists in breaking the enemy's resistance without fighting.

Good idea, but how the heck do you break the enemy's resistance without fighting? Radu wonders, when someone knocks at the door. A bit late for visitors, he thinks. "Come in."

Mehmed bursts in. His eyes are red, his clothes wrinkled, and his breath smells like wine. "How are you?" he asks.

Radu's jaw falls. "Me? What are *you* doing here?"

"I need a place to sleep. Can I crash with you?"

"But... but this is your wedding night. Why aren't you with your bride?"

Mehmed shrugs. "You were right. She's too much like Mother. I can't go there."

"But she's... what is she doing?"

"Sleeping in my bed, godamnit. Like she doesn't have her own bed somewhere. Why did they have to put her in my bed?"

Radu stares at him to see if Mehmed is joking, but he's not. He's indignant that the bride he spent the last three months getting married to is sleeping in his bed.

"But Mehmed, that girl must be heartbroken! You just left her there and walked away? How would you feel if she did that to you?"

"I'd feel just fine, thank you. I'd be delighted to be left alone. How do you think I feel?"

"You?"

"Yes. Me. I feel like an expensive stallion who failed to cover a well-bred mare. Because that's exactly what this is. This isn't love; not even lust. It's mounting. I'm supposed to mount her and get her with child, then never see her again. How would you like that?"

"Not much, I think. But this is not about me. It's about you."

"Don't you worry. Your turn will come. You'll find yourself offered some well-bred lady who'll further your chances to Wallachia's throne, and snap! You'll get locked in your own golden cage, and you'll have to do the deed to get her with child, whether or not you like her. How would you like that?"

Radu shudders. "Not me, thanks."

Mehmed laughs, then puts his arms around him and breathes in the scent of his skin. "You've been riding today."

"Of course. Like every other damned day. I..."

Radu's thoughts get blurry as Mehmed's mouth touches his neck, then his hot tongue draws mesmerizing swirls on the soft skin of his throat. Deft hands untie his shalwars and pull them down.

"What are you doing?" Radu pants.

"What do you think I'm doing?"

Radu's heart quickens and his breath grows heavy as Mehmed's mouth and hands roam over him. "I... don't know."

"I'm making the most of my wedding night," Mehmed whispers against the throbbing ache between Radu's legs.

69

CHAPTER 16
MOLDOVA, OCTOBER II, 1449

There's never been a more beautiful fall, Vlad thinks, watching the maple leaves filter the sun into golden light. The oaks, ashes, and aspens covering the hills have already turned into a hundred shades of orange and crimson, and the wild winds and freezing rains haven't spoiled them yet. But they will, maybe even today. Angry gray clouds sail the skies like warships, threatening a storm, and the leaves are so ripe they only need a sneeze to fly off, wasting all the amazing beauty God bestowed over this country.

The narrow trail through the woods is barely wide enough for a horse with its rider, so Vlad stays behind Captain Dan, the officer that Bogdan Mușat designated to lead their scout. As his introduction to battle, his uncle sent him with their avant-garde to study the terrain and spy on the enemy.

Alexăndrel's armies are close. For weeks now, they've drifted from one village to another in the south of Moldova, instead of protecting the court of Suceava up north. They're trying to gather more men, now that the harvest is finished. To reel them in, they tell them the Hungarians and the Ottomans joined to occupy Moldova, so it's their God-given duty to enlist.

Luckily, the Moldavian peasants aren't stupid. They may not know how to read and write, but they know that a brown bear would join a pack of wolves before the Ottomans and the Hungarians will fight on the same side. That never happened, and it's not going to.

They've seen the Pans, the heavily armored Polish knights on their massive horses, get ready for battle. They know that another war is coming, and no matter who wins, peasants always lose. They lose their lives fighting for rulers they didn't choose; they lose their homes and livelihood to the fires the armies set to punish them; and they lose their wives and children to enemies who look at them as prey. You can't blame them for trying to sneak away from danger, Vlad thinks, as they pass another empty village.

He suddenly smells smoke. Dozens of smoke columns rise straight up on the other side of the Siret. The river isn't deep here, but it's three hundred feet wide, hindering the army's march. Crossing over the slippery rocks while fighting the current is hard for the riders on their horses, let alone the heavy carts with supplies and those loaded with Hunyadi's bombards.

"They're here," whispers Captain Dan, as if the enemy could hear him from half a mile away. "Those fires on the other side are theirs. They're resting, cooking, and waiting for us."

"Can we get closer to count them?"

"We'd better not. They must have guards along the river; if they catch even a whiff we're here, we'll lose the surprise, which is our best advantage. We'd better head back and tell Bogdan. But count the fires. They'll give us an idea of how many they are and how spread out. I counted nine. You?"

"Thirteen. A couple are further back."

"The Pans, I bet. The Polish knights won't mingle with the lowly Moldavian peasants. Not even with the boyars, if they can help it. You've got good eyes."

They head back quietly, even though Vlad can't wait to stick his sword in someone — anyone — and draw blood. It's been too long since he's last indulged in his favorite past-times — skinning rats and impaling birds. He's been busy, for sure, but most importantly, he had no privacy. He knows that if anyone sees him enjoy himself will think him a freak. That's why he's on his best behavior around Ștefan and Bogdan and struggles to resist the blood thirst growing stronger each day.

They reach Bogdan's crowded tent. He's there with Ștefan and the Transylvanian officer heading the five hundred men Hunyadi sent. They lean over the large map held down with wine cups on the table.

"We found them!" Vlad bursts.

His uncle's side glance reminds him he's just a pup. He's here to listen and learn, not to brag.

"Tell me, Captain Dan," Bogdan says.

"They're about three hours away, on the other side of the river. They camped there to wait for us, and they chose their place well. The shore on their side is higher and steeper. Getting in the water on this side is easy, but their archers will decimate us before we reach the other shore. Then the Pans will crush whoever's left as we crawl out."

"What should we do, Vlad?" Bogdan asks.

Vlad has no clue. He's learned a lot about strategy and tactics since he's been with Bogdan, but he never planned a battle by himself. What he'd love to do is charge and kill. Paint his blade red, no matter who lives or dies. But that's not the answer Bogdan wants. The point of fighting is not killing, it's winning. And that, Vlad doesn't know how to do.

"Could we trick them into crossing the river instead, and fight on this side?"

Bogdan nods. "Not a bad idea. How about you, Ștefan?"

"We could ride north and cross, then come back south and fall behind them."

"Not a bad idea, either. Any others?"

He looks at Hunyadi's officer, a dark man with one thick brow going from one ear to the other who hardly ever speaks.

"We could mount the guns on this side of the river and start bombarding them. That ought to keep them busy. They'll either withdraw and clear the way for us to cross, or attack, and then we can fall upon them with half of our men."

"Why half?"

"The other half should find a better place to cross and fall behind them, like Ștefan said."

"I like your plan, Codru. That's a neat blend of the two, and it gives us more flexibility. Let's do it. Codru, you take your men and head north to cross the river. Ștefan, you take a hundred men and the guns. Set them in place and get them in working order on this side of the river. Make sure you get there after dark so they can't see you. No fires and no talking. The rest of us will join you in the morning."

"And me?" Vlad asks.

"You figure out how to draw them over. I'll ask you it in the morning. Now go."

CHAPTER 17

OCTOBER 12, 1449

The morning of the battle is so cold that Vlad's breath turns into steam. White with frost, the grass crunches under their feet as they follow the deep tracks the carts left behind. Hunyadi's bombards weighed them down; it must have been hard to get them through that mud, but they did. By the time Bogdan and the rest of the army arrive, the guns are set in place, camouflaged under layers of leaves, and ready to fire.

Bogdan nods. "Good job, Ștefan. What was the hardest?"

"The mud. It was so deep that the carts kept getting stuck, so it took us half the night to get here."

"What would you do differently next time?"

"I'd take fewer carts and more men."

Bogdan nods, but he's already moved on. His eyes are on the other side of the river, half a mile away. The smoke is gone, but Alexăndrel's army must still be there, waiting for them.

Vlad wonders what happened to the Transylvanians. Did they make it across the river? They won't know until they hear them on the other side. If they do. He hopes so, otherwise their plan will fall flat. Bogdan must be thinking the same thing. Magnificent in his shiny armor, with his naked face flushed with excitement and his hair blown by the wind, he turns to Vlad. "So what's your trick, Vlad? How can we conjure them over?"

Truth be told, Vlad has no trick. He thought about it the whole night, but nothing bright came to mind, so he spits out his least lame idea. "We could send one of the Moldavian peasants to tell them that our bombards got stuck in the mud just down the road. We can't move without them, so we're like sitting ducks. They may decide to cross and catch us at our worst."

"Not a bad idea, but it's not timely. It doesn't fit with our plan, and it would leave the Transylvanians stranded on the other side. So we'll go with our plan. Ștefan, fire the bombards."

Ștefan gives the order. The men attending to them fuss with their torches, fouling the air with the black, stinky smoke. One after the other, the bombards catch fire. Five deafening blasts split the air in quick succession as the massive projectiles fly across the river, carrying death and destruction. But the death and destruction fail to happen as the cannon balls sink placidly in the canopy across the river.

Angry screams tell them they're close, but not close enough. They hear fear and anger, not the agony of dying men and wounded horses.

"Aim further," Ștefan orders.

The men fumble with the long snouts of their bombards, bringing them up a tad, just enough to drop their loads a little further.

"Fire!"

Once again, the massive balls fly across the Siret like heavy birds of prey before diving into the canopy. But this time the screaming is different. It's no longer anger, it's abject fear and terrible agony. A cacophony of voices swear and pray in Polish and Romanian, and horses die screaming.

"Good job. Sounds like you got the Pans, too. Go again," Ștefan tells the soldiers nursing the bombards, but the men shake their heads. The bombards need to cool after firing, otherwise they'll crack and blow apart. They may need hours between shots.

They're right. Ștefan hasn't forgotten the battle of Giurgiu. He was there with Vlad Dracul when the Burgunds blew up their bombard and two of their men. "They need to cool down, Father. Otherwise they'll blow up."

Bogdan shrugs. "I need them now. They'll do us no good tomorrow. They may as well blow up."

The men pour buckets of water over the bombards, filling the air with steam and sizzle. They fan them with leaves and pour more water. They even spit on them, though they'd probably rather spit on Bogdan right now.

They fire again. The projectiles drop somewhere across the river to more screams of pain from men and horses, and the forest moves like it's alive.

"They're retreating," Bogdan says.

"Where will they go?" Ștefan asks.

"They'll regroup on their way out, then head north to Suceava to protect Alexăndrel and wait for reinforcements from the Poles. That would serve us poorly. We can't let them go; we must crush them now."

"Should we cross the river and chase them?"

"Yes, we should. I just wish I knew where those damn Transylvanians are."

The plaintive calls of horns split the air. The clanging of steel against steel, the curses, and the desperate screams tell them that the damn Transylvanians have arrived.

"Let's go then," Bogdan says.

His brain on fire, his naked sword in his hand, Vlad prompts his horse into the river. As freezing water reaches the horse's chest, the current pulls him over. The courser does his best to resist, but the bottom is nothing but slippery rocks and he loses his footing. Vlad leans over to steady him. The stallion neighs and sputters, then regains his footing and heads to the shore.

Vlad holds on to him for dear life. His mouth dry, his heart pumping like crazy, he lifts his blade. This is the moment he's been waiting for.

He plows into the enemy like an avenging god, but Alexandrel's men aren't into fighting; they just want to escape. The peasants on foot wear quilted tunics instead of armor and carry axes and maces instead of swords. They're no match for Vlad's blade, and salty blood spurts into his face as he cuts through arms, legs, and necks like he'd chop firewood. This is no longer a fight, it's a killing field. This vanquished army is now a dying army thanks to them all, but more than any to Vlad, who gets to kill again and again and quench his thirst for blood. For now.

By the end of the day, the forest is composted with corpses. Alexăndrel's army is just a memory, and the dead cover the ground as far as the eye can see. The few Polish Pans left alive got stripped of their armor and weapons and shuffle behind their horses, tied to their tails. They're Bogdan's captives, and they'd better pray to their Catholic God that somebody cares enough about them to pay their ransom.

The highest boyars in the land, Oancea Logofătul, and Costea Andronic, will never fight for Alexandrel again. Nor for anyone else. They'll be lucky if someone says a prayer over them and digs a hole to put them into the ground, instead of leaving them to fatten the crows.

The dead are too many to count, all fathers and brothers and sons who won't return to their homes to plow their fields, celebrate Christmas or kiss their children. But they're almost all Alexandrel's. Thanks to Bogdan's plan, they managed to crush the enemy while incurring few losses.

The new voivode thanks his men for their bravery and service, and Vlad is proud to serve under him. Father must have been like that too, Vlad thinks, but he was too young to learn from him before the Ottomans took him hostage. They also taught him plenty, but not much he could use here.

Vlad's arms hurt from all the killing. He's exhausted, but he's happier than he's ever been. First, he got to kill plenty of people and spill lots of blood. Not bad, for somebody contending with rats not long ago.

But, more crucial, he found a way to reconcile his two clashing selves that tear him apart. The heroic Vlad who lives to avenge his father, liberate his people, and uphold Wallachia to her highest greatness. And the hidden Vlad, who craves the suffering of others like others lust for sex.

That way is war.

Once he takes Wallachia's throne, which is his birthright, he can kill, maim and punish all the thieves, rapists, and traitors, get pleasure from it, and look like a hero. It can't get much better than that. Now that Vlad sees that, his life will never be the same.

"Vlad?" His uncle, Bogdan the Second, measures him. Vlad hopes he can't read his thoughts. "I've seen no one fight like you. I hope to God I never find myself on the wrong side of your sword. Good job, my son. Tell me, what did you learn today?"

Vlad sighs. What did he learn today? Too much to mention. But for one thing. "Killing people beats killing rats."

CHAPTER 18

EDIRNE, OCTOBER 1449

After living in the sarayi for years, Ali knows its every nook and every cranny, so she's quiet as a ghost in the night's silence. She learned to wait until just before the changing of the guards, when they're too tired to pay attention to every moving shadow. And that's all she is: a secretive shadow in the stillness of the night. Her silhouette skirts the gray stone walls before they turn into marble inside the sarayi, where nothing but the best will do for the sultan's women. Her heart quickens as she nears Mara's quarters for another night of forbidden love that could get them both killed.

She's Mara's eunuch, so she's entitled to be in the sarayi, but the guards will get suspicious if they see her coming late at night. Even more so if they don't see her leaving. And, if rumors start, they'll spread through the harem like wildfire. That's why Ali does her best to keep the secret, but Zambak must know something.

She's been all smiles throughout the wedding celebration, like they're the best of friends, but Ali knows better. That girl is waiting to push her off a cliff as soon as she gets a chance. And chances are easy to get, since Ali's got Mara in her blood like a disease. She can't stay away, even though she knows better. She can't wait for the last call to prayer, then the lights to go down so she can sneak into Mara's bed.

When she gets to the door, she puts down the tray of drinks she brought as an excuse. Lame excuse, really — no one will believe she avoided the guards just to bring drinks — but that's the best she's got. She lifts her hand to knock when she hears voices inside. That's odd. It's way too late for a social call.

"Why don't you just admit you love him?" Zambak's voice breaks into sobs.

"Look at me, Zambak. I don't love any man. And I never did — other than my husband, the sultan, of course. I don't know what you're talking about!"

"He's not even a man! Just a eunuch, may God burn his heart into ashes like he burned mine. You can't wait to see him, talk to him, and touch him! You think I'm blind? You no longer ask me to come over. And when I do, there's always something. You're busy, or unwell, or you're afraid someone sees us. You think I'm stupid?"

"Now, now Zambak. You know better than anyone how I love you, and how much I risked to be with you. Why would you even think I care about a man? Not even a man, but a eunuch. Come on, baby. You're being silly. Come here. Who's my girl?"

Another sob, then Mara's soft voice comforting her like you'd comfort a child.

"There. Let's wipe those tears from your beautiful eyes. How can you think I don't love you?"

Ali holds her breath, listening to the silence on the other side of the door. She should leave, but she can't. Mara's words tore her heart, though she hopes they're just meant to soothe the girl. But she's not sure. How could she be?

Well, one way would be to wait and see if Zambak spends the night. That ought to tell her something.

As if she heard her thoughts, Zambak asks: "May I spend the night with you?"

"Not tonight, love. Tonight's no good. Tomorrow."

"Tomorrow?"

"Yes."

"Are you sure?"

"Of course."

"All right, tomorrow then. But listen, Mara. Don't think that, just because I'm in love with you, I'm stupid. If you lie to me, I'll tell Murad. He may not give a hoot what his women do with each other when he's not around, but I bet he'll be eager to know if one of his wives becomes too friendly with a eunuch, especially a white one. Unless he's fully castrated, he wouldn't be the first one to recover the usage of his tool. It happened before, and it didn't end well. And the one thing Murad cares about, after the fate of the empire, is his succession. If he has even the hint of a suspicion, your little friend will end up in the Tunca, with a bag of rocks around his head. After the Bostançı basha works on him, he'll pray to be dead. And, princess or not, you're likely to join him. Murad doesn't give a hoot about your father, but even if he did, he'd still have to set an example, so nobody dares anything like this ever again."

Mara's low voice turns dangerously soft. "Are you threatening me, Zambak?"

"Just warning you."

"You think that will make me love you more?"

Silence. Her ear pressed to the thick wooden door, Ali holds her breath to listen.

"I'm sorry, Mara. That was stupid. I was angry and stupid. I didn't mean it. I'm just crazy with jealousy since I love you so much."

"Of course. I understand. I love you, too. Tomorrow?"

"Tomorrow."

Ali grabs the tray and melts into the darkness as the door opens. She leans against the wall, hoping Zambak won't hear her heart drumming so loud she can barely hear herself think. It feels like forever until the girl is gone.

"Ali?" Mara pulls her in and bolts the door. Her dark eyes sparkle and her cheeks burn with anger, but she's never been more beautiful. She pulls Ali into her arms and holds her tight. "You heard her?"

Ali nods.

"That girl is nuts. I'll have to get rid of her. But first, we need to make sure you're safe. Mehmed and his bride leave for Manisa tomorrow. You'll go with them. I'll tell Murad I sent you to look after Hüma, who isn't well, and asked for you. You'll travel with them to the Dardanelles, where they'll cross into Anatolia. As soon as you get there, find a boat to sail away from the Ottoman Empire, no matter where, whether it's to Constantinople, Genoa, or Venice."

Mara opens the precious chest encrusted with mother-of-pearl by her bed and rummages through the bolts of silk and brocade until she finds an embroidered velvet pouch. She hands it to Ali.

"I was saving this money for a new hospital. It should be enough to buy you safe passage to anywhere you wish to go. It should be enough to buy a whole damn ship. As soon as you're safe, send me a message to tell me where you are."

"How about you?"

"I'll have to take care of Zambak. But first, I need to find out who she talked to. Because she's right, you know. Murad doesn't care what his women do — he never touches most of us anyhow — but the eunuchs? That's something else. And it's easy to prove you're not a eunuch, but that would just start another mess. You'd better be gone before she talks."

"Will I ever see you again?"

Mara laughs, and her low laughter makes Ali's insides tingle. "You betcha. You know, Ali, I never liked eunuchs. They're such self-important prickless pricks. They can't screw women, so they do their best to control and humiliate them. They're supposedly doing it for the sultan, but it makes them feel good about themselves. Their power over women makes them feel manly again. I know they didn't sign up for it, but they're still assholes. That's why I've never liked them, but I've become partial to them since I met you."

Mara pulls Ali closer. She buries her hot mouth in Ali's neck and caresses her budding breasts, then unties the cord holding up her shalwars and pulls her into her bed.

"I'm not really a eunuch," Ali mumbles, her brain turned to mush as Mara's mouth finds her nexus and her hot breath sets her on fire. Ali gasps and strains to attain ecstasy, but the loving mouth pulls away.

"Thank God for that, Ali. But, since you're leaving and I may never see you again, there it is. You're special, and I love you. Don't forget that, for those who judge a woman's worth by the size of the hole between her legs, you're still a virgin, thus marriageable. In this world made for men, women are just chattel. Both my brothers are blind now, but they were useless even when they could still see. They were a couple of wanton twits, but they were Father's sons, so he sold me to Murad to save Serbia's throne for them. I was smarter, harder working, and more resilient than them both, but I was only a woman, so I didn't matter. So, stop and think long and hard before you decide who you're going to be."

"What are you saying, Mara?"

"Once you escape the empire, you'll be free as a bird. You can recreate your past in order to shape your future. You can pretend to be whoever you want, man or woman, since people seldom look beyond clothes and hair. I bet it was hard to live as a eunuch for years, but you may find that being a woman is even harder. But, unlike other women, you can decide who you want to be, so choose wisely."

Mara's greedy mouth returns to its work, finding hidden spots that melt her insides. Ali trembles under her lover's mastery until she swirls into ecstasy, wondering if any man could ever make her feel like this.

CHAPTER 19

BIGALI, NOVEMBER 1449

All over the Ottoman Empire, the late fall shrunk the days and spread the scent of fallen leaves. But here in Bigalı, where the Sea of Marmara squeezes itself into the Strait of Dardanelles before flowing into the Aegean and the mighty Mediterranean, the air smells like the sea. It's a heady combination of algae, salt, and dead fish. Tiny Bigalı, at the foot of the narrow one-mile crossing from Europe to Anatolia, is all about the angry sea that screams her rage, pummeling the sandy shore with wind-whipped waves taller than minarets.

Must be nice in summer, Ali thinks, pulling her kaftan closer.

Spooked by the sea's incessant thunder, her horse shivers under her. Happy for something to do, Ali leans over to whisper in his ear. "Hush now. Be quiet, or you'll get us in trouble. Don't you see Mehmed's mad already?"

Mounted on his fiery black stallion at the head of the caravan, Mehmed talks to a short man looking like he'd rather be elsewhere, but he can't, since he's the captain of their galley.

"What do you mean, we can't cross?" Mehmed asks, his face dark with fury.

"The wind is too strong, my sultan. Our galleys are no match for this storm. We'll have to wait until the waves die down." The man is polite and soft-spoken, but his voice is firm.

"When's that?" Mehmed asks.

"Whenever Allah orders it, my sultan. Maybe tomorrow, maybe in three days. Whenever it happens, we'll be ready to serve you."

"What about those?" Mehmed points to the two tall sail ships braving the seas. Their strained sails curve like wings, and their lean bodies cut through the waves like seagulls slicing the air.

The captain smiles. "Those are not galleys, my sultan. Unlike us, those Portuguese caravels love the wind. Our slave-powered galleys rely on the oars. The wind is our enemy."

Mehmed watches the white ships dance in the wind with wistful eyes. "When I'm the sultan, I'll build a whole new fleet of sea-worthy ships even better than those, and we'll conquer the seas."

"I look forward to that, my sultan. In the meantime, may I suggest the caravanserai down the road for you and your ladies? They must be looking forward to a bath and some warm food after traveling for so long. You too. I'll let you know as soon as the storm abates."

There's nothing else left to do. Mehmed gives the order, and the whole caravan of a hundred souls, plus the horses, turns towards the caravanserai.

The innkeeper, his shiny little eyes engulfed in fat, comes out rubbing his hands. "You honor me, my sultan. We'll get our best rooms ready for you and your ladies, and we'll feed and water the horses. But..."

"What?"

"I'm afraid we don't have room for all your escort. We'll arrange for some of them to sleep in the houses nearby. The servants might sleep in the stables?"

Mehmed nods. He dismounts and hands Rüzgar to a skinny stable boy. "Take care of him. Check his hooves and make sure he gets the best food and plenty of water. My bath?"

The innkeeper leads him inside as Mehmed's men scatter to the nearby houses to seek shelter.

Ali rides back to the cart where the women have been locked in since this morning. She knocks at the door and the curtains open a tad. "We'll spend the night here, waiting for the storm to pass. They're preparing your rooms," she says.

"How long will we be here?" Sittişah asks.

"It depends on the weather."

"I need a bath. And food."

"Soon."

"Now!" Her green eyes are ablaze with fury, just like Hüma's.

Poor Mehmed, Ali thinks, going to look for the innkeeper.

He's in the kitchen, talking to some strange, irate man. Dark curls fall over his wide shoulders, and his leather armor and skinny golden breeches cling to him like they're painted on. He's strong and sleek but for his bouffant sleeves, and Ali finds herself staring at the bulge between his legs. His stormy eyes catch her staring, and Ali blushes and looks away.

The innkeeper wipes the sweat off his face with a dirty handkerchief. "I'm sorry, sire. I have nobody."

"Sure you do. You must have somebody you can spare. I'll pay you well."

"I don't, sire. Not right now. Şehzade Mehmed just arrived on my doorstep with his bride and an entourage of a hundred. I don't have enough food, I don't have enough beds, and I really don't have enough people. I can't spare a single soul. But they'll be gone as soon as the storm dies down. Maybe even tomorrow. I'll be happy to give you a man, then."

"Tomorrow is too late. I'll leave at daylight and I need a cook. I'll pay him well."

"Let me see what I can do, sire. I'll ask around. Which one is your ship?"

"The Queen of the Seas, the best Genoese ship that ever graced the seas. The best men too, but for that addled cook who fell overboard in the storm. Stupid Greek, too drunk to hold on to the latrine."

"I understand, sir. I'll ask around and see what I can do."

The man nods. He glances at Ali one more time, and his ice-blue eyes crinkle at the corners as he studies her from head to toe. He turns to leave but stops in the doorway. "I'm Captain Giovanni. Tell your man to ask for me by name, otherwise those suckers will send him away. They'd rather cook than man the sails, the lazy bums, but I can't spare any. I barely have enough sailors as it is."

"Of course."

The man leaves, his fluffy white sleeves fluttering around him like feathers. The innkeeper shakes his head and turns to Ali. "What can I do for you?"

"The şehzade's wife wants a bath and food. Now."

"Sure she does. Tell her that the hammam will be ready for her and her ladies as soon as the şehzade is done. The food is cooking already and we'll have her rooms ready soon." The innkeeper turns to leave. He can't wait to get rid of her and get back to his work.

"Will you find a cook for that man?"

The innkeeper laughs so hard that his cheeks wiggle like jelly. "Are you kidding? I won't even look. I've got enough to do without going out of my way to help some arrogant Genoese who didn't even spend a dime in my inn. Now if you'll excuse me..."

Ali leaves him at his work and goes to do hers. She needs to help the women to their rooms, make sure their bath is prepared just the way they like it, get them drinks and food and attended to their many needs until they go to sleep. It's a lot, but she'll get it all done in time for Isha, the evening prayer.

When the women have finally gone to sleep, Ali wraps herself in her thick kaftan, pulls her turban over her ears and lies on the doorstep as usual, waiting for the place to fall asleep.

When she finally heads out, hours later, the storm is still raging. Ten steps, and she's soaked to the skin, but she pushes on towards the ships anchored in the bay. There's a dozen of them, all prancing like baby goats at the end of their anchor line. The Queen of the Seas, all dark but for the single torch at the bow, is the furthest away, dancing on the waves like a wild horse.

Ali gets as close as she can before calling. "Ahoy, Queen of the Seas."

A white shape moves under the meager cover protecting him from the rain. It's got to be the sailor on duty, Ali thinks, wiping the rain from her eyes.

"What do you want?"

"I'm here to see Captain Giovanni."

"What for?"

"He'll tell you if he wants you to know."

The man disappears, and Ali shivers in the rain, wondering how long she's got before they come looking for her. Tomorrow, maybe, if she's really lucky. If she's not, they may already be on their way. All it takes is for one woman to need something. If they call her and she doesn't answer, they'll call the guards to look, and she's barely half a mile away. Not far enough.

Ali paces back and forth under the freezing rain, trying to warm herself up. She wonders what to say to the guards if they come and find her here, but nothing comes to mind. She's frozen to the bone by the time the sailor returns.

"The captain says he's not here. Come back in the morning."

That's too late.

But it's already too late. Whistles and screams coming from the caravanserai break through the soothing sound of falling rain. Torches and oil lamps spread out, coming closer and closer. Their flickering lights turn the deep shadows into dark, hungry dragons as the shouting gets louder.

They're close. There must be a dozen of them looking for her. And there's nowhere to hide.

The sailor glances at the torches. Then at her.

"Are they looking for you?"

"Yes."

"What did you do?"

"I escaped."

The man whistles. A white dingy drops in the water and two men paddle it to her. "Jump in."

She does, just as the torches clear the last corner before the port. A dozen lights get near, and someone pushes her down to the bottom of the dingy, rushing back to the Queen of the Seas. By the time the torches reach the shore, the dingy has melted into the darkness behind the boat.

"Hey, you! Did you see a boy around here?"

"What?"

"Did you see a boy? A young eunuch?"

"Speak louder," the sailor says, as the men push her to climb the rope ladder to the deck and follow her.

"Did you see anyone here?" her followers shout.

"Yes. A boy. A while ago. He went that way," the sailor says.

A dozen torches head towards the other side of the port as powerful hands pull Ali onto the Queen.

"I hope you can cook," Captain Giovanni says, giving orders to raise the sails and lift the anchor.

"Why?"

"Why what?"

"Why did you help me?"

"I need a cook."

"Then why did you say you weren't here?"

Captain Giovanni glances at his men to make sure that all hands are on board. The rain runs down his face, and strands of wet dark hair fall over his ice-blue eyes, but he smiles as he leans over to whisper. "Because I don't want women on my ship. They're nothing but trouble. Make sure nobody else knows what you are."

CHAPTER 20

MANISA, NOVEMBER 1449

It's late fall, but the heat of the summer still lingers in the heart of Anatolia. The mornings are crisp and the evenings soft, but the days are hot, sticky, and sweaty; that's why the four hundred miles from Edirne to Manisa have been neither short nor easy. For weeks now, Sittişah stayed locked with her women in the cramped wooden carriage whose screeching wheels never miss a pothole. The darn thing may look pretty, all carved gilded wood and embroidered dark velvet, but with its curtains always drawn to avoid curious eyes, it's hot and oppressive.

To make it worse, the eunuch Mara sent to Hüma disappeared on the way. Some say he got kidnapped or killed, and some say he escaped, but none of that makes any sense. How can a sultan's eunuch disappear? Who'd dare touch him? And where could he run?

Either way, the whole caravan went berserk. They spent days at that stupid caravanserai while the guards crisscrossed the place and checked every boat looking for that dumb kid, but couldn't find him. It took three whole days until Mehmed finally gave up and ordered them to proceed forward.

"Why did we have to spend three days looking for him? Aren't eunuchs a dime a dozen?"

The old woman Emine Validé had assigned to instruct Sittişah in the Ottoman ways glanced at her sideways. "That eunuch is Hüma Hatun's personal servant, and he's precious. A white full eunuch is worth his weight in gold. Hüma left him with Mara until she returns to Edirne, but the şehzade is worried about how his mother will take this loss. She's said to be feeling poorly, and she doesn't take disappointment well."

Sittişah nodded, then pretended to fall asleep to have some privacy. Boy, is she glad to be getting home. Because the Manisa sarayi will be her new home until Sultan Murad dies and Mehmed takes back the throne, and they can move back to Edirne. May Allah in his kindness make that happen sooner rather than later, because the Edirne palace is where it's at. And it will be even better when Murad's old hags go to wherever Mehmed sends them, and she'll be the sultan's favorite, like she deserves. All these weeks they've traveled, she's been planning. She has a to-do list for Manisa, and the first thing on her list is Mehmed.

Sadly, she made no progress after that first night when he left her in his bed and disappeared. She didn't complain, of course. She kept her head up and smiled like everything was going well, but they all know. The guards at Mehmed's bedroom saw him coming and leaving in less than a minute, so they know he didn't honor her that night. And they must have told others, because she's seen a lot of faces looking at her with pity.

And that's one thing she doesn't need. She doesn't need pity — not from the validé, not from Murad's wives, not from anyone. What she needs is to get into Mehmed's bed. That's the only way she can give birth to the next şehzade. Well, there may be other ways, but she still needs Mehmed in her bed first.

Number two on her list is endearing herself to Mehmed's mother. Sittişah has heard a lot about Hüma Hatun, who sounds like she matters, even though she's just a slave. She'd make a better friend than an enemy. Especially since when Mehmed becomes sultan, Hüma Hatun will be the validé.

Number three, she'll have to show the other women in Mehmed's harem who's boss. The sooner, the better, since they're all nothing but slaves.

She's still plotting her way into Mehmed's bed as they arrive. Thank Allah! She can't wait to get out of that damn cart, stretch her legs and breathe fresh air. She smiles at the sight of the crowd gathered to welcome her. She waves and dances through the door to give them something to talk about. These are her people. She'll be their queen, and they'll love her.

A few steps, and she's finally inside the Manisa sarayi, where the welcome party is waiting. Sittişah steps in, followed by her women, and takes off her veils. The room gasps. She smiles, glad to have made an impression, but they look more stunned than delighted.

What the heck is this about, she wonders, until she sees Hüma Hatun. Looking at Mehmed's mother is like looking in a mirror.

Hüma's green eyes widen as she greets her. "Welcome home, Sittişah. How was your trip?"

Sittişah bows and kisses her hand. "It's so good to be home. I've heard so much about you. I couldn't wait to meet you."

"Me too. I'm sorry I wasn't well enough to welcome you to Edirne, but I'm glad to see you now. You're just as beautiful as Hizir Paşa's wife said."

Sittişah struggles to appear humble and fails.

"Let me introduce you to the ladies. This is Gülbahar, Mehmed's first wife and the mother of his son, Bayezid."

The smiling blonde woman seems nice enough, with her sleepy blue eyes and droopy shoulders. Not a serious contender, Sittişah thinks.

"And this is Gülşah, Mehmed's consort."

Gülşah is another matter altogether. Her skin glows like mother-of-pearl, and her lustrous black hair falls to her thighs. With her ocean-blue eyes and delicate eyebrows, she's stunning. Even worse, she's heavy with child, and just like that, Sittişah hates her like she's hated no one before. She smiles and nods as she's introduced to the others. She pretends to be paying attention, but her mind is focused on Gülşah. How to get rid of her.

The introductions over, they sit on the pillows scattered on the precious silk carpet gleaming in soft tones of green and bronze, like the forest in the fall. Sittişah has the place of honor at Hüma's left, and she has Elif, another one of Mehmed's women, to her left. Servants stream in, bending under the weight of silver trays loaded with the best that Anatolia can offer.

First come the olives: green, firm *picholine* flavored with citrus, brown pungent *Kalamáta*, woodsy dry-cured Thasos, soft-fleshed *Atalanti*, orange *arbequina* with their bitter bite. Their salty, earthy flavors make the women's mouths water, and they all fall over them like a flock of pigeons over scattered grain.

Next the breads: white crustless naan sprinkled with black sesame, white spongy *pide* baked in clay ovens, tahini sweet rolls, crusty sourdough *ekmek* glazed with egg yolk, chewy round *simit* encrusted with poppy seeds, and *somun ekmeği*, its crisp crust glowing like amber.

Then the cheeses: white goat cheese from Thrace, near the Sea of Marmara; smooth yellow cow's milk Kashar, snow-white salty feta that crumbles and melts in your mouth, tangy rich *Eski Kaşar*, crumbled *tulum* cheese served over walnut halves, and rich smoked *Düzce*, its brown crust smelling like pine.

Then the meats, sweets, and drinks, and fruit and countless mountains of deliciousness like Sittişah has never seen, not even at the wedding party. The women get busy. They pick the food off the trays with their fingers, eating on top of the bread while chirping happily like birds, but everything tastes like ash to Sittişah. The one thing she'd like to taste is Gülşah's blood. She'd like to sink her teeth into the pearly skin of her throat and rip it off like a wolf killing a sheep.

But that will have to wait.

"Are you well?" Hüma asks.

"A bit tired. It's been a long trip."

"Of course."

Hüma's sharp green eyes seek to look inside her, and Sittişah shivers. She doesn't want anyone looking inside her. Should Hüma know what she's thinking, she'd be horrified, because in the harem, jealousy is not tolerated. It's there, of course, but you can't show it. That's why the women pretend to like one another, then stab each other in the back.

But Hüma wouldn't like that. Even less now that Gülşah is about to have Mehmed's child, maybe even a son, Allah burn her in hell. I'd better get rid of her before she births the baby — one accident and boom — they're both gone, Sittişah thinks. Much harder to kill them both afterward. She might have a girl, of course, but you can't count on that. And she's way too beautiful. Better safe than sorry.

"When is your baby due, Gülşah?" Sittişah asks.

Gülşah smiles, happy to have her attention. "In less than two moons, Allah willing."

"Your first?"

Gülşah nods.

"May Allah make him healthy and strong like his father. Let me know if you need anything, I'd be glad to help."

Sittişah hopes she didn't go too far with the sweetness — who could believe such nonsense? — but they all look pleased. How stupid can these women be? Stupid enough to think that she wishes Gülşah anything but a quick death, thankfully. She'll have to make it look like an accident. She'll befriend her and gain her trust while she learns the lay of the land. There's got to be something that would work. A high tower to fall from? A well to drown in? A set of steep stairs to stumble upon?

By the time the party is over and the mountains of food have vanished, so has Sittişah's patience. She stands to helps Gülşah, whose heavy belly makes her graceless.

"We're so glad to have you here," Gülbahar says.

"Me too," Sittişah lies.

But her smile doesn't. She just figured it out. The hammam. That's where she'll kill Gülşah.

CHAPTER 21

CONSTANTINOPLE, FALL 1449

The night is soft and peaceful, now that Constantinople fell asleep. But it won't last long. The *polis*, as its people call it, like there's no other city in the world, wakes up before dawn, with the merchants' carts rumbling towards the markets to set up and be ready by the first light. At sunrise, the stalls groan under the weight of striped melons, mountains of purple olives, fragrant luscious cheeses and dying fish that flop around, looking for water. The bearded vendors cough their morning cough, then start vocalizing, warming up their throats to sing up their merchandise. They'll all be hoarse by noon, but for now, they outdo each other to entice the passers-by.

But they aren't up yet, even though the tavernas have closed their doors, sending the last party goers to sleep: the bearded men, their curly hair stuck to their flushed skin after too many cups of harsh red wine; and the tired women with their eyes magnified by kohl, their cheeks hurting from smiling, and their shoulders aching from lifting the heavy *amphorae* to pour the wine.

This time of the night is Ion's favorite. He's all alone, sitting at the long table where he first met Notaras, and he can work undisturbed by the megas doux's incessant demands, his daughter's enticing glances, and the nosy servants coming to dust, clean, and eye the records that are none of their business.

He's been doing this for almost a year, so it got easier, even though Notaras finds more work for him every day. But Ion doesn't mind. He loves his work — who wouldn't love playing with numbers? — and gets paid ten times more than he made laying bricks. And he's safe. Well, as safe as one can be in a snake pit, because that's what the Byzantine government is. And Loukas Notaras is the biggest viper of all.

Ion knew it since the day they met — the man is as slippery as an eel and just as trustworthy — but he didn't have much to lose. He's not the target of the megas doux's greed. The emperor is. And his treasury.

Constantine the Eleventh is the most imperiled men in the empire. His brothers want his throne, Loukas Notaras wants his money, and the Ottomans want his city, which is all that's left from the most glorious empire of the east. They're all after him. Still, Constantine holds them all at bay. He's got to be smarter than he looks.

Ion turns the page and sets to check the taxes paid by the bakers and the butchers when Notaras stumbles in. He pulls out a chair and sits. His flushed cheeks and red eyes tell Ion that he's had a few cups.

"How's it going?" he asks.

"Good, thanks. How's it going with you?"

"All right. Sort of."

"Problem?"

"Meh. You know Sphrantzes?"

Ion shakes his head. He doesn't know George Sphrantzes, the historian, Constantine's old friend and most trusted advisor, but he knows about him. The rivalry between him and Loukas Notaras for the emperor's ear is the talk of the town.

"He's an asshole. Don't trust him."

Ion nods. That shouldn't be hard, since he's never met him.

"You're going to see him tomorrow."

"I am? Why?"

"He has a problem with his accounts that nobody can figure. I told him I knew someone who can. He laughed at me, so I bet him ten ducats. You're going to see him tomorrow and solve his problem. If you win me the ten ducats, I'll give you one."

I get one ducat for solving the problem, and he gets nine for bragging about it. What a deal, Ion thinks. But that's how Notaras operates: he gets the lion's share out of every deal. That's why Ion wonders what's in the other set of records, the ones Notaras never showed him, locked next door.

Notaras rests his chin in his palm and studies Ion under his heavy lids. He may be half drunk, but the viper's still there, ready to strike. "I like you, you know. You're good at your job, and you never make trouble. Starting tomorrow, I'll tri... double your pay. That will make you the best paid accountant in the Roman Empire. For as long as I can trust you."

"Thank you."

"I've always been curious about Sphrantzes. He lives better than his income should allow him. Why don't you take a good look at his records, and we'll talk about them when you get back."

CHAPTER 22

AN OFFER ONE CAN'T REFUSE

It's the first time Ion set foot in Constantinople's glorious Imperial Palace, Byzantium's pride, and he can't help but notice that it must have seen better days. The palace is a thousand years old, and it looks it. Generations of Romans, as they like to call themselves, wore the stone floors into slippery smoothness. Sunbeams peek in through the gaps in the walls where the faded tapestries got too thin to hide them, and patches of green moss prosper wherever the leaks in the roof spurred them to grow.

Still, the palace didn't forget its former glory. There's gold wherever you look: the golden Orthodox crosses, the elaborate icon frames whose emaciated saints got so smoky all you can recognize is their golden aura, the holy reliquaries sitting in the many alcoves. The gold means to steal one's eye from the destitution, but Ion sees both.

Sitting at the long council table in a boxy carved chair, George Sphrantzes is not a big man. He's short and plump and about to lose what's left of his hair, but his eyes are straight and bright as he smiles at Ion. "Welcome. Are you the miracle man the megas doux told me about?"

"Not much of a miracle, I'm afraid. Just good with numbers."

"How come?"

"Numbers spoke to me since I was young. I just look at them and they make sense. Then, I was lucky enough to work with Sultan Murad's tax men. They taught me a lot."

Sphrantzes whistles in admiration. "The sultan's tax men! There's no better administration in the world. No wonder the sultan's coffers are so deep. How the heck did you end up with Notaras?"

"The sultan sent me to Wallachia with his protegee, Vlad Dracula, when he took the throne. But he didn't keep it long. When he went back, I came here instead."

"Why?"

"I didn't treasure going back to Edirne."

Sphrantzes nods. "I can't blame you. How's Notaras treating you?"

"Fairly."

The man smiles and hands him a heavy tome. "I have an extra five thousand ducats. I don't know why. I've been through it again and again. So have my men. Nothing. A stupid person would say I should be happy I'm not missing them and just enjoy them. But I know you're not stupid. You understand that having this discrepancy means that everything else in my ledgers is questionable. Your master said you'll succeed where others failed. Ten ducats weigh upon your skill. Did he tell you?"

"He did."

"And let me guess. He'll give you one and keep the other nine if he wins."

Ion nods.

"But there's more. He wants to know what's in my ledgers. So he'll raise your pay to tell him."

"How do you know?"

"I know Notaras. He's nothing if not predictable. He's been trying to look in my pants for years. He just can't believe that somebody can be honest. Just like that, honest. Maybe you can persuade him. Be my guest." He claps his hands. A young woman wrapped in a figure-hugging peplum leaving little to the imagination steps in. "Kyra, make sure that our guest here gets food and drinks and whatever else he needs. Let me know when he's done."

Kyra nods. Sphrantzes limps out of the room and Ion asks: "What happened to him?"

"Nothing. It's just his arthritis, since it's about to rain. What can I get you?"

"Water please."

He opens the first heavy ledger on the table and goes through column after column. Nothing. Page after page, it all checks out. He goes to the next, and the next, and the next.

Until he finds it. There it is: January 20th, five thousand ducats for the emperor's coronation. They aren't anywhere in the expense row. No evidence that they used it for food, or drinks, or horses, or anything else. This is it.

He rings the bell on the table and Kyra comes in. "I'm done."

"You need anything?"

"Just Sphrantzes."

He sips on his water, wondering what to do next. He won his ducat, and he's seen enough of this man's business to know that he's most likely straight. Notaras won't like that, since he's looking for dirt. Oh well. It is what it is.

Sphrantzes comes in, followed by a tall, handsome man wearing a princess tiara and weighed by so much gold he'd glow in the dark.

"You found it?"

"Yes. Here. Five thousand ducats for the emperor's coronation. Never spent."

Sphrantzes looks at it and nods. "Yep. Notaras won his bet and made ten ducats."

Ion stands to leave.

"You haven't yet met Emperor Constantine. My emperor, this is Ion. Numbers speak to him like you and I speak to each other. Lukas Notaras discovered him and took him in his service, but he's a free man. We could use somebody with his skills to keep track of our treasury. But numbers are just one of his talents. Ion spent years in

Edirne, working in the Ottoman tax system, so he knows more about them than anyone else I know. He also is an Orthodox Christian. He's from Transylvania, and he speaks Greek, Romanian, Turkish and…"

"Latin. And a little Hungarian."

"I thought you'd like to meet him."

The emperor nods. The tiara perched on top of his head wobbles, but doesn't make him look silly, which is a tall order. "You know why that coronation money didn't match?"

"No."

"Because it never got used. We had more important things to do with our money, so we decided to forgo the coronation. That's why I'm wearing this — he touches his tiara. It was meant for the sister I never had, but it's lighter on the neck. And it was free." He scratches the back of his neck and sets back the tiara, a little crooked now. "Would you like to work for me?"

"What would I have to do?"

"Play with numbers, like you are now. Teach me about the Ottomans and how their minds work. Help me keep the Roman Empire safe. It's been in danger for hundreds of years, and I'm afraid our luck is running thin."

He sits and invites Ion to do the same. His mesmerizing eyes catch Ion's and won't let go. "Ion, you must know that Constantinople is the last barrier protecting Europe from the Ottomans who would stop at nothing to wipe out Christianity. A weak barrier, I must admit, but we're the best Christianity has got left, now that Vlad Dracul is dead, Hunyadi is busy licking his wounds, and the pope is too cheap to send us anything but prayers. Prayers? I can pray myself, thank you very much. I need ships, men, and money. Especially money. I need them to reinforce the crumbling Theodosian Walls, hire soldiers, and buy provisions and weapons. I know it's just a matter of time until the Ottomans return. Whether it's Murad, his weak-minded son Mehmed, or…"

"Sorry, sir. Did you say weak-minded Mehmed?"

"Yes. That silly kid Murad abdicated to…"

"I'm sorry, sir. I'll give this to you for free: Mehmed is anything but feeble-minded. I learned with him, I fought with him, and I know him. He's not weak, and he's not stupid. Just the opposite. He'll be a greater danger to your empire than Murad ever was. Sultan Murad is old and tired, and he wants peace. Mehmed is young and hungry for glory. Whoever told you that Mehmed will be easy, they lied."

"Good to know, though it may be too early to tell. Still, will you work with me to uphold Christianity?" Constantine asks.

Ion nods. "I'll be glad to."

He doesn't tell him about Ali and Codru, his friends and partners. Why would he? He'll do his best to fight for Constantinople, since that means supporting Christianity and protecting the Romanian countries. And that's what he's here for.

CHAPTER 23
MOLDOVA, DECEMBER 1449

It's mid-December, and the days got shorter than a eunuch's pecker, here, in the north. Cold too. And, like that wasn't enough, the low sky opened, dropping tons of snow over Moldova. Covered by the sparkling whiteness, the entire country looks ready for a fairy tale. Wrapped in its glittering mantle, even the old stone castle of Suceava looks like an ugly bride bedecked in a scintillating wedding gown.

Vlad spurs his horse uphill to the grand semicircular gate. His day of hunting didn't amount to much — just one pheasant and an old hare — but it felt good to kill. That always feels good. But now he wonders if he should have stayed out and cooked them on a campfire rather than bring them back. Because, sadly, there are just a few days before Christmas, and the entire country is fasting to get cleansed for Christ's birth. Even here, at the Seat Fortress of Suceava, they haven't had a piece of meat in weeks. Nor fish, milk, or even cheese. Nothing but bread, beans, nuts, and apples. All good things, but a man needs meat. And wine.

Vlad drops his horse with a stable hand and walks across the courtyard to the kitchens, looking forward to seeing what they've got.

He knows he's late for dinner, but he hopes for something special, like maybe even a boiled egg?

He'd never thought he'd miss the Ottoman cuisine, but he'd give a lot for a roasted chicken right now. Even a fish, or some mutton. The Ottomans may have their Ramadan, a whole month they don't eat or drink during the day, but they don't fast like Orthodox do. Six weeks before Christmas, seven before Easter, plus every Wednesday and Friday of the year, plus a few weeks here and there just because. *Nobody else does this. They're not that stupid,* Vlad thinks, then chases the evil thought away. He stops to watch the fat snow fall in flakes big as feathers, covering the dirt, the ugliness and the many things in need of repair. The entire country looks like a wedding cake.

Life here isn't bad. He can come and go as he pleases, and Bogdan treats him just like he treats Ștefan. So does everyone else. But unlike Ștefan, Vlad isn't used to this.

He didn't see it, but his years with the Ottomans have changed him. He misses the hammam smelling like jasmine and roses, the rich sweets dripping with butter and honey, and the soft silk clothes. He even misses the beauty that surrounded him, though he barely ever noticed it. It's almost like he misses Edirne, and that's unthinkable. Maybe he's just bored.

With Bogdan on the throne, there's been no war. And Vlad doesn't care about the daily grind of dealing with the taxes and complaints, distributing justice, and rebuilding forts and monasteries. He struggles to stay awake through the Greek and Latin lessons. He loves the weapons training and the strategy days. But boy, how he misses a good fat rat. And a fight. And some meat.

Baba Nela, dressed all in black like the Orthodox widows, is all done with dinner. Vlad does his best to sweet-talk her, but there's no egg for him. How on earth do chickens know it's time to fast? Vlad wonders, picking up the bowl of beans with onions and paprika and a thick trencher of crusty bread.

"Not even cheese?" he begs.

Baba Nela covers her mouth to laugh. "Nope. No meat, no fish, no eggs, no honey. Nothing. But remember, Christ had it harder, and we're celebrating His birth."

Vlad wonders how she got so fat on plants alone, God help her. As for him, his old clothes hang on him, and he wasn't fat to start with.

He sits on the bench by the worn kitchen table and dips the bread in the beans, struggling not to gag. But he's hungry enough to eat anything. And they aren't that bad. As a matter of fact, they're delicious — sweet, salty and a little spicy, he thinks, wiping the plate with the last crust of bread. He drinks water, since there's no wine to be had, and wonders how he could break into the cellar to steal some, when somebody touches his shoulder.

"You're doing OK?"

Ștefan, of course.

"Nope. I'm struggling. How about you?"

"I can barely hold it together. I need a break, and I thought you might too. How about a field trip?"

"To where?"

"South. I used to have a friend in Berzunți. My milk sister was closer to me than my brothers. She's beautiful and full of fire, and your brother Mircea really liked her. I don't know where she is or what she's doing these days, but I'm hoping her parents might know. Want to ride south with me?"

His words tickle Vlad's memory. There's something he should remember. "What's her name?" he asks.

"Lena."

Ah! The girl Mircea married. *If I don't make it, take care of my wife and my child*, he had said. But Ștefan doesn't know. Darn it. This won't be easy, but there's nothing else to do.

"Of course. When?"

"The day after tomorrow? We need to talk to Father and prepare. We'll be gone for a week, maybe more."

Vlad nods. He has one day to figure out how to tell Ștefan that his best friend, Mircea, married Lena, the love of his life.

Ștefan's face lights up. "Great. I can't wait to see her, and it will give us a break from this place. I know I need it."

CHAPTER 24
TOGETHER, AGAIN

Moldova is empty in winter. Come spring, as soon as the earth's crust unfreezes, slow-moving oxen slapping the flies across their backs with long muddy tails drag heavy plows to cut deep trenches into the earth's belly to open it to the next harvest's seeds. In summer, men, women, and children brave the merciless sun to cut the golden hay with their scythes and stack it in orderly haystacks smelling like sunshine. In the fall, heavy carts piled high with hay, grain, and timber screech their way along muddy roads to stash away the wealth of the land.

But few venture out in winter. Nothing moves, other than the wood smoke rising from the sleepy houses' skinny chimneys. The villages are so gray and quiet they look like children's drawings guarded by skeletal trees.

As they ride along the frozen roads followed by the six guards Bogdan insisted upon, there's hardly any noise other than the wind whipping the snow-heavy clouds and the clatter of the horses' hooves. And their voices.

It's good to travel with a friend, Ștefan thinks, remembering the years he spent with Mircea. The long hours of mindless riding stir things you'd never dream to talk about, opening people's souls towards each other. Vlad must feel the same. "Tell me about Mircea," he asks. "I was just a kid when they sent me to the sultan's court, so I never got to know him like you did."

"That's too bad. He was just seventeen, but he was already an able general. Brave, for sure, but that wasn't it. Whenever he looked into your eyes and listened to you, you felt like no one else mattered. When he asked his men to fight, each of them felt like Mircea spoke straight to him. I've seen no one with that skill. Not Hunyadi, not your father, and not mine, though they're all great generals. Mircea alone had that gift."

"You liked him."

"I loved him. He was my best friend."

"Did you ever fight?"

"We didn't. But I hated him once. We liked the same girl. He wanted to marry her, but your father said no. 'You are a Wallachian prince; you don't belong to yourself, you belong to your country. You'll only marry to bring Wallachia a worthy alliance, to help her get ahead. Marrying a Moldavian peasant, no matter how pretty, won't help Wallachia.'"

"What did Mircea say?"

"I can't remember. I was too angry to think. But he didn't marry her."

Vlad sighs. "It looks like it's about to snow. We'd better get there before the night."

He spurs his horse, throwing snow and ice behind, and Ștefan follows. They swallow the distance as the cavalcade rushes forward. Their canter strengthens the blizzard cutting through their clothes like they're naked. Ștefan pulls his quilted mantle closer, grateful for the fox trim around his neck. They race until the horses slow down by themselves, and Ștefan moves back to Vlad's side.

"How was growing up at the Ottoman court? I was away from home too, for years, but I was with your parents, so everything was pretty much the same: the language, the food, the church. I can't imagine how it must have been to live with the Ottomans for all those years.”

“To tell you the truth, it wasn’t much fun. Most of the time, I was in jail. When I escaped from one, they caught me and put me in another. Not much to do but think. And catch rats.”

Ștefan laughs, thinking he’s kidding.

“But learning about them was worth it. The Ottomans are not like us. Every moment of their lives is ruled by Allah and the sultan. They pray when they muezzin calls, five times a day, and wash before they pray. They fast throughout the month of Ramadan, and never touch pork or wine. They all look at the sultan like he’s God, even the janissaries, which is odd, since they’re our own kids they stole from us. But they got brainwashed into thinking about the sultan like their father. There’s no higher honor than dying for him, and they’re faithful to him to their last breath. That’s why the sultan trusts them with the highest positions in his *dīvān,* up to the grand vizier. That sets them against the noble Ottomans who chase the same jobs. Have you heard of Çandarlı Halil Paşa?”

“Isn’t he the grand vizier?”

“For now. He’s been Murad’s vizier for years, but he won’t last long with Mehmed. Çandarlı Paşa comes from a noble Ottoman family, while Mehmed’s viziers come from devşirme. They’re all ambitious new converts, and he plays them against each other.”

“How’s their war machine different from ours?”

“Thanks to the devşirme and everything else they stole from us, they have more of it. More soldiers, more horses, more bombards. In every single fight, they outnumber their opponent at least two to one.”

“It was like that in Varna.”

“And Kosovo and everywhere else. They deploy their war machine according to a system. They always choose wide battlefields to surround their opponents and crush them — the opposite of what your father did at Tămășeni. Bogdan didn’t choose a terrain to fit his strategy, he chose a strategy to fit the terrain. He used the river and the woods to his advantage, and he won. He got me thinking that speed and flexibility may trump numbers. When I'll fight the Ottomans, I won't do it on their terms, like Hunyadi did. I'll pick and kill them one by one when they don't expect me. They won't even know what hit them."

Ștefan gasps. "You're planning to fight the Ottomans? I thought they were your friends. Didn't they help you get the throne last year?"

"Sure they did. But they didn't do it because they liked me, they did it because it suited them. The Ottomans are not my friends. They're nobody's friends. They're a disease trying to swallow the world, but, so help me God, I'll do whatever it takes to stop them."

"But Moldova and Wallachia are too small to fight them alone. It's either them, or Hunyadi and the Poles, like your father did his whole life."

"I know. I'll cross that bridge when I get to it."

There's the last turn before Lena's village. Ștefan's heart quickens at the thought of her. He hasn't seen her in years, and for all he knows, she could be dead. Or married. Thinking about her being married turns his stomach, and he almost wishes he stayed home, but it's too late.

The square tiny house behind the church looks empty, but for the smoke rising from the chimney. Somebody's home, stoking the fire, and Ștefan's throat tightens. Who is it? What if a man opens the door? What if she's dead? He takes a deep breath and knocks on the door.

Nothing.

He knocks again. Maybe he should have left the guards behind? Lena's parents must be wondering who they are. He doesn't want to put them off, but it's too late. They must have seen them. He knocks again.

Lena opens the door, and Ștefan's breath freezes. With her flushed cheeks bringing out the sparkle in her eyes and the thick golden braid falling down her shoulder, she's more beautiful than ever. Her eyes grow wide.

"Ștefan?"

He hugs her like he'll never let her go, breathing in her scent and relishing the touch of her hair against his cheek. His eyes moisten, and his heart swells. He's so happy he can hardly breathe. His Lena. His girl is in his arms, and all is good with the world.

"Mom?"

Ștefan steps back.

A dark-haired toddler waddles over, rubbing his eyes with his fists. He stares at Ștefan with round dark eyes and hides behind Lena's skirts.

She pushes him forward. "Ștefan, this is Mircea."

CHAPTER 25
THE UNCLE

Vlad steps back to give Ștefan a smidge of privacy. He tries to look away, but he can't. His eyes stay glued to the dark-haired toddler in the door, who's his brother Mircea's spitting image, and Vlad's heart aches with longing. The kid is blood of his blood, and he promised to cherish and protect him with his life.

His eyes move to Lena, and he can't help but wonder how she managed to ensnare both Mircea and Ștefan. Why did both these remarkable men fall for her? Mircea defied Father's orders to marry her, and Ștefan would have done the same if he could. You can see it in his eyes. He's crushed to see that this woman bore Mircea's child.

Truth be told, she is pretty, with her creamy skin, periwinkle eyes, and rich mane of silky hair. Then Vlad sees the love in her eyes as she glances at the baby, and has to admit that she's not pretty; she's beautiful. As beautiful as a painted Madonna.

But so what? Vlad rubs his icy hands and stomps his feet to the ground, hoping Stefan gets it together before they all freeze to death. Beauty is beauty, and cold is cold. There's a time for everything, Vlad thinks, frowning at Ștefan who got stuck in the door like a goddamn salt pillar, and resisting the urge to shake him awake. Fortunately, Lena picks up the kid and wraps him in her arms to keep him warm.

She turns to Ștefan. "Why don't you come in?"

Ștefan stares at the kid, then turns to Vlad for help.

"Sure, we'd be glad to come in," Vlad says. He sends their men to seek shelter, then puts his arm around Ștefan's shoulders and leads him in.

Lena closes the door and puts down the kid to stoke the fire.

Vlad squats by the kid. "What's your name?"

The kid hides behind his hands, peeking between his fingers. Vlad laughs and does the same. They study each other like that until the kid laughs and lowers his shield.

"So, what's your name, kid?"

"Mircea."

The kid studies Vlad's sword. He touches the filigreed hilt with a dirty little finger no bigger than a twig, following the intricate patterns. He glances at Vlad. "What's this?"

"My sword. It used to be my father's. You wish to see it?"

The kid nods, and Vlad pulls out the sword to show it to him. "See, this is a dragon biting its tail. And this is a cross. And see this yellow stone? It's amber. See the tiny ant trapped inside it?"

The kid nods. His wide dark eyes are so much like Mircea it's uncanny. He traces every shape and stone with rapt attention without saying a word, and Vlad suddenly realizes he's never spoken to a kid. There were no kids in prison or the janissary school. But he starts telling little Mircea about his sword, where it was made, how and when, leaving Ștefan and Lena to get themselves sorted out.

The rekindled fire warms the small room, and the smoke reminds Vlad of his nanny's house in Târgoviște. Whenever Mother was busy with some church or another, she had a peasant woman look after him and Radu. Even when they grew older, the boys would still sneak to her house. She had them sit on short, three-legged milking stools, and gave them thick slices of crusty bread and milk so fresh it was still warm from the cow. Vlad tasted nothing better, not even the finest wines.

He glances at Ștefan and Lena. They're finally talking to each other now that Ștefan came out of his frozen stupor. He doesn't look happy, but at least he's alive. And that woman... there's something about her that demands attention. There's a light inside her that goes beyond her beauty.

Vlad turns back to the kid. Little Mircea got over his shyness and started exploring him like he's uncharted territory.

The little dirty fingers checked the buckle of his belt, traced the hilt of his dagger, and they're now pulling on his mustache. "What's this?"

"My mustache. It's hair. It grows from the skin."

"Why?"

"Why?" Good question. Vlad never thought about it. "It comes with being a man. It just grows; you tame it a little, and it makes you look manly. Most men also have beards that grow from the chin, but I don't like them. They're itchy and they get greasy with food. But I guess it must be easier to clean them than to shave them. You need a barber with a very sharp knife, but you have to be careful. You can never be sure whether he'll shave your beard or cut your throat."

The kid nods like he gets it, which he can't. But the aroma of food fills Vlad's nose, and he realizes he's starving. They haven't eaten since this morning, and they rode in the cold the whole day. He glances at the table to see plates and cups, and Vlad hopes it's wine. He really needs it.

"Dinner."

Vlad stands. The kid lifts his hands. "What?"

"Up."

He wants to be picked up. Vlad leans over. The kid wraps his arms around his neck and they head toward the dinner table.

Lena's eyes grow wide. "Wow. He's never done that before. He doesn't usually care for strangers. Not that he sees many."

Vlad smiles like he doesn't care, but he tightens his arms around the kid. "It's got to be my charm."

He sits at the table with the kid in his lap as Lena serves them plates of steaming stew, thick slices of bread, and cups full of warm, creamy milk.

The flavor of the stew makes Vlad dizzy. It smells like onions and carrots and herbs. And meat. "Aren't you fasting?" he asks.

Lena shrugs. "I have so many sins, God won't care about one more. And I won't throw away good meat just because the priest says so. He can throw his."

"Where did you get the meat?"

"Joiana's calf came too early, and he wasn't going to make it. It broke my heart, but I couldn't just let it die. So, I slaughtered it and cooked it. But I have some beans if you'd rather…"

Vlad looks at the woman again and sees what he didn't before. This woman who eats meat when no one else does, even though the priest tells her she'll go to hell, is like nobody he's ever met. He starts to see what Mircea and Ștefan found in her.

"Me too," the kid says.

Vlad dips the bread in the stew and feeds him. He chews, swallows, and opens his mouth again.

This kid won't die hungry, Vlad thinks. Good for him. Like mother, like son.

"How are you?" he asks Ștefan.

Ștefan pushes his untouched bowl away. "OK. You?"

"Good." And he is. This kid gives him joy like he's never had before. And the woman is something else. "Lovely stew," he says. "The best I've ever had."

The woman smiles, and her face softens like summer rain uncovering a rainbow. "Thanks… What did you say your name was?"

"I'm Vlad."

"Vlad?"

"Vlad Dracula. I'm Mircea's brother."

CHAPTER 26
ANATOLIA, WINTER 1449

The sun is about to set on the hunting grounds near Manisa. The brown hills darkened, and their shadows grew long over the valley. It's winter, so the days are short and precious. Gone is the summer's blue sky with its blistering heat; the fall rains softened the parched earth, and the game had time to fatten through the fall. Winter is the best hunting season, and that makes Mehmed happy.

The other thing that gives him joy is having Radu with him. When he returned from Edirne after the wedding, he asked his friend to join him.

"Come with me. Manisa is my place. There, I can do whatever I want, whenever I want, without Father breathing down my neck. We'll spend the days hunting the golden hills, then at night we'll watch the stars and write poems. Please come. You have nothing keeping you here."

"But what will Sultan Murad say?"

"Who cares? You're no longer a hostage, but a valued guest. You're free to come and go as you please. Come with me," he said, burying his face in Radu's groin.

Radu gasped and panted and said: "Yes."

Still, truth be told, Mehmed felt uneasy about telling his father.

But Murad just shrugged. "Fine with me. Whatever you do in your spare time is up to you. His crazy brother Vlad is in Moldova fighting alongside Hunyadi, and he'll start pining for Wallachia's throne again. Why don't you keep Radu close, just in case? But make sure he understands the superiority of our ways and the value of our alliance. It would be nice to have a faithful ally leading Wallachia. We haven't had one of those since... forever?"

"But Father, Radu is my friend."

"I know. That's your business. Friendship comes in many shapes, and as long as you fulfill your duty towards the empire and your family, the rest is up to you."

That's why Mehmed rides the woods of Anatolia alongside Radu, who's no longer the squeamish kid he used to be. These days he's a master of the bow and arrow, and he rides almost as well as Mehmed. But more importantly, he's the best lover Mehmed has ever had.

His soft skin smells like sandalwood, jasmine, and horse — a heady combination. And with his golden hair and sapphire eyes, Radu is more handsome than many harem women. But there's more than that.

Radu touches Mehmed as if he can read his thoughts, and feels him like nobody else does, not even Gülbahar. She lays there, obedient and always ready to give herself to him any way he wants, pretending she likes it even when she doesn't. But Radu pushes him. He bites him and tortures him and possesses him in ways Mehmed never dreamed about. He'll please him like a slave, then command him like a master. Remembering it makes Mehmed's throat go dry. He wants Radu right here and now.

He signals the men following them. "Wait here. We'll be back."

He nods to Radu, who follows him into the woods. The men stay put and wait.

"What's up?" Radu asks, galloping by his side over the dry grass the sun burned into dark orange.

"I'll show you."

They enter the woods. Mehmed dismounts Rüzgar, and ties him to a branch. Radu follows, and suddenly they're all alone in the dark silence. The old forest soars like a cathedral with its tall pines like columns holding the sky, and Mehmed's heart sings.

"What is it?" Radu whispers.

"This." Mehmed drops his shalwars, liberating the throbbing flesh between his thighs. He unties Radu's shalwars and bends him over a fallen trunk, pushing him down and sinking inside him.

Radu gasps but holds on. His moans stoke Mehmed's desire, and he grabs Radu's hips, sinking inside him, thrusting his fire into him. He gasps and pants, plunging in again and again, until the heavenly release softens his knees. He plants his precious Ottoman seed inside this Wallachian man who'll never give birth to his children, then screams his joy and collapses, hugging Radu's back.

"Not so fast, my sultan. We aren't done yet." Radu rolls and Mehmed finds himself pinned to the ground with Radu sitting on his face. "There now. My turn."

Mehmed gasps, but there's no way around it. So, like a slave, he opens his mouth to the proud Wallachian flesh that stares him in the eye. He caresses it, tastes it, and loves it until the hot seed fills his mouth, tasting like salt and fish and happiness. Radu screams, then crumbles next to him and they embrace.

I'll never love anyone more, Mehmed thinks, as they rest spent in the shade of the trees. He sighs and touches Radu's cheek when the horns call. They need to return.

They help each other up. Flushed faces need wiping, leaves need brushing off from their hair, and shalwars need tying. And, more than anything, the forbidden ecstasy has to vanish from their eyes as they return to real life. Hand in hand, they walk back to their horses where a messenger awaits, his eyes wide with fear.

"What?" Mehmed asks.

The man drops to his knees, hoping his neck will last another day.

"Your... your woman, my lord."

"Which one?"

Let it not be Gülbahar, Mehmed thinks, his heart pounding. In that swarm filled with wannabees, she's the only one he cares about.

"Gülşah."

"Gülşah?"

Now which one is that? Mehmed wonders. Then he remembers. That's the one Mother pushed on him when Gülbahar got pregnant. The cheeky venetian who will soon give birth. To a son, God willing, to get Mother off his back.

"What about her?"

"She's hurt. Your mother wants you back."

CHAPTER 27

THE BABY MUST LIVE

Mehmed's sarayi is on fire. Bedraggled women and frightened eunuchs rush back and forth, stumbling over each other, and, for once, they pay no attention to Mehmed. Whenever he ventures near this place, woman after woman finds an excuse to get in his way and strut her charms, trying to entice him. That's why he avoids being here like the plague. But, thanks to the merciful Allah, today they pay no more attention to him than they do the copper braziers heating the room: they don't look at him, but give him wide berth.

"There you are."

Hüma Hatun looks tired and frail. Her mouth got thin, and her cheekbones jut out under the dark holes hiding her eyes. She's aged a lot since last summer, Mehmed thinks, and his heart twists with worry. She can't be dying. Not Mother, who's stronger, tougher, and fiercer than anyone he ever met. Maybe she's just worried, he lies to himself.

"What happened?"

"Gülşah fell. She hit her head and she's unconscious."

"The baby?"

"We don't know yet. The midwives are with her now."

121

"When was she supposed to give birth?"

Hüma's mouth tightens. "You ought to know. Not like you have a sarayi full of sons."

"You're right, Mother. I'm sorry."

"Next month."

"So it's not too early for the baby to make it."

"If she lives. If she dies, he'll die with her."

Mehmed sighs. That's too bad. If she dies, he'll have to start over and impregnate another one. Then he recognizes the horror of his thoughts and blushes with shame. "When Gülbahar had trouble giving birth to Bayezid, Akşemseddin said something about how when a woman can't give birth, one can cut her belly and take the baby out."

Hüma turns white. "And who's going to do that? You?"

Mehmed takes a deep breath to quell his nausea. "Let me send a pigeon to Edirne and ask Father to send Akşemseddin."

"Are you nuts? It will take him weeks to get here."

"You have a better plan?"

Hüma shrugs.

"I'll do that, then," Mehmed says.

"Go see her first. She deserves that much."

Mehmed avoids her eyes. Mother can't know where he was and what he was doing, but she guessed, and he feels the weight of her judgement.

In the largest room of the harem, Gülşah lies on a bed, whiter than the ivory sheets. A dozen women buzz around her, attending to her like worker bees to their queen, but she doesn't seem to notice. With her closed eyes and pale skin, she looks dead already.

Mehmed kneels next to her. He takes her hand, then leans to whisper in her ear. "You'll get better, Gülşah. You're young and strong. You'll have to get better for your son. He needs you."

A fat midwife dressed in black puts her hands on Gülşah's swollen belly and waits. "He's moving! Thank Allah, the baby's moving. He's alive," she says.

The other women turn east and fall on their knees to thank Allah for his kindness.

"How will you get him out?" Mehmed asks, wondering whether to tell her what Akşemseddin had said.

The woman looks at him like he's feeble. "If Allah in his great mercy wants it, she'll push him out. If he doesn't, she won't. There is no other way."

Mehmed nods and leans to whisper in Gülşah's ear. "Good luck. I'll be back."

Dozens of eyes burn his back as he leaves to send a pigeon to Father. Allah willing, the child will live even if his mother dies.

CHAPTER 28

A COSTLY BLUNDER

Ten steps away from the fuss around Gülşah, Sittişah sits on the narrow divan by the window. She watches Mehmed leave, and her heart quickens at the sight of his handsome face and strong, manly body. Without a doubt, her husband is the most handsome man she's ever seen. But sadly, he doesn't seem to notice her, even though he hasn't seen her since their wedding night. In that room packed with women, he only had eyes for Gülşah.

Drunk with rage, Sittişah bites her lips to stop from screaming: "Look at me, I'm here!" She wants to slap herself silly for not having finished the job. She invited Gülşah to an early morning bath, just the two of them, for a girl talk. She told the silly girl she wanted to know all about her pregnancy, and she even had a gift for her baby. Grateful and overwhelmed by her attentions, Gülşah agreed.

Sittişah went in early to check there was nobody else in the steam room, and spilled soapy water over the smooth marble steps to make them slippery. When Gülşah arrived, Sittişah held her arm to help her down the steps, then pushed her.

Burdened by the weight of her belly, Gülşah slipped and fell. She screamed as her head hit the step with a bang. Sittişah leaned over her and slammed her head against the marble slab twice more. But before she could do it again, the bath attendants rushed in.

Sittişah screamed too, pretending to panic as she helped an unconscious Gülşah. Everyone else gathered to help, and Sittişah left them to it. She took off, but one of the bath women gave her a strange side glance, and that got her worried. Could she have seen her slam Gülşah's head against the floor? Not likely. And even if she did, she'd be crazy to say anything against a royal blood princess who happens to be Mehmed's wife.

And even if she talked, nobody would believe her. How could they? A slave's word against a princess's? Nothing worth worrying about.

Still, Sittişah can't help worrying. What if Gülşah wakes up? What if she remembers and talks? That would be a disaster.

Oh well. Sittişah would say that the woman is confused. Of course, she is. She hit her head and fell unconscious, so she doesn't know what she's talking about.

Unless the slave talks, too. If they both do, then she's got a problem.

She needs to plan for that. But for now, it's all good. Gülşah doesn't look like she'll ever speak again. If she dies, Sittişah's secret will die with her, and so will the baby. Wouldn't that be a job well done?

"What are you smiling about?" Elif asks, taking the seat next to her. She's another one of Mehmed's concubines, but she's not pretty enough to worry Sittişah.

"I was just thinking how touching it is that Mehmed came to see Gülşah. He must be heartbroken seeing his favorite in danger."

"What do you mean?"

"He's got to be sick with worry about her."

"About Gülşah?" Elif covers her mouth so no one can see her laugh. "He couldn't care less about her. About the baby, sure. But he hasn't seen Gülşah since she got with child."

"Are you sure?"

"Of course, I'm sure. Here in the harem, everyone knows everything about everybody. Mehmed's favorite is Gülbahar. He'd never bed the other women if Hüma Hatun didn't push them on him. At least that's what the eunuchs say."

"But... but she's not as pretty as Gülşah."

"He doesn't seem to care. Gülbahar is the one he wants. But some say it's even worse than that."

"Worse?"

Elif's voice lowers to a whisper. "They say that his real favorite is not a woman, but Radu the Fair, the Wallachian prince he brought back from Edirne. They're always together. They hunt together, drink together, and some say they do more than that."

Sittişah's jaw falls. She stares at the woman in disbelief. "Are you saying that Mehmed is..."

Elif puts her finger on her lips, reminding her to be quiet. "Of course. He's not the first and won't be the last. Many of the paşas like boys. Some sultans, too. Some have harems full of them. So what? I don't care. I'd take that over another wife. At least he can't birth him a son and become validé."

She's got a point, Sittişah thinks, trying to wrap her mind around the idea that her manly husband prefers boys. And that she risked her future to kill a woman that Mehmed doesn't give a hoot about. Yes, there's the baby, but if it turns out it's a girl, she just wasted her time. She should have checked first.

Oh well. Now, the question is: what next? Should she get rid of Gülbahar, since she's Mehmed's favorite and the mother of his son? But how? Two accidents in the hammam will make people suspicious. She needs to think of something else. What if she compromised her instead? Maybe even with Radu the Fair? That would come in handy. She'd kill two birds with one stone. But...

A blood-curdling scream splits the air. Gülşah sits up in bed, her eyes open wide, cupping her hands around her belly. The color came back to her cheeks, and she looks very much alive.

Her face lit with joy, the midwife lays her hands on Gülşah's belly.

"Blessed be Allah. She'll give birth to this baby, like I said." She turns to Elif. "You. Go tell Hüma Hatun that, thanks to Allah's endless mercy, this baby is about to be born."

CHAPTER 29

MOLDOVA, WINTER 1449

The lead-gray sky hangs over the frozen fields. It's empty, but for the murder of black crows screaming their hate to the shivering riders. After days and days on the road, they're all cold, tired, and miserable. They can't wait to be back at the Royal Seat of Suceava and sit by a raging fire inside its thick walls.

Mulling his thoughts, Vlad rides quietly next to Ștefan. His hands froze on the reins, his butt hurts from sitting in the saddle, and his heart aches from what happened.

When she found out who Vlad was, Lena turned into ice. She took little Mircea, kicking and screaming, away. "It's his bedtime. And mine," she said, glancing at the door.

They dragged their feet, hoping for an invitation to stay, but none came. Ștefan sighed.

"How about you and little Mircea came with us to Suceava? You'd both be safer there," Ștefan said.

Lena shook her head. "We're safe here."

"No, you're not. How hard would it be for Vladislav to send a posse, you think? Once he knows where you are?"

"He won't know."

"How do you know? What if somebody talks?"

"Nobody knows. The folks in the village think I got heavy with child by some married man who doesn't want me. They know nothing about Mircea, and they don't give a damn anyhow. The only ones who cared were my parents, and they're both dead. May God rest their souls."

"How did they die?" Vlad asks.

"The black death ran through the village last summer. They were old and frail, and didn't make it. They were both gone when I returned from the Bran Monastery. So was half of the village."

"You don't have anyone to help you here. What if you get sick? Who'll care for Mircea?" Ștefan asked.

"You're right. I need to come up with a plan."

"Come to Suceava. We'll take care of you, and we'll get the best teachers for Mircea."

"I can take care of myself and him, thank you."

Ștefan insisted, but Lena refused to discuss any further and told them to go home. So, there they are, heading north.

"What do you think she'll do?" Vlad asks.

"Whatever she wants. That's what she's always done. That's probably why she won't come to Suceava. She doesn't want anyone telling her what to do."

"There's got to be more than that. She didn't like me."

"Why?"

"That's what I wonder," Vlad says.

"Did you like her?"

"Are you kidding? She's the most impressive woman I ever met. Thank God they're not all like her, otherwise they'd never need us."

Ștefan laughs. "Yep. She's not like the others. That's why she's so special to me."

"Did you..."

"What?"

"Did you... you know."

"Sleep with her? Hell no. She wanted nothing to do with me. And now I'd be afraid to ask."

"Have you…"

"Slept with anyone?"

"Yes… No. Have you?"

"No."

They ride north quietly, thinking.

"There's this place up the road," Ștefan says.

Vlad looks at him in amazement.

"You mean… that kind of place? How do you know?"

"Father told me. 'A stiff dick does your thinking for you,' he said. 'A limp dick lets your brain do the thinking. For a few coins, there are women who'll relieve you of your burden without chaining you. Don't let your dick get too stiff.'"

Vlad shifts in his saddle. This talk about sex got him heated. But he has no money. Nor anything else, of course. He's just a beggar at Ștefan's father's court.

"I have no money."

"I do."

Ștefan spurs his horse. Vlad follows. So do their men. Before long, they look at a lone house with a light hanging over the door.

Ștefan rings the bell. No answer.

"Is this it?" Vlad asks.

"I think so."

It's late, cold and dark, and they're miles away from any village. Vlad hugs himself to stop from shivering. Ștefan rings again, and the door opens.

It's almost as dark inside, but even so, the woman looks no good. She's old and fat and Vlad wishes they never came here.

"What do you want?"

"We… we're customers. We'd like to spend some time with your ladies."

The woman chokes with laughter. "My ladies. OK then. Can you pay?"

Ștefan takes out a purse and shows it to her. The woman weighs it in her hand. "Gold or silver?"

"Silver."

The woman puckers her lips and nods to the house. The boys dismount and step in, leaving the men to mind their horses.

The house is dirty and smells like smoke, but at least it's warm. The boys sit by the fire to wait for what feels like an eternity, and Vlad gets worried about a trap.

"Are you sure about this?" Vlad asks.

"No. But what have we got to lose?"

Just our lives, Vlad thinks, as five young women dressed in short white chemises shuffle into the room. They look young and scared, and Vlad feels a throb between his legs. They're prey, these girls, here for his pleasure. Any pleasure.

"What can we do to them?" he asks. It's been weeks since his last rat, and his voice is thick with longing.

"What do you mean? They're here for our pleasure," Stefan says.

"That's what I thought." Vlad looks at the youngest one, barely more than a child, but her wide eyes avoid his.

"I'll take that one."

The girl looks like she's about to cry when the fat woman digs her fingers into her arm, smiling at Vlad. "You are a man of fine tastes. She's very young and very special. You won't be disappointed."

She walks the girl like she's a dog on a chain to a small room in the back.

"Have fun." She slams the door behind her, leaving them alone.

The room is cold and dark and almost empty: a narrow wooden bed covered with woolen blankets, a high-back chair, a thin yellow candle lighting an icon of Saint Peter, his golden aura at a jaunty angle.

The girl won't meet his eyes, and that stokes Vlad's desire. She's prey, this girl, better prey than he's ever had, because she's human. He doesn't know her name and doesn't care. He didn't know the names of the rats either.

"Get naked," he says, his voice thick with need.

The girl unties the cord holding up her thin chemise, letting it fall to the ground. Her arms cover her barely-there breasts, and Vlad's breathing gets heavy.

"How old are you?"

"I don't know. Whatever you want me to be."

She's got to be young, Vlad thinks, measuring her narrow hips with jutting bones and her stick-like legs, but the dark circles around her eyes and the flat expression on her face tell him she's too old for her age.

"How long have you been here?"

"Since spring."

It's winter now, so she's been here for almost a year.

"Who brought you here?"

"My mother."

"Why?"

"I was the oldest of seven. They needed to eat."

Vlad nods. "I... I've never done this. Show me."

The girl doesn't laugh. She lies on the narrow bed with her legs spread open and looks away. "Now you take off your clothes and lie on top of me."

Vlad does, and the feeling of her body trembling under him makes him stiffer.

"Now you put your thing inside me."

His shaky hands look for the hole inside her. He guides his stiff member and pushes it in. The girl gasps as he penetrates her, and crunches like she wants to run away, but there's no place to go. He's inside her, and above her, and no matter how she squirms, she can't escape.

He grabs her bony hips and pulls them closer. She gasps again, and his soul soars. He digs his nails into her skin and she cries and sobs but doesn't resist. He finds his rhythm and pushes harder and harder to make her cry. He grabs her buttocks and crushes them in his fists like you crush grapes to make wine. She screams and he bites her shoulder until he tastes blood. The taste sends him into a haven of pleasure, and he empties himself inside her again and again until there's nothing left.

It's over. Vlad feels like he used to feel after skinning a rat, only less so, because she's still alive. But he's done. For now. He rolls off her and wipes himself on her chemise before putting back his clothes and heading to the door.

He looks back. She lies like she's dead, with her arm covering her eyes. But she isn't. She whimpers, and he wishes he could drop a coin her way, but he's got none. So he leaves her to find Ștefan and the men who are waiting.

"Was it good?" Ștefan asks.

"Not really. How about you?"

"I... felt ashamed. I'd rather do it with my hand next time. At least I won't hurt anyone."

"Me too."

That night, as they ride the frozen road to Suceava, Vlad wonders where things went wrong. The girl suffered, and he enjoyed it. She got paid for it — at least her patron did. So why does he feel like a prick?

CHAPTER 30

MANISA, WINTER 1449

The Manisa sarayi bursts with joy. Enthralled by the magic of childbirth, the women forgot their rivalries and work together to help Gülşah bring her baby to life. They've got her propped up on the walnut birth chair, but she fights them, screaming like a banshee.

"Push," the midwife says.

Gülşah screams like her insides are tearing apart. She tries to stand, but dozens of hands hold her down, soothing her, wiping her face, caressing her hair, keeping her in place. She screams again as something dark seems to pop between her legs. It vanishes, to come out further with the next scream. The midwife catches it and pulls it out. It's a beet-red baby, smaller than a cat and weirdly quiet.

Mehmed's heart skips a beat.

She wraps it in a white linen cloth and rubs him like she's trying to take off his skin, then turns him upside down and slaps the bottoms of its feet. Hard.

The baby hiccups. A sneeze, then a cry, then an indignant scream, shaking the walls, and the room gasps with delight, relishing the new life.

The midwife drops the bloodied cloth. She rubs salt on the baby, like the custom demands, to clean it and protect it from evil, drips honey on the lips so it will never run out of sweet words, then wraps it in a clean cloth and hands it to Mehmed.

A tiny red face with skin so thin it's transparent, crowned by a whisper of red hair. A toothless pink mouth opened wide in a scream. A tiny hand with five perfect little fingers grabbing Mehmed's thumb. The baby is small, red and very much alive, and Mehmed falls in love.

The room waits quietly for him to announce the sex of the baby, and the midwife opens the cloth for him to see. Right there, in between the thighs no bigger than those of a chicken, may rest the Ottoman Empire's future.

Mehmed clutches him tighter and looks at Gülşah. With her sweaty hair plastered to her skull, her skin covered in blotches, and her sunken red eyes, she's no longer beautiful. And yet she's more beautiful than ever as she awaits his verdict.

"It's a boy, blessed be Allah! His name will be Mustafa."

The room screams, and Gülşah sobs as Mehmed leans over to thank her. He kisses her forehead, then turns to hand the baby to his mother. But she's nowhere to be seen, and Mehmed's heart freezes. For Mother to miss his son's birth, something terrible must be happening.

His feet itch to run and find her, but he first must receive the women's good wishes. They come one by one to congratulate him, then move on to Gülşah to admire her beautiful baby.

It takes forever, and Mehmed doesn't care about any of this, but he knows Gülşah does. This is her moment, and he can't deprive her, so he taps his foot, waiting for the women to be done.

It's Sittişah's turn. She walks to him like she's dancing and smiles. She's stunning, and Mehmed marvels again at how much she looks like Mother, with her flame-red curls falling to her back and the green of her eyes so deeply alive.

"Congratulations, my sultan, for the birth of your son. Your wife is a lucky woman indeed."

"Thank you, Sittişah."

But, instead of going to congratulate Gülşah, like the custom demands, she leans so close that the heat of her breath warms his cheek. "I can't wait for my turn," she says, her eyes burning into his. "My turn to give you a son."

She turns to Gülşah, leaving Mehmed astounded by her audacity. She just called him out for not consummating their marriage, like it's her right. No other woman has ever done that.

Then again, she's not a slave, like the others, who only became his wives because they gave him a son. She's a princess, Sittişah. Sultan Murad negotiated their marriage, and she came with a rich dowry and a precious alliance. She has a right to expect him to honor her bed.

Sittişah smiles as she leans over Gülşah to congratulate her, but the new mother blanches as she sees her. The bliss on her face turns to fear, and she pulls her baby to her chest instead of presenting him to Sittişah.

How strange, Mehmed thinks, but then he remembers Mother, who should be here, but is not. He rushes through the last congratulations to go look for her.

CHAPTER 31

THE ONLY WOMAN YOU CAN TRUST

The long corridors of the sarayi are all empty as he races to his mother's chambers. The women must all be with Gülşah, he thinks, but they aren't. Three of them are in Mother's rooms, and they step aside to let him pass. Hüma Hatun lays in her bed, her eyes closed, her fiery hair spread over the silk pillows that used to be white. They're red now. Red with blood.

A woman holds Mother's forehead as she retches blood into a white China bowl. When she's done, she falls back on her pillows, and the women clean her face with rose water.

"Mother!"

Her tired eyes light up when she sees him. "What is it?"

"A boy. Mustafa."

"Thank Allah. Now I can die in peace."

"You can't die. You're not dying!"

Mehmed bites his lip to stop his tears. He takes the hand with the emerald ring he kissed so many times and kisses it again.

Mother looks at him fondly, and for once, there's no disapproval in her eyes. There's nothing but love, and that's even scarier.

"Everybody, out," she says, and waits until the women are gone, then turns to him. "I'm dying, Mehmed, but that's OK. I'm happy you have another son to ensure your succession. You need more, but two is a good start."

"What makes you think you're dying?"

"My stomach has been hurting for months. I haven't eaten in days, and I've been bleeding. My Jewish doctor said there's something growing inside me that eats me alive. He thought I'd be gone by now, but I hoped to live long enough to see your new son. Mustafa is a great name. I'm sure he'll make you proud, like you make me proud, Mehmed. Very proud." Her cold white hand, just skin and bones, touches his cheek lovingly and Mehmed lowers his head to hide his tears. "I wish I told you that more often, instead of always telling you how you should do better. But I always thought of myself as your trainer first, and your mother second. It was my duty to teach you, and my joy to love you, and I always put my duty first. If I could start all over again, I'd do it differently. But I love you more than my life, and I always did. Never forget."

"I won't forget, Mother."

"Now that we got that out of the way, we have some business to discuss."

"Business can wait," Mehmed says.

"No, it can't. Not this business. First, beware of Sittişah."

"Beware of Sittişah? Why?"

"One of the old hammam slaves came to tell me she saw Sittişah push Gülşah down the steps and smack her head against the floor."

Mehmed's jaw falls. "Sittişah? That's impossible! Why would she do that?"

"To get rid of Gülşah and her child, and make room for her own. I know it's hard to believe, but I've known that old slave for twenty years, and I trust her. I've known Sittişah for a couple of weeks and I don't. Do you?"

Mehmed remembers Gülşah's terrified face when Sittişah went near her. And Sittişah telling him intently that she's waiting for her turn. "I don't."

"Good. Unfortunately, I won't be here to take care of this. You'll have to do it yourself."

"What should I do? Execute her? Throw her in jail? Send her home?"

"No, no, and no. Marrying Sittişah was the price you had to pay for an alliance that will secure you Anatolia. You can't disrespect her and antagonize her family, or you'll send the Dulkadir straight in the arms of our enemies. You need to tread lightly."

"What should I do, then?"

"The first thing you need to do is to make sure she'll never give birth to your son. If she's like this before she even has a child, nothing will stop her once she has a boy. You need to protect your sons and your wives, and you can't rest while she's here. One way or another, she'll get to them. The best thing to do would be to take her to one of the other palaces — Bursa, Dometika, or wherever — and leave her there. She can't return without your permission, so that should keep everybody safe."

"Won't her family get upset?"

"Not if you treat her correctly. Give her everything she needs and make sure she gets treated with the respect she deserves as a princess and a sultan's wife. Just don't let her get anywhere near Bayezid or Mustafa."

"I understand."

"Good. Sadly, the next thing is worse."

"Worse than this?"

"Yes. And you'll have to take care of that too, since I won't be here to do it."

"What is it?"

"Did you know that Halime Hatice Hatun is pregnant?"

"Halime Hatice?"

"Yes. Your father's favorite wife."

"Pregnant? With Father?"

Hüma laughs so hard that she chokes, and red blood sprays out of her mouth. She wipes it with her silk handkerchief and turns back to Mehmed. "She's in the harem, remember? Who else could it be?"

Stupid question. "What about her?" he asks.

"If she has a boy, he'll be another şehzade, and a rival to your throne. You'll need to kill him."

An icy shiver runs through Mehmed. "A baby? I can't kill a baby."

"Fortunately, you have people who will do it for you."

"How can a baby vie with me for the throne?"

"What do you think Çandarlı Halil Paşa will do when your father dies? Will he support you, even though he hates you, or will he throw his weight behind a baby that will allow him to keep the reins of power for the foreseeable future? Forever maybe, if the new sultan dies without an heir. The janissaries didn't like you much, since you were young and impatient. Çandarlı Paşa made sure they weren't on your side, and he'll do that again. There's no way around it. You must kill the baby, if it's a boy. His mother, if he's not yet born. You can't afford to let him live."

Mehmed sighs, feeling the weight of the empire crush his soul. How can he do something so dishonorable? Lock his wife away for the rest of her life, when he's not even sure she's guilty? Murder a baby? Kill his father's pregnant wife? Is having power really worth it? He looks down, and Mother caresses his hair like she hasn't since he was a little boy.

"I'm sorry you have to do this. I know you're a good man, and this is horrific. But remember, you're not doing it for yourself. You're doing it for the empire. The Ottoman Empire cannot afford another civil war. Remember the interregnum? It lasted eleven years, ripped the empire apart, and it almost destroyed it. No matter what it takes, you must prevent another civil war."

"But Mother, what will happen to my sons when I die? Will they kill each other too?"

"They will, unless you do it for them. Power requires sacrifice. Remember that your first loyalty is not towards your brother, your wives, or even your children. Your first loyalty is to Allah, and to the

Ottoman Empire, that he blessed to spread the Muslim faith over the world. You must do whatever it takes to strengthen the empire, and a few lives are a cheap price to pay. Do you remember Aladdin?"

Aladdin, his older brother and Father's favorite, died when he was only eighteen, together with his two infant sons. Thanks to Mother. Mehmed sighs.

"Is there anything else?"

"Just one thing. Have my name carved on my tomb. Don't let it be nameless."

"I will. Anything else?"

"No. Take my ring and wear it. Don't give it to the women, but someday give it to your favorite son and tell him about me."

She closes her eyes, and Mehmed chokes. He sits, holding her icy hand. As her breathing gets fainter and fainter, he remembers his father's words: *Women are not like us. You can't trust them. The only woman you can ever trust is your mother. She'll always do what's best for you. Nobody else.*

Mehmed ran out of women he could trust.

CHAPTER 32

THE MEDITERRANEAN, 1449

Sailing in winter is not for the faint of heart. The vicious wind is so humid its chill seeps not only into your bones, but into your soul. It's not the brutal cold of the snowy Transylvanian mountains, where your piss clicks as it hits the ground, but those winters were dry and invigorating, especially when you sat by the fire with good friends and a cup of hot milk.

Here, on the ship, not so much. There's no fire, no friends, and no milk, just water everywhere. Under the ship, inside it, and all over it, since the icy drizzle that started last week never stopped.

Ali pulls her moldy coat closer, wishing she could wrap herself in her warm kaftan, but that's a no-no. The night she got on board, she exchanged her eunuch clothes for some stinky sailor's garb three sizes too big, and chopped her hair with a kitchen knife. She threw the chestnut curls overboard as if sacrificing them to the sea gods and started living as a man.

The sailors never questioned her. Nor did the captain, who never spoke to her since the night she came on board. Whenever he needs something, he sends her an order. Like when he sent word that there will be no fire because of the rough seas thrashing them around. Fire is the most terrible curse to strike a ship — Ali learned that by now — so the meals have been mostly biscuits, cheese, and dry fruit. The men glare at her, but there's nothing she can do.

That was three days ago. Ever since, they've struggled to stay afloat, and that's no fun. They're all cold, tired and short-fused, her included.

She wishes she got off in Constantinople three weeks ago. They spent a week there, unloading wine, spices, and silk, and provisioning for the next voyage, so she had plenty of time to roam the cobblestoned streets. One day she'd stopped to pray in Hagia Sophia, the patriarch's seat and the most famous Orthodox Church on earth. The cathedral was massive and dark, and all empty but for a couple of old women dressed in black praying in front of Mary's icon.

Ali dropped a coin to light a skinny yellow candle under Jesus's thin face and tried to remember the Lord's prayer. "Our father, who is in the skies, may your wish be done. Forgive our sins like we forgive the sins of those who harmed us. And..."

Nothing else came to mind. It's been years since she'd last been to church to pray, so she forgot the words. But she didn't forget her beloved father, who died way too young, leaving her prey to her mother's whims.

She tried again, closing her eyes to talk to him. "Father, I love you and I miss you terribly. I hope you are happy where you are, and I didn't disappoint you too much. I tried to do like you said, and be the best I could be, but I failed in so many ways. First, I ran away instead of looking after Mother and the boys, and I was not a good girl. But you said that being a girl was not important. Being a good human was. I did my best to be a good human, but I stopped being a girl. Sort of." She looked around to make sure nobody listened, then whispered. "You probably know about Mara. She's lovely, but I don't think you approve. I know this is wrong in many ways. She's married; and she's not a man. I'm sorry if that hurts your feelings. I'll try to get communion and do penance when I get home. But I was so lonely there, and nobody really cared, but she did. I hope you're not too upset.

And I'm not likely to see her again." She wiped her tears with her dirty sailor's sleeve and took a deep breath. "I love you, and I hope you are well. I'll see you soon, Dad."

She bowed, crossed herself, and stepped back in the noisy streets of Constantinople to buy provisions for the ship. It wasn't easy. She'd lived in Edirne for years, but she was at the palace, which was nothing like this. The entire city was a cacophony of sounds, smells, and crowds, and the market was even worse. Hard to get used to, even though the people looked busy and happy. They sold, they bought, and they sang to each other and to strangers, praising the virtues of their wares.

"Boy, you want some flour? The best flour in the world, for the hot bread of your loved one's breakfast. White and light as snow. If they eat your bread, they'll love you forever."

"Flowers. Winter roses and begonias. Beautiful scented pine, and ribbons for your loved one."

"The sweetest dried fruit. Tangy dried lemons and golden raisins and chewy dates and nuts."

"Honey. Wild flower honey, orange honey, and forest honey. The best honey on earth."

The smells, the noise, and the crowded spaces made Ali dizzy. She couldn't wait to get back to the ship where she could rest her eyes on the horizon and hear herself think. Still, she had to provision the ship for the next trip, so she returned to the market again and again.

She could have taken the money Mara gave her and left, but she didn't. She decided to stay with the ship a while longer before returning to Transylvania. From Europe, she'll find a way back home, where she can fit in.

Unlike here. Ali doesn't understand Constantinople. The locals call themselves Romans, but speak Greek. They tout their faith, but worship gold. They pretend to cherish tradition and restraint, but they party every night like it's their last, and drink wine like it's water. She gets them even less than she gets the Ottomans. The Muslims are all about Allah, Mohammad, and his teachings. That's clear. She understands that, even though it's not her thing. But Constantinople's people? She can't fathom them.

Grateful to be back on the ship, she cooked the best dinner she could: goat stew flavored with cinnamon, star anise, and coriander, fresh bread with yellow butter, and honey-drenched walnuts. The men inhaled it. But that was then. Now, they haven't had hot food for days, and they're giving her dirty looks.

She sighs and puts together another meal of biscuit and dry fruit for the sailors. At least the dry fruit is delicious — beautiful golden raisins and dates, sweeter than honey, and walnut halves. She adds a few slices of brown smoked cheese smelling like pine for a special treat. She's ready just as a sailor comes by.

"The captain wants you."

"Me?"

He nods and leaves without a word. Ali wipes her hands on her dirty brown pants, wondering what this could be about. This never happened in the weeks she's been on the ship, and it's hard to believe it's good news.

CHAPTER 33

COME WITH ME

Captain Giovanni's cabin is not luxurious. Like every place inside the ship, it's dark, dingy and cramped, with a narrow cot, a table barely big enough for a plate, and a chair nailed to the floor to stay put on rough seas. The man himself, wide-shouldered and tall enough to hit the ceiling beams, makes it look even smaller. He invites her to take the chair and sits on his narrow cot with the small table between them.

"What's your name?"

"Ali."

"No. Your real name."

She sighs. "I used to be Ana. Long ago."

"Ana, you've done a good job here. The men love your cooking and I do too. More importantly, nobody seems to wonder who you are. Nobody but me. Who are you?"

"I'm still trying to find out."

"I can understand that. Where are you going?"

"Back to Transylvania. That's my home."

"They have no sea there."

"I know. I'll get off somewhere and I'll find a way back."

146

"Why?"

"To be back home?"

"How long have you been gone?"

"A long time."

"So why go back?"

"To find myself?"

"You know, Ana, sometimes the best way to find yourself is to leave. And you're too young to know, but going back is hard to do. You're away for a while, then return to discover that the world you knew has vanished. The people you loved are no more. The things you left are gone. But, more importantly, you are no longer who you used to be. Sometimes it's best to stay away until you find yourself."

That's the longest she's ever heard him speak, and she wonders what this is about. His weather-beaten face framed by a mane of dark curls and a short beard is handsome and open, and his eyes are so warm they feel like an embrace. Something inside her shifts. He's looking at her like nobody did before, like he's a man and she's a woman. And Ali doesn't know what to do with that.

"What are you saying?"

"Come to Genoa. It's the best place in the world. The food. The wine. The people. The boats. There's no place like that on earth. You'll find a whole new world. Come check it out."

"Why?"

"Why? Because you're special. You're like no woman I ever met. And I'd like to know you better."

"Thank you. I'll think about it."

"You think I'm full of shit, don't you?"

"Yes."

Captain Giovanni laughs. "What were you doing dressed as a eunuch in Mehmed's suite?"

"I was a eunuch."

"You were not. You are a woman."

"Being a eunuch is a job, like being a cook or a captain. It's not who you are, it's what you do."

"OK. Say it is so. Still, what were you doing being a eunuch in Mehmed's suite?"

"I was taking care of his ladies."

"You know that's not what I'm asking."

"My mother sold me. She thought she'd get more money for me as a eunuch than as a girl."

"There's more to it than that."

Ali shrugs.

"You're not about to tell me, are you? So, if your mother sold you into slavery, why would you go back? To get sold again?"

Why go back? Ali didn't give that much thought, since everything happened so fast. When she left Edirne, she was too busy figuring out how to get out of there to worry about what to do next. But he's right. It's time to think about it.

If she goes back, she'll go see Smaranda, of course. And Lena. Then what? Mara gave her enough money to buy a piece of land with a little apple orchard and maybe a cow. She'd grow bees to have honey and maybe even some chickens for the eggs, though she hates those dirty beasts. They're so stupid they shit in their food and then eat it. But she could have a dog, maybe two. And she could visit her mother and her brothers.

That thought freezes her heart. She doesn't want to see Mother, even though she should. Father would want her to, and it's her duty. But Mother is the last person on earth Ali wants to see. Mother, and Hüma Hatun.

"Tell me about Genoa."

Captain Giovanni's eyes widen, then a smile lights his face, and Ali realizes just how handsome he is, messy hair, filthy clothes and all.

"Genoa is like no place on earth. They call it *La Superba*, the Proud One. It's on the Ligurian Sea, the largest port in the Mediterranean. The wind tastes salty from the spray and carries the scents of faraway places. In Genoa, the sea is your garden, right there on your doorstep. The women are beautiful and wear splendid silks and muslin, and the men are handsome and brave. We Genoese are merchants, sailors, and warriors, and we live by the strength of our sword and the power of our wit. And we are free. We have no king; we choose our doge, and he's accountable to us." He smiles again. "My city is beautiful. Also complicated and mysterious, just like you. You'd fit in well."

"What would I do there?"

"If I'd have my druthers, you'd spend your days and nights in my bed, but I'm seldom there longer than a week at the time. And my wife might disagree. So you'd have to find something else to do besides letting me pleasure you. But somebody like you, who spent years ensconced right in the sultan's sarayi has valuable knowledge that's worth a lot of money. Our Great Council would be thrilled to learn about the sultans, especially Mehmed. Not only thrilled, but generous. You'd live in a large house, wear beautiful dresses and have servants to take care of you. You'd go to parties, wear expensive jewels and meet the most fascinating people in the world. You'd travel and see the world, from Portugal to Cathay. What do you think?"

Ali doesn't know what she thinks. She'd pass on the servants, the jewelry, and the big house. But the travel? And his bed...

He leans towards her, and his hand touches her hair, running a strand between his fingers. Soft as a feather, the tip of his finger traces her cheek, her lips, her chin, and Ali feels an exquisite heat building inside her as her heart quickens. She should pull away, but she can't. She leans forward instead, and he meets her half-way. His eyes, the troubled color of the stormy sea, gaze into hers, and their lips touch, spreading fire inside her. He pulls her against him, and she melts, soft and liquid in his hold. His hard body pressed against hers takes her breath away.

His lips kiss her softly at first, then become more demanding. His tongue explores and tastes her, and her knees soften. He picks her up and lays her on the narrow cot that smells like the sea, and his body.

He kneels by the bed and opens her coat, then pulls up her chemise. His hands and lips trace the shape of her breasts and Ali gasps. She shivers, and she doesn't know if it's from pleasure or fear.

He undoes her belt and pulls down her rough woolen pants. His nimble hands find the place between her thighs where the skin is hot, soft, and exquisitely tender, and he touches her like she's never been touched before.

"You drive me crazy," he whispers against her belly, and she can't help but lift her hips to meet him.

"You want to do this?" he asks.

Ali doesn't know what she wants. "I…"

Someone knocks at the door.

"There's a ship. Looks like an Ottoman galley," a voice says, then heavy steps run up the stairs.

Giovanni lets go of her and turns to the door. "Let's talk about this later, shall we?"

He's gone before she figures out what happened.

CHAPTER 34
PIRATES

Left alone in the cabin, Ali tries to get herself together. What the heck just happened? And what else was about to happen?

She's not sure whether she's glad or disappointed that the romantic moment fell apart. She adjusts her clothes and climbs to the deck.

The men are all there. A dozen stand at the bow, aiming crossbows and muzzle-loading arquebuses at the heavy galley that fights the rough seas just ahead. The rest rush to trim the sails as per Captain Giovanni's orders, and the gunwale skirts the water as they cut through the waves.

A sudden gust of wind tilts them further, and Ali loses her footing. She stumbles and slides on the wet deck, and she's about to fly overboard when she grabs onto a line just as a firm hand pulls her back by her collar.

"What on earth are doing here? Go under. This is not the place for you to be."

Giovanni shoves her towards the open hatch and leaps to help someone else. Ali falls on her butt between two coffers nailed to the deck. She catches her breath and makes herself small. I'll be safe and out of the way here, she thinks, and stays to watch, trying to fathom what this is about. So what if there's a ship? They've met dozens, and nobody seemed to care. Are they afraid they're pirates? But then why follow them?

She's heard plenty about the Mediterranean's pirates. Sultan Murad has dozens of ships that attack Venetian and Genoese merchant vessels and raid the islands of Tinos and Mykonos to harvest slaves. Just another way to pad his treasury and keep the Genoese and the Venetians on their toes.

The heavy galley flying a red and green tughra struggles against the enormous waves that thrash her about. She leans from one side to the other, and the dozens of oars above the water make her look like a centipede on its back. But, oars or not, she makes little progress, while their light caravel with the wind in her sails slices the waves and eats up the distance. Every gust of wind gets them closer, until they're close enough to hear the heavy drum beat like a frightened heart, keeping the rhythm for the oarsmen. The men's eyes are wide with fear and their emaciated faces shine with sweat as they struggle against the oars with every drum strike.

"Shoot!" Giovanni shouts.

Three matchlock arquebuses fire in rapid succession, and the acrid smell of gunpowder covers the sea's scent as the bullets throw the galley into chaos.

The oarsmen drop the oars to cower under their seats, since they're chained to the deck so they can't run. The drums go quiet, and the overseers scatter away. Without the push of the oars, the galley rocks like a drunken sailor at the mercy of the sea.

A large man in a green kaftan aims an arquebus and fires at them, then turns to scream at his men to get back on the oars, but they're too frightened to listen. He curses and picks up another arquebus from a rack of muzzle-loaded guns and fires again. The bullet hits a bucket on the deck, just a foot from the captain, and sends it rolling. Giovanni shakes his head.

"What a stupid fool. Get him."

The first crossbowman laughs and fires. A *thunk,* and his bolt sinks deep in the arquebusier's chest. The man steps back but doesn't fall. A second bolt follows, then a third. He drops the weapon and falls on the deck.

"Surrender or die," Captain Giovanni thunders.

Heartbeats later, a dozen men stand on the deck with their empty hands held high and their faces twisted in terror.

Giovanni laughs. "Too bad. That was too easy; they took away all the fun. Roberto, take ten men and secure the galley."

Roberto, the second-in-command, is a tall man of few words who never smiles. He nods, and his men throw grapples to pull the ships against each other. Before you can count to ten, the galley is under the pirates' control. Because that's what Giovanni and his men are. They're pirates, and Ali is one of them, whether she likes it or not.

She doesn't want to believe it, but it all makes sense. Why they unloaded silks and spices in Constantinople when they sailed in from the Mediterranean, when silks always come from Cathay, so they come the other way. Why they didn't buy any cargo to take back, nothing but their provisions. Why they venture out to sea in any weather, when the other ships stay put.

Ali watches them carry the galley's load into the caravel. There's plenty of it: bolt after bolt of shimmering silk; countless bags of spices and grains; heavy coffers loaded with weapons and piles of clothes. But with everyone working, it's all stowed away before long, and they're ready to sail.

Ali wonders what they'll do with the galley and its men. It all went so smoothly it's easy to see they've done this before.

Giovanni turns to Roberto. "I'll see you in Chios."

Roberto nods, and his men release the grapples holding the ships together. They get stowed away as the two ships drift apart.

"Head north," Giovanni says. The men jump on the sails, and the caravel changes course with the ease of a bird in flight, while the old galley continues south, propelled by the dozens of oars keeping rhythm with the drum.

CHAPTER 35

DON'T TOUCH ME

Ali doesn't feel like cooking that evening. Dry tack and fruit are good enough for a bunch of rotten pirates, she thinks, ignoring their glares as she stands at the bow, braving the freezing wind and wondering what to do. Not like she has that many choices. For now, she's stuck on this darn ship. She needs to wait until they reach land, and then...

"The captain wants you."

Her heart heavy and her head hanging, she shuffles back to the cabin she left just a few hours ago. It feels like an eternity.

Giovanni sits on his bed like before, and his smile warms the room. He puts his arms around her, and after the cutting wind, the warmth of his body feels like home. She lets his heat seep in until his hands find their way under her clothes.

"Now, where were we when we got so rudely interrupted?"

"Nowhere." She slaps his hands away and sits on the chair. "You're a pirate."

His eyes widen, but he takes her cue and sits back on his bed. "You saw it, eh? Too bad. Well, I'm not exactly a pirate. I'm a privateer."

"A privateer?"

"Yes. Pirates are lawless, and they take any ship they can. I only take enemy ships. Well, mostly. The doge delegated me to wage war at sea on behalf of Genoa. Taking Ottoman ships is just another way to fight the enemy and be patriotic, you know?"

Ali stares at him.

"Plus, the occasion was too good to miss. That Ottoman ship was like a fat hog waiting to be slaughtered. We had to do it, even though it was inconvenient."

"Why?"

"Because it delays us. Instead of heading straight back to Genoa, we'll have to first return to Constantinople to get rid of this load. Then, on the way back, we'll have to stop at Chios to recover Roberto and his men. That will set us back at least a week, maybe more. But it's worth it. That ship should keep us afloat for a year."

"How so?"

"There's the merchandise — all that silk, the spices, and the grain. We'll get good money for it in Constantinople. Roberto's load is even more precious. He's got seventy strong oarsmen, then another two dozen Ottomans. Some of them will get ransomed for gold, and the rest will get sold with the oarsmen. Too bad that fool of a captain got himself killed; he was the most precious of the lot. Then there's the galley itself, which is worth a fortune."

"Don't you feel bad about selling people into slavery?"

Giovanni stares at her like she's lost her mind. "Ana, the oarsmen were slaves already. The Ottomans' slaves. They'll be better off now, since the Christians treat their galley slaves better than the sultan does. He keeps them chained to their seats, so they don't get to walk until they die. Truth be told, they don't walk much afterwards either. As for the men whipping them, I'm glad to give them a taste of their own medicine. So, to answer your question, I don't feel bad. I feel proud. Now, if we're done talking..."

"We're not done talking. What are you going to do with me?"

"Why don't I just show you instead of all this talk?"

"No. What do you plan to do with me? Will you let me go?"

"Go where?"

"Wherever I want."

"There's nowhere to go, Ana. There's nothing but water, as far as the eye can see."

"When we reach land."

"I thought we were negotiating your coming to Genoa with me."

"That was before I discovered you're a pirate."

"Look, Ana, I'm..."

"I'm Ali."

"No, you're not."

"Yes, I am. To you, I'm Ali."

He clasps his hands behind his back. "I'm not really a pirate. This was just too good to miss."

"What are you?"

"I'm Genoese. I'm a condottiere: a merchant, a warrior, and the black sheep of a noble Genoese family who shudders when they hear my name. I'm the husband of Lady Clemenza, who's happier when I'm away, and a soldier of fortune. I lend my skills to whoever can afford them. I live by the sword and I'll die by the sword someday. May God make it a fast and painless one. And I'm the man who will teach you about love."

"No, you're not."

"Why not?"

"I don't want you."

"Why not? You wanted me well enough before."

"That was then, and this is now. I'll kill you if you touch me."

Giovanni stares at her, and she can tell he's struggling not to laugh. There he is, twice her size and armed to the teeth. She stands no higher than his shoulder and has no weapon other than the kitchen knife she always carries with her — just in case. It is funny.

"You can laugh if you want," Ali says.

Giovanni smiles and puts his arms around her.

"I said no."

"You mean it?"

"Of course."

He brushes his fingers through his hair and nods. "OK. Then let me sleep. I need to be on the deck for my shift in an hour." He takes off his sword and his dagger and sets them on the table. He lays in his cot with his boots and closes his eyes.

Ali leaves, worried he'll follow her, but he's already snoring.

Three days later, when they reach Constantinople, he hands her a small purse. "This is your pay, even though you didn't fulfill your contract. If you ever change your mind, send word to me in Genoa. Or Chios."

He turns to leave, but she can't let him go without seeing his face one more time. "Who would I be looking for?"

His eyes are smiling as he turns to her. "Me. Signore Giovanni Giustiniani Longo. At your service."

CHAPTER 36

BUDA, SPRING 1450

The pride of Hungary, Buda's great castle, is brand new. Sure, the grand keep they call Stephen's Tower has been there forever, but the new castle, with its northern wing they call the Fresh Palace, the massive Roman hall with its carved ceilings and tall windows overlooking the city of Buda was built by Sigismund, the Holy Roman Emperor and King of Hungary not even twenty years ago.

The southern side of the castle is protected by its narrow zwingers, the parallel walls running along the steep hillside all the way to the Danube. The killing field between them ensures no attacker can break in unharmed. And in the west of the *Cour d'Honneur*, the aptly named Broken Tower shelters the dungeons at the bottom, and the treasury with its royal jewels at the top. And what jewels those must be, Codru thinks, glancing at the tower as he rides home to his little chambers in Buda.

His place in Buda isn't much to talk about, but that's OK, since he's barely ever home. Between training Hunyadi's guards and trying to make his way into the Hungarian nobility, all he does at home is sleep. And not well.

Ever since Hunyadi gifted him the small fief of Prod, near

Sighișoara, making him a minor Transylvanian noble, Codru has been struggling to figure out where he really belongs. His allegiance, as always, is with his friends Ali and Ion, and their mission to uphold the Romanian countries. That's why Hungary, and Hunyadi, Transylvania's voivode, who's supposedly half-Romanian but forgot that long ago, are just a distraction.

But he's too tired to worry about that tonight, with his belly full of wine and good food. It's been a grand party. Hungary's most beautiful maidens decked themselves in silk, lace, and velvet to tempt the eligible bachelors. Not many, since young men are scarce in Hungary these days. The flower of Hungary's youth was decimated in the Ottoman wars, so all that's left are old widowers hard of hearing and boys trying to grow their first mustache. The few unmarried men of the right age are all missing something — an arm, a leg, or an eye. And who knows what else?

That's why the young ladies looking for husbands are so desperate they'll even flirt with him, a newcomer nobody knows much about. They'd prefer someone of good old stock, of course, even if he's fifty, bald, and too fat to see his privates, but even those are scarce. So, suddenly, Codru became a catch, even though he's dark, foreign, and of uncertain descent. He's Hunyadi's trusted man, so he's golden.

Even this evening, one pretty girl after another batted her lashes at him, trying to entice him, and Codru didn't mind it one bit. I could get used to this, he thinks, dropping his horse at the stables and tip-toeing up the steep creaky stairs to his place.

But the widow who he rents from is still up, even though it's so late. Dressed in black, as usual, with a faded scarf wrapped around her wrinkled face, she's mending clothes in her cramped living room. She stands to greet him with a strange glow in her eyes. "Welcome home."

"Thanks."

"You have guests."

"Guests?"

"Your wife arrived. She's waiting upstairs."

"My what?"

"You wife. And your son. They arrived a few hours ago. I served them dinner, but they wanted nothing else."

Codru has no freaking clue what she's talking about. His wife? And his son? Then an old memory flashes in his mind. The woman on the Island of Lesbos. Athena. She was with child. She must have found him somehow, and she told the landlady that she was his wife. And Nikos, her son. Or is it the baby? He wonders if the kid turned out a werewolf like him. Thank God and Smaranda's potions, that hasn't been a problem for a while. But what if the kid... Well, hopefully the potion will work for him too. The woman was beautiful, loving and kind, and he owes her a debt of gratitude. And he'll pay it.

He knocks at his own door. "Hello?"

"We're here."

The voice sounds familiar, but she doesn't speak Greek. She speaks Romanian.

Codru steps in. Sure enough, the woman is waiting, like his landlady said, but she's not the sultry Greek from Lesbos. This one is blonde, blue-eyed and achingly beautiful, but for her gaze that's sharper than a razor's edge.

"Hello, Codru."

"Lena? I didn't know we were married."

"I had to tell her something to let me in. I hope that doesn't ruin your plans."

Codru thinks about the three girls he danced with, all pretty, all willing. Oh well. "Of course not. What can I do for you?"

"My son Mircea and I, we need shelter. I couldn't think about anybody else I could trust but you. Mama Smaranda told me you were here, so we came."

Codru nods, wishing he was elsewhere. "Of course. I wasn't doing much. Who do you need shelter from?"

"Everyone. We don't mean to interfere with your life, but I thought we could just hang out with you for a while as things get themselves sorted out."

"Sure," Codru says, wishing he'd taken one of those young ladies out for a walk, like they suggested. Too late now. There he is, a married man, his love life over. "How long do you plan to stay?"

"Who knows? As long as it takes to find another safe place."

"I only have one bedroom, you know. Will that be a problem?"

"Not at all. I slept in the sultan's bed for months. I have no problem sharing yours."

"How about your baby?"

"Mircea will be fine. He's slept on the floor, in the hay, in woodpiles, and anywhere else you could imagine ever since the day he was born. He's an easy kid."

Codru sighs. "Of course. I need some rest now. I had a long day and I have training in the morning."

"No problem."

Lena walks to his bedroom, checks on the baby laying on a folded blanket on the floor, making sure he's sound asleep, then gets under his covers and turns to her side. "Night. See you tomorrow."

Slack-jawed, Codru watches her take over his place. This isn't what he planned, but this is what he got. He squeezes under the covers on the other side of the bed, careful not to touch her.

"Night," he whispers, but Lena's deep, regular breath tells him she's already asleep, and Codru can't help but wonder at her guts. She came to his house pretending she's his wife, requisitioned his bed and fell asleep. Just like that. Like, really?

CHAPTER 37
SUMMER 1450

It's been a while since the evening Lena showed up on Codru's doorstep with Little Mircea, and it's not looking like they're going anywhere. And things haven't gotten easier since. If anything, they got more complicated.

He was so afraid to touch her at night that he couldn't sleep for a week, so he walked around like a zombie, wondering where to hide for a nap, when he got called to Hunyadi's quarters.

The great man smiled when he saw him, giving Codru the chills. Hunyadi wasn't a smiler. "How are you doing, kid?"

"I'm fine, thanks," Codru lied.

"You look like you need to get some sleep, my friend. No wonder, with that wife of yours."

Codru froze. "My wife?"

"Yes, your wife. Erzsébet invited her over this morning, so I got to meet her too. What a woman! She told us how you fell in love and how you saved her from the sultan's harem."

Codru's jaw fell. "I..."

"Now, now, there's no need to be modest. I bet you everyone knows about it already. Erzsébet took care of that. It's too good a story to keep it a secret. I can't believe that you kept that to yourself all this time."

Codru stammered. Hunyadi must have thought he was acting modest, but he wasn't. He was just befuddled.

"But I'm dying to know: where did you learn to howl like a wolf?"

"Howl like a... at home, in Transylvania. We, kids, had to find something to entertain ourselves on the long winter nights," Codru fibbed, thinking about what he'd tell Lena when he got home.

Hunyadi nodded. "I see. Listen, Codru, I'm mighty pleased with your work. You're reliable, hard-working, and steadfast. The stipend I gave you was enough for an unmarried man with few needs, but a family man is different altogether. I spoke to Erzsébet, and she agreed to let you and Lena use the little house in the city she inherited from her aunt. Nobody lived in it since she died, so it needs a bit of work, but you can take care of that. And I'll double your wages, starting last week."

Codru thanked him and beelined home to Lena. He found her in their bedroom, brushing her golden hair.

"How could you do that?" he sputtered.

"Do what?"

"Tell them I helped you escape from the sarayi."

"Why not? It's true. I didn't make it all the way, but that wasn't your fault."

"And the stuff about howling like a wolf?"

"Well, that's true too. Erzsébet asked me what was the first thing I admired about you, and I told her you could howl like nobody else."

Codru shook his head. He was at a loss. "How did you meet Erzsébet?"

"She came here to see me. Your landlady told everyone who'd listen that your family has arrived, so Lady Hunyadi came to pay a courtesy visit. She sat to chat with me, but she only had eyes for little Mircea. She said he looks just like her youngest son when he was just a little boy. The one who's now Đurađ Branković's prisoner in Smederevo. She misses him terribly. She wanted to see more of Mircea, so she invited us to their place. That's how I met Hunyadi. Impressive man, especially that mustache. I wonder how he gets it to stay up like that."

Codru stared at her, wondering if she was kidding, but she wasn't. She finished brushing her honey-colored hair and braided it, then wrapped it up like a crown around her head. She was so stunning that Codru's heart ached. He would have loved to hold her, but she glanced at him and her mouth tightened in disapproval.

"Get ready, or we'll be late for dinner."

"Dinner?"

"We're invited there for dinner. And there'll be news for you."

"For me?"

"Of course."

"What news?"

"You're going to war."

"When?"

"Soon."

"Against whom?"

"Against Branković. You're going to rescue Hunyadi's son."

Codru was left speechless. How did Lena know all this?

Hungary had had to pay a huge ransom to liberate Hunyadi from Đurađ Branković's grip after the second battle of Kosovo. Even worse, Hunyadi had to send his son in his stead. That had happened last year, and after they'd regrouped and licked their wounds, it was time to rescue the kid. But how did Lena know?

She shrugged. "Erzsébet told me. Amongst a few other things."

"Why?"

"She needed somebody to share her joy with, now that he finally agreed to do it. And I happened to be there."

That evening was the first time he sat at Hunyadi's table, and it was all thanks to Lena. After dinner, there was music and dancing. He watched her dance with one man after another, bewitching them all, while he drank with Hunyadi and talked war.

"I know you're worried about her," Hunyadi said, his eyes following Lena dancing with some man at the other end of the room.

"But don't be. She'll be fine, and so will your boy. Erzsébet will look after the kid, and there'll be plenty of young officers willing to look after her."

Codru frowned.

Hunyadi laughed and patted his shoulder. "Just kidding. The young officers are coming with us, remember? But I'm sure she'll be fine."

Sure she would, Codru thought. A woman who managed to talk her way out of the sultan's bed and then talked her way into his without even asking for permission could be nothing but fine.

But how about him?

CHAPTER 38

GOING TO WAR

The time has come. Hunyadi's army is leaving for Serbia tomorrow, and God only knows when they'll return. If we return, Codru thinks, heading home after a long day of training.

It's late, but every window in Buda is lit. Sure they are. From most houses, somebody will go to war tomorrow, so their families try to make the most of their last night together. That makes Codru feel even lonelier. Must be nice to have someone who cares about you, he thinks, shrugging to soften the ache in his shoulders and hoping there's something to eat at home.

He opens the door, and the aroma of Christmas bowls him over. The table is set. Lena, all flushed, is checking the oven. Little Mircea runs to hug his knees.

Codru picks him up, and the little arms wrapping around his neck melt his heart. He can't remember anyone ever cooking especially for him, nor anyone asking him to pick them up. It's like they're a real family, and they care about him.

"You're back just in time," Lena says, wiping her forehead on her sleeve. "Go get the wine from the water bucket."

Codru puts Mircea down, and the kid grabs his hand as he goes to look for the wine. It's cold, since the water well is deep and cold.

He pours wine into two wooden cups and hands one to Lena.

"*Noroc.* Cheers. To your safe return," she says.

They knock and sip. The golden wine is deep and smooth, unlike the harsh cheap reds that Codru is used to. It slides smoothly and asks for more.

"Where did you get this?" Codru asks, refilling the cups.

"From Erzsébet. I asked her where to get some nice wine to send you off and she stole a bottle from Hunyadi's cellar."

A wave of heat bursts out as she opens the oven to take out a golden roasted chicken. It's stuffed with onion, garlic, and spices and it smells so good it makes his mouth water. She cuts thick slices of warm bread, then spreads them with golden butter.

Codru sits on the long bench by the table. Mircea climbs in his lap and opens his mouth for food.

Codru laughs and gives him a bite of bread, then another while Lena carves the chicken.

"Which piece do you like?" she asks.

"The thigh, please."

She sets a leg and a thigh on his trencher. He pushes them away from Mircea, who leans to grab them.

"Let me take him so you can eat."

"He's fine here," Codru says, feeding Mircea small bites of chicken between struggling to get some for himself. "Lena, thank you for this beautiful dinner."

"That's the least I could do. You've been so generous to take us in."

"I didn't have much of a choice, did I?"

She laughs sheepishly. "Not much. Thanks, nevertheless."

They eat and drink in peaceful companionship until Mircea falls asleep.

Codru smiles at the head resting on his shoulder, afraid to move and wake him up. "What a great kid."

"He'd better be; he's the only one I've got."

Codru sighs. "Listen, Lena. If I don't come back…"

He expects her to say: "Sure you'll come back, don't even think about it," like most folks would say, but she doesn't. She's not that kind of girl. She just looks into his eyes with sad blue eyes as old as the ocean. It's like she knows something he doesn't, and that makes him shiver.

"If I don't make it back… I'd like you and Mircea to inherit everything I have. But there's a woman, far away, on the Island of Lesbos. She may or may not have a kid about Mircea's age. I spent a winter there on my way back from Constantinople."

Lena nods.

"If she has a kid, he may be special."

"Special how?"

"Like me. Special under the full moon."

The words don't want to come out, but they need to be said.

"She was kind to me. Her name is Athena. I told her I'll return some day. And I plan to. But if I don't make it back… will you go look for her and her child? And help them any way you can? There's an older boy too, a lovely kid. Nikos. I promised them to return, but I didn't," he says, his voice thick with sorrow.

Lena nods. Her blue eyes shine with tears. "I will. If you don't make it back, somehow, someday, I'll find my way to Lesbos, and I'll do whatever I can for them."

"Thank you. And Ali… and Ion. Tell them I love them. And I tried."

"Tried what?"

"They know."

Lena cleans up the table, and Codru puts Mircea to bed. By the time everything is put away and they go to the same bed they've shared for weeks, everything feels different. They are no longer the same people who slept there just last night.

"Night," Lena says. She squeezes under the blankets and turns her back to him, as usual. He lies on the edge of the bed without touching her and thinks about tomorrow. He's always looked forward to battle, but this time he's sorry to leave them. This woman and her child made his dull life richer, like love always does, and it hurts to leave.

He turns to his side, thinking about the people in his life. His parents had no use for him. But then he met Ali and Ion, who are closer to him than his brothers. Athena in Lesbos and her son, who gave him shelter and love. Then Mama Smaranda and Hunyadi. And now Lena and Mircea. He was lucky to find so many friends who care.

He's half asleep when Lena turns around and spoons his back, putting her arm around him.

Codru holds his breath, waiting for more. But there's nothing more but her hold, which is strong and sweet and it brings tears to his eyes.

"Good night," he whispers, but she's asleep already.

CHAPTER 39

MOLDOVA, AUGUST 1450

Fat white clouds float over the deep blue sky like swans gliding over still water. The green canopy whispers in the warm wind that smells like summer, filtering the harsh sunlight into shimmering green. Busy bees gather pollen from the hearts of the daisies, forget-me-nots and red poppies scattered through the hayfield. Lying on his back under his favorite old oak, Ștefan wonders if it's time for dinner.

Life in Moldova is sweet in summer. The months he's been back home have been the best of his life. He's with Vlad, who's like a brother, and Father, who teaches them both how to lead. Father even co-opted him as a co-voivode.

"But Father, I'm not good enough."

"Good enough for what?"

"To rule with you."

"You're not ruling with me, kid, you're learning from me. And, hopefully, you'll rule after me. Pretending to share the throne will make it easier for you to keep it if I die, or grab it when I lose it. People will know you. Not only our Moldavians but also Hunyadi, the Poles, the Ottomans, and everyone who matters. That will smooth your path to the throne."

"But Father, you're young and healthy. You're not going anywhere."

"I'll go wherever God sends me. In life, you should always prepare for the worst and hope for the best. There are no guarantees. Starting tomorrow, we'll share Moldova's throne. Remember that you're a voivode, and act accordingly."

Ștefan did. He tried hard to listen to the men who instruct him in history, philosophy, geography, and languages — but what he loves best are strategy and tactics, and weapons practice. Same with Vlad, who shares his classes. They do their best to outdo each other.

Father was pleased. "You boys are the future of the Romanian countries. I'm glad you get to grow up and learn together. I wish we had a Transylvanian too. They also need leadership."

"But Father, Transylvania belongs to Hungary."

"Sure it does. Transylvania belongs to Hungary just like Greece, Bulgaria, and Albania — other than what Skanderbeg managed to keep — belong to the Ottoman Empire. They didn't have a choice. We, the Moldavians, and the Wallachians, kept our traditions, our faith, and our language. The Transylvanians couldn't. Those Huns overtook them, and they lost their country. Transylvania has more Romanians than it has Hungarians, Saxons and Székely put together; still, they're treated like an inferior minority. The Huns even tried to steal their faith and turned some of them to Catholicism, may God make them pay for their sins."

"Uncle, did you know I was born in Transylvania? My childhood friends are still there. I also met some Transylvanians in Edirne. This boy, Isa, who's magic with numbers. And Ali, a eunuch in Murad's harem. They both spoke Romanian."

Bogdan's eyebrows went up. "Did you say a Transylvanian eunuch?"

"Yes. He was..."

"Are you sure?"

"Of course."

"Really. I guess that could happen, but I've never heard of one."

Ştefan knows about Ali from Lena. That evening in Berzunţi, before she kicked them out, they talked about their past, and Lena told him about her friend Ali, the eunuch.

"I hope she's OK. I wonder how to get in touch with her," Lena had said.

"Him, you mean."

"Of course."

Ştefan had thought she sounded off. But he forgot all about that when he'd asked her to come to Suceava.

"Are you nuts? I'm not going anywhere with Vlad. I don't want that lunatic killing my baby."

"What are you talking about? Little Mircea is blood of his blood!"

"That's just what I'm talking about! Mircea is an heir to the Wallachian throne. Killing him would clear his path."

"You're losing it, Lena. Can't you see he loves the kid?"

"No. I'm not going anywhere with him. If you want to know where I am, you'll have to swear not to tell him."

Ştefan had, of course. What else could he do? He needed to know where and how she was. She's still in his heart, even though she married his best friend. No matter what, she's still his Lena, unlike any other woman he ever met, and his heart aches with love for her.

So he kept his promise. But Lena's secret stands between them, and he wishes he had nothing to hide.

His stomach rumbles, telling him it's time for dinner. He gets on his horse just as Vlad arrives at a gallop.

"What?"

"We've been looking for you for hours. Your father wants you."

"Why?"

"The Poles are coming. We're at war."

CHAPTER 40

ANOTHER KIND OF WAR

To discourage unwelcome visitors, the Suceava Fortress is perched on top of a steep hill. It's a clumsy square built seventy years ago by Peter Muşat, one of Ştefan's forefathers, and it's not pretty. And it's not meant to be. It's utilitarian rather than cozy, with seven foot thick walls of piled stones held together with mortar thickened with ground rocks and bricks, and surrounded by a ten foot deep ditch wherever the hill isn't too steep to climb.

The large room in the middle isn't much larger than the small dark chambers, the cellars, and the keep. Still, it's big enough for the heavy wooden table surrounded by ten straight-backed chairs, all empty but for the one where Bogdan the Second, Moldova's voivode, pores over maps at the head of the table.

He smiles at the boys, but his clean-shaved face is strained with worry. So much so that Ştefan feels guilty for spending the day playing hooky instead of standing by to help.

"I'm sorry, Father, I..."

"No worries. Be seated, boys. We have to talk. Did Vlad tell you?"

"War?"

Bogdan nods. "The Pans gathered at Lvov and crossed our northern border to join Alexăndrel in Camenița. Manoil, the greedy boyar from Hotin, joined them too. They're three days north, with five times more men than we have. All trained and well equipped."

Terrible news, Ștefan thinks, remembering Vladislav's attack on Târgoviște. They were betrayed, the fortress fell, and Vlad Dracul and Mircea died.

"What will we do?" he asks.

"What would you do?"

"I'd look for help."

"From where?"

"Hunyadi?"

"I already did. I asked for his help in February, then again in July. I even promised to not take back Chilia, our port on the Danube by right, without his permission. He said he'd help, but he didn't. And Buda's far away, while the Pans are here."

Ștefan turns to Vlad for help.

"What if we negotiated with the Pans? Alexăndrel is just a kid. He can't help them when the Ottomans head north again," Vlad says.

"I tried that too. The King of Poland was thinking about annexing Moldova, like they did with Ukraine, but decided against it. He'd rather have it as a buffer against the Ottomans. I even offered to pledge allegiance and pay tribute, God burn his greedy soul, but he'd rather have Alexăndrel, who's his nephew, and a child with no will of his own."

Vlad turns to Stefan, but he's at a loss. Thank God that Moldova's fate doesn't rest on his shoulders. Only now, with the danger so close, can he see how much he has to learn.

"So, what do we do, boys?" Bogdan asks.

"I guess we'll have to fight," Ștefan says.

Bogdan laughs. "I guess so, too. Fighting it is, then. But how do we win? The Pans' heavy cavalry is already on our land. They're supported by heavy infantry and a long convoy of supply carts, and led by Odrowąż and Koniecpolski, their most famous generals. They crushed the soldiers I'd left to guard the border."

Vlad scratches his head. "Uncle, do you remember what you did at Tămășeni? You used the terrain to make their size into a weakness. Can you do that again?"

"Good thinking, Vlad. So: Lesson one. Don't fight unless you must. Lesson two: If you do, choose your place and your time. They expect us to barricade ourselves in Suceava, so they think they'll surround and crush us. And that's just what would happen if we stayed here. But we won't." He leans over the table to unroll a map and puts his finger on the green space in the middle. "This is where we'll fight them: in Crasna. It's the perfect place. Right in the middle of the country, tucked between two rivers and old forests. Too tight for the Pans to fully deploy, but perfect for us to hide."

"But how will you get them there?" Vlad asks.

"Easy. We just make sure they can't go anywhere else. This morning I sent messengers throughout the country, asking our men to meet us there. They'll burn the fields and poison the wells on their way, forcing the Pans to head in that direction. In the meantime, we'll harass them every day and night to keep them tired, hungry, and thirsty. We'll cull them one by one when they go to look for food and water. We'll take the laggards and kill those who venture too far. In a month, we'll have them exactly where we want them."

"Why a month?" Stefan asks.

"Our men need time to get there. They'll leave their homes and walk there from every corner of the country. That takes time."

"How do you know they'll come?" Vlad asks.

"I don't. But I hope they will."

"What if they don't?"

"If they don't, Alexăndrel will sit on this throne next month, and we'll start over. If we're still alive."

His heart heavy, Ștefan turns to Vlad, who's stunned too. This plan sounds insane. They've never heard of anything like this before. But they have nothing better.

"You'll each take a hundred riders and head north. You'll coordinate, but work separately. One team can rest while the other fights. Slowly but surely, you'll drive them to Crasna, just like sheep dogs lead their flock to the fold. I'll meet you there in a month."

"What will you do, Father?"

"I'll stay here to keep their spies from suspecting our plan. I'll offer them better peace terms, to make them think they've got us by the short hairs. A month from now, they won't know what hit them."

CHAPTER 41

MOLDOVA, SEPTEMBER 4, 1450

As August turned to September, the days shrank and chilled, and the leaves started turning, up in the mountains. But down here in the Albeşti River valley near Crasna the canopy is just as thick as ever, so it was easy to hide Bogdan's army — thousands and thousands of peasants coming from Moldova's every corner.

They had already harvested the wheat when Bogdan's call came, so they left the rest standing and got their sickles, axes, and maces. They kissed their women and hugged their kids, then headed to Crasna on foot. It took days for some, weeks for others, but today, on the fourth day of September, they're all here. The thousands of men who were just peasants yesterday are now Moldova's Great Army.

Vlad holds his horse tight and studies them. Short, bearded and unsmiling, they're clothed in quilted vests instead of armor, covered with tall sheepskin hats instead of helmets, and they carry sickles and scythes instead of swords. Seeing them makes Vlad sick with worry.

For him, an army is an orderly squad of disciplined janissaries in bright red uniforms, with pointed helmets, carrying bows and arrows, and kilijes sharp enough to cut a falling feather. But this? His faith in Bogdan is all but gone.

"See them?" Ștefan whispers.

"Yep."

"It's even worse than I thought. I fought with Mircea and your father's Great Army, but at least they were mounted on ponies. And they had weeks to train together, not like this. I sure hope Father knows what he's doing."

"Sure he does. Wasn't he right about everything else? He said he'd have them here just as we harassed the Pans into coming this way, and it worked like magic," Vlad says, with a confidence he doesn't feel.

Ștefan's lips tighten. They both know it was more sweat than magic. For a month now, they've been taking turns to ambush, harass and drive the Poles nuts with their unexpected nightly attacks, until the Pans didn't dare go to sleep any more. They didn't kill that many, but put the fear of God in all the others. They must be tired, hungry, and ready to go home by now.

Resplendent in his shiny bright armor, Bogdan stops by. His chestnut stallion dances under him, and his face glows with joy. "Did you hear?" he asks.

"What?"

"The Poles sued for peace. They want me to give the throne to Alexăndrel in 1453, when he's fifteen, and pay them seven thousand golden coins a year in the meantime. In exchange for that, they'll go back to wherever they came from and let us be."

"What did you say?" Stefan asks.

"Yes, of course. What else did you expect me to say?"

The boys glance at each other. That's the safe thing to do, of course; it would buy them time to get ready. But they still feel deflated. Yes, their army looks like it's here to harvest, not to battle, but they've put so much work and hope into this fight that it's hard to move on.

"OK," Ștefan says.

Bogdan laughs. "Are you kidding? Now that we've got them where we want them? No way! We fight tomorrow morning at the crack of dawn."

CHAPTER 42

SEPTEMBER 5, 1450

By the time the inky sky starts fading towards East, Bogdan's Great Army is ready. Right at the edge of the woods, the men stand as still as the trees, their weapons ready.

Ștefan with the cavalry stands ahead of them. A thousand men, all experienced riders, armed with swords, bows, and maces, and mounted on nimble mountain ponies used to fighting.

Vlad is as restless as his gray horse that dances in place. His men will spearhead the attack on the Poles and draw them in towards Ștefan and his men. He glances at them: five hundred of the best riders Moldova ever had. Like him, they learned to ride before they could walk, and they're raring to go.

Vlad's heart drums in his chest. His mouth turns dry and his hands tremble with the need to fight. He looks up the hill at Bogdan for the order.

Bogdan raises his sword. The blade glows red like a torch in the sunrise, and Vlad flies like a bat out of hell. The wind in his face, the sword in his hand, he gallops towards the field where the Poles spent the night. His men follow, and the earth shudders under the hooves that tear it apart.

The guards sound the alarm, and the Poles' army wakes up in a hurry. Tall tents spit out disheveled Pans looking for their weapons. Sleepy men stumble against each other while Vlad and his steadfast Moldavians converge over them, howling like a pack of hungry wolves. Without their heavy armor, long lances, and massive destriers, they're easy prey, the Poles, and the wolves have a bloody feast.

But before long, they get themselves together, and the battle heats up. Everywhere around Vlad, his men fight for their lives. Steel clangs against steel, horses neigh, and wounded scream.

A giant Pan on a red horse lifts his sword to the sky and brings it down over Vlad like he's splitting a log. But Vlad's gray leaps aside, and his sword sinks into the soft spot between the helmet and the armor like it's butter. But it's not. A fountain of fiery blood erupts, thick and salty, into Vlad's face, pleasing him beyond anything he's ever felt with a woman.

The red horse runs scared, dragging its rider behind him, but another fighter takes his place, then another and another. Vlad and his men fight like demons, killing, maiming, and crushing enemy after enemy, but before long, the Poles are everywhere. Thousands of them, all better armed and armored than Vlad's men. Once the surprise vanished, they surround the Moldavians to cut their retreat and butcher them to the last.

Vlad wants to stay and fight. Oh, how he wants to stay and fight! But he can't. He must pull back and draw them after him.

He signals the retreat and turns back. His men follow at a gallop, heading back to the river, where Bogdan and his Great Army are waiting.

Vlad reins his horse to let the Poles catch up. He waits until they're close enough, then gives the signal for his riders to scatter, letting the heavy-armored Pans face Ștefan's light cavalry. Mounted on his chestnut, up on the hill, Bogdan watches.

Vlad rides up to him, and his men follow. They reform behind the voivode, ready to get back into the fight as soon as he gives the order.

"Good work, Vlad," Bogdan says, keeping his eyes on the Poles, whose mad cavalcade has stopped to reform.

Thousands of proud knights in shiny armor holding six-foot lances topped with their colors, their armored destriers dancing under them, fall into formation facing the Moldavians on their mountain ponies.

The silence is so heavy you could cut it with a sword as the two cavalries face each other. The wind ceased, and the birds went quiet, like the whole world stopped to watch.

A knight gives the signal. The sharp lances drop their tips like one to aim at the Moldavians' hearts. Two more breaths, and the heavy knights surge ahead at full speed, a wave of steel and rage hellbent to crush Ștefan and his men into oblivion. They gallop faster and faster, rocking the earth with the weight of their anger. Seconds later, they're close enough to skewer Ștefan and his men. Vlad's heart thuds in his chest as he watches his best friend face certain death. He itches to fly to his rescue, but Bogdan's voice keeps him put.

"No. Let him be."

The Pans' lances are only feet away from the Moldavians, ready to pin them like they're meat when Ștefan gives the order. His men spring aside, splitting like a river around a rock, and open the Poles' way forward. The heavy knights' momentum is too high to stop. The entire cavalcade barges into the forest, where the Great Army is waiting.

The Moldovans kneel behind the trees, so the Pole's lances go above their heads as the men start their grim reaping, cutting the horses' legs with their sickles like they're hay. The legion of proud knights melts and crumbles as the Moldavians take them down. The peaceful woods have turned into a gruesome killing field. Blood spurts, horses fall, people scream, and dirt flies as the earth gets ripped apart by the dying horses' hooves. It's a harvest of death like Vlad has not yet seen.

It goes on, and on, as the proud Pans fall like ripe fruit at the peasants' feet.

Their arms must be hurting, Vlad thinks, yearning to jump in and cover himself with blood and glory. He covets his share of the kill. His horse feels his need and prances under him, but Bogdan raises his hand.

"No. Stay put."

The voivode watches something far from the battlefield. Vlad wonders what he's looking at when he sees a dark cloud of riders coming from the north, angling to fall behind them.

"What's that?" he asks.

"Betrayal. Their carts left yesterday, with most of Alexăndrel's men. Somebody called them back. If we don't go, they'll catch us from behind. It's time to go."

"Go where?"

Vlad isn't done. He didn't get his fill of blood. He needs to get in there and kill, but Bogdan would have none of it.

"Time to go."

He gives the signal. The horns sound the retreat, and Moldova's Great Army vanishes like it was never there while Bogdan, Vlad, and Ștefan ride back to Suceava with their men.

"Will they come back?" Ștefan asks.

"Sure, but not soon. We won't have to worry about them for a while, but we still need to worry about everything else."

"Like what?"

"Like the Ottomans. Hunyadi. And treason. Especially treason. That can come any time, from anywhere, and cut us down."

"Is there any way to prevent it?" Vlad asks.

Bogdan shakes his head. "Not that I know of. If you find it, let me know."

CHAPTER 43

MANISA, JANUARY 1451

Rüzgar's hooves clatter on the sun-baked empty road as he gallops, his body more responsive between Mehmed's knees than any lover's. They fly through the desert, leaving a cloud of dust behind. The hot wind burns Mehmed's face and parches his throat as the desert sucks up every drop of water. A hundred feet down the road, a dark man in a white djellaba pounding a stake in the ground turns and smiles, showing the blinding white of his teeth.

"This stake is for you, my sultan. I'll get another for your lover."

He pounds the stake once more, then turns to grab him.

Mehmed gasps and opens his eyes as Radu shakes him gently.

"Wake up. Someone's at the door."

Mehmed shakes his head to clear it, then throws the silk sheets over Radu to hide him. Not much point in that, since the guards know Radu sleeps in his bed every night, but why embarrass them?

"Yes?" he croaks.

A messenger walks in, dusty like he's been riding for days. He carries a scroll bearing Çandarlı Halil Paşa's elaborate seal. He must be coming from Edirne, but the message is not from Father, Mehmed thinks, as he breaks the seal.

183

My Sultan,

*I have to sadly inform you that your father, our beloved Sultan
Murad the Second, much blessed by the merciful Allah, died
suddenly last night.*
*Three days ago, he suffered an attack that left him impaired. His
doctors believe that it was caused by the sultan becoming overexcited
when he met a dancing dervish on the bridge over the Tunca. Ever
since, he couldn't move or speak. He died peacefully this morning.
We kept his death a secret, and we told everyone that the sultan is
resting and should not be bothered. I took care of the most urgent
affairs, but we eagerly await your instructions.*
With my respect and best wishes,
May Allah bless you day and night,

Çandarlı Halil Paşa,
Grand Vizier of the Ottoman Empire

Numb from head to toe, Mehmed stares at the message and reads it again, struggling to grasp its meaning. Father is dead, and he'll never see him again. He'll never be able to show him he's worthy, and he deserves to be a sultan. On the other hand, if Father is dead, that means that he, Mehmed, is the sultan. Or does it?

He needs help.

He pulls the sheets off Radu to hand him the message, and the guards look away, pretending not to notice. Radu finishes reading, drops the scroll and jumps out of bed to get dressed.

"Let's go. Get our horses ready, Zaganos Paşa. And a hundred men."

Zaganos Paşa bows and leaves. Mehmed stares at Radu.

"Where are you going?"

"We are. We're going to Edirne to take your throne. Get dressed."

Mehmed stares at his friend like he's never seen him before. In the blink of an eye, Radu got dressed and pulled on his boots, ready to go.

He's no longer the sweet, soft-spoken boy Mehmed used to know. Just like that, he took charge of the situation, and Mehmed.

"Why the big rush?"

Radu glares at him like he's feeble. "Remember Çandarlı Paşa is not your friend? He sent you the message about your father's death because he had to. But he waited for three days when your father was so sick he couldn't move or talk, and he didn't call you? You could have rushed to Edirne to see him alive, but that didn't fit in with the grand vizier's plans. He doesn't want you for a sultan because he knows you'll take charge. He'd rather have your baby brother, who has years to go before he can rule. That would give Halil Paşa plenty of time to cement his position and possibly take the throne for himself."

"But my brother's just eight months old. He can't be sultan."

"That's just it. But if Çandarlı Paşa presents him with the Sword of Osman and declares him the sultan, the moment you go back to Edirne to take your throne he can call you a traitor and execute you. We need to get there before that happens."

They jump on the horses waiting outside and set on the road to Edirne before the break of dawn. Radu leads the way at break-neck speed. Mehmed follows, but his heart isn't in it. He remembers Mother's words.

"You have to kill the baby."

CHAPTER 44

EDIRNE, FEBRUARY 1451

The horses' hooves swallow the dusty road. For three days and nights, Mehmed and his men stopped at the caravanserais along the road just long enough to refresh their horses and moved on, and on, day and night, until everything blurred into a daze of exhaustion. But now they're finally closing on Edirne. It took them weeks on the way over, when Mehmed brought Sittişah from Edirne. Mehmed shudders, remembering her. It's been a year since he put her away, like Mother said. He left her in Dometika, the palace where Bayezid was born, and hasn't seen her since. Thank Allah!

But he can't avoid her letters. She writes to him every week, and her calligraphy is so perfect it tugs at his heart. Her letters are even worse. They got more and more tearful every month, and the last one made him feel so bad he almost allowed her to return.

My dear lord and master,

I think about you every day and every night, and I pray to Allah to keep you in his favor and bless you with good health and great successes against the infidels.

I so wish I was blessed to see you and breathe the same air as you do.
I wish I could hear your voice and bask in the pleasure of your smile,
and I hold hope that someday you will make it be so.
I don't know what lies my enemies told you to make you send me
away, but they are just that: lies. I did nothing to harm you.
Everything I ever did was meant to gain your favor and bring you
happiness. Whoever says something else is lying, to separate us and
keep me away.
Every morning at sunrise I listen to the caged birds in the sarayi sing
about their loneliness without their loved ones, and I cry with them,
wishing I could be with you.
Until I could not see them suffer any more. I freed them all yesterday.
They flew away together, happier than they've ever been. The
servants look at me like I'm crazy, but the new silence in the castle
makes me think about how happy they are together, and gives me
hope that someday soon you will liberate me too so that I can come
and be with you.
Your most loving and obedient wife under Allah,

Sittişah,
Princess of the Dulkadir

That letter brought tears to Mehmed's eyes. He grabbed a piece of paper to write her back, but then he remembered Gülşah's terrified face, Mustafa's premature birth, and his mother's words. His heart heavy, he left her where she was, because she may be a danger to his sons. And now, here he is, thinking about killing his baby brother. How's that any better? He sighs.

Radu turns to him, his eyes heavy with worry. "What bothers you, my love?"

They've been riding side by side for days, followed by Zaganos Paşa and the men, but they haven't talked in ages.

"How can you tell?"

"I know you better than anyone, and I can feel your anguish in my heart. What is it?"

"Mother said I have to kill the baby. Otherwise, he'll grow to be a threat to my throne and jeopardize the empire. We can't afford another interregnum, and a baby's life is a cheap price to pay, she said."

Radu turns white. "That's awful."

"What do you think?"

"I don't know, Mehmed. I hate to think that your mother was right, but she was a wise woman and she had your best interest at heart. On the other hand, it's a terrible crime to kill your brother. Blood of your blood, and bone of your bone. Your father's son. I have... I have sometimes thought about killing my brother, but I'm glad I didn't have to do it. Not yet."

CHAPTER 45
THE NEW SULTAN

The million stars studding the midnight sky shiver with cold high above the Edirne Castle. A sharp wind from the north cuts through Mehmed's velvet mantle and his chainmail armor, going through his chemise like it's nothing. The stone walls with their arched wooden gates offer little protection, and Mehmed can't wait to get inside and warm his hands around a red-hot brazier. But first, the gates have to open.

Once again, Zaganos Paşa lifts the hilt of his kilij to strike the metal plates of the gate. The clatter of steel against steel shatters the night's silence, so loud it could wake up the dead, but apparently not loud enough for the guards, Mehmed thinks, and signals Zaganos Paşa to strike again.

"Who's there?"

"Sultan Mehmed and his men," Zaganos says, even though they all know the guards saw them miles ago from their watch post in the tower. This is just a convoluted song and dance that gives Çandarlı Halil Paşa extra time to decide what to do, because he couldn't have been expecting them yet. It takes a messenger a week to ride from

Manisa to Edirne, but Mehmed made it in three days. He must be ahead of the grand vizier's schedule, whatever that may be.

The heavy bolts screech, the hinges wail, and the massive gates open slowly to the palace courtyard. The flaming torches affixed to the gateposts make the courtyard seem even darker. The flickering lights throw ominous shadows that might hide soldiers waiting to kill.

His throat dry, his heart racing, Mehmed spurs Rüzgar forward. The black stallion steps into the darkness and the others follow, closing around him. Behind them, the gates slam shut and the bolts scream their way back in, trapping them inside.

Frozen in the middle of the courtyard, surrounded by his men, Mehmed waits for his eyes to get used to the dark. A few heartbeats later, and there they all are: Çandarlı Halil Paşa and his father's other viziers stand under the eaves, as still as chess pieces.

Mehmed awaits, but nobody moves. He counts to twenty, then urges Rüzgar forward until he's just two feet away from Şehabeddin Paşa, the chief of the eunuchs.

"Why do my father's viziers stand aloof, Paşa? Call them and tell Çandarlı Halil to take his accustomed place."

Nothing happens.

Mehmed dismounts. He takes off his leather glove, then steps forward to offer his hand, heavy with his mother's emerald, to the grand vizier. Palm down, for a kiss.

Çandarlı Paşa stands unmoved. They measure one another as the entire court stands to attention in frozen silence. All eyes stay glued on the two men facing each other, and hands reach for their weapons.

Mehmed's eyes sink into the grand vizier's, willing him to bend, but he won't. In deadly silence, the old man stands straight, his spine steel, his eyes daggers.

Mehmed smiles. His right hand waits for the kiss, but his left reaches for his dagger. He's so mad with rage he can almost taste the salt of Çandarlı Paşa's blood as his fingers close around the hilt. The paşa's eyes follow his hand. One, two, three heartbeats and Mehmed pulls out his dagger just as the grand vizier takes the offered hand in both of his to kiss the emerald, then touches it to his forehead in submission.

"Welcome, my sultan. I will serve you well."

Mehmed smiles and slides the dagger back into its place. "I know you will. You've been my father's most trusted advisor and my teacher for so many years. I know there's nothing in your heart but love for Allah, the empire, and me. I will never forget what you taught me. That's why I'll…"

The place freezes, watching Mehmed's fingers caress the hilt of his kilij. He didn't forget the disrespect and the put-downs, nor the grand vizier's betrayal when he called Murad from retirement and ousted Mehmed. Çandarlı Paşa opposed everything Mehmed ever tried to do, especially his yearning to conquer Constantinople, and neither of them has forgotten.

But Mehmed needs him. To secure his power, to bring the janissaries into the fold, and to lull his enemies into a false sense of security, he needs the grand vizier. For now.

"I reconfirm you as my grand vizier. I expect you to serve me with the same wisdom, faith, and honor as you did my father."

His face ashen, Çandarlı Paşa falls to his knees and kisses the emerald ring once more. "I won't disappoint you, my sultan."

Mehmed smiles. "I know, Çandarlı Paşa. I'll make sure you won't."

CHAPTER 46

EDIRNE, FEBRUARY 3, 1451

The imperial room is so full you can hardly see the marble floor. No matter where you look, there's nothing but bright brocade, shimmering silk, and rich velvet, making it look like a garden in bloom. But there's no garden; just a fancy crowd, since every dignitary for hundreds of miles came to offer his condolences, pay his respects, and assure the sultan of his faith. But they're all done now, and the room is waiting for the rest in deadly silence.

That was the easy part, Mehmed thinks, sitting on his father's throne. It's his again, and so is the Sword of Osman resting on his knees. His fingers trace the filigree, gathering strength from the symbol of power and faith that inspired every Ottoman sultan for more than two centuries. He caresses the toothless lions making up the guard and tightens his fist around the skinny, curved handle. The fuss is almost over. There's only one thing left to do.

He glances at Radu, who sits with the other dignitaries on a low divan under the windows. Radu nods in encouragement, and Mehmed takes in a deep breath and turns to Ali Bey, who guards the door.

"Bring the women."

The eunuchs leave to get Sultan Murad's women. By tradition, they

192

all must come to congratulate the new sultan. But the truth is that they come to learn their fate. Now that their husband and master, Sultan Murad, is dead, their life will never be the same.

The first wife, Hatice Halime Hatun, comes first, of course. She's short and plump and dressed in black from head to toes, but for the narrow split of her jellaba over her teary eyes. She shuffles to Mehmed's podium and drops to her knees, lowering her head and wringing her hands. "Congratulations for taking your throne, my sultan. I know the Ottoman Empire will be safe in your powerful hands. Your father would be so proud of you!"

"Thank you, Hatice Halime Hatun."

"I am… I am heartbroken to lose your father. We were married for twenty-six years, and he blessed me with two wonderful sons. I pray every day that his soul watches over you, and over Ahmed Çelebi, your young brother. I know your father will find pride and joy in your deeds."

Mehmed hopes so, even though he feels neither pride nor joy in his heart.

"I wish you a long and prosperous reign, rich in memorable victories, just like your father's."

"Thank you, Hatice Halime Hatun."

"May I… May I present to you your brother, my son Ahmed? He's a lovely baby, and so much like your father. Seeing him will give you joy. Now that your father is gone, the baby is the only light left in the night of my soul. Thank merciful Allah for blessing me with him. I believe holding him will give you solace."

"I will see him tomorrow."

"Thank you, my sultan. You are most kind." Hatice Halime touches her forehead to the floor in gratitude.

"Hatice Halime Hatun, you have been my father's faithful wife for many years. He had much affection for you, and he must have been sad to leave you. This is why you will…"

The room stops breathing. What will he do with her? She's no longer that young, but she's still the mother of Murad's son, and a princess of royal blood, Isfendiyar Bey's daughter.

"You will marry Ishak Paşa, Anatolia's governor. He will treat you with the kindness, love, and dignity that you deserve."

The room gasps. If she leaves for Anatolia, who will look after her baby? She can't take Murad's son, the young şehzade, to another man's harem. Ishak Paşa himself looks struck by lightning. This is an honor he can't refuse, even though he already has four wives, the most Allah allows. He'll have to get rid of one of them.

Stunned by the news, Hatice Halime drops to the ground in a heap. On Mehmed's sign, two eunuchs help her up and take her back to the sarayi.

The next one to come is Mara Branković, Sultan Murad's third wife, and Mehmed's favorite person in the sarayi. She's the daughter of the Serbian despot and his Byzantine royal wife, and she's related to every crowned head in the world.

"Mother Mara."

"Congratulations, my sultan. I'm glad to see you back. Your father would be so proud of the man you've become."

"Thank you, Mother Mara."

"I know that the Ottoman Empire will grow and prosper under your reign."

"Thank you, Mother Mara. I'm glad to see you again, and sad to see you go."

"Go where?"

"You will go back to Serbia, to your family who missed you for so many years. You will help us strengthen our ties with Serbia and the rest of Europe. I rely on you to represent the Ottoman Empire at Europe's courts, and I hope you'll be able to convince them that we want peace, not war."

The crowd gasps.

Astounded, Mara wavers. "Why are you sending me away, Mehmed?"

"I'm setting you free. You've always been kind to me, ever since I was a child. I'm grateful and I want you to live the life that you choose."

"What if I choose to stay here?"

"I hope you won't. As much as I treasure your counsel and love having you near, I need you to help me mend our relations with Europe. I need peace in the West for what I must do, and you're the only one who can get it."

Mara moves aside to make room for Murad's concubines, who are to be disposed of. One by one, they share their grief and congratulate Mehmed. He listens to them patiently, then marries them off to the last one to his dignitaries and officers.

The ceremony is almost over when a heart-wrenching scream comes from the sarayi, then another and another. Behind the carved wooden screens, someone's heart is breaking apart.

The crowd gasps and stares. Two eunuchs head to the sarayi.

"Stay here!" Mehmed says.

They freeze in place and listen to the agony. So does Mehmed. He did what he had to do, but he's not proud. His heart aches for his baby brother and the unfathomable grief of his mother. It's a terrible price to pay for being sultan, even though he didn't do it for himself. He did it for the empire, but that doesn't help him feel any better. He sits quietly and listens until the screams die down into sobs, then silence.

"Ishak Paşa."

"My sultan?"

"You'll leave for Anatolia tomorrow with my father's casket. You'll take a caravan worthy of him and stop along the way to let his people mourn and pay their respects. You'll distribute money to the poor as a last token of his generosity."

"Yes, my sultan."

"You will take Hatice Halime Hatun with you, and you'll treat her with the dignity and the respect she deserves. And..." He stands and glances at the silent screen. "You'll also take the baby's coffin."

CHAPTER 47

CONSTANTINOPLE, SUMMER 1451

Perched on the northern slope of Constantinople's sixth hill, the Palace of Blachernae has been the residence of the Byzantine Emperors for over three hundred years, starting with Emperor Alexios, who moved here from The Great Palace and rebuilt the place. His successors fortified the massive outer walls and built imposing new halls to host the Roman dignitaries. That's why they called it The New Palace, even though some of it was seven hundred years old. But that was long ago.

Today, the council room's walls are covered in precious tapestries, rich rugs, and enough gold to steal your eye from the crumbling walls and the leaks in the roof, Ion thinks, searching for a comfortable position on the high chair whose sculpted back digs into his ribs, and thankful for the pillow under him.

This is his first council meeting, and he's only here because Emperor Constantine told him to be. Everyone else is either old nobility, or a big shot in the Orthodox Church, and they give him dirty glances. All five of them but for Sphrantzes, who sits to his left by the emperor's empty seat.

Ion shrinks under the glares, wishing he was somewhere else.

Fortunately, heavy boots resound on the stone floors, telling him the emperor is coming.

But it's not the emperor. It's his old master, Loukas Notaras, who freezes in the door when he sees him. "What's he doing here?"

The dignitaries snicker, glad that Notaras asked what was on everyone's mind. Constantinople is not the Ottoman Court, where any kid from devşirme can grow up to become the grand vizier, if he's worthy. Here, in the Roman Empire, as they like to call themselves, they believe everyone should know their place. Traditions matter above all. That's why the Eastern Roman Empire has lasted for a thousand years, while glorious Rome got overcome by barbarians and became a distant memory. Or so they say.

"I asked him to be here," the emperor says as he enters the room, and they all stand and bow. Because here, the emperor is not a mere mortal. He's thought to be God's ambassador on earth, and therefore sacred.

But that's too much for Notaras to take. When Ion left him to serve the emperor, he felt personally insulted. So much so he didn't even pay him the ducat he'd promised for winning his bet with Sphrantzes.

"Let the emperor pay you if he thinks you're so special," he said.

Ion hasn't seen him since, and didn't miss him. With his oily hair stuck to his head and his shifty eyes, the megas doux isn't much to look at anyhow. But he's not here for his looks. He's here for being the emperor's right-hand man and first advisor, and he glares at Ion with narrowed eyes.

"Why?"

"Because I want to use his expertise and his advice. That's why," the emperor says.

"But how do you know he's not an Ottoman spy? He worked for the sultan for years. How can we trust that he's not still in his service?"

The emperor sits in the tall gilded throne at the head of the table. "You took him in first, Loukas, remember? He was with you for months before he came to us. How come you didn't worry about him then?"

The megas doux's mouth tightens to nothing as he sits at the emperor's right and opens his book to take notes.

"What's on today's list?" the emperor asks.

"The first thing is Murad's death. Mehmed was crowned sultan. He killed his baby brother but kept Çandarlı Halil Paşa as his grand vizier," Sphrantzes says.

Notaras nods. "That's good news, my emperor. Çandarlı Halil Paşa is an old friend of Constantinople, and he'll do his best to temper Mehmed's youthful exuberance, in case he thinks about heading our way. We should congratulate him and maybe send him a gracious gift to remind him who his loyal friends are."

The emperor nods. "Not a bad idea. But first we'll send Mehmed our condolences as well as our congratulations, and we'll reassure him we are his friends and want nothing but peace."

Sphrantzes intervenes: "We should also remind him how glad we are to continue extending our hospitality to his uncle Orhan, Bayezid Yildirim's great-grandson. At the moment, Orhan is the only potential rival to Mehmed's throne, and he's our lucky break. We've been getting three thousand silver aspers a year for his upkeep, and we hope Mehmed will continue his contribution."

"How about we up it some? Our coffers are empty, and the sultan can afford to pay five times that much," Notaras says.

Sphrantzes shakes his head. "Not yet. Let him settle first and show him we are his friends. We can always increase our demands next year."

The emperor looks at Ion. "What do you think?"

Ion's cheeks catch fire as all eyes gather on him. "I... his coffers are empty, too. After the coronation, he'll have to pay the janissaries an extra bonus, besides the extraordinary expenses he'll incur for Murad's funeral. I don't think it's a good time to increase our demands."

Notaras scowls. "What do you..."

The emperor cuts him off. "I agree. We'll leave that for next year. What's next?"

Sphrantzes clears his voice. "Ensuring the succession to the throne of Constantinople. We've been looking for a suitable empress for years, and Murad's death just opened an amazing opportunity. Mehmed released Mara Branković from the harem. She's a most eligible candidate: she's beautiful and well connected. Even Mehmed respects her and listens to her advice. She'd be the perfect wife for you."

Notaras turns red. "You've got to be joking. You want the emperor of Constantinople to slobber over Murad's leftovers? And she's too old. She's got to be forty, and she never had kids. She must be sterile. And a Muslim, to boot!"

"She's thirty-five. And she never converted, so she's still a Christian. Orthodox, like us. They say the marriage was never consummated, that's why she didn't have kids."

"Yeah, like you would know! She was married to Murad for fifteen years. Why wouldn't Murad mount her if she's as beautiful as you say?"

"Murad had plenty of other wives and concubines. It's not like he was short of women."

"Enough!" The emperor turns to Ion. "You know anything about her?"

It so happens that Ion knows a lot about Mara from his friend Ali. She couldn't stop talking about Mara, her beauty, her humor, her kindness. If he didn't know better, he'd think Ali had a crush on her. "She's said to be beautiful, and very kind, Emperor."

Notaras snorts. "How would you know? They let you check her out in the sarayi, perchance?"

"No, sir. But my best friend was a eunuch in the sarayi and he worked for her."

Constantine sighs. "OK, then. Send the Serbian despot a message and see. One way or another, we need to secure the succession, and this woman sounds as good as any. What else?"

"The churches' reunion."

Nodding at the other end of the table, the old Patriarch Gregory, all black but for the scraggly white beard covering his chest, snaps to attention. "The Orthodox synaxis is unquestionably against the union, my emperor. I did my best but couldn't persuade them. 'We won't subject ourselves to the papal rites and bow to those Catholic heretics. We'd rather die in our own faith than lose our soul,' they said. The best I could do was talking them into another meeting, should the pope agree."

"Do they understand that the churches' union is our only chance to get help from the west? We can't fight the Ottomans alone, and the pope refuses to even discuss any aid before we negotiate the union," the emperor says.

Notaras shrugs. "There's no guarantee they'll send any help, anyhow. And our people don't want the union. Push them too hard and you'll lose their support."

"Don't push them enough and we'll lose Constantinople," Sphrantzes says.

"You're an alarmist, as usual," Notaras says.

"And you're a contrarian, as usual," Sphrantzes answers.

The emperor had it. He stands, and the gold of his clothes steals the light from the room, but his dark eyes are worried. "That's enough. I'll see you all next week. Ion, come with me."

CHAPTER 48
CONSTANTINE'S TREASURY

Ion follows the emperor through a maze of dilapidated rooms, stone stairs smooth with wear, and windowless hallways. Flickering torches sit high in iron rings, throwing mysterious shadows over the gray stone walls and enticing Ion to linger and look at everything, but Constantine walks with the firm pace of someone who's walked this way a thousand times.

"Watch your step here," he says, lifting his torch to light the missing step, then keeps going, deeper and deeper into the heart of the hill. Ion follows him closely, wondering where they're going. He'd better not lose him, or he'll never get back.

He's a tall man, Constantine, and handsomely dressed in purple and gold. So much so that he glows from head to toe from all the crosses, diadems, and embroidery covering him. He's grandiose, and a living God to his people, but Ion feels sorry for him.

His hunched shoulders carry the weight of the empire — what's left of it after the Ottomans gobbled it piece by piece. The Eastern Roman Empire lasted for a thousand years and used to be the pride of Christianity, but all that's left of it is this half-empty city, and the tiny despotate of Morea in the Peloponnese. Everything else vanished like water in the desert, leaving just the Red Apple ripe for picking. And it won't be long.

One last set of steep stairs and they stop at a metal-plated wooden door, with lock after lock hanging like grapes from its many bolts.

Constantine hands Ion the torch, grabs a key-ring from his robes and unlocks. "Come in."

It's nothing but a moldy cave, carved deep inside the mountain, so it has neither windows nor doors other than the one they came through, and empty, but for a couple of coffers at the far end. Nothing here but the rough rock walls and three Orthodox icons leaning against the walls.

"You know what this is?"

"No."

"My treasury. What's left of it. This is all we've got left to pay for food, soldiers, ships, and everything else. Nothing more."

Ion stares at the empty room of the golden empire and can't believe it. "This is it?"

"Yes. Or at least that's what the megas doux tells me. He's the keeper of the finances, so he tells me what I owe and what I get. And, somehow, what I owe is always more than what I get. We are in trouble."

Ion nods, wondering about Notaras' second set of records that he never got to see. "I see."

"I've been emperor for a year, and I can't remember a day without being told that we can't afford something. We can't afford ships, soldiers, armor, or cannons. We don't seem to afford anything. One wonders what happens to all the money flowing into the treasury."

Ion has no answer. He has suspicions, but that's not enough.

Constantine sighs. "I'd like you to look into that. I'll help you as best I can. I hate money, but I know it's the root of everything. And we need cannons, soldiers, and ships, because Mehmed is coming. The best we can hope is to delay him, but, sooner or later, he'll pound at the gates, and we need to be ready. Thanks to the Theodosian Walls, Constantinople withstood twenty-three assaults, including Murad's, but I'm afraid we're running out of time. We need to prepare. Please help us."

Ion's heart warms up for this tired man who speaks like a real person as they sit on the floor next to each other. The Emperor of Byzantium talks to him like they're buddies.

"May I ask you a question, Emperor?"

"Of course. You can ask me to get naked for all that I care. What is it?"

"Why me? I've been with you for just a few weeks. You don't know me, and I don't know much about you. You have so many wise people around you. Why me?"

Constantine laughs. His laugh echoes in the empty cave like a hundred people are laughing, and not one is having fun. "That's just it. You're new, not steeped in a thousand years of Byzantine tradition. We need a fresh voice. I know I do."

Ion nods. "I'll do my best for you, my emperor. I'll find you money if I can, and I'll advise you the best I can, with my limited knowledge. I'll be faithful to you."

"But?"

Ion has a hard time saying it, because it's unkind, and maybe even untrue. "But Constantinople will fall."

"How do you know that?"

"I… know things."

Constantine nods. "Have you heard about the prophecy?"

"No."

"It says that Constantinople's last emperor will have the same name as the first. That's my name. His mother's name will be the same as the name of the first emperor's mother. That's Helena, my mother's name. They also call it the empire that will last a thousand years. And our thousand years have expired."

"Why fight, then?"

Constantine looks at him, and his eyes glow luminous in the torch light. "Because it's my duty. I'm responsible for every life in the city. It's my job to save them, and preserve our faith, our traditions, and our way of life that makes us who we are. I'll do whatever it takes, even if the odds are a million to one."

"I understand."

"And you? What are you fighting for?"

Ion thinks back about his days of training in Kronštadt, then his days in Edirne. "I'm fighting for my people, Emperor. The oppressed, enslaved, and hurt, too many to count."

"Who are they?"

"The Romanians."

CHAPTER 49

LITTLE SISTER

When Ion finally heads home that evening, he doesn't know whether to be happy or sad. He found a use for Ali, who's been like a thorn in his side for weeks now. But he'll be sorry to see her go.

It hasn't been long since she came back into his life. Dressed like a boy, though only an idiot could think her a boy. In the time they'd been apart, she bloomed into a woman he couldn't keep his eyes from.

He was leaving the palace one evening when a dirty beggar grabbed his sleeve. "Evening, sir. Would you happen to have an extra coin?"

He met her ocean-blue eyes, and the earth shifted. "Ali?"

"Yes, sir."

He gasped. He looked right and left, then grabbed her arm. "Mother will be livid. How could you do this to her? You've been gone for weeks. Where have you been?"

"I've…"

He didn't listen to a word she said, but dragged her through the gates, telling the guards she was his little sister. They shrugged and let them pass, so he took her to his rooms where he hugged and kissed her, as filthy as she was, swearing to never let her go.

"How did you get here? And what are you doing?" he asked.

"Whatever I can. How about you?"

He shook his head and let her be. Still a pain in the ass, like she'd always been. But she was his pain in the ass, and he felt happier than he'd been since... probably the last time he hugged her. His heart soared. Ali was there, and everything was right with the world.

He studied her in the candlelight, from the greasy hair sticking to her head and dirty face to the shapeless boots way too big for her feet. Her chemise topped with a moldy brown kaftan swelled around her chest and her hips, hugging curves that had no business being there, and his heart quickened.

"You make a lousy man."

She looked him up and down and smiled. "You think you have room to talk?"

He remembered he'd had a long day, and he could do with a wash and some clean clothes. He laughed. This was his Ali, just like she'd ever been: a woman who didn't know her place, a pain in the ass, and the love of his life.

That happened weeks ago. She never told him where she was coming from or where she was going, but he was happy to have her, at least for a while. Getting her to wear women's clothes was a pain. She tightened her lips and spat: "Why?"

"Because you don't look like a man. In that garb, any idiot can see you're a woman. They'll wonder what you're up to."

"You're saying I look like a woman?"

Ion stared at her chest and nodded. She stomped her feet and left, but the next day he came back home to find her dressed in an ugly black skirt.

"You're happy now?"

Not exactly. To be really happy, he'd have to see her lying in his bed wearing nothing but a smile. But that doesn't look likely. Every time his hug lasts too long, she pulls away. And that one time he didn't let her go, she kneed him in the groin so hard that he walked bent over for two days. She made it clear that his bed was of no interest to her, so he stopped pushing. But he still wonders how long she's going to stay. She's like a bird perched on a branch, ready to fly the minute it suits her, and he'll be left empty again.

But for now, he found her a job.

CHAPTER 50
AT HOME

Ion's kitchen isn't big, but it has everything Ali needs to cook their meals, and she loves it. These two weeks in Constantinople have been the happiest ever, because, for the first time in her life, she's free. There's nobody to tell her what to do, when, and how. Ion tried, of course, but she couldn't care less. He does what he wants, and so does she. For now.

She chops the onions and the carrots and adds them to the goat meat sizzling over a quick fire. She throws in three bay leaves and half a spoon of cinnamon, then pours in some white Greek wine, and just like that, the place smells like the dreams of angels.

She only stopped here in passing; she'll head back to Kronštadt as soon as she gets her legs under her. She can't wait to get back home to Mama Smaranda, but after her boat adventure, she needs some rest and healing.

She's glad to be out of Edirne, and delighted to be with Ion. She knew she'd find him at the palace, since Mama Smaranda knows everyone's whereabouts and finds ways to send messages when needed. It's cumbersome, but it works. That's how she found out that Lena joined Codru in Buda, so she joined Ion in Constantinople. She

208

knows only too well how hard it is to be a lone woman without a home.

She was bummed she didn't make it to Genoa and Venice, since she was looking forward to seeing the city of a thousand islands, the masquerades, and the doge with his horned hat. But it wasn't meant to be. After taking the Ottoman galley just off shore of Lemnos, the pirate ship returned to Constantinople, and she left.

But there's no point in thinking about that now. Here, she's safe, and she has time to decide what to do, she thinks, as the door opens.

Ion comes in, glowing like he found treasure. He picks her up and holds her so long that she wonders if he forgot the last time she kneed him in the groin; then he sets her back down.

"I got you a job."

Ali straightens. She wipes the sweat off her forehead with her sleeve, refraining from hitting him with the wooden spoon. "A job? I didn't know I was looking." She turns to stir the bubbling stew that fills the room with wonderful aromas and resists the temptation to pour it over Ion's head. Nah. It was too much work. And they'd go hungry for dinner.

"I've got you the job of your dreams. Come here and listen."

She nods, but doesn't get any closer.

"You'll be a housekeeper in Loukas Notaras' home."

"What a splendid idea. I always dreamed about being a housekeeper."

"Loukas Notaras is the megas doux, the first man in the empire after the emperor. He holds the keys to Constantinople's treasury. I worked there for months, but I couldn't get anywhere near his second set of ledgers, or to most of his house. But as a housekeeper, you can. We could expose him as the fraud I know he is, so the emperor can recover everything that Notaras stole. That would help Constantine to no end. He could buy guns and ships, and hire soldiers to protect the empire." His eyes shine with hope as he stares at Ali, trying to infect her with his enthusiasm, but she's not buying it.

"And how is this my problem?"

"Saving Constantinople from the Ottomans would mean a victory for Christianity. If we can hold Mehmed at bay, we'll uphold not only the Orthodox Church, but an empire that lasted for a thousand years."

"And what does that have to do with me?"

Ion stares at her. "You don't want to uphold Christianity?"

"What for?"

Ion opens his mouth, then closes it back to search for the right words. "Think about it, Ali. Once they take Constantinople, Christianity's last outpost in the east, they'll head west through the Romanian countries. There'll be nothing left to stop them."

Ali stirs the stew. She presses the onions and the carrots with the long wooden spoon, and they give. Dinner is ready.

She grabs a cloth to pick the pot hanging over the fire and sets it on the table, on top of the cutting board, then gets wooden bowls and spoons from the corner shelf. She carves thick slices from the crusty bread she bought this morning and serves the stew, then brings small bowls of yellow butter and silky sour cream to the table. Reaching for the bottle of Retsina, the white Greek wine smelling like church, she pours it into cups.

"Time to eat."

Ion sits on the bench on the other side of the table. He leans over his bowl and inhales the aroma of herbs, goat, and cinnamon, and sighs. "I'd marry you for nothing but your cooking, Ali. But I wouldn't mind the rest of the package."

Ali laughs and lifts her cup. "To health, luck, and success."

Ion nods and they knock. "Will you do it?"

"I don't know. Housework doesn't sound like fun, and I'm not quite sure what the point of it is. But I'm thinking."

Ion nods, dips his spoon in the stew and blows on it to cool it, then tastes it. "How did you ever learn to cook like this?"

"I didn't. It's a matter of imagination."

"Well, your imagination isn't bad."

He wolfs down the stew, then has seconds. He finally pushes the bowl aside. "Ali, will you do this for me, please?"

His honest face is so open that Ali feels bad about all the things he doesn't know about her.

"Why?"

"I believe in the emperor. I know he's doing his best for his people and Christianity. And I believe that supporting the Byzantine Empire will help support our people."

"You think he'll win?"

Ion sighs. "I don't. I'm afraid that Constantinople will fall, but I hope I'm mistaken. Will you help me anyhow?"

Ali sighs. Not like she's got something better to do. "When do I start?"

"Tomorrow morning. I arranged for him to see you tomorrow at eight."

"I'll be there."

They talk little that evening. Ion pores over some ledgers while Ali mends an old shirt, thinking about how sad it is that they've grown so far apart. Ion is hell-bent on helping Constantine, even though he thinks he'll lose, in some vague hope to help Christianity.

But Ali doesn't much care about Christianity. The church never did much for her. She'd rather help women, the many women who have no say in their lives and are slaves to the whims of their men. It's sad to see how far they grew apart.

CHAPTER 51
MOLDOVA, OCTOBER 1451

Life in Moldova is sweet in the fall. The warm spring rains have been kind to the seedlings; the summer, long and lusty, loved the crops into a heavy bounty. The sweet fall cherished the fruit of the earth into ripeness. Here, one could get used to being lucky.

The peasants finished harvesting the wheat, the vegetables and two crops of hay. It's time for the grapes, their heavy golden drops of heaven bending the vines dressed in rusty leaves. Time for the earth's most beloved fruit to turn into joy. Once harvested, the grapes get crushed into wine to celebrate the weddings, which have been on hold — unless emergent — since spring.

The Moldavians cherish a good party. Passers-by get invited to partake of the food, the wine, and the dancing, no matter who they are. That's why Mircea, Vlad, and Bogdan stopped in the little hamlet of Răuseni on their way back from their hunt.

Bogdan never hunts, since Moldova's voivode has more serious things to do than play. But the boys talked him into it — just this once. The country's safe, so they only took a few guards. And after hours of rambling through the woods and plowing through mud, the boys got a huge boar, the biggest Vlad has ever seen. They tied it by its feet behind a horse and headed home, when they fell upon the wedding and were invited to join.

"Why not?"

So they did. After a few cups of new wine, Bogdan looks happier than he has in ages. So does everyone else, honored to have the voivode share their joy. Her dress a touch tight over her middle, the blushing bride gazes awestruck at her new husband who looks at her like she hung the moon. But the black-clad priest drones on and on, until the folks can't take it anymore.

"The food's ready, Father," someone shouts, so he blesses the couple to get the party going.

Up in the field by the church, wooden saw-horses hold up long wooden boards covered with white cloth, make-shift tables that bow under the weight of the food: round breads larger than a cart wheel, sweet white cheeses, jars of pickles, and butter. Black-clad women and girls dressed in white with ballooning sleeves they embroidered themselves and colorful half-skirts that cover their front and rear load the tables with roasted chickens, golden pies and steaming bowls of fragrant tripe soup and the pickled hot peppers that go with it.

Under the tree by the well, three sweaty musicians play like the devil is chasing them, thrilled to be the center of attention and count the coins landing in their upturned hats. The new red wine flows like water, straight from the barrel into the wooden cups. Three cups in, and the dancers get going. The young men dance together in a row, their heels pounding the earth with the music, then the girls twirl in. Their blooming skirts bare strong white legs, their heavy braids whip their backs and shy eyes exchange furtive glances as the youths mingle and romance blooms under the old people's indulgent watch. This wedding is just the first of many. Others will follow before the long harsh winter clutches the village in its snow grip.

"Go dance, boys," Bogdan says, as the mother of the bride refills his cup. "Have fun, but don't touch the girls, no matter how pretty. You shouldn't do that unless you plan to marry them, and you know you can't. Play it safe. No dark corners, no foul play. Respect these girls like they're your sisters, because some of them may be."

The boys stare at each other.

"What's he saying?" Vlad asks.

"That any of these girls could be my sister. I hope Mother doesn't know," Ștefan says. He's got his eyes on a redhead with a rich chestnut braid thicker than his wrist and eyes as green as spring. "I'll take that one."

Vlad shrugs. He's not into dancing, but he doesn't want to be a party pooper. He meets the fiery eyes of a curvy brunette, standing under an old oak tree. She covers her smile with her hand but doesn't look away as she whispers to a blonde with downcast blue eyes.

Vlad heads towards them. The brunette looks him in the eye, but the blonde looks down. Vlad smiles and nods, then takes the blonde's hand and pulls her to dance. She reminds him of his Sophia, now Gülbahar, the girl he still dreams about. She's beautiful and tame, and she yields when he pulls her close.

They dance and drink and dance again, then switch partners and dance some more. The gypsy musicians live up to their fame of being the best in the world. Sweat pours over their strained faces like rain, but they don't miss a beat, and swing the dance like they'll never stop. It's the best party the boys have ever seen, but the wine poured lead in their feet. They lead their disappointed partners back to their friends and head back to the table to find Bogdan gone.

"Where is he?" Vlad asks a woman pouring drinks.

"The bride took him out for a dance."

The boys laugh and drain their cups.

"What do you think?" Ștefan asks.

"Pretty girls, your Moldavians. I wouldn't mind a roll in the hay with any of them, but your father wouldn't approve."

"Isn't that funny when he's worried about any of them being my sister?"

"He must have been less prudent when he was young."

They sit in pleasant companionship, watching the dancing girls who look even prettier after all the wine, when a ruckus suddenly starts. It sounds like a fight.

"Too much wine, you think?" Ștefan asks.

"Maybe. Or just folks who can't hold their drink."

They wait for the shouting to fade, but it doesn't. The screams get so loud that the musicians stop. So do the dancers. A handful of people head south to see what's happening, when a guard rushes to them.

"What's going on?" Stefan asks.

"Your father. Your father is... is in trouble."

They grab their swords and run to join the action. Blades clang, people scream, horses whinny, but it's hard to tell who's who in the darkness. A handful of riders fight at the edge of the forest as Ștefan and Vlad search for Bogdan, but the voivode is nowhere to be seen. Just two of his guards, fighting a dozen armored men.

"Father! Father!" Ștefan shouts.

One of their guards stops his horse next to him and lends him a hand to mount behind him. "Come. Now."

"Are you crazy? I need to find..."

"You father's dead. I saw his head sit on top of a stake. Yours will too, unless you come with me now."

"But..."

"No but. You come or you don't."

"My cousin?"

The man whistles, and another rider comes for Vlad.

Ștefan clings on to the rider's back, and the horse takes off at a full gallop. It's dark, and he's drunk, and he feels like a coward running away. Soon, they leave the fray behind and there's no noise other than the horse's hooves.

"What happened?" Stefan asks.

"Your uncle."

"Which one?"

"Petru Aron. He's been waiting for his time, and he decided tonight was the night. His men pulled us away from your father, and your uncle's guards murdered him. Next, they'll come after you, and we can't defend you here. We need to get you out."

"Where are you taking me?"

"You tell me. Where will you be safe?"

CHAPTER 52

THE FUGITIVE

Safe? Where can he be safe? Now that Father…

Ștefan holds on to the man, his thighs sore from gripping the galloping horse, and tries to think about a safe place. And only one comes to mind.

"Take me home. To the Seat Fortress of Suceava."

Where else could he go? With Father gone, Ștefan's life isn't worth more than the boots on his feet. As for Vlad, he doesn't know what happened to him. They lost him in their mad gallop through the forest.

"Are you sure?" The man's voice is heavy with doubt.

"Where else?"

"I don't know, but I bet your uncle sent troops to the fortress. If they're lucky, they're under siege. If they're not lucky, they're dead."

Dead? Mother, his brothers and sisters, the old guards and the cooks, and everyone else he's known since he was a child? They all came to Suceava when Father took the throne. They can't be dead. If he couldn't save Father, he might still get there in time to save them.

He chokes a sob thinking of Father. Not the wise, patient father who always listened and taught him so much, but Father's severed head skewered on an eight-foot lance. The bared teeth, the bloody

217

mouth, the dead eyes still open. Stefan caught a glance of him as they fled, and the shame of running instead of staying to fight will burn his soul forever. He doesn't know what he can do to atone for his cowardice, but he'll try.

"Father, I swear I'll find your killer. I'll butcher him and scatter his remains for the wild beasts to feast on, so nobody can find them again. I promise to raise a church where you died, and dedicate it to the St. John the Baptist's beheading. I'll endow it with lands, rivers, and fishing ponds so the monks can pray for your soul day and night." The whispered promise makes him feel better, but it gets the guard worried.

"What did you say?"

"Nothing."

Ștefan bites his tongue and holds on to the man as they keep heading north. After galloping for miles and miles with two men on his back, the horse grew tired. His step grew slow and uneven, but he keeps trudging until Ștefan hears something behind.

"Did you hear that?"

"What?"

"Something behind us. Sounds like horses. Maybe it's my cousin with the guard?"

"Unless they're your father's killers. The odds aren't good, and this horse is about done. What would you like to do, Your Highness?"

He sounds snarky. Maybe he's tired and troubled. Or maybe a grown man riding shotgun like a woman inspires no confidence or respect. Either way, Stefan had better do something. It's high time to stop behaving like a frightened orphan and act like a voivode. Make Father proud.

Ștefan eases himself to the ground. "You go ahead. I'll walk the rest of the way."

"But you can't outrun the riders! They'll catch you in no time."

"I can't outrun them, but I can out-think them. Go on. If you make it to The Seat of Suceava, tell them to bolt the gates, raise the bridge and let no one in. No one, you hear?"

"How are you going to get in, then?"

"I'll find a way. Go."

Ștefan slaps the horse's rump. The animal picks up the pace to a slow canter and disappears in the night.

The hooves behind him get louder. And somewhere behind the old trees looming over Ștefan like clawed black monsters, there's a light. They're getting close, and they have torches. He'd better out-think them soon if he wants to live.

He looks around for shelter. A few feet ahead, there's a little meadow between the trees. No bigger than a barn, but it's large enough to let him see the stars above and help him hide his trace in the dark. He runs around it to leave his scent everywhere and confuse the dogs — if they have them — then climbs the tallest tree, but it's not easy. His boots slide on the trunk, and his dangling sword gets caught in every branch, so he has to free it again and again. But Ștefan is good with trees — he's climbed them a thousand times whenever he played hooky and hid from his teachers. And the scare blew away the wine's fog. He climbs higher and higher until he melts into the canopy.

It's so dark he can't see his own hands, so Petru Aron's men, with their eyes burned by the torch light, have no way in hell to find him here. Unless they have dogs. But there's no point in worrying about that now.

He leans over a thick branch overlooking the meadow that gives him a good view and makes himself comfortable. If he's lucky, he'll be here for a while.

CHAPTER 53

A FRIEND IN NEED

Ștefan lays in the darkness, wondering where to go if he escapes. And how. He's got no horse, nothing but his sword and the clothes on his back, and Father's killers are searching for him. Sure they are. He was Father's co-voivode, so he's got the best claim to Moldova's throne. But a claim isn't enough to get you the throne, even if it's enough to get you killed.

Going to Suceava is tricky, but where else could he go? Vlad Dracul is gone, so Târgoviște is no longer safe. He could try Berzunți, but Lena's no longer there, and last he checked, nobody knew where she went. He could try to cross the mountains to Transylvania, then Hungary, and put himself under Hunyadi's protection. Or head south to the Ottoman Empire.

Voices, then a light burns his eyes. When he opens them again, the men are right below him, in the meadow. Six of them, on tired horses that slowed down to a walk. The leader lifts his torch, and three men dismount to look for his trail. The others wait.

"I told you he'll go home," a voice says, and Ștefan's heart freezes. Is that Vlad? He leans further to check. It's him indeed. There's no trace of the guard who helped him flee, and he's unarmed, but he's calm and unhurt. But for the lack of a sword, he could be riding with friends.

"How do you know?" the leader asks.

"I know him. I've been with him day and night for more than a year. I know what he does, I know what he says, I know what he thinks. I can hand him to you. The Seat too."

The man stops his horse below Ștefan's branch to check the woods. He glances at Vlad and spits to the side.

"Why? They took you in and treated you like one of their own. Why would you betray them?"

Vlad laughs a bitter laugh that turns Ștefan's stomach. "One of their own? Are you nuts? They treated me like a beggar. Everything was about Ștefan. Everything was for Ștefan, as they groomed him to become Moldova's voivode. Ștefan got to share his father's throne. Me? I got his leftovers. When there were any."

A wave of fiery anger chokes Ștefan. He's burning to jump off and slice Vlad into tiny small pieces. Stupid, he knows, but this betrayal from a friend who used to be like a brother drives him mad. May not be as bad as Petru Aron killing his father, but it's personal and mortifying. He takes a deep breath and forces himself to stay put, hoping they won't hear the drumming of his heart.

Vlad looks up, and for a split second, Ștefan feels like he's looking straight at him. But that can't be. He did nothing to give himself away. He's one with the darkness, afraid to even breathe.

He checks his sword with his right hand and his dagger with his left. They're there. Good. He'll wait for the posse to be gone, then follow, though Suceava doesn't look good. If they didn't take it yet, that damn Vlad will sell it to them to save his hide. They all know and trust him there, so they won't hesitate to open the gates and lower the bridge to let him in.

"Ștefan and I spent a lot of time together," Vlad says. "We studied together, fought together, and partied together. But even then, he always had to be the boss. He'd say: 'You climb up that tree and jump on the fat one when I tell you, and I had to do it. Like I didn't have a mind of my own, you know?"

Ștefan's jaw falls. Nothing like that ever happened.

The man ignores Vlad to look into the darkness that swallowed the others. "Hey, you there. Did you find anything?"

A skinny man returns and points to the path the guard took. "This way, I think. They rode north."

"I told you." Vlad looks up again.

"Come back, you two, we found the trail," the leader shouts. "Time to go."

Vlad nods. "Indeed. Come on, Ștefan!"

He spurs his horse and tramples the man who walked back from the forest. The man cries a dreadful scream, then goes quiet as his throat turns into a blood fountain carved with his own dagger. His torch drops to the ground and hungry flames lick the dead leaves, setting them ablaze. The wind whips the flames over the ground, lighting the night into blood-red. The horses spook.

Ștefan lets go of his branch. He grabs on to the hilt of his sword and drops through ten feet of thin air on to the fat captain. He clutches the man and drags him to the ground as his left hand searches for his dagger. He pulls it out and sinks it into the man's throat. The dagger goes in like it's butter, opening the windpipe and letting the life gush out of it. The captain gasps, then dies, and Ștefan lets go of him to grab his sword.

Another rider rushes him, his battle axe lifted like he's downing a tree, but Ștefan rolls to his side and the man misses. He lifts his axe again, but Vlad's blade hisses as it slices the air, and the man's head rolls under his horse's hooves, leaving the headless body in the saddle.

Two more men rush back from the forest, their eyes popping out at the killing field lit by the blaze. They stare at what's left of their comrades on the ground, and at the headless one in the saddle. One flees, as the other bends to retch in the bushes.

Vlad's sword finds his neck, and the man's head rolls to the side as blood and vomit burst out of his severed throat.

Ștefan jumps on a horse to chase the one who escaped. He's over him in a heartbeat, and the man falls to his knees, asking for mercy.

"Please, spare my life, and I swear ..."

Ștefan doesn't get to hear what he swears because his angry sword has a mind of its own. It slices the man from the left shoulder to the right elbow, and the body parts fall to the ground like pieces of a rag doll. Ștefan wipes his sword on the man's pants and pushes it back in its scabbard.

Back in the meadow, Vlad is searching the bodies.

"What are you looking for?"

"Anything. Money, papers, weapons. We have a long way to go, and not much to keep us going. Our lives, their horses, and the weapons. But anything we have could come in handy, and anything we don't could tun out deadly."

Ștefan dismounts to search the captain's body. There's a bag of money — the price of Father's life — and a firman with the seal of Moldova, proclaiming him a captain in Voivode Petru Aron's army, and asking all to grant him any help he needs.

"Take his ring, too. He doesn't need it anymore, but we might."

Ștefan spits on the dead hand to loosen the ring — an irregular orange stone with a little ant frozen inside — and puts it on. They gather the horses, tie the spares behind them, and they're ready to go.

The fire's almost out, now that the dead leaves are gone, and so is the light. They need to get used to the darkness again.

"Where are we going?" Ștefan asks.

"Damn if I know. Anywhere that isn't here. We'll figure it out on the road."

"The Seat?"

"The Seat will be better off without you. If you're there, they'll put it through fire and sword. If you're gone, they may let them surrender peacefully and live."

He's right, Ștefan thinks. He gets his foot in the stirrup to mount his horse and notices he's missing a boot. And they're his favorite boots, made of soft yellow calf skin.

"Darn."

"What?"

"I lost my boot."

"Look under the tree you were in."

Sure enough, the boot is there, a little charred but still working. He pulls it on.

"How did you know it was there?"

Vlad laughs. "The better question is: How did I know *you* were there? I saw your boot as we arrived, so I thought: If he's up there, the two of us have a chance. I couldn't have done it on my own."

"What if I wasn't there? What if I'd just lost my boot?"

Vlad smiles. "Then I was signing up for a terrible day."

CHAPTER 54

CONSTANTINOPLE, OCTOBER 1451

Constantinople is cold and wet in November. With winter on its way, the days grew short and gray, so the sun is about to set and the narrow streets are thick with people as Ali heads home after another day at Loukas Notaras' house. But, with luck, this was the last.

She did her routine in the morning — sweeping, dusting, laundry — all women's jobs that she hates. But she's not doing this for fun. Not even for the few meagre coins Notaras pays her, acting like he's cutting them out of his flesh every week. Like Ion said, this is about saving Christianity, even though Ali isn't sure it's worth saving. But she promised Ion she would help.

And she has to admit to herself that she loves danger. She thrives on the rush she gets when she opens a drawer she shouldn't and closes it right before getting caught. Or when she tries the keys Ion gave her in the lock of the room she's not allowed in. The dry mouth, the pumping heart, the heat between her thighs — they remind her of her nights with Mara. That makes her wonder how much of Mara's magic was because of the lethal danger they were in.

Still, she misses her like she'd miss a piece of her soul. Not only for the pleasure they shared, though Mara took her closer to heaven than anything else Ali ever did. She misses her friendship, her wit, and her wisdom.

But there's no time to think about that right now. She buys bread from a skinny man balancing a massive basket of flat breads on his head, then red apples and green olives for dinner. Because, even though she works all day, every day, she's still in charge of cooking, shopping, and cleaning. Ion hasn't yet discovered that these things are needed to survive.

"What did you do before I came?" Ali asked him one evening.

"What do you mean?"

"What did you eat? How did you clean your clothes?"

He stared at her with wide eyes. "I ate food. I stopped at tavernas."

She sighs and rolls the hot flat breads, then slips them in her bag with the apples and olives. That's dinner, taken care of. That, and the cheese they have at home. It will have to do, since she's too tired to cook. And too angry.

Being a woman sucks. She was better off as a eunuch. People treated her with respect, and they didn't invade her like it was their right.

She was washing the Notaras' laundry this afternoon. Nasty to touch other people's dirty undergarments, but that goes with the job. Like the sweat, the cracked hands, and the back always aching. She leaned over the washing tub to wring the sheets when something touched her under her skirts.

Without even thinking, she twisted and back-handed the intruder, then slogged him with the wet sheet in her hands. The man screamed and fell on his butt. Ali prepared to kick him when she realized he wasn't a man. It was Jacob, Notaras' youngest son. Thirteen years old, the apple of his mother's eye and his father's pride, the lad thought she was there for his pleasure.

"Stand up," she ordered.

His eyes wide, his right cheek on fire, he sat staring at her.

"Stand up. Now."

He stood and stepped back. "Whoa! Aren't we overreacting?"

"You may be. I'm not. Next time you touch me, I'll cut off your dick. You understand?"

He stared at her in disbelief. "What?"

"Next time you touch me, I'll cut off your dick. I may feed it to you or I may not. It depends on my mood. But I promise you'll never piss like a man again, and you'll never fuck a woman. You got that?"

His face white, his eyes wide as saucers, he ran off without another word.

Ali finished that sheet, then the others. She was hanging them outside to dry when Notaras stopped by. He watched her work and waited until she was done before speaking.

"I believe that you and my son had a misunderstanding?"

"Not at all. I think we understood each other quite clearly."

"He says that you hit him and told him not to touch you again."

"That's correct."

"Do you understand he is my son?"

"I do. Do you understand I am your housekeeper, not your whore?"

Notaras' eyes widened. He took in a deep breath. "You're overreacting."

Ali smiled politely and grabbed the laundry basket. "Did he tell you what I said?"

Notaras glared at her, his oily face purple. "He did."

"Well, if you think I'm overreacting, just let him touch me again."

She dropped the basket and left with her head held high, but she doubts she'll be welcome back tomorrow.

Ion won't be pleased. He'll tell her she blew things out of proportion. She should have told the kid to go away and get on with her business instead of making a fuss, he'll say, and just thinking of that makes Ali's blood boil.

They're in a quandary. Ion is her best friend, but he doesn't understand her or care about her goals. And she doesn't really care about his. Still, she tried to help him, while he doesn't even know her dreams. Oh well. Such is life, she thinks, as she puts dinner together.

When she's done, she goes to clean herself up. She glances in the foggy metal mirror, pinches her lips and her cheeks to look less tired, and brushes her red curls into a bun. Looking better might help, but she doesn't hold much hope.

WOMEN AND MEN

The door slams.

"I'm home," Ion calls.

Ali puts down the mirror and drags herself to the kitchen. Ion takes her in his arms and hugs her tight. She feels his desire press against her, but he kisses her cheek and lets her go.

His blue eyes glow with the joy of seeing her. "Boy, am I glad to see you! You're the best thing that happened to me all day."

Ali smiles thinly at being called a thing, but she knows he means well. She opens the wine, a cheap Greek that smells like the woods at home, and fills the cups.

"*Noroc*." Cheers.

"*Noroc*."

They drain the cups, then Ali brings in their modest dinner: flat bread with feta cheese, olives, fruit, and wine. Ion won't even notice she didn't cook, but she knows it and feels guilty, and she gets mad again.

Ion sips on the wine and picks at the food without noticing it.

"How was your day?" Ali asks.

"Terrible. Just terrible."

"Why?"

"The treasury is empty. We have no money to buy anything, and that freaking pope won't even talk about sending us help before the churches unite. The patriarch tried his best, but the priests and the faithful want none of it. They'd rather have the Ottomans than the Catholics. That means there'll be no help from the west, and we are in trouble." He spits two olive seeds and bites into a piece of crumbly feta. "And like that's not bad enough, we got news from Smederevo. Your friend Mara rejected the emperor's hand. Imagine this: the Emperor of Constantinople proposed to Murad's widow, and she said no. What is that woman thinking? She'd rather live in some Serbian backwater with her decrepit father than be Constantinople's empress."

Ali's eyes widen. "Mara is in Serbia? I didn't know. I didn't even know the emperor proposed to her."

"He did, against his advisors' counsel, and she refused. Can you fathom the humiliation?"

Ali can. But more importantly, her beloved Mara is free and out of the Ottoman Empire.

"Where is she?"

"Who the hell cares about that stupid woman? Somewhere in Serbia, I guess. Smederevo probably."

"What makes you think she's stupid?"

Ion stares at her like she's lost her mind. "Are you kidding? She refused the Emperor of Constantinople's hand. She's got to be insane."

"Why?"

"He's handsome, kind, and the head of an empire that lasted for a thousand years. As for her, she's a widow, not a virgin, and she's past her prime. She has no children, so she might be sterile. Even so, he asked her. She should be over the moon, but no. If that's not insanity, I don't know what is."

Ali struggles to keep her cool, but it's not easy. "What if she said yes?"

"She'd be the Empress of Constantinople. She'd live a pampered life and wear silk and gold and jewelry, and she'd do whatever she wants."

"Like what?"

Ion shrugs. "I don't know. Walk around and look at the Bosporus? Eat tasty things? Wear rich clothes?"

"What would she have to do for that?"

"Just make children."

Ali nods. That's all it takes to live a pampered life. Just make children. "Sorry you had a rough day."

"It's OK. It's nice to come back home to you, even though this dinner isn't quite like your others. But you may have been tired. Maybe tomorrow."

He empties his cup and stands up to go to bed.

"Ion?"

"Yes."

"I may not be welcome back at the Notaras' house tomorrow."

His face darkens as he listens to her story. "You realize how much trouble I went through to get you into that position?"

"You mean bent over the washtub? No. Why don't you tell me about it?"

Ion shakes his head. "I never realized you're so hot-headed. I hope you haven't squandered your opportunity to find out what's going on with Notaras. If you go back and apologize, he might take you back."

"Ion, do you know what you're saying?"

Ion shrugs a shoulder, like Ali's question isn't worth shrugging both.

"That kid had his hand between my legs. And I should apologize for that?"

"Not for that. But for… hitting him. And threatening him. That was really over the top."

"Ion, what would you have done if you were me?"

"I'd say something like 'get over it, dude, let's go have a drink.' There's no need to get into that kind of histrionics. You women are so dramatic," he says, and goes to bed.

It's sad, really, Ali thinks, as she packs her stuff.

CHAPTER 56

EDIRNE, OCTOBER 1451

The fall softened Edirne's heat, dyed the leaves red and burned the grass to coppery hues, but the gardens are still blooming. The heady scent of the late roses and the bitter fragrance of the chrysanthemums mingle with the smell of smoke and dead leaves carried by the wind. Here and there, low branches bend under the weight of heavy yellow pears, making Radu's mouth water.

He sits with Mehmed on the marble bench by the fountain, enjoying the sun on his face as they play chess in the garden. The game, not so much, since he's not much of a chess player. He cares more about the intricate beauty of the carved pieces than the game. The whites are made from elephant ivory and the blacks from ebony, and each is a work of art. The shahs, with their fierce eyes and embroidered kaftans, the rearing horses, the wrinkly elephants, and even the janissary pawns, are all different. This set took years to make and is more expensive than its weight in gold.

Radu picks up the white vizier and marvels at the detail of his dress, from the carefully wrapped turban to the tiny upturned slippers. He'd be precious enough to display in the palace on its own, but he's just one of many. Every pawn has a unique expression, and every horse a different stance. Radu marvels at the beauty in his hands.

"Where did you get this?"

"Jahanshah, The Shah of Tabriz, sent it to me as a coronation gift. For them, chess is almost a religion. Nobody plays better. But they've been doing it for a thousand years. Stop fooling around, will you? Play."

Radu sighs and makes the only move he can see. "*Şah,*" he says, knocking down Mehmed's horse with his vizier.

Mehmed glances sideways, his smiling green eyes shaded by his red curls. "You're sure you want to do that?"

"Of course not. I'm never sure. I'll never be as good a player as you are, but I have to take my chances."

"That's true, but chess is not a game of chance. It's warfare. It's a game of strategy and psychology, just like war, but more so. No matter how well you plan your campaign, there'll always be surprises: lousy weather, enemy traps, your army's unforeseen weakness. Not in chess. The board is the board, the rules are the rules, and it all boils down to knowing how to exploit the opponent's weaknesses, whatever they are. Impatience, misinformation, arrogance. Or short vision, like yours." In one smooth move, Mehmed takes Radu's vizier with his elephant.

Radu stares at his orphaned team and sighs. "I should have thought better."

Mehmed laughs, and it's wonderful to hear him laugh like he's young, happy and carefree, not the sultan of the largest empire in the world where there's always some fire to put out.

"You should have, shouldn't you?" He takes Radu's hand and kisses his palm, and Radu's insides melt with the heat.

"I love you," Mehmed whispers, and Radu's heart softens with joy.

"I love you too," he answers, then moves his elephant.

"*Şah.*"

Mehmed smiles and takes his elephant with his pawn. Radu sighs, wondering what to do next, when Zaganos Paşa bows in front of the sultan.

"My sultan, I have news."

"Urgent?"

"That's not for me to decide, my sultan. That's for you. But I'll wait if you want me to."

"Go ahead."

Zaganos Paşa is Mehmed's favorite vizier, even though he's not old Ottoman nobility, like Çandarlı Paşa. A few years ago, Zaganos Paşa was just one of the Greek kids brought by devşirme. But his hard work, quick wits, and loyalty to Mehmed raised him high in the Ottoman bureaucracy. "Our spies in Constantinople have been hard at work. It appears that the emperor proposed to princess Mara."

"Mara? Our Mara?"

"Mara Branković, your father's widow. She said no."

Mehmed's eyes are about to pop out of his head. "Of course not. After being married to Father, how could they even think she'd consider the Byzantine's proposal? That's insane. Can you believe this, Radu?"

Radu shrugs. "He must have thought that being the Empress of Constantinople was an attractive proposition, but it looks like he was mistaken."

Mehmed shakes his head. "That's crazy. What else?"

"The union of the Christian Churches fell apart. The Orthodox want nothing to do with the Catholics. They'd rather rip out each other's throats than unite. And without the union, Europe won't send them any help."

"Excellent. Anything else?"

Zaganos Paşa clears his throat. "It appears... it's not confirmed yet, but it looks like the Byzantine will increase their demand for money to keep Orhan locked up. Your uncle has an insatiable appetite for wine and women, and Constantinople is out of cash. Their treasury is empty, their tax base is almost gone, and Notaras bleeds the treasury like a leech. The messengers asking you to double the three thousand aspers Sultan Murad was paying are on their way."

"Thank you, Zaganos Paşa."

The paşa bows and leaves, and Mehmed stands to pace. His mouth narrowed, his fists tightened, and his green eye pierce Radu like it's his fault.

"Seriously? More money for that old drunkard? I already give them three thousand aspers as agreed by my father, and they want me to double that? You've got to be kidding."

Radu stares at the chess set, wondering if he could move a piece without Mehmed noticing.

"Luckily, thanks to Mara, we signed a three years peace treaty with Branković and Hunyadi. And there's nobody else in Europe I need to worry about. You know what that means?"

Radu shakes his head.

"That frees me to take Constantinople. I finally tamed the damn Karamanids to have peace in Anatolia, and I made peace with the Hungarians and the Serbs. I can put everything I've got into taking the Red Apple. My time has finally come." Mehmed sits back, his cheeks flushed with excitement. "There's nothing I want more. I can finally take that darn city and make it mine, no matter what it costs." He smiles at Radu. "What do you think?"

"*Şah,*" Radu says, taking the black vizier with his horse.

Mehmed knocks his elephant with a pawn. "*Şah-mat.*"

CHAPTER 57

THE BORGO PASS, OCT 1451

It's like a church up here, Vlad thinks. Towering pines, straight like pillars, cleanse the air with their incense breath and shroud the ground in shade. Their needles soften the trail, dampening the hooves' clatter and softening their voices. It's so quiet up here that they whisper, though there's no one to hear them but the trees.

They've been riding for three days, always up. Each day gets shorter, each night colder, and now they've hit snow. It's not yet November, but up here, in the heart of the Carpathians, the seasons are nothing like down in the plains.

"How much longer?" Ștefan asks. He rides behind, all wrapped up in his mantle, but for his blue eyes and frosted mustache.

Vlad changes the reins from his left to his right and sticks the frozen hand into his armpit to warm it up. "Not long now," he lies.

He never took the high mountain pass cutting through the Carpathians from Bistrița to Vatra Dornei, joining Moldova to Transylvania, so he doesn't know, but it can't be that long, can it? And it can't get much higher, otherwise they wouldn't call it a pass. The darn thing should avoid at least the highest peaks.

"We're almost at the top, and it gets warmer as we head down," Vlad says.

They ride in silence, listening to the wind rustle the pines, when a sudden gust shakes the branches and covers them with snow. Vlad wipes his face, then grabs a handful of snow and eats it to cheat his hunger.

"Are you sure about this?" Ștefan asks.

"About eating snow?"

"No. About going to Transylvania. What if Hunyadi finds out we're there?"

"He's got nothing against you. And I did nothing to him. Yet."

"Yes, you did. You took the throne from his protégée, Vladislav, remember? With the Ottoman's help."

"That was three years ago, and that's a lifetime these days."

"You think he forgot?"

"No, but he's got bigger fish to fry. After he got crushed in Kosovo, then captured by Branković, the Hungarian diet kicked his ass and took away his titles. He's no longer regent, nor even the voivode of Transylvania. After all this, wouldn't you rather worry about your stuff than about me? And there was nowhere else we could go. We're lucky we got out of Moldova alive."

"How about the Ottomans who helped you get your throne? They might do it again."

Vlad spits to the side. "That was Murad, but he's dead. Mehmed is nothing like his father. He and I hate each other, and I'll kill him some day unless he kills me first. So no, the Ottoman Empire is not the place to go."

They keep on riding as the light fades. The day turns to dusk, and another long night with no food and no shelter is coming.

Vlad hears his stomach growl and starts wondering if Ștefan was right. What if, instead of heading east through the Carpathians, they made their way south and cross the Danube to take their chances with Mehmed? But it's too late now; they'd better figure out how to make it through tonight.

They're almost four thousand feet high. The trees got smaller and thinner, and soon enough they'll be gone. The high alpine meadows offer no shelter from the wind, Vlad thinks, as a random gust whips snow into his face. He narrows his eyes to keep it out, but he tears so hard he can hardly see. Not that there's much to see. Nothing here but frozen snow, and Vlad's heart sinks.

He turns to Ștefan. "What should we do?" He's led their escape up to now, but he's losing his grip.

"Let's stop for the night. Otherwise, the horses will break their legs and we'll break our necks. Let's find shelter."

"Where?"

Ștefan gets off the path to look. "Here."

Vlad follows. It's just a hollow, barely big enough for them both, surrounded by low shrubs that offer slim protection. But it's better than nothing.

They dismount and tie the horses to each other, hobbling the first one so he can't go far, then drop in the hollow back-to-back to share body heat. Vlad clenches his chattering teeth to keep from biting his tongue.

"Want some wine?" Stefan asks.

"What?"

Ștefan hands him a leather flask. Vlad takes a thirsty sip, and the harsh red warms him inside. He wipes his mouth on his sleeve and returns the flask. "Where did you get it?"

"From the captain."

"And you kept it a secret?"

"I thought I'd save it for when things got worse."

"And now?"

"They can't get much worse."

The wine softens the chill. The sky above looks close enough to touch, and it's studded with a million stars. Some are big, some small, some blink red, some are almost too faint to see. Vlad wonders which is his, and where will it take him? His happy days in Suceava are over.

Bogdan is dead, and his family... who knows? He and Ștefan are on their own, and they have nobody but each other.

As if he heard his thoughts, Ștefan whispers: "I wonder what happened to Mother. And my brothers."

Vlad would like to give him hope, but he can't think about anything hopeful to say. But for one thing. "Ștefan, will you be my blood brother?"

There's no answer, and Vlad waits and waits, wondering if his cousin heard him. He may not want to share this sacred allegiance with him. After all, few people like Vlad. But Ștefan was his friend. Until he dragged him here.

"Yes."

Their daggers gleam in the star-lit night. They kiss the blades, pull up their sleeves and look at each other.

Vlad goes first. He slides the blade over his left wrist to score the skin. The second cut makes the wound into a bleeding cross. It burns, but the blood is warm, and it feels good on his frozen skin.

Ștefan does the same, and they kneel facing each other. They touch their arms, letting their wounds kiss and their blood mingle.

Vlad looks in Ștefan's eyes. "I swear to trust you and love you and help you whenever you need it, so help me God."

"I swear to be your friend and your brother and trust you and help you whenever you need it, so help me God," Stefan says.

There's power in the words, and magic in the sharing of the blood. But even more, there's hope for the future. They're bound with a tie that no mortal can break. As long as they're alive, they'll never be alone again.

CHAPTER 58

A HIGH CLIFF

Sadly, the magic vanished by the morning. After another night with no food or fire, Vlad and Ștefan wake up frozen stiff, and hungry.

"We'd better get out of here if we want to make it alive," Vlad says, saddling his horse.

Stefan nods. "Thank God the horses are in better shape than we are. They dug for grass under the snow, and these hairy coats kept them warm through the night. I wish I could say the same," Stefan says, mounting and heading back to the path. One way or another, they need to find shelter tonight.

They trudge uphill, wondering when this darn pass will finally cut across the mountain, when they find themselves on top of the world. They reached the top of the pass, and the whole Transylvanian plateau opened to their eyes like a picture framed by the snow-topped mountains stabbing at the clear sky. The morning sun softens the pines' velvety green cover, gilds the red maples and the oaks, and warms the fertile brown fields down below. Tucked between the meanders of a glittering river, the tiny houses huddled around a white church steeple look like children's toys. They're far below, but seeing them gives them hope.

"See? I told you we were close," Vlad says.

Ștefan gives him a side glance. He says nothing, but Vlad knows what he's thinking: How long will it be before we get down there to sit by a warm fire and get something to eat? But he's wise enough to keep his thoughts to himself.

They get their fill of the view, then head down, and it's a debacle. The way up was hard, cold, and slow. The horses struggled, and they did too. It was hard to not know where you were going or how long it would take. But it didn't compare to this.

The path downhill is sheer ice. The horses slip and slide. Every step is a struggle, so going down is even slower than going up. It took them three days to reach the top, but they won't have three more to get down. They have one, if they're lucky, because the cold and hunger sap their strength at every step.

The trail gets even steeper. Vlad's heart jumps to his throat as his pony loses his footing and skates. The horse recovers and takes three more steps, then loses his ground, slips, and crashes on the ice. Vlad jumps off at the last moment and slides down on his belly after the horse that can't stop.

Vlad tries to grab on to the ground with his nails, but there's nothing but ice to hold on to. He skins his fingers, straining to claw into the ice, but he fails. He loses his grip and follows the horse, sliding faster and faster towards the cliff's edge.

"Your dagger!" Ștefan shouts.

Vlad pulls out his dirk and stabs the frozen, dirty ground like he wants to kill it. The blade holds.

Vlad stops, hanging by the strength of his arm. His heart races, and a rush of heat fills his veins as he listens to the horse scream, swallowed by the void. He hangs over the bluff, hoping his trembling arms will hold, as Ștefan grabs a rope and ties it to the nearest tree. He throws the other end to Vlad.

It's way too short. Vlad can't reach it without letting go of the dagger.

Ștefan grabs the rope letting himself slide down over the treacherous ground. His steps are small and calculated, and he's slower than slow, but his old calf-skin boots stick to the ice like limpets. It feels like forever until he makes it to the rope's end, but he's still too far.

He lowers himself to the ice, holding on to the rope with one hand and reaching toward Vlad with the other. He crucified himself on the ice, Vlad thinks, more grateful than he's ever been.

"OK."

Vlad clutches Ștefan's arm, and they grab each other's wrists. He pulls out his dagger and shields it, then grips the ice with his left hand and feet, pulling himself up. Inch by inch, he crawls out of the icy ravine towards the path. Five more steps.

He tries to be smooth since Ștefan, who acts as his anchor, feels every jar and every pull through his whole body as he lies on his belly with his face on the ice. It's not easy, but step by step, Vlad makes it to the path.

"Your turn," he says.

Ștefan tries to stand, but his boots fail. He slides and falls on his face, jarring the rope, which starts to give.

He holds on to Vlad's hand and gasps. "I can't."

The path is a sheet of ice, so Vlad can't pull Ștefan without sliding himself. He looks for something to hold on to, but there's nothing close enough. The nearest tree is too far, and the horse is gone. There's nothing to grab.

He takes out his whip, the one thing nobody knows about. He wears it around his body, and its closeness gives him succor. Using it has saved lives, since it stopped him from killing many people. Seeing the bloody welts on their bodies was enough. He didn't want Ștefan to know about it, because he knows that inflicting pain is wrong and weird, but he's got nothing else. He wraps one end of the whip around his arm and throws the other to Ștefan. "Lie there until I grab on to something." He crawls on his knees and gets hold of a branch. "I'm ready."

Holding on to the whip, Ștefan pulls himself up while Vlad holds steady. Muscles tremble, sweat slicks their palms, and their hearts pummel in their chests with the struggle, but, inch by inch, Stefan gets back on the trail.

They catch their breath, gather the remaining horses, and get ready to go.

"You're lousy with knots," Vlad says, packing Ștefan's rope.

Ștefan glances at the whip. "You're lousy with relationships."

They lead the remaining horses down the path. It's safer and warmer down here, but not fast, and there's still a long way to go. As the day dies, the cold, the hunger, and the misery return with a vengeance. The villages look even farther away than this morning. The exhilaration of saving each other's lives vanished, and exhaustion takes over.

I can't make it through another night outside. I just can't, Vlad thinks. His hunger eats him from inside, and every bone in his body aches from the cold. He's so hungry he can't think straight, and he'd give anything for a warm fire and a bite to eat, but there's nothing. Nothing but the bitter cold and the darkness descending upon them. Still, they go on because none of them can bring himself to say: "Let's stop." It's cold, miserable, and hopeless.

Until Vlad sees a light.

CHAPTER 59
THE HERMIT'S PROPHECY

A faint glimmer of light blinks somewhere in the mountain's darkness, but it vanishes as soon as Vlad looks at it.

He turns to Ștefan. "Did you see that?"

"See what?"

Has he started imagining things? But no. It's back. Right there, to their left. "A light. That means people."

"Right."

They step off the path and muddle towards it, dragging their horses, until they find it. It's a cave, its opening above their heads and faintly lit.

"Hello?"

A thin silhouette in a tattered cassock shows up. By his frock and unkempt beard, he's got to be a hermit monk.

"Hello?"

"We're two tired travelers looking for shelter for the night. Would you kindly take us in?" Vlad asks.

"Come on in."

They hobble their horses and climb the hanging rope ladder to the cave, more hopeful than they've been in a while. The hermit welcomes them with a nod and a smile, but his white eyes stare into nowhere.

"Who are you?"

"I'm Vlad, and this is my cousin Ștefan. We're two lost travelers who haven't seen a human face in days, and we're grateful for your hospitality."

"You're most welcome. I have seen no one in ages. People seldom venture here in winter," he says, shuffling in along the wall.

He looks like he's seen nothing in years, Vlad thinks, following him with Ștefan in tow. The cave's mouth leads to a tunnel so low they need to walk bent over, before opening into a large round room smelling like smoke. Not much inside other than a table, a chair, and a narrow bed covered in furs. But the skinny candle under St. George's icon on the wall and the fire at the far end make it feel inviting and warm.

"Enjoy the fire while I fetch some wine," the hermit says.

Vlad and Stefan sit by the fire, warming their frozen feet and hands. Unfreezing hurts like hell, but the dancing flames fill them with hope.

The hermit returns with a flask and three cups. "Pour it, will you? I can't see, and it's a pity to spill it. That wine is ten years old, and it deserves better."

Vlad fills the cups. "Thank you, Father. I've never been happier to see a human being. Thank you for your kindness and your hospitality."

"Thank you for coming. It's been a while since I talked to anyone, so I'm delighted you stopped by."

They drain their cups, and the hermit brings bread, dry sausage, cheese, and pickles. The cheese is moldy and the bread's a bit stale, but Vlad can't remember eating better food. They eat in pleasant silence, letting the fire's warmth comfort their bodies and the wine mellow their souls.

"How long you've been here?" Vlad asks.

The hermit shrugs. "Who knows? I started my penitence of solitude and prayer after King Sigismund was crowned Holy Roman

Emperor. I'd fought for him, so I had the blood of many on my hands. That may be why the good Lord saw fit to take my eyes. He lent me his vision instead. That's why the village folks often come to me to seek advice on their future and ask me to pray for them. They bring me food, wine, and candles to keep me through the winter. Would you boys like to know your fortunes?"

"Sure," Vlad says to humor him, even though he doesn't believe in prophecies.

"Give me your hand." He takes Vlad's hand and brings it close to his face. His gnarled fingers trace every crease and feel every mound as he mumbles softly to himself. He takes his other hand and does the same, then lifts his white eyes. "You wish to know?"

"Of course."

"Your burning wish will come through. Before long, you'll be a voivode again and you'll fulfill your oath. You'll avenge your kin and you'll take more lives than any other voivode ever did. You'll rule through death and bloody terror, but Wallachia will be safe under you. Your name will travel the world and frighten your enemies. People will remember you for centuries, because there has never been a prince like you, and there won't be another. But you won't be happy. You'll die by treason, like your father and brother, and like them, you'll never have a proper tomb. Your enemies will hate and malign you, but your people will never forget you. The world will speak about you for centuries from now." His face shrouded, the hermit lets go of Vlad's hand and grabs his cup.

The silence is so deep it hurts. The cave grows colder, and a shiver runs down Vlad's spine, but he tells himself there's nothing to worry about. Just a crazy drunk hermit telling him the same story he told many others. "Thank you," he says.

The hermit nods. "I know you don't believe me, but one day, you'll remember tonight and know it's the truth. Beware Snagov's marshes."

He sighs and turns to Ștefan, who's sitting by the fire. "How about you?"

Ștefan hesitates, but gives him his hand.

The hermit takes it and feels its every crease and mound. It feels like forever till he speaks. "You, too, will fulfill your wish. Some day. Unlike your blood brother, you'll have to fight long and hard to take Moldova. But when you do, it will be for half a century. You'll avenge your father and you'll strive to give your country peace, but you'll have to do it by the sword. Your people will love you, so much so they'll call you a saint. But saints don't fall for the sins of the flesh, like you will. Still, your soul will soar forever."

The hermit sighs and drops Ștefan's hand. "This has been the furthest God lent me his eye to see the future, but now I'm spent. You're safe here. Good night."

CHAPTER 60
BUDA, FALL 1451

A harsh evening breeze smelling like snow rushes in from the north, bringing dark clouds and ruffling the few leaves left on the branches. Fall hangs by a thread, and winter is coming.

But nobody cares about that, because they're getting ready to party. After God only knows how many wars that spilled the blood of Hungary all over Europe, from Bulgaria and Serbia to Albania and Moldova, the Hungarian army is coming home.

That news put a sparkle in the women's eyes, a blush in their cheeks, and a fresh spring in their step. There's joy and rush all over Buda as women do what women do when their men are due home: clean, cook, and make themselves pretty. The excitement has spread like a fever all over town.

Lena caught it, too. The little house Hunyadi gave them sparkles. She cleaned it like her mother used to clean for Easter: she scrubbed the pine-wood floors with homemade soap and hot water until the hundred-year-old planks looked like they'd just been cut from the tree. Her cracked hands hurt, but it was worth it.

She took out the carpets, hung them on a low tree branch, and beat them within an inch of their lives, choking in dust. She whitewashed the walls and cleaned the wooden frames of the icons with a soft cloth dipped in milk, like Mother used to do. Then she cooked and baked and cleaned again. And now she's ready.

"What are we waiting for, Mother?"

Mircea's almost four, and he's the spitting image of his father: dark-haired, with fierce green eyes and a proud little body. Even his chin juts forward, just like Mircea's used to. Lena sees him every time she looks at her son.

But little Mircea doesn't know a thing about his real father. He's too young to understand, let alone keep a secret, so he thinks Daddy's coming home from war. And, truth be told, that's not too far-fetched. Codru gave them shelter and provided for them. They've been a family in every way, but one, Lena thinks, and a yearning wakes up inside her.

Funny how she didn't give a hoot all those nights she slept in Codru's bed. She slept like a baby, and he didn't touch her. But now, her heart quickens at the thought of sharing his bed. Maybe she shouldn't have wasted all that time. Life is too short. What's she saving herself for, anyhow? Mircea is as dead as they get, and she's still young. She'd better make the most of it, since tomorrow holds no guarantees.

She smiles at little Mircea.

"We're waiting for your father. He's coming back from war."

"Did he win?"

Did he win? Maybe? Lena isn't sure. The intricacies of European politics befuddle her. She heard Hunyadi signed an armistice with Serbia's despot and recovered his son. Her friend Erzsébet is over the moon with joy, and that's good enough for her.

"Of course. Your father is a brave warrior. He always wins."

"What did he fight with?"

"What did he fight with? A horse, of course."

Mircea rolls his eyes and huffs. "What weapons, Mother?" He's barely up to her hip but already patronizes her like a man.

"A bow. And a sword."

"What's the name of his sword?"

The name of his sword? Are you kidding me? I didn't even know that blades have names; otherwise, I'd have baptized my axe, Lena thinks. She still carries it everywhere she goes, and for good reason. But that's not what this is about. This is about Codru. "It's a secret. He didn't tell me, but he may tell you when he returns."

Mircea nods. "Of course. You can't tell this kind of secret to a woman. They don't know how to keep secrets."

"Who told you that?"

"György."

György, their neighbor across the street, is seven, and Mircea looks up to him like he's God. He returns home and shares pieces of György's wisdom like they're nuggets of gold. They sting Lena like nettles because György's family is Hungarian, Catholic, and noble, so they look down their noses at everyone who isn't. But they tolerate Lena, since she's the wife of Hunyadi's captain. And Mircea needs friends, so Lena learned to bite her tongue.

"György has a lot to learn about women. Other things, too. Women can keep a secret better than anyone."

"Really?"

"Absolutely. You want to know my secret?" Lena asks, polishing the last cup.

Mircea's eyes grow wide with curiosity. "Yes."

Lena smiles and messes up his black curls. "Well, you can't. Because women can keep a secret even when men can't. Go tell György that women can keep secrets better than men."

"But Mother..."

"Go."

The boy runs out on his chubby little legs. "György! György! My mother said that women can keep secrets!"

Lena laughs and takes a last look around. Everything's ready. The chicken in the oven fills the house with aromas of rosemary, onions, and garlic. Yesterday, she baked fresh bread and cozonac, the Romanian sweet bread stuffed with raisins. It's neither Christmas nor Easter, but she couldn't think of anything more festive. She glances in the polished mirror by the window and rubs a slice of red beet over her lips and cheeks to give herself some extra glow. She's ready.

She grabs her sewing basket with clothes that need mending, pulls out a pair of socks, and sits by the fire. She pushes the thick needle in and out of the knitted brown wool, so rough it itches, dreaming about his smile when he sees her.

She'll lean in close and hug him just a touch too long. But then let go. A girl can't start lovemaking without looking like a whore. But she can give subtle signs to get the man going. Then they'll play hide-and-seek through the evening in front of Mircea. But tonight…

The chicken smells ready. Lena opens the oven. It's beautiful and golden and has to come out; otherwise, it will dry. She sets it on the table, hoping it won't be long or the food will get cold.

She remembers to check the wine sitting in the bucket of water she had just pulled from the well. It's good and cold.

She glances out the window again, then sits back to mend a chemise, wondering what's taking so long. Soldiers have been arriving since noon, but Codru is a captain. He may have more work to do before he can come home.

She mends another pair of socks, then another, until she hears steps at the door. But they're light and fast. It can't be him.

It's little Mircea come home. "I'm hungry. What's for dinner? Where's Father?"

"He got delayed. He'll come as soon as he can."

It breaks her heart to cut up the chicken before Codru sees it, but she's got to feed the kid. She gives him a wing to gnaw on, then a cup of milk with buttered bread and honey. When he's done, she washes the food off his face and puts him to bed.

"Where's Father?"

"He's an officer, so he has work to do. But I bet he'll be here when you wake up." She covers him to his chin with his blue wool-stuffed comforter and kisses his forehead. "Good night, and sleep tight."

"Tell me a story."

She can't think about a story right now, since all her thoughts are at the door. But Mircea won't sleep until she does, so she sighs and sits on his bed, caressing his hair. "There was a girl…"

"Was she a princess?"

"No. She was just an ordinary girl."

"Was she pretty?"

"Pretty enough. She needed to escape from the palace."

"What was she doing in the palace?"

"She got kidnapped and locked there."

"By whom?"

"By the Ottomans. So, she wanted to escape and ran away into the woods, but fell into a trap."

"Did she get hurt?"

"A little. She waited in the trap, hoping someone would come and save her. But they didn't. A hungry bear came instead, and he wanted to eat her. She got scared. But, just as the girl thought she would have to fight the bear, an enormous wolf chased him away, then sat by the trap to watch and keep her safe."

Thank God, he fell asleep. She kisses his cheek and returns to sit by the door. She grabs her work and waits.

The shadows grow thicker and thicker. Lena stares into the darkness outside, forgetting about the socks and the needle. The chicken gets cold, the wine warm, and she's still waiting. Her eyes mist, and her heart aches. She's so alone.

She remembers her parents. The Black Death took them too soon, but at least they were happy, though they were often apart. Father spent his summer in the mountains with the sheep; Mother looked after the house and the cows in the village. But they looked happy when they were together. Maybe. Who knows?

Lena sighs, wishing she'd asked Mother about her marriage. But she didn't, and now they're gone. So is Mircea, and Ali, wherever she may be if she's alive.

And Codru is late.

CHAPTER 61
SAD NEWS

Lena doesn't know how long she's waited until she hears heavy, slow steps at the door. Her heart skips a beat, but it's not joy. This is not the step of a man rushing home. This is the walk of somebody who'd rather be leaving than coming. Lena bites her lip and watches the door.

Somebody knocks.

"Come in."

Hunyadi shuffles in, and he's ten years older than he used to be. His somber face is gray, his mustache limp, and his eyes avoid hers.

"Hello, Lena. May I sit?"

Lena pulls a chair. "Wine?"

He nods.

Lena fills two cups and drains hers without knocking. Whatever he has to say, it's not good news. She may as well be ready.

The wine runs warm and smooth down her throat and chokes her. She's not used to wine, since she seldom drinks anything but water, but today isn't just any day. Today is a day to stay alive.

Hunyadi's shoulders sag. He sighs and looks away.

"Tell me," Lena says.

"Codru isn't coming."

"That I know; otherwise, he'd be here instead of you. Is he dead?"

"I don't know."

"You don't know?"

He sighs, looking older than ever. He empties his cup. "He's gone."

"Gone where?"

"I don't know. We were fighting Jiskra. The Hussites sheltered themselves in a fortified monastery in Lučenec. From there, they made incursions into Upper Hungary, marauding the countryside, and there was no way to ferret them out. So, one night, Codru took three of his men and went to capture someone to show us a way in. They never came back. We saw the three men's bodies hanging from the Hussite tower the next day. But not Codru's. We looked high and low but couldn't find him, so we still don't know whether he was killed or taken prisoner. I hoped Jiskra would ask for a ransom if he had him, but he didn't, and nobody knows anything."

Lena nods and pours more wine.

Hunyadi sighs. "I'm sorry, Lena, but I think he's dead. We'd have heard if Jiskra had him, but we heard nothing. It's like he vanished into thin air."

"Was it a full moon?"

Hunyadi stares at her like she's lost her mind. "What?"

"The night he disappeared. Was there a full moon?"

"Not that night. Two nights later, I think. But there was so much light that I wondered if they could get near the monastery without being spotted, but then the clouds set in. Why do you ask?"

"The last night with a full moon, I had a weird dream. I wondered if it was then," she lies.

Hunyadi puts his hand on her shoulder. "I'm sorry, Lena. Codru was a brave young man and my best captain. I'll miss him, but I know you'll miss him much more."

Lena sighs. Her heart aches, her eyes burn, and she wishes he'd leave her alone. But he's not done.

"I want you to know I'll care for you and little Mircea. You can stay here for as long as you wish. But if you wish to leave, I'll gladly help."

"Leave? Where?"

"Codru's estate in Prod will come to you and Mircea. Prod is just a small village, but it's beautiful and safe if life here in Buda is too much for you."

"Thank you. I'll think about it."

She needs to be alone, but he won't budge.

"Is there anything you need? Anything I can do for you?"

"No, thanks. I'm good."

She stands up, wishing him to get moving, but when he finally does, she feels terrible. The celebrated Hunyadi is just a tired old man. He wants to help her because he feels guilty about her husband's death. Of course, Codru wasn't her husband, but he doesn't know it. And doesn't need to.

"If there's anything Erzsébet or I could do..."

"Thank you. I'll let you know."

Lena swallows the lump in her throat and struggles for air. It's too hot inside, even though the fire died long ago.

She corks the wine and puts it away, then covers the chicken and puts it in the pantry. Thank God winter's coming, so it's cold enough to keep for a few days. They'll eat it tomorrow.

She wraps the bread and the slices the cozonac to take them to church tomorrow. Other than Sundays, when the faithful drop something in their bowls as they leave mass, the poor always struggle. They'll make good use of it.

By the time she's done, the darkness fades, but the walls feel like they're closing around her, so she steps out on the porch to breathe fresh air and watch the city wake up.

A hoarse rooster calls the morning, and, down the road, two more answer. Carts loaded with fruit and vegetables squeak on their way to the market, bringing food to feed Buda's people. Somewhere far away, an owl screeches and the eerie sound reminds her of home.

Should she return to Moldova? Vlad must be gone now that

Ștefan's father is no longer voivode. She could live in her old home and bring up Mircea in her village. He'd grow to be a shepherd, like her father, instead of Wallachia's voivode. Or should she go to Transylvania and live as Codru's widow? Nobody would ever need to know the truth.

Or should she stay here, in the only home Mircea remembers? He was too young to remember Moldova, but here he has friends. And they'd be safe under Hunyadi's protection. Vlad will never come here after Hunyadi helped Vladislav take his father's throne. He must be back with the Ottomans, scheming to take Wallachia.

"Mother?" Mircea stands at the door in his bare feet. His eyes wide open, he shivers in his thin chemise, and sucks on his thumb. She dipped it in bitter tea over and over to stop him, but he still does it when he's upset.

She picks him up and pulls his thumb out of his mouth.

He buries his face in her neck. "Where's Father?"

She kisses his dark curls and sighs. "Sorry, baby. He didn't make it."

CHAPTER 62

EDIRNE, FEBRUARY 1452

The hammam's steam is heavy with scents of rose and eucalyptus and so thick Radu can barely see beyond his nose. But that's how it should be. The hammam is the realm of heat and water, where the song of the fountains covers the servants' steps, the hushed conversations, and the moans of the men subjecting themselves to the bath attendants that restore dirty, achy bodies into cleanliness and beauty.

Laying on the warm marble slab with his forehead on his arm, Radu abandons himself to the hands of the masseur who scrubbed every inch of him with the rough, soapy loofah to remove the sweat and the dirt and tame his skin into silky softness before massaging his aches. This is one of Radu's favorite things, right there with smelling roses and loving Mehmed. But today, he can't let himself drift into the bliss. The message he received this morning weighs on his heart and troubles his mind. He read it again and again but still doesn't know what to do, even though he learned it by heart.

Kronštadt, January 1452

My dear brother,

I trust you are healthy and well. I hope life was good to you in the two years I haven't seen you. I didn't expect it to be so long, but, as you know, life gets in the way.

You must have heard that our uncle, Bogdan the Second of Moldova, perished at the hand of his own brother, the traitor Petru Aron. That treasonous, cowardly act happened at a wedding we were invited to. Our cousin Ștefan and I barely escaped with our lives.

After an arduous journey through the mountains, we finally arrived in Transylvania and stopped in Kronštadt, a Saxon fortress just north of the main pass to Wallachia. I'm doing my best to avoid Hunyadi's wrath while endeavoring to gather support for my claim to Wallachia's throne. Some Wallachian boyars left their homes and chose to live on this side of the border rather than swear fealty to Vladislav, the murderous traitor who killed our father and our brother. A few promised to support me, but that's not enough. I need more to swing the Wallachian State Council in my favor.

That's why I am in need of help.

I need to gather an army and equip it with weapons, horses, and good armor, and none of that is cheap. And, since I have less money than a church mouse, I wonder if you'd be willing to pitch in?

Some money would be awfully good. But, even better, I wonder if you'd speak to your friend, Sultan Mehmed, and get him interested in my cause? His father, Murad the Second, supported me with men and weapons. Maybe the son could do it too. I know he cares about you. If you could talk him into supporting me, we'd both fulfill our duty to our country and avenge Father and Mircea.

I'm sure our Father's legacy and Mircea's martyrdom weigh on your soul like they do on mine. I also know that, given his affection for you, Mehmed would lend a kind ear to your supplication. That is why I look forward to your positive response and brotherly help.

Yours, for God and for our country.

Your loving brother, Vlad

Radu sighs and struggles to push Vlad's message out of his mind. He tries to focus on the firm, skilled hands kneading his muscles to soften the stress in his shoulders, but he can't. That letter bothered him in so many ways.

First, it reminded him of Vlad. He hadn't heard from him in ages, so he sort of hoped he'd stay lost, but no. Not Vlad. He's back and, as always, pressures Radu into doing things he doesn't want to do. Like asking Mehmed for favors.

He also didn't like Vlad's insinuation about his relationship with Mehmed. Nor the hint that he neglected his duty to avenge Father and Mircea. All in all, he liked nothing about that letter: neither what it said nor what it implied, the tone, or the sender.

And he especially disliked that it made him feel like a lazy, good-for-nothing bum compared to his brother. Again. Being Vlad's brother has never been fun.

The masseur's hands descend from his shoulders to his back, then lower. The iron hands soften, turning slow and sensuous as they reach Radu's most sensitive parts. Radu's mouth turns dry, and his heart races, pumping blood into the throbbing ache between his legs. He gasps and rolls over to see Mehmed's face, his green eyes glazed with desire, only inches away.

"I sent the man away."

He leans against Radu, and his slow, loving hands caress every inch of his body until they can't take it anymore, and they embrace, hidden by the steam.

CHAPTER 63
WALLACHIA'S BLOOD

The fat white candles' flickering lights reflect in the golden cups and silver plates, sending playful twinkles throughout Mehmed's quarters. The low table sitting in the middle of the precious Isfahan carpet bows under the weight of platters loaded with deliciousness: garlicky leg of lamb with mint, ya`khni — a fragrant stew thick with eggplant, onions, and tomatoes whose scent fills the room; fragile cataifs, nests of thin noodles dripping with butter and honey; and fragrant soft yellow pears with skin so thin they melt in Radu's mouth like butter.

Sitting cross-legged on a blue pillow, Mehmed wipes his fingers on his embroidered cleaning cloth before picking another crispy strip of lamb. His green eyes sparkle, and his cheeks are flushed with Hungarian wine and the joy of celebrating a year on the Ottoman throne with no major disasters.

Radu lifts his cup. "Congratulations, my friend. I'm proud of you."

He ate little, but drank more than his fair share of the terrific wine, which helped. A little. It softened the sting of feeling like a loser. He drains his cup again, and Mehmed watches him with worry.

"Are you OK?"

"Yep."

He lifts the cup to have it refilled, and Mehmed frowns. "What's up, Radu? You've moped the whole day, and you're getting drunk on purpose. What's this about?"

Radu sighs. The wine didn't totally numb his feelings, but it lessened his inhibitions. That's why he talks to Mehmed like he never would were he sober. "My brother."

"Vlad? What about him?"

"He wrote to me from Kronštadt. He's maneuvering to take the Wallachian throne."

"So what? What's that to you?"

"He... he wants me to ask for your help."

"I see. Is that it?"

Radu sighs. "I... I feel like I'm wasting my life. I eat, I drink, and I write poems. I ride good horses, and I have you when you're not too busy. But what am I doing with my life? What's the point of my existence? For years now, Vlad has been fighting to retake Wallachia and avenge Father and Mircea while I spent my days drawing in the rose garden."

"What would you like to do instead?"

"I'd like to be useful. I'd like my life to matter. I'd like the world to be better because of me."

"But you're only sixteen!"

"You were a sultan when you were twelve!"

"And look what good it did to me! My father sent me back to my hole when I was fourteen, and I've struggled to climb out of it ever since."

"You're the sultan. The fate of countries and people's lives depend on you. Your everyday decisions mean life or death. You're shaping the future of the world while I pet my cat."

"Leave Sari out of this, will you? None of this is her fault."

Radu laughs, but he's not kidding. He squirms as Mehmed's knowing eyes search his soul.

"OK. Let's talk then. What do you want? You want Wallachia?" Mehmed asks.

Radu's jaw drops. He told no one, but he's been thinking. As Vlad Dracul's son, he's just as entitled to be voivode as his brother Vlad, even if Vlad is older. In Wallachia, like in the Ottoman Empire, the throne doesn't automatically belong to the eldest son. Any son of a voivode can claim it, and then it's up to the boyars to choose. They may need an army to persuade them, but still. Snatching Wallachia's throne from under his brother? Radu smiles.

Mehmed reads him. "Well, you can't have it. Not yet. You're not ready, just like Vlad wasn't ready when he took it last time. That's why he lost it in two months and barely escaped with his life. Same with me. I lost mine in two years, and I'm still living with my shame."

Radu wilts.

Mehmed shrugs. "I said not yet. If that's what you really want, you'll have to put in the work and learn how to rule. How to read and lead people. How to gain their trust and keep it. How to scare them straight and get rid of them when you must. There's a lot of work you have to do. Are you willing to do it?"

Radu doesn't know what to say. This all came so fast. Does he want it? Is he willing to do the work? Is it worth it just to spite Vlad?

Mehmed puts his arm around his shoulders. "Listen, Radu. Why would you want Wallachia's throne? It's nothing but a pain. War, always war. The Wallachian boyars are a bunch of hyenas ripping the country apart. They betrayed one voivode after another. Wallachia is nothing but a battlefield between the cross and the crescent. With Hungary on one side and us on the other, you'll never get peace. That's why I'm considering occupying it and annexing it to the empire like Father did with Bulgaria, Greece, and Albania. Your people would be better off under Ottoman rule."

Radu's heart freezes. "No!"

"Why not?"

"Wallachia is my country! Our Orthodox faith, our Romanian language, and our thousand-year-old traditions make us who we are.

Wallachia is my homeland, and my father and brother would roll in their graves if I let that happen."

Mehmed leans forward. "If that's how you feel... But why would you want Wallachia's throne? What would you do with it besides pissing off your brother?"

"I'd... I'd try to bring them peace and a better life. I'd teach them the good things I learned at your court without destroying who they are. And I'd avenge my father and my brother."

"So you really want it?"

"I do."

"Are you willing to do the work?"

"Yes."

"OK. Then go get me Çandarlı Halil Paşa."

"Now?"

"Now."

It's almost midnight. Radu wonders if Mehmed is kidding, but he's not; he's waiting for him to get up and go. He really wants me to wake up the grand vizier and bring him over. But why? Radu thinks, but he knows better than to ask.

He heads to the door. Like Mehmed said, it's time to do the work.

CHAPTER 64
THE GRAND VIZIER'S NIGHT

It's past midnight in February, a cold, foreboding night, rare here in Edirne. Yesterday's rain froze into a slippery sheen that spooks the horses, and the streets are empty but for the wind. Around here, long winter nights are not for gallivanting around. They're for staying at home and making children.

But Radu isn't in the child-making business. The freezing wind whips his face and tears his eyes, but he's still warm inside from the wine. He gallops with his dozen janissaries towards the grand vizier's home, wondering what he got himself into.

Çandarlı Paşa never liked him. He always looked at him like he was a spoiled brat and Mehmed's play toy. He doesn't like Mehmed either, but he's always polite to him — after all, he's the sultan. But that doesn't apply to Radu. To him, Radu isn't any better than a eunuch slave, even though he's a prince of Wallachia.

Radu tried to endear himself to the man, but that got him nowhere. Çandarlı Paşa ignored him, unless he threw him a wilting glare. And if he didn't like him before, he'll like him even less now. But Radu has a job to do.

They stop in front of the vizier's home. One of the men knocks at the door, but nobody answers. He strikes again until an old servant, his eyes swollen with sleep, cracks the door open.

"What…"

Radu pushes the door open and steps in. The place is dark and silent. "Go fetch your master."

"The grand vi…"

"How many masters do you have? Go get him. Now," Radu barks.

The man scuttles away, and Radu ponders how easy it is to be an asshole. Not his thing, but if there's ever been a time for it, it's today. He'll have to play the role of Mehmed's ruthless general and treat Çandarlı Paşa like he's garbage.

He walks around the lavish living room, admiring the thick cinnamon carpet warming the marble floor and the Murano chandeliers, wondering where Çandarlı Paşa got his money. But he's just the latest grand vizier from a noble family who watched over the interests of the Ottoman Empire and its treasury for half a century. They've always been rich and powerful, and they got more so with every year.

Until now. Radu doesn't know what Mehmed wants the paşa for, but he's not waking him up to thank him for his service. Çandarlı Halil Paşa must know there's a solid chance he won't make it back home. He's done it to others; tonight, it's his turn.

Heavy steps, then Çandarlı Paşa appears, but he's not his magnificent usual self. Instead of his rich embroidered kaftan, he wears a linen chemise; his wrinkled face is weary, and his thin hair messed up from sleep. But his steely eyes are as sharp as ever, and he sighs with relief upon seeing Radu. "Allah be blessed, it's just you, Mehmed's little prince. Good to see you, but you should find a more appropriate time. My assistant will get you an appointment." He turns to head back to his bed.

Radu bites his tongue to keep from apologizing and promising to pick a better time. Mehmed sent him here for a reason, and Radu needs to show he's more than a good roll in the hay. "I'll keep that in mind, Çandarlı Paşa. But Sultan Mehmed wants you now."

"Now? What for?"

"He'll tell you if he chooses to. Let's go."

The vizier's eyes narrow, and he pales. "Now?"

"Yes."

Çandarlı Paşa sighs. "Let me get dressed."

He steals out of the room, and Radu wonders if he should have sent his men to watch the house and cut his escape. But where could he escape to? The entire empire knows him, so there's no place he can run to. He'll have to face his fate, whatever that is, but that's not Radu's problem. His job is to bring him to Mehmed, and that's precisely what he'll do.

When he returns, the paşa has recovered his dignified self: gold-embroidered kaftan trimmed with black fox, a white turban with an ostrich feather held in place by a sapphire the size of a child's fist, and eyes sharper than Damascus blades. He carries a melon-sized velvet bag, and Radu wonders what's in it.

As they ride to the palace, the vizier searches Radu's face. "What does he want me for?"

Radu forgets his asshole role. "He didn't tell me, but I'd be worried if I were you."

For the first time, Çandarlı Paşa looks at Radu like he's a real person. "Will I make it out of there?"

Radu avoids eye contact, feeling bad for this old man who spent his whole life doing his sultan's deeds and is about to lose his head. "I don't know, Paşa. But if he wanted to kill you, he would have probably sent the Bostanji Paşa, not me."

"Why did he send you?"

"To try me? This may be as much about me as it is about you. I wish you luck."

Çandarlı Paşa nods, and they speak no more. But as they near the palace, Radu has the strange feeling he somehow betrayed Mehmed, though he can't figure out how.

CHAPTER 65
THE SULTAN'S PLAN

A hundred candles are burning in the throne room, and the flickering lights make it feel eerie. The golden throne is empty; so is the rest of the room that looks huge without the usual crowd. There's no one there but the sultan and his guards.

Wrapped in a gold-embroidered red kaftan, Mehmed leans over a table piled with maps as if he didn't hear them coming, but Radu knows better. The clatter of the heavy boots on the stone floor is loud enough to wake the dead. Mehmed is just showing Çandarlı Paşa who's boss.

The grand vizier stops at the door, waiting for the sultan to invite him in. He waits and waits until he can't take it anymore and clears his throat.

Mehmed keeps up the game for another minute, then turns and greets him with a smile. "How nice to see you, Çandarlı Paşa. I trust you are well?"

"My sultan, I..."

"I'm glad to hear that. What would I do without your wise counsel if you fell ill and died?"

The grand vizier turns green at the hint, but Mehmed acts like he didn't notice. He sits on his throne and looks the vizier up and down.

"You were saying?"

Çandarlı Paşa steps to the foot of the throne. He kneels to kiss Mehmed's hand, then drops his heavy velvet bag at his feet.

"What's this?" Mehmed touches it with his toe, and the bag topples sideways with a clatter.

"It's a gift for you, my sultan."

"A gift for me? It's not my birthday."

"It's the anniversary of your coronation. And it's... the tradition for dignitaries to bring gifts when summoned to the throne. Especially if it's the middle of the night."

"Open it, Radu."

Radu unties the string and empties the bag at Mehmed's feet.

Glittering diamond bracelets, golden crosses studded with precious stones that must have belonged to some rich Christian, sapphire rings, golden ducats, and a ruby big enough to choke on, roll over the floor, stealing the light. The candles' flicker sets them on fire, and Radu's eyes hurt from their light.

Mehmed laughs. "You want to buy your life, Çandarlı Paşa? Is this what you think your life is worth? Don't you know I can kill you and keep the bribe? Because that's what it is. A bribe. Who'd stop me?"

Çandarlı Paşa shrinks to a pitiful old man under Mehmed's disdainful gaze, and Mehmed loves it. He holds the moment, watching him squirm, until Radu can't take it anymore. He collects the jewelry, drops it in the bag, and ties it back.

Mehmed claps his hands. The noise resounds like an arquebus shot in the empty room, and two guards rush in, their hands on the hilts of their swords.

"Bring pillows for my friends to sit on," Mehmed says.

Çandarlı Paşa wavers.

"Take your bag, Paşa. This is not about your money; it's about your faith. I need to trust you and know we're both fighting the same fight.

Otherwise..." He looks at the guards dropping the pillows. "Otherwise, I'll have to go on without you."

"I've always been faithful to the empire, my sultan."

"Sure you have. But now I need you to be faithful to me. And my goals." Mehmed stands to pace. "It's time for me to fulfill my destiny. Constantinople, the Red Apple, is ripe for the picking, and I'm ready to harvest. Will you be on my side?"

"I'm always on your side, my sultan."

"I need you to do everything you can to help me take Constantinople. Everything. I want you to lend me your wisdom, connections, and diplomacy to help me take it. I need you to swear nothing will be more important, more urgent, or more vital than taking Constantinople. Starting today, and until the day I'll sit in my new mosque in Hagia Sophia, nothing will take precedence over the Constantinople campaign. Nothing."

"Yes, my sultan."

"You swear?"

"I swear."

"Good. Because if I fail, you die. Future generations will remember you as the grand vizier who failed to take Constantinople. Men will spit when they utter your name, and dogs will piss on your tomb. You get it?"

Çandarlı Paşa drops to his knees and touches his forehead to the floor. "Yes, my sultan."

"We'll build a new fortress on the European side of the Bosporus Straits. We'll erect it right across from Anadolu Hisari, the fortress my grandfather Bayezid built, because that's where the Straits are narrowest, and we'll call it Rumeli Hisari, The Throat Cutter. Rumeli and Anadolu will control the passage of ships to or from Constantinople, so the Romans won't get any help from the west, and they won't have a way to escape. Come see."

Rumeli Hisari's irregular shape reminds Radu of the calligraphy of the prophet's name. It's shaped like an irregular heptagon, and grows straight from the rock, reinforced with four large towers and a few smaller ones. The grand vizier studies it with narrowed eyes and sniffs.

"This shouldn't take more than a few years to build. We'll have to strike coin, then gather troops and equip and train the..."

"The Rumeli Hisari will be done by the fall." Mehmed's voice is colder than ice.

"This fall?"

"Of course."

"But there isn't time to gather materials and..."

"The materials are gathered already. There's lime, beams from Ereğli and Izmit, and plenty of stone from Anatolia. I also got a thousand masons and just as many lime slakers and workmen on standby."

"But how will you..."

Mehmed shakes his head. He puts his finger on the largest tower by the gate. "Oh, no. Not me. You. This tower is all yours, Çandarlı Paşa. You'll build it with your men. The other towers will be Şehabeddin's, Zaganos's and Sarica Paşa's. I'll take the walls. The men will work harder and faster if they compete."

"I see."

"This summer, we build Rumeli Hisari, then start the blockade in the fall. This winter, we watch them starve and shiver. We'll take the Red Apple in spring."

The grand vizier sighs. He's aged a lot since yesterday, and Mehmed sees it.

"Go get some sleep, Paşa. Tomorrow we have work to do."

He leaves, and Mehmed turns to Radu. "What do you think?"

"That was masterful."

"Thanks. Tell me: Why did I send you to get him in the middle of the night? After all, this could have waited till tomorrow."

"To scare him?"

"Why?"

"To make him do what you want him to?"

"But why? I could threaten him, and he'd do whatever I told him. Why tonight?"

"I don't know."

"Because this way, he expected to die, but he didn't. He ended up better off than he expected, so he'll be grateful rather than resentful. He'll be glad to do what I want. You understand?"

"I think so."

"See, Radu, we don't respond to what happens to us, but to how that compares to what we expected. If Çandarlı Paşa expected a gift and got what you saw, he'd be pissed. But he expected to die, so anything short of that is a gift."

Radu nods, hoping someday he'll be as wise as Mehmed.

Fat chance.

CHAPTER 66

SERBIA, SPRING 1452

Leaning against the rough, cold rock at the cave's mouth, Codru looks beyond the rusty iron bars, willing the sun to go down. Now that winter's finally over and the days grew longer, he has a few more hours before the full moon rises, and he can't wait.

A soft wind shakes the wild plum trees pink with blooms, snowing fragrant petals over the new grass. A stubborn red-headed woodpecker drums holes in an old dead trunk. A thousand bees loaded with pollen and drunk with nectar zoom from flower to flower to gather sweetness. Codru's mouth waters, remembering the taste of honey, and his belly growls like he hasn't eaten in ages. Because he hasn't. Night after night, he's watched the skinny crescent of the moon grow bigger, and he decided that, no matter what, he'll stay awake and find out what's going on under the full moon. That's why he didn't eat or drink for two days.

He's been locked here since the fall. That fateful day, when he took his men to spy on Đurađ Branković's troops to find a way into the monastery that sheltered them, they fell into a trap.

As soon as they approached the dark walls, all the bells started ringing and a hundred torches came out of nowhere, surrounding them.

Codru and his men stood back-to-back and fought valiantly, killing one enemy after another, but the attackers were too many to prevail. Codru's men fell one by one, slaughtered by swords, skewered by lances, and trampled by the armored horses. When he was the only one left standing, Codru pulled back against the wall, panting and bleeding. His arms ached from killing, and his brain searched desperately for an escape.

"Give up!" the enemy captain shouted. "Give up if you want to keep your life."

Codru didn't bother to answer. The Serbs weren't known for their mercy, and he had killed so many they'd never let him live.

"Come on, man, don't be stupid," the captain said. "You can't beat us all. What's the point of wasting your life like that?"

Good question, Codru thought, weighing his choices while holding up his sword, ready to slash those who ventured too close. He could charge them and get himself killed. He could stay put and wait to get killed. Or he could stick his dagger in his heart and save them the trouble. That would ensure they couldn't catch him alive and torture him into betraying his people.

He was still mulling over his options when the captain shouted. "Too bad, man. You're a fierce warrior, and we could use someone like you. But you're clearly too stupid to live. Go ahead, boys. Let's get this over it."

The five men surrounding Codru lifted their swords, but nobody stepped forward. They'd seen him fight, so they knew the odds were that they'd be the first to die.

Annoyed, the captain shook his head and glanced behind him. "Archers? Nock your arrows."

A dozen archers grabbed arrows from their quills and readied their bows. One by one, they pulled taut the string and aimed.

It's over, Codru thought. I'll die the death of a thousand cuts, and I'll look like a dead hedgehog instead of a werewolf. But no one who cared would see him, especially not Lena. Not that it mattered. He could look like a weasel for all that she cared, but the thought that she wouldn't see him cut to pieces gave him solace.

"Shoot," the captain said, and a flock of arrows converged on Codru like vultures on a corpse.

The first one whizzed by his ear; the second parted his hair. The third one buried itself in his neck, and a spurt of thick, salty blood filled his mouth.

It's over, he thought. Lena's face with her periwinkle eyes crinkled at the corners and her soft hair smelling like lavender filled his mind. He sighed and readied himself for the last arrow, the one that would send him to a better place.

"No! Stop!" someone shouted, and the world went silent.

The captain looked at something behind Codru. "But why? He's almost dead," he said.

"He's not dead yet. I claim him. He's mine, and nobody dare touch him," the voice said, as Codru's world went dark.

CHAPTER 67
BABA CLOANȚA

Codru woke up in a cell. Monastery? Prison? Hard to tell. It was small, white, and quiet. And empty, but for an old woman whose ugly face lit up in a smile when he opened his eyes. She pushed back the black scarf covering her thin white hair and nodded.

"You woke! Good! I'd started to lose hope. You took a long time to come to, especially for someone of your... persuasion. I expected you to be down a day or two, but weeks? Never mind, though. You're back, and that's all that matters."

"Where am I?" Codru asked.

"In Đurađ Branković's Serbia, may Queen Moon and King Sun torch him to ashes before his soul burns in hell. You're in the Tumane Monastery."

Codru looked around. Stone walls, barely whitewashed, empty but for the Orthodox crucifix above the wooden door. Under him, a straw mat. Over him, a woolen cover making him sweat. He threw off the cover, and the old woman laughed.

"Feisty, aren't we? Good. That means you're getting better. Soon enough, you should be back to your usual strapping self. Lia?"

A young woman stepped in. Her dark eyes were worried, and her movements swift. "You called?"

"I did. Our young... hero here woke up. Go get me the yellow potion. And some food."

The girl's eyes widened. She glanced at Codru, then turned to the woman. "The yellow potion, you said?"

The old woman frowned. "What's with you? You lost the usage of your ears? Just because this young... man here opened his eyes? Get me the yellow and make it quick. We'd better be out of here before Durad's men find out he woke up. Otherwise, they'll start asking him questions, and by the time they're done with him, he'll be of no use to anyone."

The girl disappeared, and the woman turned to Codru. "You were too ill to remember, but I saved you from being killed. That stupid captain wanted you dead, but he yielded and let me have you. It took you a while, but I'm glad to see that my care paid off."

"Who are you?" Codru asked.

"I'm a Vlach. Call me Baba Cloanța."

What's a Vlach? Codru wanted to ask, but he was drained. And, truth be told, he didn't much care. The only thing he cared about was escaping this darn place, but not now. He'd only been awake for minutes, but he was already falling asleep.

The door opened, and Lia returned with a tray. She set it on the floor and handed him a golden drink.

"What's this?"

"A potion that will help you rest and heal," Baba Cloanța said. "Drink that, then eat. Your body needs nourishment to heal."

He took the cup, looking into the girl's watchful eyes. *Something's odd about this*, he thought, but his brain was too fogged to care. And the woman had already saved his life, so he lifted the drink to his lips.

"Don't you have somewhere else you need to be?" Baba asked, and Lia gave him one last glance, then squeezed out the door without a sound.

Codru sniffed the drink. It smelled like chamomile and plantain, and though he hated them both, he knew from Mama Smaranda they'd help with healing. The drink tasted like honey, so he drained the cup and set it down.

"Good. Have some soup now," Baba said, handing him a steaming bowl of chicken broth with herbs and spices, so flavorful it made his belly growl. Codru drunk the stock straight from the bowl and licked his lips. He set it down, feeling worn out and faint.

"You need to rest now," Baba said, covering him to his chin. "That's the only way you'll recover your strength."

Codru's brain buzzed with questions. Who are you? Why are you helping me? What's going to happen next? But he was too drained to talk.

"Don't worry, you'll find out in due time," Baba said as if she'd heard his thoughts, and blew out the candle lighting the cell.

CHAPTER 68
THE CAGED WOLF

W hen Codru woke up again, he was locked in this cave, and he never left it since.

That was five moons ago. It's got to be, since he marked every day on the wall, but he's never seen the full moon. One way or another, he slept through his shift — if there was a shift — every time. That never happened before.

Once a month, the full moon's magic turns him into a *vârcolac,* a werewolf, filling him with restless energy. When the full moon calls, he has no choice but to follow, even though he knows he can't reach her. Her magic is too strong to resist, so he runs for miles and miles, until his chest is ready to burst and his paws are too raw to go on, and still he keeps running. He can't stop until the first rays of sun break the spell, turning him back into a human.

Even Smaranda's potions can't take it all away. They stop the change, so he keeps his human shape, but he never sleeps. His soul yearns for the moon, making him anxious, moody, and restless. And his shadow shifts to that of a wolf, so he has to keep it hidden.

But ever since he left Hunyadi's camp, he missed every full moon and slept like a normal human, even though he didn't drink Smaranda's potion. What the heck happened? It's like the kiss of death drained his werewolf blood and turned him back to a human. Or is it?

He hasn't seen the cave door open yet. They come every morning, and pass him food and water through the grates. When it got freezing in winter, they gave him blankets to keep him warm. Sometimes it's Baba Cloanța, sometimes Lia or another girl who brings his daily food, but nobody ever comes in. And nobody answers his questions.

"Where am I?" he asked. Baba didn't answer.

"Why am I here?" Baba said nothing.

"How long will you keep me?"

"As long as it takes," she said, and she left.

"As long as it takes to what? What are you waiting for?" he shouted, but she was already gone.

The girls are even worse, because they don't speak at all. They just stare at him with terrified eyes, like they expect him to blow through the bars. If only I could, Codru thinks, but there's no way. He couldn't do it even as a werewolf, because the bars are thick and stuck in the rock, and the grate is bolted and locked with four heavy locks that would inevitably break his teeth.

He studied every inch of that rock, looking for an opening, or at least a crack, but there's nothing. The dark end of the cave is nothing but solid rock, and the layer of dirt by its mouth is no deeper than a couple of inches. He broke his nails digging into it, but he didn't get far. There's no digging a tunnel under that door without tools, or at least iron claws, and he's got neither.

He kept thinking and searching and marking the days on the wall. Then, one day, he found something. Not much — just a clump of fur stuck to the mattress. It was rough and dark at the ends, but gray at the root. And it smelled of wolf.

That's mine, he thought. That's my werewolf fur. I've been wolving out all this time, I just didn't know it. They must be giving me something to put me to sleep.

That's why he stopped eating and drinking. He wasn't sure how long they kept him down, so he stopped eating three days before, and drinking two. He threw the food and water at the bottom of the cave and left the empty dishes, so they wouldn't smell a rat, and he's now waiting for the sun to go down.

CHAPTER 69

BLOOD MAGIC

I t felt like forever until the trees' shadows grew long and the sky darkened, telling Codru it was time. He sighed and lay on his mattress with his eyes half closed, pretending to sleep, but he'd never been more awake. Through the thick metal bars, he watched the graying of the day and counted the beats of his heart. Way too fast. He slowed his breath to quieten it, but he worried. Can he lay still and pretend to be asleep when the moon summons him? Won't his paws take off on their own to follow her call? He doesn't know, but there's only one way to find out.

The sky turns black, and the shifting starts. Codru's heart quickens, and his bones melt to lengthen. His achy hands sprout dagger-like claws, and his mouth morphs into a long, strong muzzle. It's got to be worse than teething, he thinks, feeling his teeth lengthen into fangs and his ears stretch above his head.

His paws itch to go, so he's got to use all his will to keep still. But... now that he's got his power, maybe he could chew through the bars? Or dig through the rock with his claws? Or rush and break the door with his werewolf strength?

He's about to jump up when his keen ears hear voices, and soon

282

after, he glimpses a flicker of light. It's too late now, so he closes his eyes and struggles to quiet his heart.

"Everything looks OK," Baba Cloanța says. "But for..."

"But for what?" Lia asks.

"I don't like the pace of his heart. It's too fast."

"You think there's something wrong?" another voice asks.

"I don't know, but I'm worried. He's never been like this since we got him here. I wonder if he's ill? They say rats can carry the Black Death. Or maybe a snake got in and bit him?" Baba answers. "Whatever it is, it would be a pity to lose him."

"What if he's just pretending?" Lia asks.

"Pretending to do what? To have a racing heart?"

"Pretending to be asleep. What if he's awake?"

"After the potions we gave him? Are you serious?"

"What if he didn't drink them?"

"Why wouldn't he? You think he wants to die of thirst?"

"Maybe... maybe he suspects something?"

Baba Cloanța sighs and shakes her head. "You, girl, are too smart for your own good. He's been here for months, and he never suspected a thing. And now, all of a sudden, he figured it out? For no reason? Come on! He's a damn strong *vârcolac,* but nobody said he was smart."

Someone rattles the door, and Codru creaks open an eye, watching them under his lashes. There's a bunch of people at the door, all women, all young. Baba tries the door and checks the locks.

"All's well here. Let's get this done. Everyone ready?"

The women nod. Two of them raise sharp metal-tipped lances to stop him if he tries to escape. Two more, behind them, hold bows.

"How about you? Are you ready?" Baba asks.

Lia frowns. "I guess you only die once. But don't forget you promised to kill me if he bites me," she says.

"I won't forget, though it would be handy to have your own friendly *vârcolac* rather than go through all the trouble to get blood from this one."

"And you'll give me a black wedding?"

Baba nods. "I sure will. I'll get you the most handsome young man in seven villages, and I'll wed him to you before your funeral. You'll have the finest wedding this county ever saw."

"And a white dress?"

"The dress, the musicians, the tombstone, the *pomana* for the living and the dead — you'll have it all. And I'll make sure your groom stays chaste for the year. Otherwise, he'll join you in your tomb."

Lia nods, and Baba unlocks the locks, one after another then pulls the bolts. "Go," she says, pushing the door open just a crack.

Lia slips in, and the bolts slam back into place.

It all happened too fast for Codru to react, but he's surprised that the hinges didn't squeak. They must have oiled them to make sure that I don't wake up, he thinks, watching the young girl through his eyelashes.

Her eyes glued to him, she steps closer carefully, watching his every breath. Codru closes his eyes and struggles to slow down his heart and calm the blood rush in his ears.

She grasps his back paw, and Codru labors to soften his muscles and stay limp. There's a quick slash behind his knee and hot blood spurts into the vessel she brought. Seconds later, she lets him go.

She rushes through the door, which is already open. The locks slide back before Codru figures out what to do.

"Good job," Baba says, watching him through the grates, and Codru keeps his breathing even and his heart slow.

"What will we do if it still doesn't work?" someone asks.

"It has to work. It's true *vârcolac* blood, for God's sake. The magic of the moon flows through it. It will work; I just need to find the right recipe."

"But what if it doesn't? After all, you've been trying for months."

Baba Cloanța scratches her head. "If it doesn't, we'll try his seed."

CHAPTER 70

CONSTANTINOPLE, SUMMER 1452

After a long, ugly winter and a short moody spring, summer brought Constantinople's gloomy walls back to life. It came with a bright sun that returned the glow to the old gilded roofs, warm rains that cleaned the streets of muck, and a soft breeze smelling like hope. The wheat in the fields is turning to gold, the vines bend under the weight of ripening fruit, and the birds sing of love and joy of life.

Ali is glad. The dreadful, long winter pushed her deep into hopelessness and despair. For months, she did nothing but go to work and come home, wondering when it would all be over. And hating herself for not leaving.

That ugly day back in November, Ali packed her stuff, as little as she had, and put on the old beggar clothes she'd kept in the bottom of a coffer, thinking she may need them someday.

It turned out she'd been right. Ion was oblivious to the plight of women, who men see as chattel rather than humans. He had no clue what upset her. The kid stuck his hand up her skirt? So what? What's the big deal? Nothing's so terrible you can't fix it over a cup of wine.

But Ali got hurt to her core. By Notaras' kid, who thinks she's a toy; by his father, who expects that spreading her legs goes with the little he pays her for the laundry. And, worst of all, Ion, who's like her brother, doesn't think that any of this is worth fussing about.

That awful night, Ali grabbed her bag and dragged it to the port. Not much happened in the middle of the night, but the morning would come soon, and dozens of ships would sail to faraway places. She considered sailing away to never return to Constantinople, which she loved and hated.

But sail to where?

To anywhere. Anywhere had to be better than this. She could sail to Braila or Kiliya, the Wallachians' ports on the Danube, then head north to Kronštadt. She'd then go home to Mama Smaranda, to breathe the incense of the pines and be herself with someone she trusts.

And then? She'd settle for a quiet life in the forest, picking herbs and leaves, and learning to make potions. She could finally understand the witches' craft and use the power she felt inside her, but she'd never known how to reach.

Or she could sail to Smederevo and find Mara. She's got to be back home, living with her father, after leaving the harem and rejecting Constantine's proposal. Ali misses her terribly, and she's yearning for Mara's arms around her. But what would she do there besides sharing Mara's bed? Is that a life she could settle for?

Or she could sail to Genoa and look for Signor Giovanni Giustiniani Longo. For months, she's felt foolish to have left because he was a privateer. He was right after all — the oarsmen were slaves already, and changing masters couldn't harm them any worse. As for the men with the whips, they deserved to taste their own medicine. But Giovanni was married, and Ali wasn't into sharing. And he must have forgotten her long ago.

She'd sighed and pulled her coat closer to keep the sharp wind from cutting into her, then leaned back against the cold wall, waiting for the morning.

Truth be told, she was better off than most women. She could come or go as she pleased. Unlike most women, she didn't have to do what anyone told her to please the man in her life. Even Mara, who's a princess, got sold to Murad. When he died, she was lucky Mehmed let her go, but now she's back with her father, ready to be sold again. Ali wished she had been a fly on the wall the day Constantine's proposal arrived. How did she dodge it? And how will she escape the next one?

Ali was lucky. She could choose her future. She could become a potion-brewing forest witch, a kept woman warming someone's husband's bed, or the favorite of an Eastern princess. But none of that felt right. She was too young to settle; she first needed to decide what her life was about, then live true to it.

The sky faded in the east, then turned to bruised purple and blood red above the leaden Black Sea. Soon enough, the ships would wake up to prepare for their journeys. She could get a passage wherever she wanted since they all needed cooks. She could travel the world and see with her own eyes all the fantastic places she'd learned about in her geography lessons. To Cathay, where they make silk out of worms, or to England, where armored knights knock each other off tall horses with their lances, or to Rome, where cattle graze between the Roman Forum's marble columns, or to Egypt, where a stone lion buried in the sand tries people with riddles and eats them if they can't answer. Well, maybe not there since she's not good with riddles and she doesn't fancy getting eaten by a lion, even a stone one. But she could go someplace she's never been and live a new life she never dreamed about.

Or she could go home, like Father would want her to.

She remembered Mother, and a rush of hot blood went to her brain. There was no one else on earth she hated more. That was a dark secret she'd never told anyone since people thought mothers were sacred or something. Still, she could return home to Mother and her brothers and... and do what?

Ali shook her head. She wanted to see Mother just a tad less than she wanted to see the food she ate last week. That helped. She still didn't know where to go but knew where she wouldn't. Home.

She stuck her frozen fingers in her armpits to warm them and watched Constantinople come alive. Workers headed to work, vendors set their stalls, fishermen's boats returned heavy with catch, and she envied them all. Their life was straightforward, and they all knew what to do. All except her.

The ships started coming alive. Sleepy sailors climbed up from down below, rubbing their eyes, and began fussing with the sails, and Ali's heart itched for adventure. The wide world was waiting. She could go anywhere she wanted. Even Africa, where they rode bumpy camels instead of sleek horses.

"Hey, you."

An important-looking man dressed in a blue velvet tunic and breeches so tight they looked painted on frowned impatiently at her.

"You, boy. We need a cook. You know anyone?"

"Where are you going to?"

The man is tall and handsome, and his eyes are kind. "We're going to Lisbon, the best place in the world. The food is good, the wine cheap, and the women soft and kind. We'll then set sail to discover new territories nobody has set foot on before. There'll be loot, lots of loot. Gold, and silver, and pearls. Just one journey and a smart fellow could build himself a good life. Do you know of anyone?"

Ali was tempted. Oh, boy, was she tempted. She could go to new places she had never heard of and see things no girl like her had seen. She could sail into an adventurous new life.

But her purpose was here. She needed to stay and fight for change right here, in the old world, where men thought of women as chattel. Even Ion. She needed to stay put and make a difference.

"No, sorry. I don't know anyone."

She grabbed her bag and headed home. If she was going to fight for women, she might as well start at home.

CHAPTER 71

A RELUCTANT SPY

But that was all months ago, before the winter, when Constantinople still thought it had all the time in the world. Before spring, when Mehmed built Rumeli Hisari to choke the Bosporus and starve Constantinople.

Ali returned home, and life went back to its old pace: cooking dinner and working for Notaras. Because, strangely, he didn't fire her.

When she returned to work the following day, nothing had changed besides Notaras' furtive glances and the fact that she never saw the kid again. But Ali knew they watched her. She felt their eyes on her every moment of the day, whether she cleaned, cooked, or did the laundry.

But not today. Notaras was leaving as she came. He headed to the port. Rumor has it that Mehmed's Throat Cutter will be finished today, so everyone went to watch like there's anything to see other than the red walls growing taller. But they think they'll fire the big guns to celebrate, and they all want to see that.

There's no one inside as Ali heads to the kitchen. Her first jobs are to clean the dirty dishes off the table, stoke the fire, and clean the floors. She keeps her ears pricked to listen as she works, but she doesn't hear a thing. They must be gone to see the guns, she thinks. This may be the opportunity she waited for.

Pretending to be dusting, she wanders through the whole house. There's nobody but the cat.

She grabs the ring of keys hanging by the door and tries to unlock Notaras' private study. No luck. The heavy wooden door is locked, and no amount of shaking will get it open.

She moves on to the bedrooms. The master's room is first. It's small and lit by a single narrow window. And it's empty but for the four-poster bed and the massive metal-plated chest sitting next to it, holding a candlestick. She tries to open the coffer, but it's locked.

She takes out her keys again and tries again.

The fourth one screeches and twists. The lock gives.

Her heart drumming in her ears, Ali holds her breath to listen, but there's nothing.

She opens the chest. It's packed to the brim with bolts of precious silks and brocade. She takes them out one by one, marveling at the sheen of the green silk, the color of the stormy sea, that looks alive when the light strikes it. It's beautiful, as are the others, but that's not what she wants. She piles them on the bed, ensuring she has them in order.

Ali is almost at the bottom when she finds a leather bag between the bolts. She empties it on the bed. There's a pile of gold: bracelets, rings, pins, pendants, all glowing in the meager light of the room. And between them, a key.

Ali doesn't know if it's the key she's looking for. She needs to try it, but can she leave everything here like this? Surely not. She puts everything back just as she found it, even though she knows it will take her forever to put the key back. But she can't risk leaving everything out, in case someone returns before she's done. She locks the coffer, makes the bed, and returns to the study.

Her mouth dry, her heart racing, Ali tries the key in the door that frustrated her for months. The lock clicks. She opens the door to a windowless dark room. She needs light.

She grabs a candle, lights it from the fire in the kitchen, and returns. The room is small and dingy, like a closet, and lined with wooden shelves bowing under the weight of books and ledgers.

Ali picks one, then another. She glances inside, but she doesn't know what to look for. There are dozens, and they all look the same. She can't take them all. So, which one should she take? The oldest? The newest?

She sighs. After all this trouble, she finally got to what she came here for and doesn't know what to take. What the heck?

There's a dusty old chest in a corner, no bigger than a stool. She tries to open it, but it's locked.

This is getting old.

She tries the key and curses. It won't fit. And the chest is too large to steal. Dang it!

She sighs and pushes it back, then hears a noise. Someone's coming.

Ali grabs a random book and hides it inside her chemise, then rushes out and locks the door. She's sweeping the floors as Notaras walks in. "What are you doing?"

"Cleaning."

"What do you need the candle for?"

Oops. The candle, still lit, sits on the table. "A friend died. I just found out today, so I lit a candle for him."

"Here? Not in church?"

"I didn't have time to go to church this morning, since I came here to clean. You can deduct the money for the candle from my pay."

"Be sure that I will."

Notaras' eyes on her are heavy with suspicion as she keeps sweeping a floor that needs no cleaning, hoping that he can't hear her heart beating like a drum. He tries the door of the study. It's locked, thank God, but the key is still in her pocket, and she's got no prayer of putting it back in its place. Not with Notaras here.

"Who was this friend?"

Ali looks in her mind for a friend. "Lena. My friend Lena. She died in childbirth," she says, praying that Lena is safe and she's not sending her the evil spirits.

"You said it was a man. "

"I didn't."

"You said 'Him.'"

"That's the baby. It was a boy. He died, too, so I lit the candle for his soul. He didn't get baptized." Ali sighs, sending a prayer for Lena and her boy and waiting for Notaras to leave so she can disappear. She knows he didn't believe the rubbish she told him. He'll be up to his coffer looking for the key in no time, and then he'll know for sure. And she's still got the book, digging in her belly and her breasts.

She stops sweeping and heads to the kitchen, which is closer to the door, hoping the book won't fall out. The only thing holding it is her thin belt, which is not meant to carry weight.

She cleans the kitchen table, listening for Notaras' steps, but he's not going anywhere. He stands there watching her as she finishes cleaning the table, then puts away the dishes.

When he finally leaves, Ali blasts through the door, holding the book against her chest. She runs like she's chased by the devil until she gets home, slams the door behind her, and leans against it. She catches her breath, then takes out the book and opens it.

CHAPTER 72

THE WRONG CATCH

"Are you kidding me?" Ion asks, staring in disbelief at the illuminated Bible Ali got him. "Out of everything there, this is what you got?"

Ali's brain is so hot with fury that she can't see straight. "Yes. Feel free to return it and get whatever you want. There." She slams the key on the table, forcing herself to stay calm, but it's just as easy as stopping a storm. She's so angry her mouth is too dry to swallow. But it's not Ion's fault. He has no idea how that went. So, she tells him. "He knows I took the key. He may not know what else I took, but he's suspicious. I may need your emperor's protection if Notaras accuses me of theft."

"Will you go back and try again?"

"Are you out of your mind? Nothing in the world will get me back there."

Ion's shoulders slump, and his face falls. He doesn't argue but looks so dejected that Ali's fury melts, and she feels terrible.

"Listen, Ion, what exactly is the point of all this? I've been trying for months, and I couldn't find those ledgers. I still can't. And even if I did, what good would it do?"

"If you found them, I could go through them to find the missing money. I'm sure Notaras skims the taxes and steals the money from the treasury. I know it like I know I'm breathing. I just can't prove it."

"If you could, what would you do?"

"I'd tell the emperor."

"And what would he do?"

"He'd probably demote Notaras and confiscate his estate."

"And then?"

"We'd have more money for guns and soldiers and supplies."

"Listen, Ion. I tried. I couldn't make it happen. If they catch me, they'll put me in jail unless Notaras kills me first. And we're doing all this to demonstrate to Constantine that the megas doux is stealing him blind? Unless your emperor is stupid, he already knows it and pretends he doesn't."

"But he has no proof!"

"He doesn't need proof to remove a thief from holding the keys to his treasury. He just needs balls. And I can't get them for him no matter how hard I try. He needs to grow his own."

Ion stares at her like he's never seen her before. "Are you really going to quit? After everything we've been through?"

"Not at all. This was never my fight; it was yours. I tried to help you, but I had enough. I need to move on to do something useful."

"Like what?"

"I don't know. Do you have any ideas?"

"How about if you spoke to the emperor?"

"About what?"

"About Mehmed. You know him better than any of us. Maybe you could help the emperor better understand Mehmed and enlighten him about what's happening."

"It's obvious what's happening. Mehmed built a fortress to block the Bosporus, and he's getting ready to take Constantinople. Which part of it is hard to get?"

But in the end, she agreed.

Ion paced as he watched her get ready. She washed her face, brushed and braided her hair, then put on her coat.

"OK."

"This is it?"

"What?"

"You'll go like this?"

"Like what?"

"That worn gray coat. And the old shoes. You're dressed like you're going to Notaras to clean."

"What would you like me to dress like?"

"Don't you have something more... fancy? You're going to see the emperor."

"No, I don't. This is my coat, and these are my shoes. And if the emperor doesn't like them, he can look elsewhere."

Ion's tight lips tell Ali he's not happy. He'd like a more charming sister to introduce to the Roman Emperor.

But she gave up charms, and she's all he's got.

CHAPTER 73

CHARMING THE EMPEROR

But the emperor didn't seem to mind Ali's ratty clothes. Seated on his tall gilded throne with the seal that must dig into his ribs, he smiles at Ali and offers her a seat, then signals the servant to pour tea.

Ali takes it all in. She's never seen so much gold in one room, not even at Edirne Palace. There, they had marble, tiles, and carpets, but here it's all about gold. The dark stone walls are crammed with smoky icons in heavy gold frames. The dead emperors' portraits glow in gold, and so do the carved crosses hanging all over the walls. The candlesticks are gilded, too, as are the tea cups set with precious stones and even the emperor himself. His golden collar sits like a wagon wheel on his shoulders, holding up the heavy golden brocade aprons covering his front and back. They've got to weigh a ton, Ali thinks, wondering how he can walk carrying all that weight. Still, above all the gold, his tired face is open and kind, and his smiling eyes study Ali with interest. He's not young, but he's handsome, and Ali understands why Ion cares so much about him.

"Good to meet you, Ali. Ion tells me you know Mehmed."

"I do."

"How come?"

"I worked for him for a few years."

Constantine's eyes widen. "You worked for him? As what?"

"I was one of his eunuchs."

Constantine chokes on his tea, and Ali refrains from hitting him across his back to help unchoke him. It wouldn't do to strike the Roman Emperor, not even to keep him alive.

"One of his what?"

"Eunuchs. In the sarayi."

Constantine looks at her, then at Ion, then back at her.

Ali shrugs. "It's a long story, but yes, I know him. What can I help you with?"

"Tell me about him. How is he?"

"He's extraordinarily bright and has no trouble making decisions and sticking to them. He's loyal to his friends, but he's obsessed with greatness. To feel worthy, he must surpass all his ancestors' successes. And some of them are hard acts to follow."

"What are the things he loves?"

"He loves riding and hunting with his falcons. He also loves chess, which to him is like training for war. He loves planning, and he's a student of people."

"Does he love women?"

"He loves his wife Gülbahar, Bayezid's mother. But no, I don't think he's particularly interested in women, but he takes them to his bed to make him sons. The one person he really loves is my friend Radu, Vlad Dracul's youngest son. They grew up together, spend days and nights together, and some say they're much closer than friends should be."

Ion gasps. "Ali!"

"What?"

"You can't talk like that."

"Why not?"

"Because... because it's against God's law. And it's not natural."

Ali's eyebrows furrow. "Maybe not to you. But it seems pretty natural to them."

"Are you sure about that?" Constantine asks.

"Pretty sure. It's a poorly kept secret. Everybody knows it at the Ottoman Court."

"I wonder if that could come in handy," Constantine says.

"How so?"

"Like maybe threatening to let the cat out of the bag if he doesn't let us be?"

Ali laughs. "The cat's been out of the bag forever. Even his mother and his father knew it. Mehmed's wives do, too, but he couldn't care less about what anyone has to say. Not that anyone dares to say anything."

"How about Radu? Would he care?" Ion asks.

"Maybe. But then, so what?"

"We could pressure Radu into convincing Mehmed to leave Constantinople alone."

Ali shakes her head. "Listen, Emperor. If you think anything you could say or do will dissuade Mehmed from attacking Constantinople, think again. He's obsessed with taking Constantinople, and he's never been closer. Now that Rumeli Hisari is almost done, he'll gain control over the Bosporus and start the blockade. Then he'll start the siege. No amount of talking will make him go away. You'd better get ready."

"How are you so sure?" Ion asks.

"I know Mehmed. He's like a dog with a bone, and he can't let go. I can only think of two things that could save Constantinople. The first one would be to hold on and manage to keep him at bay, for a few months at least. The Ottomans hate long sieges, especially far from their supply lines."

"What's the second?"

"The second is having someone attack him somewhere else. In Anatolia or Albania, or wherever. That would force Mehmed to leave, since he can't keep his army here to hold a siege while the Ottoman Empire is threatened elsewhere. Your allies could help you from afar, even if they can't send you help here."

"You're a very sensible young lady," Constantine says, studying Ali without seeming to notice her worn coat or her shoes. His eyes move from her eyes to her lips, then lower, and Ali blushes. "Where did you learn all these things?"

"First, at home in Transylvania, then at the palace school and the sarayi. I heard many interesting conversations while I carried trays and poured wine."

"Yes. When you were a eunuch at the Ottoman court. What an extraordinary situation. I'd love to hear more about it sometime."

"Of course, my emperor. I would be honored."

"Come back, please. Ion, thank you for introducing your lovely sister to me. Next time, you don't need to trouble yourself. She and I can just chat on our own."

Ion nods, but his face darkens. He doesn't seem pleased to see how well the emperor and Ali get along.

CHAPTER 74

CONSTANTINOPLE, AUG 31 1452

Standing on his galley in the Bosporus, Mehmed contemplates Rumeli Hisari's proud towers stabbing at the sky and he can hardly hold his tears. *This has got to be the most beautiful castle on earth,* he thinks. There's never ever been anything like it. She's gorgeous, unpredictable, and full of promise, like a beautiful woman, but her lush orange curves silhouetted against the deep blue sky fill his heart with love like no woman ever did.

Because this one is his fruit. Not the fruit of his loins, but the fruit of his spirit. He designed her out of love. Out of love for Constantinople, the city he covets more than he ever wanted a woman. Even more than he desires Radu, though that's hard to contemplate.

"Isn't she beautiful?" he asks.

Radu smiles. "Of course, she is. And the sunset..."

"Forget the bloody sunset. We're talking about the castle. MY castle. She'll help me bleed Constantinople until it crumbles into dust so I can resurrect it. Just look at those towers!" He's more passionate about those towers than he's ever been about breasts, and the castle brings him more joy than his children, his wives, and even his lovers.

The fortress blooms like a rose, opening towards the wide tower in the middle. Her crenelated walls climb gracefully towards her heart; the slim lower towers, like a queen's ladies-in-waiting, are there to enhance her beauty. Her safety, too. Between them, those walls hold more cannons than any other castle in the world. And the Basilica.

That was a fateful day, when Orban landed on Mehmed's doorstep, even if he didn't know it at the time. He had finished his divan meeting, and the dignitaries were leaving when the guards brought in a strange man. His hair stuck out, his wrinkled face was smudged with soot, but his eyes glowed with hope. He wasn't alone. The youth beside him, still a kid, carried a bag of scrolls.

"Who's this?" Mehmed inquired.

"Some crazy foreigner with a kid. He said he'll help you take Constantinople," the guard said.

That was enough for Mehmed. He called them in, even though Çandarlı Paşa and even Radu looked out of sorts.

"What do you have for me?"

The man burst forward with a bunch of scrolls, but the guards grabbed him before he got close to the sultan and he froze in his tracks.

Mehmed pointed to the table in the middle of the room. "What have you got?"

"I have the mother of all cannons, my sultan. The cannon that will take Constantinople for you, Your Highness. I have the Basilica."

"What's the Basilica?"

The man smiled sheepishly. "That's what I call her. She needed a special name, since she's like no other gun on earth. The Basilica will be the largest cannon ever made. Her barrel is twenty four feet long and can throw projectiles weighing a thousand pounds further than a mile. I'm unsure how much further, because she still needs to be built. But I've finished the design, and I know she will help you pick the Red Apple."

Mehmed nodded. "I see. You're from..."

"Hungary."

"Catholic?"

"Yes."

"Therefore, Christian."

"Of course."

"Of course. So, if you're a Christian — and you know I'm not — why did you come to me? Doesn't your Christian God want you to save Constantinople instead of crushing it? The Romans aren't Catholics, but they're Christians. Orthodox Christians, not Muslims like us. So why bring your invention to me instead of taking it to Constantine?"

Orban looked down, and his face darkened. "I went to Constantine."

"And?"

"He can't afford me. He said his coffers are empty, and he can barely stay alive. He offered us an IOU that he'd pay as soon as you withdraw your troops from Constantinople."

"And?"

Orban shrugged. "That wasn't good enough."

Mehmed smiled pleasantly and pushed the plans aside. "So, you came to me, of course."

"Of course."

"Who's the young man?"

"My son. He helped me with everything, from the beginning to the end. He's the one person who could build the Basilica without me if need be."

The son, a youth with blushing cheeks, smiled and bowed. They both looked like nice and decent folks, and made Mehmed very glad that he was not a Christian. *Being a Muslim isn't always easy, but one thing is sure: for us, faith always trumps money. I'd never lend my allegiance to the enemies of my faith just because the people of faith cannot pay. That's why the Christians will fail. Their true allegiance is not to their God, but to their purse. That's why I'll take Constantinople. Not because I'm smarter, braver, or further thinking, but because my allegiance to Allah is complete. Nothing matters more to me than conquering Constantinople for Allah's greater glory. That's why I'll win*, he thought. He nodded and smiled at the kid. "I'm glad you came to me. How much did you ask Constantine for?"

Orban bowed and mumbled something.

"How much?"

Orban cleared his throat. "Ten thousand ducats."

Mehmed smiled. "That's a lot of money, my man. Way more than anyone would pay for something that hasn't yet been built. What if you can't build it? What if it doesn't work? What if it blows apart when you fire it?"

Orban's shoulders slumped. He shrunk into his rags and rolled his plans, looking defeated. Mehmed watched him squirm until the man turned to leave.

"I'll pay you twice as much to have the Basilica up and running in three months. And I'll double that when we take Constantinople," Mehmed said.

"Three months is a short time. May I..."

"Of course. You may also try to go back to Constantine. Three months."

Orban bowed deeply. "I'll be back."

"I'll be here."

That was many moons ago. Now, the Basilica sits in Rumeli Hisari, ready to change the world, and Mehmed has never been so in love.

CHAPTER 75
FOR LOVE OR FAITH

The Rumeli Hisari is almost ready. For months, five thousand men have worked as if chased by the devil, competing to build the towers. Mehmed promised to pay the winners twice as much of the others, which got them all cracking. The giant towers are almost done now, but there's still no clear winner. The curtain walls are almost ready, too. One more week, and it will be done, Radu thinks.

"How will you use it?" he asks Mehmed.

They stand holding hands on top of Çandarlı Paşa's tower, the tallest of them all, watching Constantinople's evening golden glow shimmer across the water. A salty summer breeze caresses their faces, bringing the scent of the sea. White seagulls dart about, screaming their plaintive cries over the rhythmic sound of the waves. It's a magic moment together after the incessant hassle and bustle of the last few months, and Radu's heart bursts with love.

Mehmed smiles. "I'll cut Constantinople off from the world. I'll tax every ship going in or out of their protected Golden Horn, and I won't let those that carry weapons, soldiers, or supplies go through. This winter we'll starve Constantinople to weaken their resolve and willingness to fight and make it an easy target in spring."

"What will you do if the ships don't stop?"

"Sink them, of course. That will give the cannon masters a chance to practice for next year, when we take Constantinople. The Bosporus is narrow here, barely half a mile, and the current is swift, so the ships will be easy targets. We'll have no trouble stopping any reinforcements they get from the west, if any. Because truth be told, those hypocrites don't give a hoot about Constantinople. The pope dismissed Constantine's pleas for help, saying he wanted the churches to unite first. What a joke! A thousand-year-old Christian civilization, the whole Eastern Roman Empire, is about to get swallowed by us Muslims, and the pope is preoccupied with uniting of the churches."

As much as he loves Mehmed, Radu is still a Christian, and Constantinople is the home of his faith. This hurts.

Mehmed touches his shoulder. "Radu, let's get this straight: When Constantinople falls, it won't be because of me. It will be because of the Christians. They're a bunch of short-sighted, mercantile, self-centered cowards. Any idiot can see that once I take Constantinople, nothing will stop me from heading west to take the rest of the Christian world. Still, they won't lift a finger to help Constantine. Isn't that amazing?"

Radu's blood heats to a boil. "You really think you have room to talk?"

Mehmed's eyes widen. "What are you talking about?"

"Remember last week when Constantine sent you his emissaries to talk peace? You didn't even listen. You sent him their heads in a bloody bag."

Mehmed is so outraged he stutters. "Are you nuts? I was doing Constantine a favor!"

"Seriously? How exactly is that a favor?"

"I made it abundantly clear, beyond a shadow of a doubt, that I'm not interested in peace. Not now, not ever. If the emperor wants to save his city, he must surrender. Now. I was honest with him, unlike his so-called friends, who promise to help him if he jumps through their hoops but won't really commit. Constantine and his city would be better off if his Christian friends were half as blunt as I am.

"Because I know — and you do too, unless your faith has fogged your brain — that nobody will come to help Constantine. Nobody. Not the pope, who wants the union but not the trouble the Orthodox bring, not Hunyadi, who's still licking his wounds, not the Genoese, since he's out of money. Just look at Orban, the cannon maker. He's a Christian, but he works for me to crush Constantinople.

"The city is doomed, and the sooner Constantine understands it, the better off they'll be. If he surrenders, I will let his people go, and I'll take the city without plunder. That won't be easy, you know, since my army counts on the loot. They expect money, gold, and women. Boys, too. Forbidding the plunder will make me unpopular. They may even revolt, but I'll risk it if Constantine agrees to surrender. But will he?"

Radu sighs. "I don't think so. But even if he doesn't, you don't have to act like a savage."

"A savage? Me?"

"You and your troops. Will you really let your men plunder and rape the city?"

Mehmed's fallen jaw closes with a snap. "You have a better plan?"

"How about showing them mercy and letting them go?"

"And how am I going to reward my men? You think they're risking their lives for their janissary salary, which gets thinner every time I mint new coins? No, my friend. They're here to get rich. That loot will keep them safe when they're too old to fight. I can't deny my soldiers their customary rights to save a city that defies me. That's why I offered a chance to surrender." Radu sighs, and Mehmed looks at him with worry. "Listen, my friend. I know Christians are your people, and you care about them. But you need to open your mind and think beyond that. Christianity is a rotten religion that has run its course. I hope you see the light and come to us. Please convert and receive Allah's mercy and love."

Mehmed puts his arms around him, but Radu can't stand his

touch. Even the beloved scent of his skin turns his stomach. He's angry, guilty, and torn; the last thing he wants is love. He'd much rather fight.

Mehmed hugs him close. His breath quickens, and he sneaks a hand into Radu's shalwars, but Radu slaps it off and pushes him away.

Mehmed sighs. "I'm sorry you're upset, but I understand. This must be hard for you. How about we talk about this tomorrow?"

Radu shakes his head. "No. Enough is enough. We'll never talk about this again, but let me put it straight to you now. I've been a lousy Christian and a terrible son to my father and my country. I ignored her to fall in love with the Ottoman Empire — its beauty, its comfort, its sophistication. I loved it more than I did Wallachia. If my father saw me, he'd roll in his grave. But abandoning God to become a Muslim? That's like shedding my skin to turn into a wolf. I can't, and I won't. I am who I am, and if you don't like it, feel free to find someone else for your nightly romps."

Torn between love and guilt, Radu turns his back to Mehmed to gaze at Constantinople. He never cared much about his faith, but now that the Orthodox Church is in danger, he's distraught that he ever helped Mehmed.

If Christianity falls, it will be his fault.

CHAPTER 76

TRANSYLVANIA, 1452

Summer gave way to the fall, and the hot days are over in Transylvania's green hills. Thick frost whitens the grass in the morning, and the long nights come with spooky shimmering shadows and mysterious calls in the dark. Unseen creatures roam the woods, whooshing, whispering, and hissing all night long, getting Vlad's heart racing and stirring something inside him like he's touched by magic.

"What was that?" He gasps, when a piercing howl splits the air.

"What was what?" Ștefan asks, spurring his horse forward.

They've been here for months, hiding in some place or other. They barely made it when the Kronštadt burghers threw them out after Hunyadi threatened death to whoever sheltered Vlad. He was lucky they let him go instead of offering him to Hunyadi like a trussed chicken. But, since hate is often stronger than fear, they found someone else to give them shelter. They're now the guests of a boyar who left Wallachia and settled here, in the Amlaș, waiting for someone to topple Vladislav, the usurper.

They're hunting today, and the hounds caught an old deer's scent and went crazy. They're all gone, so Ștefan and Vlad sit perched on their horses, watching the full moon pour its silver light over the forest and waiting for the hounds.

The woods are so tranquil they're magic, and Vlad can't help but feel moved. "What a beautiful country. The shimmering stars and the softness of the silent night smelling like incense and mushrooms. Don't you love it?"

Ștefan shrugs. "Sure. But what are we waiting for?"

"The dogs, of course."

Ștefan cuts his sharp blue eyes towards Vlad. He's not good with waiting, Ștefan. For him, it's easier to do things, whether right or wrong, than wait. Ștefan is a storm waiting for a place to land. Vlad used to be like that too, but his years in jail, first in Tokat and then in Eğrigöz, taught him patience. He doesn't like it, but he learned that patience is a weapon. Just like striking, it just takes more work.

"You know damn well I'm not talking about the dogs," Stefan says. "What are we doing here? We've been hiding for months while my father's killer sits on Moldova's throne, and Vladislav the second, who killed your father and brother, rules Wallachia. And we've done nothing but hunt."

"We're waiting for the tide to turn."

"How? Why? What do you expect to happen?"

Vlad shrugs, wishing he knew. "I don't know, Ștefan. All I know is that I must be ready when it happens. Whether Mehmed gets killed, Hunyadi falls out with the Hungarian diet, your uncle Petru Aron's horse throws him and breaks his neck, or Vladislav chokes on a chicken bone — I don't know. But, sooner or later, something will change the tide, so we'd better be ready when it does."

Ștefan smirks. "Petru Aron is your uncle too, you know. He's your mother's brother, like my father was."

"I know. But he only matters to me because of you. I never met him and don't plan to, even though I'd gladly kill him if I had a chance. But he stands between you and your throne. He's yours to take on."

"I can't wait. But doing nothing is killing me. How much longer will we sit on our hands while..."

Somewhere to the left, the dogs scream, calling them to the trail. Vlad and Stefan spur their horses, racing into the depths of the woods. Ștefan's mount stumbles and he falls behind. Vlad pushes his horse forward.

The forest grows darker and darker under the thick canopy. Low branches claw at Vlad, pulling him off his horse, but he leans forward, holding on with his thighs and laying his cheek on his neck. He's one with his horse as they fly through the forest like an arrow.

Until they find the light.

Something glows in the woods, spooking the horse. He rears, and Vlad struggles to hold on.

An old stag stands still between the trees, staring Vlad in the eye. He glows like gold, and the star between his antlers burns Vlad's eyes with its light. The dogs see him, and they cry and cower.

Vlad lifts his bow and grabs an arrow.

He pulls back the string, closes his left eye, then lets out a breath and softens his fingers, ready to let the arrow go, when the stag speaks. "Put down that arrow. You have no fight with the deer; your war is with your enemies, and they're on their way. Betrayal looms. Get ready, little brother."

Vlad's heart freezes. "Mircea? Is that you?"

But the stag has already vanished. The dogs start yapping; a clatter of hooves closes in, and Ștefan arrives.

"Did you see that?" Vlad whispers.

"See what?"

"The stag."

"What stag?"

Vlad glances at Ștefan to see if he's joking, but he's not. He's damn serious and quite pissed.

"We need better dogs," Ștefan mumbles, heading back.

Vlad follows, but something calls him, and he glances back. Hanging upside down from a branch, a round-eyed bat wrapped in his leathery wings stares at him.

The bat is smiling.

CHAPTER 77

THE HOT SPRINGS

Nestled in the heart of Transylvania between pine-covered mountain ridges, the tiny hamlet of Geoagiu is not found on most maps. It's older than dirt, but it's only home to a few dozen people, and they're old. The youth perished in the many wars, so the old folks struggle to make do. The fields somehow get plowed, the cows milked, and the sheep sheared, but little life is left.

The tiny church is built from river rocks and old bricks stolen from the thousand-year-old Roman ruins nearby, and its stinky hot springs are said to cure illness and relieve pain. That's why sick people from everywhere have been coming here since Jesus was born. The engraved Roman plates declare it a place of pilgrimage and healing, but Vlad is wary. He feels that this place wants him to fail. That's silly, of course, since places have no souls nor plans. I've been hiding for too long, he thinks, slowing his horse to wait for Ștefan.

"Let's stop here for the night," Ștefan says. "Should be good enough."

Vlad nods, though something tells him to move on. But they've been traveling for hours, and the sun is about to set.

They left Sibiu this morning, and they made good time. They're heading to Buda, Hungary's capital, to meet The Man. Hunyadi himself invited Vlad over.

Ștefan frowned when he heard. "Are you sure? I wouldn't trust Hunyadi further than I can throw him, and I couldn't throw him far. I'm afraid he's more likely to kill you than help you."

Vlad shook his head. "I don't think so. His love affair with Vladislav the Second is over, since that filthy usurper started paying tribute to Mehmed. That's not why Hunyadi put him on Wallachia's throne. He may not be ready to get rid of him just yet, but he's looking at options. And I'm one."

They headed to Buda, but Vlad felt someone watching him the whole way. He kept looking back, but nothing seemed amiss. Still, now that they reached the tiny hamlet and opened the inn's door, a wave of unease stirs inside him, telling him to beware. The innkeeper, a thin-lipped Hungarian, measures them with narrowed eyes.

"You're going where?"

"To Buda, to see Hunyadi."

The man rolls his eyes. "Isn't everyone? Why they all think Hunyadi has the magic touch to make a nobody into somebody, I can't imagine. But that's not my problem. Can you pay?"

Their money bag has thinned, but Vlad throws the man a couple of coins. "Enough?"

The man nods, suddenly friendly. "We'll look after your horses. You rode the whole day; you must be tired. Why don't you try the healing springs? They'll help your aches and pains and clean you up. People come to them from far away. They're that way, just a short walk away. You may as well go now, while we fix your rooms and cook your dinner. You'll thank me when you return."

They hand their horses to the stable boy and head to the springs, which are easy to find by the steam rising in the air. The yellow, murky water smells like rotten eggs, but its bubbly heat promises succor, and Vlad hasn't had a hot bath since he left the Ottoman Empire. He checks out the largest pool. It's big enough for five men to lie in, and it sits right at the edge of the forest, surrounded by flat stones that the water dyed yellow and orange.

Vlad and Ștefan take off their weapons, boots, and dusty clothes to step on the slippery stones into the steaming water. It's so hot it sears their skin, but the heat soon turns to relief. Vlad sinks all the way to his chin, rests his head on the lip of the pool and closes his eyes. Ștefan gasps, but the heat softens him too. He lies next to Vlad to listen to the silence.

Vlad looks at the stars, wondering which one is his and where it will take him, though he knows only he can shape his future. But not tonight. Tonight, he'll let the hot water melt the aches in his back, listen to the crickets, and enjoy Stefan's company.

"This is something else," Ștefan says, sinking in the water to his chin. "Smells awful, but it feels heavenly. I didn't know something like this existed."

"Much like the Turkish baths, though they smell better. They're man-made and come with servants, soap, and masseurs."

"You miss the Ottoman Empire?"

"Are you kidding? I miss it like a hole in the head. But they have some good things. Like the hammam."

"What else?"

"Their discipline. Their emphasis on values instead of money. Their incredible interrogation techniques. But I wouldn't be one of them if you paid me."

"Why not? You seem to like a lot about them."

"About their traditions, not about them. I don't care for them one bit. They're consumed by their faith. Can you imagine praying every day, five times a day? Whenever they hear the call to prayer, they'll stop whatever they're doing, wash, and pray. Unbelievable. And they all think with one brain: the Prophet's. They have no mind of their own; they're like a flock of sheep waiting for slaughter."

Stefan shrugs. "They've done pretty well for a bunch of sheep."

"Until someone slaughters them. And that's going to be me."

Ștefan smiles. "That's a plan. I'm with you."

They lay without talking, enjoying each other's company and the healing heat that melts away their aches. It's a rare moment of repose, and Vlad's eyes start closing when he hears something jangle.

"Did you hear that?"

But Ștefan's already out. All naked, he pulls out his sword from its scabbard.

"May be just visitors coming to soak in the springs," Vlad says, but he grabs his sword too.

"Let's do a little laundry," Ștefan whispers, and throws his cloak into the water. Under the moon's dim light, the dark cloth looks like a body in the pool.

Vlad does the same, and they melt behind the trees, buck-naked and armed to the teeth.

CHAPTER 78

A NAKED FIGHT

The cadence of the hooves slows down as they near. Someone looking for the hot springs, unless they're looking for them. Hidden in the shade of an old oak and breathing softly through his mouth to make no sound, Vlad wishes he wasn't naked. The nakedness makes him feel vulnerable, even though he's got both his sword and his dagger. An icy gust of wind hits him from the back, making him shiver, and he clenches his teeth to stop them from chattering.

"They've got to be close," a raspy voice says in Romanian.

"Be careful. The innkeeper said they took their weapons."

"How worried can they be? They left their horses behind, and they don't even know we're after them."

Dead leaves rustle in the darkness.

"What was that?" the first man asks.

"What was what?"

"That noise."

"I didn't hear a thing."

"Sure you didn't. You're deafer than a bishop. Something stirred in the forest."

"Come on, man. It's a damn forest, full of rabbits, squirrels, deer, and bears. They all move. And the darn wind. Get over it, will you? They're just a couple of snot-nosed kids who don't even know we're after them. They won't know what hit them. Slow down everybody. Get off your horses and tie them to the trees. We'll walk the rest of the way. Surprise is our best weapon."

They creep, rustling the dead leaves, but the pool of water reflecting the moon stops them in their tracks.

"There they are," someone whispers.

"Neculai, Ciolac, and I will take the one on the left. You, Gheorghe, and Dan take the one on the right. Be fast and show no mercy. Vladislav wants Vlad's head."

"How about the other one? Nobody wants him."

"He's out of luck. He should have kept better company."

They sneak towards the pool, tall shadows holding swords that glimmer in the moonlight.

"I'll take the left. You take the right," Vlad whispers.

"OK."

The men give up their secrecy and leap towards the pool, slashing at the floating cloaks as Ștefan and Vlad creep from behind.

Vlad's first enemy is still in the shade when Vlad slides his dagger across his throat from behind. He kills him like he'd kill a chicken. The man whimpers, then crumbles to the ground without a word. A hot fountain spurts from his severed neck, splashing Vlad from head to toe. He tastes the salt and the iron in the blood, and it's the best thing he's ever tasted. He bubbles with joy as he closes on the next one. He glances right at Ștefan to see his first kill dropping like a bag of grain. As white and silent as a wraith, Ștefan wipes his blade on the man's chest and moves on.

There's something unreal about fighting naked, Vlad thinks. He's never done it before, but bathing in fresh blood exhilarates him and gives him strength. It's like a magic shield giving him vigor. He follows the other two men in the moonlight.

"Watch out," the first one says, hacking at Vlad's cloak to kill it. The next one pushes closer to help. He slips on the wet rock, but doesn't get to fall, since Vlad's blade severs his throat before he hits the ground. The man gasps, a weird noise between a sigh and a cough.

"I told you to be careful," the first man says. "Are you hurt?"

"No," Vlad answers, dropping the dagger and lifting the sword. "I'm good."

He glances at Ștefan, who's still in the shade. He also dumped his dagger for his sword, but he's still got two to go. The man ahead of him turns around, and his eyes pop out of his head.

"What the…?"

Ștefan's sword sings as it slices the air, so that's all the man gets to say before the moonlit blade carves him from the shoulder to the hip. Blood bursts, painting Ștefan's pale body dark red.

Vlad lifts his weapon sideways to behead his last foe when the man turns to look back. His jaw falls, and he stares into Vlad's eyes, paler than a ghost. "Who are you?" he asks.

Vlad smiles, and his sword severs the man's head from his body before he understands what happened. The bearded head rolls to the ground like a ripe cantaloupe while the body still stands. Vlad wipes his blade on his tunic before what's left of the man crumples into a heap at his feet.

"Save the last one," he shouts at Ștefan.

"Why do you always have to have all the fun?" Ștefan asks, his bloody blade glowing in the moonlight. "Why didn't you keep yours?"

Vlad nods. "Come on. I'll let you have the next one."

The man glances from one to the other, his eyes like trapped rats. He lifts his long sword, but his hands tremble as he stares at them.

Ștefan smiles. "I'll let you live if you drop the sword. Don't feel you have to, though. My cousin already owes me a lot."

The man's crazy glare moves from Ștefan to Vlad. His eyes are huge and white as he gawks at the two naked men who killed his partners and now gang up on him. Livid with terror, he drops his sword.

Ștefan sighs. "He's all yours."

"Who sent you?" Vlad asks.

The man crumbles into a heap at his feet. "Please let me live. It's not my fault…"

"Who sent you?"

"Vladislav."

"Why?"

"To kill you."

"How did you find me?"

"The innkeeper told us where you were."

"What next?"

"We were supposed to bring your head back to Vladislav, so he knew we'd done the job."

"How did you know it was me?"

"Dark he said. Green-eyed, he said. But we were going to bring you both anyhow. Just to be sure."

Vlad nods at Ștefan. "Good enough. He's all yours."

Ștefan shakes his head. "Nope. I promised to let him live if he spoke. He spoke."

"You're going to let something like that get in your way?"

"My vows are important to me. I have no throne, no army, and no money, so my word is all I've got these days. How about you?"

Vlad shrugs. "Your call."

He turns to the man. "Stay here. You can leave tomorrow morning. But tonight, if you want to stay alive, catch a nap and try the waters. They're wonderful."

As they ride away on the men's horses, Ștefan asks. "Would you really have killed that man after vowing to let him live?"

Vlad smirks. "We'll never know, will we?"

CHAPTER 79

CONSTANTINOPLE, FALL 1452

A frightful winter looms over Constantinople. Every new day is shorter and drearier than the last, Ion thinks, hustling home under the frozen rain whipping the stands along the narrow street. Here, in Constantinople, you can tell the seasons from the street merchants. Right now, the tables bow under the weight of red apples, bumpy quinces as hard as rocks, glowing amber grapes, and more cheeses than you can count. In spring, it's all green: tiny radishes peek between bunches of green leaves, bearded green onions, and fresh garlic with long leaves like thin green blades, all pretty enough to put in a vase. And crispy lettuce and lacy parsley and fragrant celery and pink wild strawberries, everyone a tiny flavor bomb. The summer belongs to the long, plump tomatoes, prickly cucumbers, dark-blue eggplant with hidden veins of purple, and fat green melons with ruby-red flesh sweeter than honey.

Just thinking of them makes Ion's stomach grumble, and he wonders what's for dinner tonight. Did Ali cook, or did she buy olives, hummus, and wine? His mouth waters, and he picks up the pace, looking forward to dinner and seeing her freckled, bright face.

Today sucked. It's been another lousy day with no good news for the empire's treasury — other than the lack of disasters, and Ion can't wait to get home to their tiny place behind the bazaar.

The door is locked. Bummer. Ion wonders where Ali went and how long until she brings dinner. He looks around the kitchen for something to eat, but there's nothing. The kitchen smells like many things, but none of them is dinner.

He scratches his head, wondering where she could be. Shopping? But it's almost dark. She should be back any moment. Unless she left. The thought freezes his heart. She can be like that, Ali. She gets something in her head and just goddamn disappears. Not forever, thank God, but still.

He waits and waits. Nothing happens. When he tires of sitting, he lies in his bed and leaves the door open so he can hear her.

He awakes to the door slamming shut. Ali is home.

She looks a tad flushed, but her eyes sparkle, and she smiles. "Hi. Sorry, I'm late."

Ion sighs. "I'm glad you're safe. I was worried. Where have you been?"

"At the palace. Constantine invited me for dinner, and I think I had too much wine."

Ion's jaw falls. "You dined with Constantine?"

Ali takes off her soggy coat. Underneath, she still wears her old dress, which is too big and shiny from too much ironing, and Ion feels strangely reassured.

"How did that come about?" he asks.

"I went to gather some plants from the gardens and..."

"What plants?"

"Healing plants from the garden."

"What garden?"

"The palace gardens. So, I gathered..."

"Why would you gather plants?"

"For the wounded. The war is about to start, and many will get hurt. And I learned a bit about healing, remember? Sadly, I forgot my incantations and most of my potion recipes, but I can still help with wounds and burns. And I know how to relieve pain. When the war starts, I want to do my share, so I need to get ready. So, I've been gathering plants and drying them to make ointments and potions…"

"How long have you been doing this?"

"Since I ditched Notaras."

Ion suddenly realizes he never wondered what Ali does the whole day after he leaves for work in the morning and doesn't come back before dinner. He vaguely thought she cleaned their place, shopped, and cooked dinner. In all these months, it never crossed his mind to ask.

"So, you gathered plants."

"Yes. Then the rain started, and I sheltered under the eaves, waiting for it to stop. I don't mind getting wet, you know, but the plants get moldy and rot."

"And then?"

"Constantine passed by. He asked what I was doing, and I told him. He invited me for dinner. Boy, what a dinner! His treasury may suck, but his cook doesn't. And that wine! We had suckling pig with salad and a yummy spongy omelet he called *sphoungata* and honey cakes and…"

Ion's stomach growls. "Stop this, will you? I didn't have dinner, you know? What happened next?"

"I'm sorry."

"Sure. So, what did you talk about?"

"He wanted to know about the Ottomans. He asked me about Mehmed and Radu and about my job as a eunuch. He seemed to have trouble wrapping his mind around it."

"What did you tell him?"

"I told him I was a fake, but I was lucky enough to get out of there before I got caught."

"Did you tell him about Kronštadt? About our mission?"

"Of course not. Are you crazy?" Ali looks indignant. Her outrage would be even more convincing if the hiccups didn't make her stutter every other word.

"Did he make passes at you?"

"Passes?"

"Did he try to get into your pants?"

"May I point out that I'm wearing a dress? Thanks to you, of course. You said I couldn't pass for a man."

Ion sighs. "Come on, Ali. Did Constantine try to get you into his bed?"

"Not exactly."

"What's that supposed to mean?"

"Well, he didn't ask me to his bed. But he told me he was in dire need of a wife, and he wanted to know if I happened to have any royal blood. Apparently, the son of God can't marry a commoner."

Ion laughs. "What did he say when you said no?"

Ali smiles, and the light in her eyes warms his heart. "I didn't. I haven't mentioned it, but I happen to be Alexandru the Good's granddaughter. That makes me a first cousin to Vlad and Radu."

Ion frowns. "Are you drunk?"

"A little."

He stares at her, wondering what to think. "Are you serious? Are you really their cousin?"

"Yep."

"What did Constantine say?"

"He said he'll talk to Sphrantzes, who's the authority in all things imperial, and he'll get back to me."

Ion sighs and stares at Ali, scratching his head. Is she really of royal bone? And if she is, would the emperor really marry her? It's too much to digest. He'll think about it tomorrow.

But dinner?

"What do we eat?"

Ali smiles. "I ate, thanks. Why don't you get yourself something?"

CHAPTER 80

A STARTLING PROPOSAL

Ali's head feels like an overfilled water bucket the next morning. Her brain smashes against the inside of her skull whenever she moves, making her sick. Every heartbeat shoots a flash of pain into the swollen veins of her temples, and the light burns her eyes. The smell of the neighbors' cooking turns her stomach, and she wishes Constantine was less generous with his wine.

But, thank God, she gathered enough willow bark for an army, so she makes willow bark tea and endeavors to drink it. But her stomach twists and climbs to her throat, and that nasty tea wants to come out. She pushes it away and remembers Smaranda's hangover cure and her wise words. "The best cure for hangover is pickling juice. And tripe sour soup. The vinegar helps with the nausea, and the salt pulls out the water swelling the brain. And the garlic keeps away the vampires. But it's often best to let them suffer, so they learn to be more careful next time. Teaching folks a lesson serves them better than giving them relief."

She must have been right, but Ali has no stomach for lessons right now. Her hands shake, her head is about to blow up, and the nausea turns her inside out. And that's not even the worst.

The worst is that she can't remember whether she agreed to marry Constantine.

Sure, he's the emperor, and he's good-looking and all that, but she's not into marriage. Marriage is about swearing to obey your husband and making kids, and she's not into any of that. As a matter of fact, she didn't think she was into men at all, but meeting Signore Giovanni Giustiniani Longo taught her otherwise. It's been more than a year, but her heart still quickens when she thinks of him. And that's every day. Whenever she looks at a man, she compares him to the pirate, and they all come up short. And that's fine, since she needs a man like she needs a hole in the head.

The pickling fluid does its job, taming Ali's hangover enough to let her work on the plants she gathered yesterday. She should have done it last night — get them out, sort them, and set them to dry — but she didn't. She'll have to do it today.

She takes them out of her bag. There's mint, good for upset stomachs, heartburn, and diarrhea; chamomile, soothing for sore throats and cleansing for wounds; and chrysanthemum, good for the kidneys. She looked for poppies, but it's too late. Thank God she collected plenty in summer, because there's no better medicine than the milk of the poppy.

The ripe capsules bleed a heavenly milk that melts away the pain and puts people to sleep. Nothing works better to help people out of their misery, and there'll be plenty of that when the war starts. Whether they win or lose, Constantinople's soldiers will do their best, and Ali plans to do her share to relieve their suffering.

The last few months have been harsh in the city. After finishing Rumeli Hisari, his new fortress, Mehmed took charge of the Bosporus Strait like it's his back yard. He throttled the traffic to Constantinople down to nothing, and stopped all the ships bringing supplies, soldiers, or whatever else doesn't meet his fancy. Ever since his cannons sank the first Genoese galley, then rescued its sailors from drowning just to impale them on Rumeli Hisari's walls, nobody else dared to brave his blockade. Nothing can come in: no weapons, no soldiers, no wheat. A harsh winter is on its way, and Constantinople stands alone.

Ali sighs and hangs a bunch of mint over the stove. She grabs the chamomile to do the same when the door opens.

That's strange. It's not noon yet, and nobody but Ion ever comes here. Has Notaras finally come after her? Ali checks the dagger hidden in her boot and squeezes behind the door.

Ion shuffles in, his shoulders hunched under the weight of the world. "Ali?"

"I'm here." She slides her dagger back into its place. "What happened? I thought you went to work?"

"I did. But then I thought about something and came to speak to you. Can you spare a moment?"

Ali glances at the plants she's piled everywhere. She needs to deal with them, then go shopping and cook dinner, and she's already late, besides feeling like damaged goods. "If you don't mind me dealing with my stuff while we talk?"

"Not at all." Ion sighs and sits by the table with his chin in his hand, watching her.

Ali sorts the plants, bunching them loosely by type, then ties them together with string and hangs them on the hooks above the stove. The fragrant herbs make their place smell like an apothecary: lavender, chamomile, and mint, just like Smaranda's cottage, and the thought brings a smile to her face. She also needs some St. John's Wort, but she didn't find any. Must be too humble a plant to belong in the emperor's garden.

She glances at Ion, who sits scratching his head. He rubs his face, then scratches his ear, and Ali wonders if something bit him.

"Would you like something for your itch? I can make you an ointment. With mint and..."

"What itch?"

"You've been scratching."

"No thanks, I'm good." He crosses his hands on his chest and sighs, staring at her with his honest, worried eyes. "Ali. What about we got married?"

"Married? To whom?"

His mouth tightens, and his words come out clipped. "To each other. I marry you, and you marry me."

Ali wonders if he's sick. She touches his cheek, but he doesn't seem hot. Maybe he hit his head? She checks him carefully, but he looks fine other than being worried.

"What for?" she asks.

Ion's face darkens, and Ali feels bad. "I mean, we are like brother and sister, aren't we? We can't marry," she says.

"We aren't really brother and sister. We're not related at all. We can marry if we so choose."

"But your emperor thinks we're brother and sister. If you tell him otherwise, he'll think you lied. You'll lose his trust and your job, and you'll have to go elsewhere."

Ion sighs, taking this in. "How about we get married but not tell him?"

"What for?"

He blushes, and Ali wishes she'd kept her mouth shut, but he just won't leave her alone.

"To be together?"

"But we are together every day. Getting married won't get us any more together than we are."

Ion's eyes slide down to her mouth, then her chest, and she sighs. He's thinking about bed. That's too bad. She loves him dearly, more than she loves her own brothers, but she has no use for him in her bed. She'd take Constantine before him, and she'd take the pirate before either of them. She doesn't want to hurt him, but that's a no-no.

"I'm sorry, Ion. You stayed here for this war, and I agreed to help you. We're facing the most important war in the history of Christianity, and we have more important things to worry about than who to sleep with. I love you, but not in that way."

Ion sighs. "Are you going to marry Constantine?"

"I hope not. I just hope I didn't agree to it last night."

CHAPTER 81

BUDA, FALL 1452

The grand ballroom of Hunyadi's castle is the stuff of fairytales. Glowing marble walls rise from the shiny floors to the vaulted ceilings, so high they vanish in the darkness. Heavy velvet curtains hug the arched windows framing Buda's starry sky. Flickering candles reflect in the polished mirrors, throwing moving shadows behind the dancers tormenting the dance floor. Everything here glows, glitters, and gleams, from the women's bejeweled ears to the Murano chandeliers.

Standing alone in a corner, Lena pasted a smile on her face as she watches the dancers. She hopes her old blue dress doesn't look too shabby between all the golden brocades and blushing silks. She wasn't planning to be here tonight, but Erzsébet wouldn't take no for an answer.

It's been almost a year since Codru disappeared, and Lena has settled into her lonely life in Buda like she never lived elsewhere. Mircea's almost five, a lively kid who makes his mother proud. And life here isn't bad. Thanks to Codru's bequest, Lena can put food on the table and still have time to care for her son. But she hasn't yet made it to Lesbos, and that unfulfilled promise weighs her down.

She told no one, but she's still waiting for Codru to return, because she can't believe he's dead. He's the strongest man she's ever known. As a matter of fact, he's not even a man; he's a werewolf, so nobody could kill him unless they had a silver bullet or stabbed him with a silver blade. Maybe he got wounded and captured. Or perhaps he ran away for some reason, but he might still return. But, as month after month passed without news from him, she started losing faith.

The Hunyadis have been nice to her, and they never fail to invite her to their parties and introduce her to all sorts of men who try to get under her skirts. But she's not interested. She's still hoping for Codru's return, which is downright silly, since she didn't give a hoot about him when he was around. But life is what it is. And she's not interested in sharing her bed; she only cares about her son.

"Come tonight," Erzsébet told her that morning. "There's someone I want you to meet. You won't be sorry."

Lena smiled and shook her head, but Erzsébet would have none of it. "I insist. You must come tonight. And look pretty."

Lena didn't want to be rude, so she did her best. She donned the blue dress she hadn't worn since the dinner with Codru. Not a hard choice, since that's her only ball gown. She braided her hair and pinned it around her head into a crown, painted her lips with red beets, and lined her eyes with charcoal to make them look bigger, like the Muslim women who enhance their eyes with kohl. All in all, she went out of her way to look pretty.

And it worked. Her neck may not sparkle with diamonds, and her dress may not glitter with gold like the others, but the eligible Hungarian men swarmed around her, and the women glared at her, green with spite.

Lena smiled, danced, and acted charming, but her heart wasn't into it. The Hungarian nobles wouldn't kick her out of their bed, but marrying her? Not so much. She's neither wealthy nor noble, so she's not a catch. But it feels good to be wanted, so she may as well have fun.

Someone touches her arm. It's Erzsébet. "Lena, I have someone special to introduce you to. This young man once fought with your husband and remembers him well."

The man bows. He's tall and well-built, with clear blue eyes, an upturned blond mustache, and golden curls falling to his shoulders. And a crooked smile that touches Lena's heart.

"This is Ștefan Mușat, the son of Bogdan the Second and soon-to-be Moldova's voivode. Things in Moldova are murky right now, but he should get his rightful throne before too long."

Ștefan's eyes on her feel like a caress. He bows deeply and kisses the tips of her fingers, and Lena's heart melts. Oh, how she missed him!

"I'm so glad to make your acquaintance, my lady. You are even more beautiful in person than everyone said."

His eyes smile into hers, and she yearns to hug and kiss him, but that's not for here and now, even though he's the only man in the world she can trust. She curtsies. "I'm glad to meet you, too. I used to live in Moldova. I had a milk brother who meant the world to me, and his name was Ștefan, like yours. Have you met him, perchance?"

"Ștefan is a rather common name in Moldova, isn't it? And I've been a fugitive from my country. I still am. But I'll look for your brother when I return."

Lena nods. "He's a fugitive too. Life in Moldova isn't easy these days. If you ever meet him, please tell him that I love him, I miss him, and I can't wait to see him again."

Ștefan bows deeply and steps aside to make room for a dark-haired man to take his place. The man's green eyes sparkle with glee as they sink into hers.

"What a pleasure to meet you again, my lady. I've been looking forward to it for years. Your husband's name is Mircea, you said?"

Lena chokes. He's toying with her. But she must play his game to keep her son safe. "No, sir. You must be mistaken. My husband's name was Codru."

"Oh, really? Please forgive me. I misunderstood. I thought you were my brother Mircea's wife and his son's mother. My mistake. How is your husband?"

"My husband died fighting."

"I'm so sorry. He was a brave man. How is your son?"

Lena wonders how to get rid of him, but nothing comes to mind. "My son is well, thank you."

"Mircea, is it? He must be almost five. Is he still a good eater?"

Lena's eyes swing around for help.

Fortunately, Erzsébet is on her way. "Young men, let me introduce you to a few lovely ladies who are dying to meet you. Sadly, Lena is still in mourning. But there are..."

She slips her arms under Ștefan and Vlad's arms and drags them to the lone ladies hanging out along the walls, and Lena sighs with relief.

She sighs and leans out the window, looking into the night. What a total disaster! First, because Vlad may try to harm little Mircea to rid himself of a potential rival. And second, because, if he lets the truth come out, she's cooked.

Hunyadi and his wife have been kind to her and little Mircea. They sheltered them, thinking they were Codru's family. But they aren't. They're Mircea's family.

What would Hunyadi do if he found out that little Mircea is the son of the prince that his men blinded with hot pokers and buried alive? And the grandson of Vlad Dracul, whom they killed in the marshes of Bâlteni? Would he let him grow up into a man and seek revenge? Or would he kill him like he did his father and grandfather?

Vlad is a threat to little Mircea, but Hunyadi is, too. If he finds out, her son's life is in danger. Lena needs to hide him before it's too late. But where?

She could go back to Moldova, or to Codru's estate in Transylvania. But he'd find them there. Maybe cross the Danube to Mehmed? She needs to think.

She heads towards the door when a hand grabs her arm. It's Vlad, of course, and his devilish eyes glow with glee. "Please allow me to escort you, my lady. I so wish we could talk. I can't wait to learn how my brother's son became the offspring of some Transylvanian peasant. But there's no rush. I'll be here for a while, and I can't wait to see little Mircea. Tomorrow?"

Lena nods.

"I'll be there tomorrow at noon," Vlad says, kissing her hand with unmatched chivalry.

Her heart racing, Lena flies through the door. She's wondering how to kill him without getting caught.

CHAPTER 82
RUN

Buda is asleep by the time Lena makes it home. The old neighbor who looks after Mircea is snoring peacefully by his side, so Lena wakes her up and sends her home.

"Should I come back tomorrow?"

"I'll let you know."

She waits for the woman to be gone before starting to pack. She can't take much. There's no way to find a carriage before the morning, so she'll have to leave on foot and find a horse on the way. She can only take what she can carry, and she has to carry Mircea if she wants to move fast. And he's a chunky kid, so she can't take much besides him.

She unlaces her ballgown and throws it on a chair, then opens the coffer holding Codru's stuff. She puts on brown woolen breeches, a linen chemise, and a dark cloak. His wide leather belt is way too big, so she wastes precious seconds she doesn't have to hammer a nail into it and make a new hole. That's loud as heck, so she glances at Mircea. He's still asleep, thank God.

Her moneybag goes on the belt. So does Codru's spare dagger and her faithful ax. She wraps a change of clothes for Mircea in a blanket, ties it around her back, and she's ready to go.

But for one thing.

She looks in the polished mirror and releases the braid wrapped around her head. It falls down to her hip, dark-gold and thicker than her wrist. It hurts her heart to lose it, but she has no choice if she wants to keep Mircea safe. She grabs a kitchen knife and hacks at the braid until it falls off. She packs it with Mircea's clothes and runs her fingers through what's left of her hair. The uneven, loose curls fall no lower than her shoulders, and look like they've been chopped with an axe. Oh well. She wipes a tear and sticks Codru's sheepskin hat on her head. It's so big it falls to her eyebrows, but it hides her hair and keeps her warm.

She picks up Mircea, who's warm, soft, and heavy in his sleep, and ties him in a blanket around her shoulders. He mumbles something and puts his chubby arms around her neck. His head falls on her shoulder, and she prays to God to give her strength to carry him.

She glances back at this place that has been their home for years, wondering if she'll ever see it again. Probably not. This is just the latest escape out of many, all dangerous, all meant to keep Mircea safe. And all worth it.

She sighs and opens the door. Silent as a ghost, she steps into the night.

Two men step forward.

Lena gasps and reaches for her axe, but they're faster. They grab her and drag her back inside, slamming the door shut.

She fights and claws and bites. They let her go, but block the door.

"I told you," Vlad says.

"You were right. I owe you a golden ducat. I'll pay you as soon as I get my hands on one. Hi, Lena," Ștefan says.

"What the heck are you two doing here?"

"We came to visit." Vlad drags a chair to block the door. "I told Ștefan you'd take off. He didn't believe me, but I knew. You were too fast to agree to see me tomorrow. I knew I'd come and find the nest empty. Why?"

"Why what?"

"Why did you run away?"

Lena scowls. She unties the blanket and lies Mircea back in his bed. His thumb in his mouth, dark curls falling over his white face, he's still asleep, thank God, despite all the noise and commotion.

"He looks just like my brother," Vlad says, touching the dark curls with his finger.

Lena wants to shove him away, but there's no point. He won't hurt him now, with Ștefan watching. She drops her bundle and takes off her hat.

The men gasp.

"What on earth did you do?" Ștefan's eyes widen with horror, and Vlad's mouth falls agape as they stare at what's left of her hair.

"I got a haircut. So, to what exactly do I owe the pleasure of your unexpected visit?"

"We wanted to speak to you," Vlad says, sitting on the chair at the door.

"Don't worry, I won't go anywhere without Mircea. So, what did you want to talk about?"

"Why are you hiding from us?"

"I'm not hiding from you. I just felt like a change of place."

Vlad laughs. "Come on, Lena. You can do better than that. What exactly is your problem?"

Lena glares at him but doesn't answer.

Ștefan does. "She's afraid of you, Vlad. She's afraid you'll hurt Mircea."

"Me? Hurt Mircea? Really?"

Lena looks away.

"Why on earth would I hurt Mircea? I love the kid. The last time I ever saw my brother, before little Mircea was born, I swore to take care of his child as if he was my own. And that's what I would do if his crazy mother wouldn't keep kidnapping him and dragging him all over the world."

"I don't believe you," Lena said.

"Why not? I've done nothing to him. Or to you."

"I know your reputation. You wouldn't stop at anything to take Wallachia."

"Absolutely. And I will. I swore to catch Vladislav and make him eat the tongue that ordered Father and Mircea killed. And that's just the beginning. I'll make him suffer more pain than he made Father and Mircea go through, and I'll destroy those who helped him. They'll be sorry they were ever born. But that has nothing to do with little Mircea. He's not a rival to the throne. He's just a kid, my nephew, and the spitting image of my brother. He's the last person I would ever hurt. Can you get that into your thick head, woman?"

His irked voice is loaded with truth, and his ugly green eyes look straight into hers. Lena glances at Ștefan, who leans against the wall between them.

He nods. "That's the truth, Lena. Vlad is a terrible enemy, but he's a loyal friend. I wouldn't be here without him, and I trust him with my life. Vlad is not a threat to Mircea. Let him be your friend."

Lena sighs. She glances at her son, wishing she knew what to believe. But she doesn't really have a choice, does she? They're here.

She sighs. "I wish you came sooner. It took me years to grow that hair."

CHAPTER 83

SERBIA, FALL 1452

The summer's over, and the winter must be close, Codru thinks, rubbing his hands and blowing the steam of his breath over his frozen fingers to warm them. He wonders if the full moon is close. He tried to keep track of it by marking the days on the wall, then crossing them off in rows of seven to count the weeks and the months, but he must have missed a few. Or double counted. And one day is all it takes to throw off the count, as he knows only too well.

He hasn't seen the full moon in months. That night they stole his blood, he got thinking. He remembered he had heard about the Vlachs long ago, from Mama Smaranda, but he forgot it all until they talked about the black wedding.

It was the winter he'd returned from Lesbos. He was staying with Mama Smaranda and Lena, and they went to a funeral in the village. The old man had drowned in a well.

When the black-clad priest finished the long-drawn-out service in church, four neighbors carried the coffin to a freshly dug grave at the cemetery's far edge. They opened the cover to stuff a head of garlic in the dead man's mouth and pound nails through the soles of his feet, nailing him to the coffin. They threw a shovel of gravel in his coffin, then covered it back before lowering it into the grave.

Lena's jaw fell. "Why are they doing this?" she whispered.

"Because he killed himself. His neighbors worry he'll turn into a *strigoi*, and come back from the dead to drink their blood and turn their cows barren."

"And how does all this help?" Codru asked.

Smaranda shrugged. "The nails are supposed to keep him from walking, and the gravel is to keep him entertained. He'll take so much time counting the pebbles that he won't have time to wander. As for the garlic, I'm not sure. I know it wards off vampires, but as for the *strigoi*... Maybe they think he'll stink so bad they'll smell him from afar."

"That's weird," Lena said. "We don't do any of that in Moldova."

Smaranda laughed. "Of course you don't. But this is Transylvania, where any woman might be a witch, any man a *vârcolac*, and any bat a vampire. And if you think this was strange, you should see what the Vlachs do. But you won't, because they keep their black magic under wraps. No wonder, with the church on the lookout for witches to burn."

"Who are the Vlachs?" Codru asked.

"They're people living south of the Danube, in Serbia and Albania. They speak Romanian and they're Orthodox, like us, but they're more into magic than into religion. They teach their magic from mother to daughter, and their whole lives revolve around it. They worship the moon and the sun, and some say they worship the devil, but I don't think that's true. But they seem to worship the dead and they do some weird stuff."

"Like what?"

"They craft love potions from a girl's monthly blood, and give it to the intended to drink. Instead of cemeteries, they bury their dead in their gardens. They make oblivion elixirs from the water they wash blind kittens with, and use the water from washing the dead to make revenge potions. There's more, but the strangest to me is the black wedding."

"What's that?" Codru asked.

"Whenever a young person dies unwed, they wed them before their burial. They have a wedding party with food, wine, and music that may be bigger than those of the living. After that, the dead person's spouse must be chaste for a year, or they'll join them in the tomb."

"That's creepy," Lena said.

"How do they get anyone to marry a dead body?" Codru asked.

"I don't know if they persuade or threaten them. But few ever say no, because the Vlachs possess powerful magic. And after the year's over, they can do whatever they want," Smaranda said.

That had been many moons ago, but when he finally remembered, Codru understood why the Vlachs spoke Romanian, not Serbian, like Branković's men, why the soldiers let him live when Baba Cloanța told them to, and why they kept him there.

They wanted his blood because it was magicked by the moon, so they thought it would strengthen their potions, but it didn't work out. At least not yet. They said they'd try again the next full moon, so he might get a chance to escape. But how?

He decided to forgo eating and drinking for two days before the full moon to be ready. He'd wait for them to unlock the door, then he'd beat Lia to it. It shouldn't be that hard, he thought. He was a goddamn werewolf, and she was just a human.

Or was she?

Codru remembered Smaranda's words: "The Vlachs have powerful magic they pass from mother to daughter." Lia had to be a witch.

So what? Witch or no witch, she only had two legs. And he'd have the surprise going for him. And the moon's strength. One way or another, he'd beat her to that door.

And he'd better. Baba Cloanța said that if his blood didn't work, they'd try his seed next, and the thought of it made him shiver. How would they harvest it from him?

CHAPTER 84

THE LAST FULL MOON

Codru spent the next month getting ready. He studied the cave door and was glad to see it opened outside. If they opened it just a crack, he should be able to blow his way through a bunch of women. They'll have weapons, of course, but so what? He was bigger, stronger, and faster, and he could handle a few scratches. And they wouldn't wish to kill him, or they'd lose their supply of werewolf blood and whatever else they wanted from him.

But they could still use the water they'd wash him with... and his skin, and teeth, and heart... and other things.

That thought sent a shiver down his spine, but he shook his head to clear it. Better think about what he could do and how, rather than worry about what they'd do with his body. He won't care anyhow.

For days and days, he leaned against the grill to learn the lay of the land. He couldn't see far because of the trees, but the cave had to be in the side of a mountain, south of the Danube. Sooner or later, he'd reach the river if he ran down and north. Sooner rather than later, since as a werewolf, he was fast as the wind. Once he reached the Danube, swimming across should be a breeze, and after that, he'd be home free. From Hungary or Wallachia, getting home to Buda should be easy.

And Lena...

He heard steps and ran back to his mattress, pretending to sleep, but watched the grate under his lowered lashes. It was Lia's turn to bring him food and water. He watched her squeeze the jug and the pot through the bars and collect the empty ones he'd left there. After she straightened, she stood to watch him for a while, her dark eyes sad, the corners of her mouth turned down, and Codru wondered what she was thinking. She'd been worried he was faking his sleep, and still she came in to steal his blood, risking her life, as long as Baba promised her a black wedding. Strange girl, Codru thought, wondering if he could find a way to touch her heart and have her set him free. Not likely. She was Baba Cloanța's most trusted assistant. And she didn't have the keys.

He kept counting the days and marked them on the cave wall one by one. He watched the moon wane and wax again, growing into its silver glory.

Two days before the full moon, he stopped eating and drinking, so when the time came, he was ready.

Ten steps from the mattress to the door. That's like two werewolf leaps, Codru thought, and lay on the straw bed with his eyes on the door. As he waited, he thought of Lena. He hadn't seen her in so long. Was she still in their little place in Buda? Was she ever thinking of him? Or had she moved on and responded to the affections of some other man courting her? The thought stabbed at his heart like a knife, and he forced himself back to here and now.

The air chilled, and the light faded. The sky turned gray, then black, and the moon made her call.

But this time, it was the call of freedom. Codru delighted in the pain of his shift like never before. His heart full of hope, he watched his fingers turn to claws and his skin turn to dark fur. The searing ache of his bones melting and stretching to wolf him out turned into joy.

He lay his muzzle on the mattress, watching the door. Before long, the women stopped by the grate to peek in, like last time. Baba raised her torch and studied him, then the cave. She checked the bolts and the locks.

"It all looks good," she said. "You all ready?"

The women raised their lances and their bows.

Baba turned to Lia. "Are you ready?"

Lia turned to Codru and studied him intently. Her teeth worried her lip. "Do you really think he's asleep?"

Baba Cloanța shrugged. "Look at him. He'd be climbing the walls and howling to high heaven if he wasn't. He's a *vârcolac*, for the Moon's sake. He can't resist her call."

"How about his heart?"

"What about it?"

"Can't you hear it drumming like mad? Why would it race like that if he was sleeping?"

"It's the moon, I tell you. His blood feels the call, but the potion's magic keeps him down. His brain is fogged, but his heart knows."

"Are you sure?"

"Of course I'm sure."

"Let's do it then."

Baba unlocked the locks, one after the other. She pulled the first bolt, then the next, then the next.

Codru's heart pummeled like crazy as he waited to pounce.

Baba Cloanța pulled the last bolt. She cracked open the door.

Lia slipped her head in, her enormous eyes watching him.

Codru's breath froze.

Lia gasped. She slammed the door shut and pushed the bolts home.

"He's awake."

CHAPTER 85

THE WEREWOLF'S RAGE

That happened many moons ago. Five, by Codru's count, give or take a few days. But, since he hasn't seen the moon since, he can't be sure.

When the gate slammed shut and the bolts banged back into place, a rage like he'd never known stole his mind. His brain drowned in boiling blood, his heart thundered in his ears, and his sight darkened with fury.

He howled until the mountains answered with their echos, foamed at the mouth and clawed at the door, jarring the iron bars. He bit them and shook them and chewed on them until his muzzle filled with blood. He ran and slammed himself against the grate, again and again, to shatter it.

The bars resisted.

He left the grate and moved on to the floor. He dug the ground with his iron-like claws like he was looking for the mother of all bones. In seconds, he got through the thin layer of dirt and reached the rock. But tough as they were, his curved claws were no match for the mountain's hard core. He dug and howled and bled, but that got him nowhere.

Still, he kept at it until his claws broke, his paws bled, and his heart turned hollow.

When he finally stopped, he turned to the door. The Vlachs were gone. They must have fled when they witnessed his wrath. That should have made him feel better, but it didn't. It made him fear what was coming.

Wilted inside, he lay by the grate watching the moon. His bleeding muzzle on his shredded paws, he watched her glide across the sky, knowing that she'd soon be gone and his strength with her. Come sunrise, he'll be nothing but a prisoner with no hope and no plan. His heart burned, and his eyes did too. He'd have cried if he could, but werewolves don't know how to cry.

The sunrise brought him back to his human form, though much worse for the wear. His werewolf rage gave way to human misery: broken nails, bleeding teeth, bruised bones, shredded skin. But none hurt as bad as his despairing heart. He fell asleep and woke up shivering, with Baba Cloanța and Lia staring at him. They didn't look pleased.

"Look at you," Baba said, her mouth puckered in disdain. "The all-mighty werewolf, defeated by a bunch of women. How does it feel to be you?"

Codru didn't answer. He wished he was still a werewolf to lick his wounds, but since he wasn't, he had to contend himself to washing them with the water he avoided yesterday, hoping the poison wouldn't touch him through his wounds. And if it did, so what? God knew he could do with some sleep to forget about everything that happened.

"*Sa-ți fie rușine!* Shame on you!" Baba spat, pushing back the black scarf tied around her chin.

Codru was too tired to argue, but he was curious.

"*Rușine?* Why? What do I have to be ashamed of?"

"You tried to fool a bunch of women and attack us. I saved your life, healed you, fed and sheltered you, and this is my reward? Shame on you."

Codru didn't think he'd ever laugh again, but laugh he did. He laughed so hard he couldn't stop, bloody mouth and all, until he choked.

"You're crazy, woman. Bat-shit crazy. You imprisoned me, poisoned me, and stole my blood, and you think I should be thankful? You're nuts. Unless you're worse than nuts. You're evil and stupid, and for that, there's no cure."

Baba darkened with fury. She sputtered and moaned and tried to curse him, but Lia dragged her away.

Codru sighed and leaned against the grate, looking out. His ire spent, he listened to the wind sing through the branches, watched the birds fly across the sky, and breathed the smell of the grass, wondering what was coming.

He found out when they came, boarded the door, and left him in the dark.

CHAPTER 86
EDIRNE, WINTER 1452

It's mid-winter. The short, ugly days are cold and gray, calling for early nights and sleeping-in because here in Edirne, winter is for rest and renewal. That's when the rich earth pours its strength into the new seeds, bewitching them to sprout in spring; laughing women look after the children, hoping that the coming year will bring more; and bearded men sit around hot braziers, drinking mint tea and talking about old friends and new wars.

Not this winter. This winter, the winter of 1452, the Ottoman Empire is fiercely getting ready for war. From morning till night, sweaty blacksmiths pummel shapeless lumps of red-hot iron into razor-sharp blades; red-clad janissaries spar to hone their skills with their weapons; and the palace's fat cooks bake mountains of hardtack to feed the army. The mints in Edirne, Bursa, and Amasya mint new silver akçe with sultan Mehmed's name on one side, and a prayer for the empire's glory on the other. The new coins are shiny, but lighter than the old ones, because the treasury must pay for the tons of grain, the thousands of sheep ready for slaughter, and enough cloth for uniforms to wrap the earth a dozen times.

Everybody everywhere talks about the war of wars and nothing but the war, and Radu has had it. He's so fed up with that darn war he wants to puke.

But Mehmed is more obsessed with it than anyone else. Day and night, he stares at his maps and studies his forefathers' campaigns against Constantinople, trying to understand why they failed.

Even now. The Edirne throne room is empty but for the table covered in scrolls and the three copper braziers endeavoring to take the bite out of the air and failing. It's late, it's cold, and it's time for dinner, but Mehmed didn't notice. He stares at his map and scratches his head with his quill.

"There have been twenty-three campaigns against Constantinople. Twenty-three! And they all failed. Why? And how can I ensure mine won't?" he mumbles.

Radu sighs. "You've already built Rumeli Hisari and throttled their supply chain. You've commissioned the largest gun ever built, isolated Constantine from any possible help, and gathered the Ottoman Empire's largest army. I'd call that a good start."

But Mehmed doesn't laugh. He stares at an old map of Constantinople, more precisely at the Theodosian Walls, the five-layered defense structure surrounding the city on all sides but the one towards the Golden Horn, the city's sheltered harbor. Without the city's permission, no ship can get in there, since a mile-long iron chain cuts it off from the sea.

"How can I get my boats inside the Golden Horn?"

"Why would you?"

"The wall is weaker on that side. It would be easier to break through."

Radu sighs. "Come on, Mehmed. Enough is enough. There's another day tomorrow. Let's have some fun." He puts his arms around Mehmed and kisses his neck. His hands wander down to the bulge between his thighs and stroke the warm silk. Before long, Mehmed loses track of the chain and the Theodosian Walls to focus on Radu's hands pleasuring him. He unties his shalwars and turns around.

"I hope nobody comes to find us," he says.

"Why not?" Radu tastes his lips, then his neck, then savor the salty skin of his belly.

"Because it wouldn't do. Not in the throne room."

"Why not?" Radu whispers against his groin, and Mehmed forgets about the throne room and slides into his mouth. Radu loves him slowly and gently, pulling away the further Mehmed pushes. The faster Mehmed moves, the slower he responds, delaying his pleasure until Mehmed screams and crumbles.

"My turn."

Radu turns him around and bends him over the map, with his chest over the Theodosian Walls. Holding on to his hips, he pushes inside him. Slowly first, to feel him opening, then faster and faster until he bursts into a frenetic release.

Panting and spent, they lay embraced on the throne in a rare moment of contentment, because happiness has been hard to find these days. With fingers as soft as rose petals, Mehmed caresses Radu's cheek. He kisses his eyes and whispers in his ear. "Will you come with me?"

"Of course."

"Will you fight alongside me and give me everything you've got?"

Radu stays silent for a long time. Constantinople is his spiritual nexus, the home of Hagia Sophia, the patriarch's seat. The city is to him what Mecca and Medina are to Mehmed. Radu has never been too religious, but destroying his people's faith doesn't come easy. Bad enough when Mehmed demolished the Orthodox Church rising where Rumeli Hisari sits now. He used its bricks to build his new fortress and slaughtered those who dared to protest. But helping him make Hagia Sophia into a mosque?

"I don't know, Mehmed. I don't think I can do that."

Mehmed's smile vanishes, and his loving eyes turn to steel. His cheeks are flushed with anger as he adjusts his clothes. "Get off my throne, will you?"

Radu does. He watches Mehmed turn his back to him and get back to his maps as if their lovemaking never happened. Radu's eyes burn, and his heart aches. That damned Constantinople is tearing them apart.

"Mehmed, what if things were the other way? What if I was going to war, and I asked you to fight against your religion? What if I wanted you to help me destroy your most beloved mosque and turn it into an Orthodox Church? Would you do it? Would you betray your people's faith for me?"

Mehmed turns from his maps. His eyes are green ice as they meet Radu's. "But we aren't there, are we? I am the Sultan of the Ottoman Empire, and you are a beggar prince trying to grab Wallachia's throne. You need me to take it, while I don't need you to take Constantinople. But faith is faith, and trust is trust. I need to know that you'll support me unconditionally, even if it's not easy. One way or another, we'll both have to choose."

CHAPTER 87

CONSTANTINOPLE, WINTER 1452

Winter subdued Constantinople. The brief fall came and went, and the dreariest winter there ever was clutched Constantinople in its merciless grip. The days are grim and gray, with leaden skies and sharp rains that freeze you to the bone.

Mehmed's blockade locked them out of everything that used to bring them joy. Things are expensive and scarce, from silks and furs to flour and wine, because they're all brought in from far away, so everything costs its weight in gold. Many go to bed hungry, and the siege hasn't even started.

Ion pulls his cloak closer and hurries through the empty streets, worried he'll be late for the council. He skips the deepest puddles and avoids the slippery cobbles. Like everything else in the city, the roads are falling apart. Constantinople, the City of Gold, the thousand-year-old capital of the east, is half-abandoned. Those who could leave are gone. Half the city's houses are empty and falling apart, and everything inside them got plundered: valuables, clothes, furniture, even doors. They got sold, used, or fed someone's fire. The polis is eating itself.

Ion makes it to the meeting just in time. He sits before the emperor appears, ignoring Notaras' poisoned glare. The megas doux's spite has no end, but the others are used to Ion by now. They pay him no more mind than they do the servants pouring wine.

The emperor arrives, resplendent as always in purple brocade and glittering gold, with his tiara on his head. The council stands and bows, as fit for God's son on Earth, but Constantine looks tired and old. Watching him, Ion understands how their positions differ. He came to help, but he's free to leave and go wherever he wants. Constantine will die here. His empire will soon be his tomb.

"What do we have today?" Constantine's voice is flat and toneless. He's lost hope. He'll still do whatever he can, but he no longer believes that his empire can be saved.

Sphrantzes stands. "This is the Papal Request. Before sending us help, the pope wants us to hold a united Christmas service to show our commitment to the churches' union."

"I object," Notaras roars.

If looks could kill, Sphrantzes would be history, Ion thinks, watching Notaras' eyes throw daggers at Sphrantzes.

"Why?" the emperor asks.

"The vague hope that the pope may send us help if we agree to subject ourselves to this humiliation isn't worth our people's wrath. If we bend over to please the pope, they'll revolt, and we'll no longer have a city to fight for. As for me, I'd rather see Constantinople full of Ottoman turbans than the Catholics' poisoned crosses."

"What do you think, Sphrantzes?"

"I appreciate my noble colleague's point of view. But if we are to hold any hope for help from the west, we'll have to do it. I don't know if it will get us help, but if we don't do it, we'll stand alone. And alone, we can't win."

Notaras rolls his eyes. "Of course not. That's why I said over and over that we shouldn't rush into war. We should try to mollify Mehmed and change his mind. We have friends in his camp who can help us. The grand vizier, Çandarlı Halil Paşa, is an old friend of Constantinople who wants to stop this stupid war. We need to help him appease Mehmed."

"And how do you propose to do that?" the emperor asks.

"Gold. Gold is always the answer. A few bags of gold sent to the sultan and maybe a couple to Çandarlı Paşa may be all we need to avert this disaster."

"And where, pray tell, would you get this gold?"

"The treasury, of course."

Constantine laughs like Ion hasn't heard him laugh before. "Oh, Notaras, you are precious. Our treasury is empty, and I thought you knew that. You're the megas doux, aren't you? We don't have enough gold to buy a pig for Christmas, let alone a sultan and his grand vizier to boot. There's no gold in the treasury. Any other ideas?"

Notaras sits back, his face dark with disapproval.

"So we'll do the joined service. Thank you, Sphrantzes. What else?"

"As for your marriage..."

"Don't worry about that. We have more urgent things to attend to. Anything else?"

Sphrantzes clears his voice. "We requested help from the west, as you directed us. We sent letters to the pope, Hunyadi, Venice, Genoa, and every other place we could think about. We only have two answers."

"Yes?"

"Hunyadi said he would consider sending us help if you agreed to cede him our Black Sea forts, Silivri and Misivri."

"Consider, he said?"

"Yes."

"Tell him to bite me. What else?"

"The Genoese. They'll send two ships with grains, weapons, and seven hundred men. The captain comes from the best Genoese families, but few of them speak to him. He's said to be an outstanding soldier and a master in defending walled cities. He's brave beyond belief, but he's a ladies' man, a privateer, and a pirate. He even took some of their own ships; that's why they don't want him there, but they'll send him to us. We'll have to negotiate the price with him and his men."

Constantine nods. "An interesting man. What's his name?"

"Giovanni Giustiniani Longo."

CHAPTER 88

CONSTANTINOPLE, JANUARY 23, 1453

Constantinople is god-awful cold in January. The rain never stops, and the streets are slick with ice in the morning. The heavy sky is empty, as if the sun went somewhere else, leaving the shivering people to the winter dread.

But nobody complains about the weather today. The people forgot they are cold. They even forgot they're hungry and frightened. They forgot about anything else but the Genoese ships.

The white dots of the sails had barely appeared on the horizon, and the whole Constantinople climbed up the walls to wait for them. Bright smiles light the tired faces, and bitter hearts fill with hope.

"It's the pope. He sent them. Seventeen ships loaded with soldiers and everything," a short man says, glancing at the sails while balancing a tray loaded with fragrant flatbreads just out of the oven on his head.

The woman sweeping the street before her sweet shop laughs at him. "Go away. That pope wouldn't send seventeen ships loaded with dirty laundry. Not to us. The Catholics don't care about us. They wouldn't give a hoot if Mehmed made us into shish kebabs, smothered us in tzatziki sauce, and fed us to his men wrapped in your breads."

"But they say that after we had that Catholic mass..."

"And what a mess that was. You know nothing about papists if you think they'll send any help without expecting something in return." She returns to her shop and slams the door, and the man turns back to the ships.

The blind beggar in the corner tugs his ear. "They still have to make it through the Strait, where Mehmed's guns are waiting."

The man with the flatbreads stares dumbfounded as the blind man unglues his eyes from the ships to sit against the wall. He takes off his hat and sets it at his feet for people to drop coins.

Ali laughs. She knew he wasn't blind, just like the cripples by the church door weren't crippled. She saw them walk when no one was watching. Here, in Constantinople, the business of a beggar is a commerce like any other. The more impaired and uglier, the better, since people look away and feel guilty. They'll drop a coin in the hat to assuage their guilt.

But, blind or not, the man is right. Rumeli Hisari's guns have already sunk two Venetian ships that refused to pay Mehmed's new toll. What a pity it would be if they sank these Genoese ships everybody's been waiting for like they're the Holy Grail. In the weeks they've been waiting, the two ships became seventeen, and the seven hundred men became ten thousand. That's how gossip works.

But Ali knows the truth from Ion: there will be only two ships, if they're lucky. Constantinople's folks will be disappointed. But they'll be even more so if those two don't make it, so Ali hopes against all hope that they will.

She's going to the palace to meet Constantine. He asked her to stop by, but didn't say why, and Ali is terrified. She fears he will ask for her hand, as thin as her royal blood is, since his empire is under siege, and royal princesses are scarce for the moment. He needs to plant his seed and secure his dynasty; in case he dies and the city survives. And Ali happens to be there and available.

She sighs and drags herself away. She'd rather wait to see the ships, but that would make her late, and you can't make the emperor wait.

But, one way or another, they'll be done soon enough to see what happens.

Constantine is waiting in the throne room. From his twinkling tiara to his imperial purple shoes, Constantine sparkles in imperial splendor, but his eyes are tired and worried.

"Thank you for coming, Ali. I have a matter of utmost importance to discuss with you."

Ali sits in the chair he pulled out for her. He covers her hand with his and looks into her eyes. It's nice, like when a friend holds your hand, but there's no sparkle, Ali thinks, glad that she trimmed her nails this morning. She knows he likes her and wishes her well, but his agenda is not her problem.

"You know what I asked you here for?"

Ali hesitates, then decides he deserves the truth. How he takes it is up to him. "You need an heir to carry on your dynasty in case you die, but the city survives. Since you don't have many prospects, you decided to honor me with your attention."

Constantine drops her hand, looking guiltier than a toddler caught stealing a baklava. Ali wants to laugh, but she refrains. Barely.

The emperor clears his voice without meeting her eyes. "And... what do you think about that?"

Ali smiles, but he's not looking at her. He's looking through the window towards the Bosporus. The ships must be close, Ali thinks. We'll soon find out if they make it.

"I'm sorry, my emperor, but I'm not interested. I'm not keen on children, but even if I were, I wouldn't want them just to keep alive an old dynasty that has nothing to do with me. And, to be honest, I find you attractive, but not attractive enough."

Constantine's face shifts from shock to outrage, melts into misery, then settles for a smile. "Well, that will make Sphrantzes happy. He thought this was a lousy idea."

"Ion did, too. He was not a fan."

"No wonder. You know, Ali, you're way too pretty to be his sister. But you aren't really his sister, are you?"

Ali blinks. "I'm the best sister he's got."

Constantine laughs and pats her hand. "Thanks for being straight with me. I knew it was a long shot, but I had to do what I had to do."

Ali nods. "Thank you, my emperor, for honoring me. Now, how about we go see those ships?"

CHAPTER 89
THE MIGHTY SHIPS

They walk the dark corridors side by side, then take the worn stone steps to the tower. They're both winded when they get to the top, but it's worth it. The old Tower of Belisarius has the best view of the Bosporus Ali has ever seen. A whole new world opens to your eyes from up above. The street merchants roaming the streets down below look like busy little ants. The lush Galata colony raises across the Golden Horn's sheltered waters like a garden. Beyond the narrow ribbon of the Bosporus Strait, the Sea of Marmara opens as blue as can be. But that's far away, beyond Mehmed's twin castles leaning towards each other like two stone monsters trying to throttle the Bosporus between them.

The Genoese carracks made good use of time. They got so close that Ali can distinguish the men on the decks and count the sails. They dance with the wind and lean so low the gunwales skirt the water, then right themselves and lean the other way. Ali's heart fills with awe. They're beautiful, the Genoese ships with their snow-white sails blooming high on their masts. Sleek and trim and fast.

"They're nothing like the Ottoman galleys. Or even our ships," Constantine whispers.

He watches in wonder as the ships sway and swing on the water, getting closer and closer to Mehmed's cannons. The twin fortresses, Rumeli Hisari on one side and Anadolu Hisari on the other, stalk them like two hungry cats teaming over prey. And the prey's odds aren't good, as witnessed by the loaded stakes on Rumeli Hisari's walls. The vultures still fight over what's left of the last ship's crew — bloody skulls with empty eye sockets, warning the daring what to expect. Every single boat since then stopped to pay the toll. Some were allowed in, and some weren't, but not one braved the Strait. For good reason.

The carracks dance over the blue waters like white water birds, stirring something inside Ali. Their dangerous dance is mesmerizing, and Ali's heart drums in her chest as the white sails near the place of reckoning.

"See how they harness the wind that buys them speed and strength instead of relying on oars like our galleys do? That's marvelous to watch."

Ali is too busy watching to answer. They've got to be close to firing range, she thinks, as the water splashes just ahead of the first ship. Seconds later, they hear the cannon.

"It's starting."

Constantine's breath comes out raspy as he stares at the ships, more eager than he ever looked at her, and Ali knows she made the right choice. Other than making him an heir, Constantine has no interest in her, and Ali feels relieved.

The first carrack changes course as swiftly as a bird in flight. The following splash, heartbeats later, comes in the precise spot she used to be, but no longer is. Her crew surely knows what they're doing. That channel is narrow and fast, but the ship flies through it like she has wings instead of sails, and the cannons struggle to keep up.

They change course again. Ali doesn't know why until the water splashes just a foot behind their stern.

"How did they know it was coming?" she asks.

His eyes glued to the boat, Constantine shakes his head. "I don't know. But whoever runs that boat, I want him on my side."

The first ship is half through the channel when the second reaches the firing range.

"I hope they change target and let her through," Constantine says, but the next splash comes two feet off her bow, and she changes course again. Mehmed's men are hell-bent on stopping her from breaking the blockade, so they focus on her, giving the second one a break.

But she's about to escape the fire. Another two-hundred feet, and she's free. Every man, woman, and child in Constantinople cheers for her. The first ship to break Mehmed's blockade has almost made it, and they're drunk with joy.

But she does the unthinkable. Just as she's about to be out of danger, she completely reverses course and turns back into the channel.

Constantinople gasps. People scream, yell, and cry, cheated of their glee to see her sailing in. Angry watchers spit into the wind, cursing and throwing rocks at her, even though she's too far to reach.

Constantine's knuckles whiten as he grips the wall. "Are they crazy? What the hell are they doing?"

"They're drawing the fire to themselves to help the second one get through."

Constantine throws her a side glance. "How do you know?"

"I just do."

Sure enough, the jilted cannons can't forgive the first ship, which is still — barely — within reach and ignore the other. The water boils around the first carrack like the sea is on fire. She dances left and right and left again, avoiding the blows as if she knows where they're going, while the second ship sails straight into the Golden Horn. The first one tacks once more, then follows, blowing her horn as if she's giving Mehmed the finger.

"Wow. Whoever that captain is, I want him," Constantine says. "I've seen nothing like that. It was like he could read their thoughts. What a brilliant man."

"He surely is smart. Cocky, too."

"Let's go meet him," Constantine says, heading down the stairs, and Ali follows. She has a thousand things to do, but she can't resist the temptation to see that man.

"What if he's an asshole?" she asks.

"What do you mean?"

"What if he's a pirate, a killer, or someone who abuses women?"

Constantine shrugs. "That's too bad. But, if I had to choose between a man who could save my empire and the hurt feelings of some woman I don't know, she's out of luck. I'll do what's right for my empire, and I'd hire that man if he's the devil incarnate."

CHAPTER 90
THE GENOESE

The Imperial throne room is jam-packed with people waiting for the heroes. And they're not ordinary people — the beggars, the merchants, and the stable boys are out in the port, and they'll get to see them first. They're already cheering out there, and Ali wishes she could go there, too, but Constantine drags her behind him as he makes his way to the throne.

The Byzantine Empire's highest dignitaries have gathered to honor the heroes: the megas doux, Loukas Notaras, with his oily hair falling over his spiteful dark face; George Sphrantzes, Constantine's advisor and best friend, short and chubby, frowning as he sees her in Constantine's wake; and even Ion, who stares at her like she's got three ears. They're all here to meet the men who came to save the empire.

They were eager to see them before, but today's performance, when they put Mehmed's cannons to shame, gave them hope. These are not ordinary men. Maybe, just maybe, their outstanding bravery and incredible skills can help Constantinople survive its predicament.

"That was something else," Sphrantzes says, taking his regular place at the emperor's right. "The Genoese weren't lying when they said that man is worth his weight in gold."

Loukas Notaras slips him a dark look. "Really? So what, pray tell, did he do? He didn't do Mehmed any harm. And, the way he went, he was lucky to escape unharmed. Returning to take the fire, that was foolish."

"I beg to differ. That was wise. That's why we have two loaded ships instead of one."

"So, you're saying that the second ship's captain is no good? You're likely right. The second is no good, and the first was lucky."

"There's just no pleasing you, is there, megas doux?"

Constantine looks at him with pity and Notaras turns away. He wants no war. He has better things to do than fret about Constantinople's future, like worrying about his fortune. Some say he's the wealthiest man in the Balkans — Constantine and Mehmed included.

Half-hidden behind Constantine, Ali seeks a way out. He dragged her there, then forgot about her, and now she's stuck. She squeezes through the crowd towards the door, and she's almost there when the cheers peak and the sailors trickle in, cutting her retreat.

They're dirty and tired, but their eyes glow with joy. They fulfilled their mission and brought the ships all the way from Genoa, through the Tyrrhenian, the Mediterranean, the Aegean, and the Sea of Marmara, then sailed the Bosporus to Constantinople under the fire of Mehmed's cannons. After thousands of exhausting, dangerous miles, their job is done. They bow in front of the Byzantine emperor, who stands and bows back.

The council looks at him with worry. The last Roman Emperor, a demigod, bowing to some Genoese illiterate peasants? But that's his greatness. Unlike any other noble Ali knows, Constantine is a decent human first. He recognizes these men's bravery and is grateful for their service to his people.

Next come the soldiers, and they're a different breed. Covered in heavy armor, they carry shiny shields, bows, and swords and advance in perfect formation, like they've been practicing for ages.

Constantine nods and smiles but doesn't bow. They're not the ones who sailed those ships. Their work hasn't yet started, but Constantine is grateful for their willingness to help his city.

The procession is done. Ali squeezes towards the door, ready to sneak out, as two more men come in.

They're neither soldiers nor sailors — or maybe they're both. The first, a massive man in chain-mail armor with metal plates to the chest and back, dwarfs the door. The top of his feathered helmet touches the arch, and his shoulders block the light. He looks familiar, Ali thinks, but the memory eludes her. The second is more human-sized. He wears a well-worn leather tunic and steps with the effortless grace of a large cat. Dark curls frame his tanned face, and his storm-colored eyes smile.

Ali stops dead in her tracks as if struck by lightning. Her knees weaken as she watches him walk towards the throne.

"And you are?"

"We are the captains of the ships, my emperor. We brought you supplies, and seven hundred soldiers. I wish it was more, but that's all we could muster. We came to help you through the siege."

"Thank you for coming. What is your name, sir?"

"Signor Giovanni Giustiniani Longo, at your service."

CHAPTER 91

A MAN WHO MATTERS

The little house feels too tight tonight as Ali sets the table and reheats yesterday's stew. She adds a plate of bread, wine, and fruit, too preoccupied to notice she's serving raw eggplant and cucumbers instead of fruit. Ever since she snuck out of the palace, she's been in a haze, and she can't think about anything but Giovanni.

It's been years since she saw him last, and she didn't spend them dwelling on him. But seeing him again gutted her to the core. That man is still like no other she has ever met. Just seeing him cut her at the knees. She wishes it wasn't so — he's nothing but a pirate and a cheat — but his velvety voice is still music to her ears. She can't believe she could ever turn him down.

But that was years ago; since then, he must have had a hundred lovers besides his noble wife. He wouldn't even know her if they met, Ali tells herself. There's nothing to worry about. The past is the past, and it's over. But he upended her life just by landing here, and she struggles.

"How do you know him?" Ion asks, sipping his wine like he doesn't care, and Ali remembers he's here.

"How do I know who?"

365

"Giustiniani. How do you know him?"

Ali sighs. She'd rather not tell him, but there's no point in lying. "He saved me from a tight spot. When I escaped Mehmed's caravan, I looked for a ship to take me, and they did."

"Then what?"

"Then he turned out to be a pirate. They took a ship with me watching and killed a man."

"So?"

"So what?"

"What did they do next?"

"They did what pirates do. They took the men into slavery and sold the cargo and the ship."

"What did they do to you?"

"To me? Nothing."

"How come?"

"What do you mean?"

Ion looks at her like she's feeble-minded. "Did they rape you? Sell you? What did they do to you?"

"They dropped me in Constantinople, and they let me go."

"Why?"

"What do you mean, why?"

"Ali, the slave trade is more lucrative than trading gold these days. A young virgin with your looks would bring in tons of money. And they just let you go?"

"Yes."

"Why?"

"I wasn't a virgin. I was a cook."

Ion chokes on his food and wipes his mouth. "And they never knew you were a woman?"

"I don't think so. The men didn't."

"And the captain?"

"The captain..." Ali remembers Giovanni's cabin. His warm lips over hers, his powerful arms holding her. Him, laughing when she threatened to kill him. Him, going to sleep and letting her go. "He just wasn't that interested."

Ion nods and pushes his plate to the side. "I see. May I suggest that next time you do leftovers, you don't salt them again?"

"Sorry. I didn't realize."

"Of course not. Ali, how much does this man matter to you?"

Ali looks away. "I don't know. But does it matter?"

"Well, it matters to me. And maybe to Constantine. And probably even to the man."

"I see. I'll think about it."

She does that night in her bed. She remembers the tall ship flying like a bird between the cannon balls, the white sails skirting the water, and the carrack turning back into the fire to save the other. She remembers his laughing eyes, the softness of his touch, the taste of his kiss, and she feels hollow inside without him.

CHAPTER 92

CONSTANTINOPLE, JANUARY 1453

The throne room is somber, despite the flickering candles reflecting in everyone's gold: bracelets, rings, gold embroidered brocade, even the emperor's pilon. The only one devoid of gold, other than Ion, is Giovanni Giustiniani Longo. Everyone else sparkles, even the patriarch, Gregory the Third, whose unkempt gray beard hangs over his black frock. The heavy gold cross studded with rubies and diamonds resting on his rotund belly sparkles whenever he takes a breath.

It's like they're trying to show how rich they are, Ion thinks. Except they aren't. Well, Constantine isn't. But Notaras? And the patriarch, who holds the keys to the church's coffers? They're showing off for the pirate, trying to look important and wealthy and put him in his place.

But the man's not impressed. Leaning back in his chair, wearing a scuffed leather armor and half a smile on his weather-beaten face, the Genoese ponders one dignitary after another like he can read their thoughts. He's not young, but he's savvy and formidable, and he makes Ion feel like a boy.

Ion sighs. Just as he thought that this winter couldn't get any worse. The foul weather, the Ottoman threat, the shortage of food, and the west sitting on their assets. And now, to top it off, this Genoese pirate who stole Ali's heart is about to charm the emperor. Constantine looks at him like he's a tree ripe with fruit.

"We're so glad to have you, Signor Longo. We've heard so much about you. They say you are a specialist in defending walled cities."

"That I am. Amongst other things. How many men have you got?"

Constantine clears his throat. "Not that many, in fact. But..."

"I'd call it seven thousand. Is that accurate? Mostly untrained militia."

"Close enough. Your informers did a good job. But they're all enthusiastic and hopeful..."

Giustiniani laughs. "Keeping informed goes with my job, Emperor. But hope? Not so much. In my line of business, hope will get you killed. Enthusiasm too. My men and I, we're all about harsh reality."

"Adding your forces to ours..."

"We're talking about protecting fourteen miles of walls, correct? With seven thousand people."

"If you put it this way..."

"Is there another way?"

"The western powers will come to our help. They just need to understand how serious this threat is. And our walls withstood a thousand years of attacks. There's no reason to believe they'll fall to an inexperienced and impatient sultan."

Loukas Notaras can't keep it inside anymore. "I'm sorry, my emperor, but I disagree. We should not underestimate Mehmed. He's as dangerous as it gets. He's a hungry young wolf looking for a kill."

The pirate lifts his wine cup to Notaras. "I cannot but agree with you, sir. You are?"

"I'm Loukas Notaras, the megas doux."

"To your wisdom." Giustiniani empties his cup, and Ion's heart sinks, seeing Constantinople's presumed savior agreeing with the man who wants to give up.

Notaras smiles. "So, you agree we should do whatever we can to make peace?"

The Genoese shakes his head. "Oh, no. Of course not. We need to crush them. The sultan won't agree to peace unless we force him into it, and that's a long way away. But I agree with you that Mehmed is hungry for glory and the most impatient sultan there ever was. He staked his entire empire against yours. He'll conquer Constantinople or die trying, no matter what you offer him, even if it's a thousand virgins or a hundred boys, which he seems to prefer."

The throne room gasps. These Christians can't believe that a manly man could look to another man for love.

Loukas Notaras scowls at Longo with disgust. "You clearly don't know what you're talking about. Real men don't care for boys."

The Genoese smiles. "I'd have a chat with my spies if I were you, megas doux. It looks like your old friend, Çandarlı Halil Paşa, forgot to mention Mehmed's preferences. Ask him next time you meet him secretly like you did at Ziraki's tavern, on Christmas Eve. And I'd be more careful if I were you."

Notaras' face darkens, and the council gasps. All eyes turn from Notaras, whose constant push for appeasement makes his secret meeting with Çandarlı Paşa smell of treason, to the pirate, who knows things no one else does. They all start speaking at once.

The emperor waits for them to stop. When they don't, he slams his cup on the table, spilling his wine, and the room goes silent. "Let's not get distracted. Signor Giovanni Giustiniani Longo, will you take on the task?"

"Fourteen miles of walls; seven thousand untrained people. And not much money. Correct?"

The emperor nods. "Sadly, I'm afraid so. But I have a special offer for you, should the city survive this assault. If we make it through, I'll give you the island of Lemnos to use as you choose. You can keep it, sell it, or use it as an outpost against the Ottomans."

"Mine, forever, no matter what?"

"Yes."

Longo nods and offers him his hand. "Emperor, your wish is my command. My men and I will live or die protecting Constantinople. We won't spare our effort, our lives, nor anything else to save the Roman Empire. Our odds aren't great, but the odds that lead to big victories are never great. We'll fight with you and see you through, or die, so help me God. And I'll forgo my pay until then. But if you want my men to fight for you, you'll have to pay."

"But... we have no money."

"You have gold."

The emperor glances at the icons in their golden frames, the crosses studded with gems, and his own garb, gilded enough to shine in the dark. "We'll pay your men." He turns to the patriarch, whose eyes grew wide with worry. "Melt the crosses. The icon's frames. The relics. We'll melt every piece of gold we own to mint coins and pay Christianity's saviors. We'll give everything we have to save our city. There." The emperor removes his rings and bracelets and drops them on the table. He takes off his tiara and drops it with the rest, then scratches his head. "Boy, that feels good. I've been wanting to get rid of that silly thing for ages." He turns to his dignitaries, daring them to do the same. They all avert their eyes until Sphrantzes puts his own adornments on the table. The patriarch sighs and takes off his cross, then the others follow, dropping their baubles in the pile. Even Notaras, his face pained and his glare hate-poisoned, drops his rings with the rest.

The room fills with excitement. The emperor bows. "Thank you, all. If we make it through, it will be worth it. If we don't, we won't miss it. We'll be too dead to care. Thank you for contributing to our defense fund. These men are here to help us, but this is not their fight. It's ours. Our gold for their lives — we've got a good deal."

The Genoese stands. "Thank you, my emperor. My men and I will do our best for your city. We'll live or die with it. Thank you for rewarding my men."

He walks out, and something about him gives Ion pause. He's met many leaders, from Murad to Mehmed and Constantine, but this man has something no one else has. He's a force like a storm is a force.

Whether or not you like him, it's easy to see why Ali fell in love with him.

"This man is something else," Sphrantzes says. "I've never seen someone like him. I wonder if all the Genoese are like that."

"Are you insane? This man is fixing to take over the world. That's why the Genoese want nothing to do with him. He's a freaking pirate," Notaras says, glancing longingly at the pile of gold on the table.

Constantine follows his eyes and sees his tiara. He sighs. "I'm so glad I got rid of that thing. I always thought it made me look like a sissy, but I couldn't ditch it without a reason." He removes his aprons — the front and the back, both heavy with gold — and his massive golden collar and drops them on top of the pile. "That feels better. At least I won't die looking like a moron."

Ion wishes he had something to contribute, but he's got nothing but his clothes, shoes, and the dingy rooms he rents for more money than they're worth. Then he remembers the golden pin he won at the palace school math contest. It's a gold diamond-studded question mark, the only precious thing he's ever owned. It's tiny compared to everyone else's offerings, but it's all he has. He takes it off and drops it on the pile.

Constantine smiles. "Ion? Thank you for making a difference."

And just like that, Ion is reminded that what we do matters.

CHAPTER 93

EDIRNE, MARCH 1453

A bright sun smiles over Edirne, bringing up the roof's gold, brightening the gardens, and charming the caged birds into singing like they're free. Spring has finally come.

It's been a long, busy winter, its short days filled to the brim with things needing doing, meetings, and work. This whole winter, they prepared for war. From dawn to dusk, the blacksmiths forged weapons, the janissaries trained, and the viziers kept their long noses in the maps, looking for a way into Constantinople's heart. Little time was left for leisure, so Mehmed hadn't hunted in ages, but today, he asked Radu to join him for a hunt.

Radu looked at him askance. "What? No meetings with the viziers? No troop inspections? No watching the new ships being built? No writing letters to appease Hunyadi and keep him out of your way?"

Mehmed shrugged. Radu was right. It had been a rough time for them. For months, they barely saw each other. Which was good.

Mehmed understands Radu's resistance to join his war against his forefathers' faith, but can't condone it. He needs every one of his men to be committed, especially Radu, his friend and soul mate. But the troops are leaving tomorrow, so Mehmed will try one last time to bring

Radu to his side. Or he's done. "They'll wait. I'm leaving tomorrow and I don't know when I'll return. Possibly never. I'd like to spend some time with you if you won't join me on my campaign."

Radu nods. "It will be my pleasure, Mehmed. What are we hunting for?"

"Whatever we find. Spring is a bad time to hunt since the beasts — bears, deer, or foxes — look after their young. It's a sin to kill a mother and leave her cubs starve to death. But the males are now useless. Hunting them will leave more food for the others. So, let's go for the males."

"How will we know them?"

"They'll be the only ones who don't look starving."

Unlike humans, where men look after their wives and children, and they'd die to keep them fed, most females of the forest care for their young all alone, and they often die doing it. *Human females have it good,* Mehmed thinks. He tries to imagine Gülbahar and Gülşah chasing deer in their djellabas to feed the kids, like wolves, and the thought makes him laugh.

"What's so funny, my sultan?" Radu asks.

"I imagine Gülbahar and Gülşah hunting for their kids, and that's funny."

"Not in my country. Our women often bring up their kids without a man."

"That never happens here. If a man dies, another man will take responsibility for his wives and his children. See, Radu, that's one more way our country can teach yours."

Radu tightens his lips and spurs his horse forward, splashing mud behind him, and Mehmed lets him go. *It's sad that all our love and friendship came to this,* he thinks, pushing Rüzgar forward. The young green leaves started showing, filtering the sun into green light, and the mellow wind smells like spring. They ride deep into the forest by the Tunca's edge, watching her brown waters roar down below. Scared by the noise, a flock of gray birds takes off.

"Are you ready?" Radu asks.

"Pretty much. I still hope they'll surrender, but that's not likely. Too bad that Constantine chose to die with his empire. The man is supposed to be brilliant. If he surrendered, I'd let him run Constantinople in exchange for a healthy tribute. He could keep his city intact and his people alive. But he doesn't get it."

"But you'd melt their church bells into cannons and take their kids into devşirme."

"Of course. But that's not too much to ask."

Radu shrugs. "It looks like it's too much for them."

A moving shadow catches Mehmed's eye. He tightens his knees around Rüzgar and nocks an arrow into his bow, ready to release it, but Radu's arrow is already gone. A thunk and a groan tell them it hit its target. The second one follows before Mehmed figures out what they hit.

"What was that?"

"A deer."

"How do you know?"

"I saw him."

Mehmed is unconvinced. They ride to the forest's edge, just above the ridge, to find a massive stag. An arrow sprouts from his neck and another from his side. His eyes glassy, his proud antlers tangled with the branches, he chokes on the blood gurgling in his throat.

Mehmed looks at Radu with new respect. They've hunted together more times than he can count, but Radu has never been the one to get the game. And now he got a trophy.

"Good for you," he says, as Radu dismounts to end the stag's suffering.

The ride back is silent. They're within sight of the palace before Mehmed speaks again. "Will you join me, Radu?"

"Why? You have more than a hundred thousand men, and outnumber Constantine ten to one. You have the largest gun ever built, a bunch of viziers, paşas, and spies, and everything else you need to win. Why do you need me?"

"Because you're my friend and the only man I can fully trust. I need you by my side to help me, support me, and tell me the truth, whether or not I like it."

Radu's mouth tightens, and his blue eyes narrow as they meet Mehmed's. "Have you thought about what that means to me? Have you ever considered dropping your obsession with Constantinople to please me?"

Mehmed's mouth falls open. "Drop the siege? You mean drop the war? And let Constantinople be?"

"Exactly."

"You're kidding, yes?'

Radu shakes his head. "No."

"But I can't do that. Everything I do, and everything I am, is about Constantinople. I can't be who I need to be without it. That city is the key to the empire I'm destined to lead. I'd rather cut off my left arm than forego Constantinople."

"And I'd rather cut off my dick than help you take it."

That night, Mehmed lies awake in his bed, thinking about Radu. It's unbelievable that his best friend abandoned him, but that's precisely what happened. After all these years together and everything he did for him, Radu ditched him like trash. Mehmed's heart quickens and his blood heats to a boil. His rage consumes him, and he wants to gorge out Radu's eyes, but he can't. He calls his guards.

"Bring me a boy. Blond. A virgin."

He lays in his bed, dreaming about every kind of painful revenge he can inflict on Radu until the guards bring the boy. He's young and pretty, with silky blond hair falling to his shoulders and wide blue eyes. He stares at Mehmed as the guards push him down to bow.

"What's your name?"

"Mirko."

"How did you get here?"

"My parents sent me to serve the sultan."

"Are you ready to do that?"

"There's nothing I'd rather do, my sultan."

"Good. Drop your pants and bend over."

The boy stares at him, and his mouth falls open.

"You mean..."

"Yep."

The boy unties the string holding his shalwars and bends over the bed.

Mehmed's hand pushes his head down until the boy's cheek rests on the bedcover, and he can't see his face, just the blond hair, so much like Radu's. He tries a finger in his bottom, but the boy is tight as can be.

Mehmed spits on his hand, rubs it against him, then drops his shalwars and pushes in. The boy sobs, and Mehmed's heart beats faster. He holds on to the bony hips, pushing inside him. His eyes closed, he dreams about hurting Radu until his release comes, and there's nothing left.

CHAPTER 94

CONSTANTINOPLE, EASTER MONDAY 1453

It's April, and the long winter nights gave way to warm spring days fragrant with jasmine and lilac. The air rings with the birds' love calls, and by the side of the road, yellow dandelions and purple crocuses spring to life, making the grass look even greener.

Mehmed lifts his face to the mellow breeze, hoping it will bring some relief to his troops. After long weeks of marching all day and inhaling each other's dust, his men are getting tired. They had enough of setting camp every day, sleeping under the open sky, and eating hardtack.

Mehmed is tired too. He can't tell anyone, but these weeks have been even harder on him than on his men. Unlike him, they don't carry the empire's weight on their shoulders. To gather the hundred thousand soldiers marching on Constantinople, Mehmed had to expose the Ottoman Empire's soft underbelly. He depleted the troops in Anatolia, where the Karamanids can't wait for him to turn his back. He left even less in Rumelia, where Hunyadi yearns to rebuild his sullied reputation, and Skanderbeg is ready to stab him in the back. He signed peace treaties with them, of course, but he knows as well as they do those treaties aren't worth the paper they're written on. His foes will attack him as soon as they can if they think they can win.

But he had to gamble everything on Constantinople. His fate, and the fate of the Ottoman Empire, hinge on whether he wins or loses the city.

"Don't do it, my sultan. It's too risky," Çandarlı Halil Paşa implored, when Mehmed withdrew troops from Anatolia. "You can't trust the Karamanids."

"I have to do it."

"But why? Our informers told us that Constantine has fewer than ten thousand men. We don't need a hundred thousand troops! If you only take fifty thousand, you can leave twenty each in Rumelia and Anatolia, plus another ten to guard Edirne, and we'll still outnumber Constantine five to one. And we're talking well-trained janissaries and sipahis, not a bunch of dirty peasants, merchants, and bakers armed with hot water and rocks!"

"The more men we have, the faster we'll take the city. And the faster we can return before our enemies can harm us."

Çandarlı Paşa shook his head. Mehmed knows his argument is weak, but he can't tell him the truth: He must take Constantinople now, no matter what. Even if that means losing Albania, Serbia, and half of Anatolia. They don't matter to him like the city of his dreams. As a matter of fact, they're a pain in the ass to keep, since they're so far from Edirne, and across the freaking sea.

As if Mehmed didn't have enough worries, he feels that Çandarlı Paşa's allegiance has started to fray. It's been a couple months since Mehmed sent him home with his head still on his shoulders, and he forgot. He may need a reminder, Mehmed thinks, knowing that this war is not earning him any friends.

He left without Radu, but took the boy. He remembers Radu every time he calls on him, and his heart is still poisoned with betrayal. His best friend and soul mate refused to stand by his side in the fight of his life, for the sake of a stupid religion he never cared about. Hard to believe his love mattered so little.

Up ahead, someone shouts, then another and another. They've arrived.

The golden city of his dreams rises straight ahead, gilded by the setting sun, and Mehmed's soul soars. He forgets about Çandarlı Paşa, Hunyadi, and even Radu, as his heart bursts with love for his city. And his army.

Karaca Bey, Rumelia's governor, had his men cut down the city's vineyards to open the way and make room for Mehmed's camp. Boat after loaded boat brought the azaps and the sipahis sent by Ishak Paşa, Anatolia's governor, and landed them under Rumeli Hisari's protection. The Rumelian troops came from the west, led by fifteen hundred Serbians on their splendid horses. The three hundred boats from Gelibolu under Admiral Suleiman Baltaoğlu rock gently in the Bosporus, sheltered by Mehmed's twin fortresses. They're so many they make Constantine's navy in the Golden Horn look like an afterthought. The dozens of tall siege machines and heavy cannons are already set in place. So is Orban's Basilica.

It took two months, fifty oxen, and two hundred men, plus an entire contingent of road builders to bring the Basilica from Edirne. But look at her now, shining like a golden queen among dozens of smaller cannons.

And his men. What used to be Constantinople's vineyard turned into a field of Ottoman uniforms spreading as far as the eye can see, all waiting for Mehmed's orders, and make his heart soar.

They pitched his tent behind the large guns, high on the Hill of Maltepe, facing the St. Romanus city gate. He has twelve thousand janissaries around him: the Anatolian to his right, the Rumelians to his left. And down below, a hundred thousand men await his orders.

The time has come.

"Zaganos Paşa."

"My sultan?"

"Take my peace offer to Constantine. Tell him that, should he surrender, his people can leave the city with their belongings. No hair from their heads will be harmed, and the city will be spared. But if they don't, I'll put Constantinople through sword and fire. Nobody will be safe. The dead will be lucky, since they won't live to see their houses plundered, their daughters sold and their sons killed. It's up to him."

Zaganos Paşa grabs the scroll Mehmed wrote and re-wrote until he felt happy with every word, and gallops to the St. Romanus's gate with his men carrying the messengers' white flag, while Mehmed awaits.

He studies the city walls. These are the famed Theodosian Walls he's been obsessing about since he was only twelve. They're even more impressive in reality than on the map.

The five-layered defense comprises an inner wall around the city and an outer wall surrounding it, plus a deep moat and two killing fields in between. No wonder it lasted for a thousand years.

The solid inner wall is eighteen feet thick and thirty six feet high, faced with limestone blocks and filled with mortar made from crushed bricks and lime. Nine bands of brick strengthen it inside, bonding the stone façade to the mortar core and increasing its endurance against earthquakes and cannons. Its ninety-six towers are fifty feet tall, and their battlement terraces let the defenders pour death and destruction over any invader strong enough to break into the killing field between the walls.

The outer wall is six feet thick and crowned with a battlemented walkway. It's thirty feet high and reinforced with forty tall towers. That outer wall alone is a formidable defense, good enough to thwart Father's siege in 1422.

Then there's the outer killing field by the moat. The moat alone is sixty feet wide and thirty feet deep, with another crenelated wall serving as the first line of defense.

Sure, there are gates. Nine of them. But they're closed, and it doesn't look like the emperor plans to open them soon.

The longer Mehmed studies the walls, the heavier his heart gets. They must have worked on them throughout the winter, because the thousand-year-old bricks look like they just got laid last week. The cracks and missing stones Mehmed remembered are all gone. The emperor's men worked hard on the city's defense, and that doesn't bode well for surrender.

Up on the highest tower, Constantine's yellow flag with the black double-headed eagle flutters in the breeze. In its shade, men in glittering armor watch Mehmed, and he remembers about that Genoese pirate. They say he's like a god in battle, and nobody has beaten him yet. Neither him nor his condottieri, who swore to protect Constantinople to their last breath. And those are not peasants armed with pitchforks and sickles; they're Genoese mercenaries, well-armed and as experienced as they get. But there's only seven hundred of them for fourteen miles of walls. How could they possibly make a difference?

Mehmed spurs Rüzgar towards the Golden Horn, the half-mile-wide strip of water where two creeks join to flow into the Bosporus, and ogles it longingly. The harbor is cut away from the Bosporus by a heavy mile-long chain stretching from Constantinople's Acropolis to the Tower of Galata to keep the enemies out and the Romans' boats safe. Mehmed lusts after that harbor, but, even more, he covets the walls, which are weaker here. Not weak, mind you, but they're nothing like those Theodosian Walls he loves to hate.

He paces, waiting for Zaganos Paşa with Constantine's answer, and his excitement dies down. What if Çandarlı Paşa was right? What if he fails after risking his empire for this? Everyone else did. Twenty-three attempts to take the city and none of them succeeded. How can he return to Edirne defeated? And face Radu?

His heart heavy, Mehmed turns to see Zaganos Paşa. His face shrouded in darkness, the vizier shakes his head.

This is it. The moment he's prepared for his whole life is finally upon him. Time to rise to greatness or die.

Mehmed lifts his kilij, and a hundred thousand people fall silent to listen.

"Fire the guns."

CHAPTER 95
THE PIRATE

The weather no longer matters in Constantinople. Between the gunpowder smoke and the dust fouling the air, they don't even know if it's sunny or cloudy. The air is gray, thick, and heavy with dirt from the crumbling walls, and it sticks in Ion's throat.

The thousand-year-old empire has never seen something like this. It's like they fell straight into the depths of Hell. Day after day, Mehmed's cannons fire at them from dawn to dusk. Plus a few shots in the night, just to ensure the defenders can never get a full night's sleep.

Every day the thick walls that stood through a thousand years and twenty-three assaults shake, shiver and crumble. The outer walls were the first to succumb to the devastating blows of the thousand-pound cannon balls. The rest followed. The inside walls, the holy churches, the people's homes, even Constantine's Grand Palace, struggle to stay put while the earth shakes under them like a wet dog. It's like living through fifty earthquakes a day.

The walls crumble, and heavy tiles fall from the roofs, crushing those unlucky enough to be under them. The empty buildings turned to piles of rubble as their bricks got taken to fix the holes in the walls.

The others are about to follow suit. It's an all-out assault like nobody has ever seen, not even Giustiniani.

The new *prōtostratōr*, the high military commander, as Constantine titled him, meanders from one post to the next, from one gate to the other, from one wounded man to the next, lifting them out of misery. He's never scared, never tired, and never angry. It's like he's not human, and that pisses Ion off no end.

Ion is up on the walls to see the fight, even though he has no business there. He should be down in the treasury, counting money. But he climbed to watch Giustiniani instead, struggling to see what's so special about him. Why did Ali fall for him? And the more Ion watches him, the more pissed he gets.

He's about to go to his work when Giustiniani turns to him. "You're Ion?"

"Yes."

"Where are you from?'

"Transylvania."

"Really?"

"Yes."

"Amazing. I've never been there, and I've been everywhere else. But they're a little short of seas there. Do you grow fangs at night?"

"Not me. My brother does, but only under the full moon."

Giustiniani laughs and moves to the next post, where a man got knocked down when a stone fell from the wall. He chokes with dust and bleeds from his ear. Giustiniani helps him up and rips a strip of his chemise to wrap his head.

"Hold here," he tells Ion.

Ion puts a hand on the bandage and looks away as Giustiniani wraps the man's head. "See, you want to do it tight, but not too tight. You want to stop the bleeding, but not the blood circulation. How are you doing, my man? Should I help you to your home?"

The man stares at him. "Are you the pirate?"

"I guess so."

"It was wonderful what you did with that ship. I've seen nothing like that."

"Neither have I. So, you want to go home?"

"Nah. I'll be OK. And Pirate?"

"Yes?"

"You're OK."

Giustiniani laughs and pats his shoulder, then walks to the next post, a hundred feet away, to check on the defenders. It's on the southern side of the wall, by the gate of Selymbria. As it happens, Ion was there when the council divided the gates, assigning each gate to a defender, so he knows Selymbria is not Giustiniani's to look after.

"Didn't you get the San Romanus' gate?" Ion asks, then wishes he hadn't.

"Yes. So what?"

"So why aren't you there?"

"I've been there. And I'll go back. But for now, I'm here. Whose area is this?"

"Notaras' maybe? Or Orhan's? I don't know."

"Neither do I, but does it matter? They aren't here, and I am. You can't really protect a city by dividing responsibilities. Have you ever heard that a chain is only as strong as its weakest link? We can't win unless we all do the best we can. For things to work out, everything must be everyone's responsibility. They don't know it, but I do, and I try to lead by example."

Ion sighs. This man makes him feel small without trying.

"You want to help?"

"Of course. But I don't know much."

"That's OK. Nobody cares how much you know until they know how much you care. We all need help."

That's how Ion spends the rest of the day following the pirate from one post to the next, from one wounded man to the next. They stop to pick up rocks the cannons knocked out of the wall and push them back where they came from; they help the wounded; they check the locks on the gates. Every once in a while, they glance at Mehmed's army with its smoking cannons, then get back to whatever needs doing. By the end of the day, Ion is so exhausted he can barely walk, but Giustiniani looks no worse for the wear.

As a bloody sunset slaughters the sky and the cannonade slows down, Ion hopes they're done for the day.

Giustiniani glances at him and smiles. "How're you doing, my man?"

Ion nods, too tired to talk.

"Good. Let's check the ammunition and make sure everyone has what they need for tomorrow."

Ion follows, his legs heavy as lead, wondering where this man gets his strength. He's not young, the pirate. His eyes are surrounded by deep laugh lines, and his dark curls are streaked with white. He's got to be forty if he's a day, but he shows no sign of slowing down, while Ion's feet burn like he's walked on hot coals. He's tired, cold, and thoroughly fed up, and looks for an excuse to take off, as he follows Giustiniani down the steps.

The pirate glances back. "You OK, pal?"

Ion nods, and the man taps his shoulder. "You're doing a fantastic job. Come on, I'll buy you a drink before we go to check on the basements."

CHAPTER 96
A FREAKING HERO

Constantinople has only been under fire for a week, but it feels like a year. The never-ending cannonade, the heart-wrenching screams of the wounded, the dust in their throats, and the lack of sleep are taking their toll on the Romans. People's hopes are running thin.

The gloom and misery also infected the imperial council. With the gold gone, the dignitaries' bleak faces match the martyrs' in the now frameless icons: long and dreary. They sit around the council table like they'd sit at a wake, just less joyful, Ion thinks.

"Any news about the ships?" the emperor asks. The pope's Genoese ships bringing supplies and reinforcements have been due for weeks, but there's no sign of them yet.

Sphrantzes shakes his head.

Loukas Notaras sneers. "I told you they won't come. Just another unfulfilled promise from those damned Catholics after we gave them what they wanted."

"What exactly did you give them?" Giustiniani asks.

"The united Orthodox and Catholic mass. They insisted on it as a precondition to sending help. So we bent over and did it, even though it enraged our people and humiliated our faith. And now the darn pope sits on his thumbs, watching us perish."

"We aren't exactly perishing. We held on through a full week of incessant fire, and we're still holding on," Giustiniani says.

"Did you happen to look at the wall this morning? Did you notice how the wall around your St. Romanus gate is almost gone? It was your task to defend that, I believe. You may want to get around to doing that."

"Neither I nor anybody else can protect the wall against the massive blows of that monstrous cannon," Constantine says.

"Well, then. If your brave defender here can't defend us, it may be time to surrender, like I said long ago. Mehmed won't be as generous as he was, but he may still give us terms we could live with. Otherwise, we'll all die here like a pack of rats. The walls are crumbling. We're running out of food. The Genoese aren't coming, and our people's morale is at an all-time low. What on earth are we waiting for?" Notaras spits.

Constantine rubs a hand over his face. "We need to pray. God, in his wisdom, will send us help when He chooses to."

"IF He chooses to. But why would he, especially after that Catholic mess we shoved down His throat?"

At the end of the table, the old patriarch crosses himself and looks at Notaras with fear. "You are committing blasphemy, my son. Watch yourself. I'll see you in confession on Sunday."

"You might, if we're still here on Sunday. But it doesn't look good. Even if Mehmed doesn't break through, our own people may well revolt against us any day now. They're losing faith."

Constantine sighs. "If the ships arrive, they will gain courage."

"And if they don't?"

"The megas doux has a point," Giustiniani says. "You can fight with a hungry army, with a naked army, even with a poorly trained army, as long as they have their morale. But you can't fight with a *hopeless* army. Losing hope is the end. So, I guess we need to give our men some hope."

"How?" Notaras asks.

"Why don't you all meet me at the St. Romanus' gate? The one I was supposed to defend?"

He leaves, and they stare at each other, wondering what he's up to. Sphrantzes follows him, then Constantine, Ion, and the others.

There, just inside the St. Romanus' gate, they find a Giustiniani none of them has seen before. He's covered in armor from head to toe, complete with gorget and helmet. His face shield open, he stands ahead of two dozen of his men, all in plate armor like him. They're armed with crossbows and swords, and they carry rectangular shields that reach from their knees to their shoulders, all marked with the Genoese red cross.

Giustiniani lifts his sword. "Are we ready to fight?"

"Yes, we are!" his men answer.

"Are we ready to crush the enemy?"

"Yes, we are."

"Are we ready to spill their blood to protect this city, and show the faithless whose side God is on?"

"Yes, we are!"

They holler, striking their swords to their chests and thumping their feet to the ground to make more noise, pumping themselves up for the fight.

The entire city watches.

"Open the gate."

The tall arched gate of St. Romanus screeches open for the first time in weeks, and time stops. The wind dies down, the birds go quiet, and the cannons stop firing.

Inside the wall, eyes grow big and mouths fall agape. They can't believe the Genoese left the shelter of the wall. They're two dozen against a hundred thousand Ottomans with cannons. Nobody has ever seen anything like this.

The Genoese walk away from the wall and fall into formation. From Ion's spot up on the wall, they look like toy soldiers. Ion's heart quickens seeing them face Mehmed's entire army, and he wonders what's next.

A formation of red janissaries deploys from the Ottoman camp and marches towards them. There are only a hundred or so, a tiny fraction of Mehmed's army, but they outnumber the Genoese five to one. And they're the best-trained soldiers in the world.

As they get close, the janissaries spread out to surround the Genoese and cut their retreat. That's easy to see from up on the wall, but they may not see it down there, Ion thinks, since Giustiniani and his men stand frozen like statues.

"They'll surround you," Ion screams, but they can't hear him, because everybody else is shouting too. Sphrantzes, Constantine, even Notaras. The whole Constantinople yells at the top of their lungs, covering the roar of Mehmed's troops.

The janissaries get closer. Deployed wide, they're closing in.

The Genoese wait.

Five hundred feet. Four hundred. Three hundred.

The Genoese wait.

Two hundred. One hundred.

The janissaries lift their kilijes and rush them.

"Allah U Akbar! Allah U Akbar."

Giustiniani lifts his sword.

The first row of Genoese drops to their knees behind their shields like one. A cloud of arrows flies above their heads, sinking into the janissaries storming them, then another and another. In less time than you'd take to say the Lord's prayer, half the janissaries are writhing on the ground.

The Genoese drop their shields and lift their swords to attack.

They aren't fast, the Genoese, under fifty pounds of heavy armor. Nothing like the nimble janissaries in their chain mail. But they're strong, precise, and ferocious. Their long swords cut through limbs like they're kindling. The chain mail doesn't even slow them down, while the curved Ottoman kilijes slide harmlessly over their heavy armor.

One after another, the bloodied janissaries fall to the ground like a flock of sheep slaughtered by wolves. The condottieri stay put. They're slow, efficient, and merciless.

It feels like a week, but it couldn't be more than the time to burn a skinny candle, and no janissary is left standing. The Genoese are covered in blood from head to toe, but unharmed. They lift their swords towards Mehmed and scream.

"For God."

They turn around towards the wall.

"For the city."

They turn to Giustiniani, his muzzle face shield open, his white teeth sparkling in his blood-splattered face, and they lift their swords once more.

"For our captain."

He lifts his sword to them. "For the best fighters God created. Let's go. I'll buy you a drink."

The sultan's cannons forgot to fire as the gate of St. Romanus closes behind the victors. The city of Constantinople watches in awe as the condottieri walk back, laughing.

"You're getting slow in your old age, Giustiniani. You should thank God I was there to save your sorry ass," one says.

Giustiniani laughs and slaps his back. "Like you have room to talk. Thank God those janissaries were slower than molasses."

Ion glances back to see Ali gazing at the pirate like she never looked at him. Oh, how he wishes he could hate that man!

CHAPTER 97
THE BASILICA

Through the red haze of his rage, Mehmed can barely see the St. Romanus' gate slam shut behind the last Genoese. He's so angry he can hardly breathe, and his heart beats like it wants to tear off his chest.

Those mercenaries, that scum that fights for money instead of giving their blood for their faith and country, massacred every one of the janissaries he sent after them and didn't lose a single man. He wouldn't believe it if he didn't see it with his eyes.

But he did. And so did every one of his men, who were already tired and antsy after more than a week of siege with nothing to brag about. This will crush their morale, like it crushed his. Mehmed's blood boils in his head and he's so furious he can't see straight. Still, he has his men to think about, so he spurs Rüzgar forward, lifts his sword, and shouts. "We will destroy those mercenaries. We'll put Constantinople through sword and fire and make them sorry they were ever born. We will avenge every one of our men who are now with Allah, rejoicing in the many gifts He has for them."

He considers mentioning the seventy-two virgins that Allah saves for his braves, but he refrains. The men are tired and hurt. As things stand, they may see those virgins as an extra chore rather than a reward. He'll save them for a better time, he thinks, and goes to check the cannons.

The guns stopped firing when the gate opened. That was a mistake. A well-planted cannonball amid the Genoese formation would have saved him all this heartache. But what happened, happened. You can't go back, only forward. He must punish the city for everyone to see to lift his men's morale.

"Fire."

A hundred sweaty cannon men lean over their machines, soothing them like they're babies. They check the ropes that swaddle them, making sure they're tight enough. They bathe them in olive oil, inside and out, to lessen the friction and help them cool. Finally, they light the fuse to the gunpowder behind the cannonball. The killing machines are really simple: you light the gunpowder, it explodes, and it spits out the cannonball along its well-greased track, towards the target.

Two dozen cannons fire. A dust cloud envelops the city, so thick they can't see the result. It takes a while to settle, but when it does, the wall around St. Romanus' gate got shorter.

"Fire!"

They fire again, and again, and again. When the dust finally settles, it's obvious that the wall is barely standing. They're finally getting the break they need, Mehmed thinks, and his heart fills with joy. His men's screams tell him they noticed it too, and they can finally see their way to the heart of the city. Mehmed swells with pride. He'll obliterate those faithless mercenaries who humiliated him.

"Fire!"

The cannons blast again, but the noise changed. And there's little dust. When it settles, seconds later, the wall is still standing.

"What happened?" Mehmed asks.

Zaganos Paşa eyes narrow with concern. "The Basilica didn't fire, and she always does the most damage."

"Why not?"

"Orban says she's overheated, and he needs to let her cool."

"What?"

Mehmed stomps to the Basilica. Orban, smelling like smoke and covered in soot from head to toe, is bathing the enormous gun in olive oil like a midwife would clean a sultan's firstborn, only more carefully.

"What's going on?"

"We need to let her cool, my sultan. We overheated her. She's only supposed to fire six times a day to have time to cool, but we overused her, and now... see these cracks?"

He points to a handful of deep cracks in the gun's enormous body. They're big enough to stick your finger in, despite the thick ropes holding the barrel together.

"I'm afraid they're about to expand. We need to let her cool. We can fire her again tomorrow, I hope. And..."

"Orban."

"Yes, Sultan."

"Would you rather have your head on your shoulders? Or at your feet?"

"My sultan..."

"If you want to keep your head on your shoulders, you'll fire this gun right now. You hear me?"

"Yes, my sultan. But..."

Mehmed doesn't wait to hear what the man has to say. He steps away to stop himself from killing him, but his fingers clutch the hilt of his kilij. *Chill down now*, he tells himself. *Be patient. Count to one hundred before slicing Orban's throat. Allah will see how patient you are, and he'll give you help.*

Twenty, twenty-three, twenty-four...

"My sultan?"

Çandarlı Halil Paşa faces him, and Mehmed's grip on his kilij tightens further. "Those mercenaries were not good for our men's morale."

No shit, Mehmed thinks, as his brain keeps counting. "You're right, grand vizier. We'll have to correct that."

"How about stepping back, my sultan? We could offer Constantine some reasonable terms if he agrees to pay a tribute, and let him be in charge of his city, but keep the forts we took on the Black Sea. We can still make this into a victory."

Sixty-seven. Sixty-eight. Sixty-nine.

"I don't think so, Çandarlı Paşa. They'd all think we got chased away."

"What do we care what they all think?"

"I thought you wanted to improve our men's morale?"

Eighty-eight. Eighty-nine. Ninety. Mehmed's fingers grip the hilt tighter as he turns back to Orban with Çandarlı Paşa in tow. The man is still oiling the gun, but his assistant has the torch ready to light the fuse.

"I'm ready," the assistant says, and Orban wipes his forehead with his sleeve. His dirty face is falling apart, like there's nothing but the skin holding it together, and his dilated eyes scream fear. For a moment, Mehmed wonders if he should let the gun rest, like he asked for, but it's too late. The assistant lifts the torch towards the fuse, and Orban crosses himself and throws himself to the ground, rolling away from the Basilica.

Nothing happens.

Mehmed feels reassured until he realizes he didn't hear the cannon fire. He glances at St. Romanus' gate for the charge to strike, but there's nothing. He turns back to the Basilica, but something lifts him off his feet, twists him and throws him through the air. He crashes to the ground.

When he opens his eyes, he sees only darkness and hears nothing but the maddened beat of his heart. He can't remember where he is and why he's here.

Then he remembers. The Basilica. Orban was right. He should have left it to cool.

CHAPTER 98

CONSTANTINOPLE, APRIL 20, 1453

Mehmed struggled to see, and couldn't hear at all for three days after the Basilica blew up. Even now, a week later, his head still hurts, and his ears are bleeding.

His Jewish doctor tried a dozen potions, from the gallbladder of a hare to mandrake and opium. He plastered Mehmed's feet in fox fat and herbs, and managed to bring back his hearing in the right ear. The left one's still bad, so he wanted to burn it with a hot iron, but Mehmed said no. Truth be told, he almost wishes he was deaf, because none of the news he got lately has been good.

First, that frontal attack against the damaged gate of St. Romanus. When he realized the Basilica had blown up, so bringing down that wall was not likely, he decided to catch the defenders unaware.

He sent his assault machines with his best janissary units to conquer passage over the damaged wall. But those damned Genoese came out again and fought like devils. They littered the field with janissary bodies until the dirt turned red with the blood of his men, and they didn't lose a single fighter.

Mehmed followed the fight from his hill. He saw his janissaries fall under the mercenaries' broadswords. He watched his ox-hide covered siege machines burn to the ground from Greek Fire. He saw his burning men jump out of them and break their necks. And, worse of all, he witnessed the damned Romans rebuild the tower overnight.

"How can that be? How is that even possible?" Mehmed thundered.

The dozen viziers aligned in front of him lowered their eyes. They said nothing, but Çandarlı Paşa's silence spoke louder than words. He'd warned him, again and again.

But Mehmed didn't listen. The grand vizier wanted to keep his men safe, but his army wasn't here to be safe. They're here to take Constantinople, and Mehmed would gladly give a hundred thousand lives, if that's what it takes. Still, the field is littered with his men's bodies, but there's no sign of progress, and Mehmed chokes with rage.

As if that wasn't bad enough, Zaganos Paşa brought a message from their watchmen at the Dardanelles this morning. They saw a Genoese fleet pass into the Sea of Marmara, heading toward the Bosporus Strait. They must bring the supplies the Romans are waiting for, and they're arriving just when nobody thought they would. Just to ruin his plans.

"Are you sure?" Mehmed asked.

Zaganos Paşa shrugged. "I didn't see them, but our men seem sure. If they're right, the ships should be here by the day after tomorrow. Sooner, with good wind."

The Genoese ships aren't driven by oars, like the heavy Ottoman galleys. The Genoese sail nimble caravels, tall carracks, and curvy galleons that fly dozens of sails to harness the power of the wind. And that's both their strength and their weakness.

"We need to stop them. Admiral Baltaoğlu?"

The old fleet admiral climbed through the ranks from lowly janissary to Admiral of the Navy for a reason. His nickname, Baltaoğlu, means "Son of the battle axe" after his favorite weapon, and it fits him well. He's not young, Süleyman Baltaoğlu, but he's wiry and strong like an oak, and he has never failed Mehmed yet.

"My sultan?"

He's gray-bearded and sharp-eyed, and his narrow, weather-beaten face makes him look like a human blade. Mehmed is glad he rebuilt the Ottoman Navy and put it under him.

"I need you to stop the Genoese ships from getting into the Golden Horn, no matter what."

"I'll do that, my sultan."

"How many ships have you got?"

"A hundred and forty."

"They say there are four Genoese ships. Just four. Can you handle that?"

"They won't get through, my sultan. We'll send them to the bottom of the sea. The fish will feast on their flesh, and we'll feast on the fish and grow stronger."

"Good. But if you don't…"

"I will."

"But if you don't, the fish will feast on your flesh. I, personally, will make sure that you don't see the light of another day. Got it?"

The old admiral nods, looking put out, and Mehmed wonders if he's been too forceful. But it's too late and the battle should start soon.

The wind blows strong through the Bosporus Strait, whipping the flags above Constantinople's towers. The Genoese ships must be close.

"They're here," someone screams.

Mehmed heads to the high point that gives him the best view of the Strait. To his left, the Golden Horn. That's where the Genoese must sail to shelter with the other Roman ships. His new fortress, the Rumeli Hisari, is straight ahead on the Strait, the half-a-mile strip of water joining the Black Sea to the Marmara. The Marmara, to his right, is no bigger than a lake, but it opens to the Mediterranean, connecting Constantinople with the rest of the world. That's where the Genoese are coming from, but they still have a long way to go. Baltaoğlu and his fleet stand between them and safety, blocking their entry into the Golden Horn.

Tall and handsome, the Genoese galleons with their high-flying white sails look like brides holding hands. They're bigger than Mehmed's ships, but there's only four of them, for Allah's sake! Four against a hundred and forty. That's thirty-five to one, Mehmed calculates. Every Genoese ship has to steer clear of thirty-five Ottoman galleys fighting for Allah, who would do anything to stop her. The combination of math and faith makes Mehmed giddy. There's no way, absolutely no way, they can get through.

The heavy drums start their low rumble, punctuating the rhythm the oarsmen must keep, and Baltaoğlu's ships cut the galleons' way. The low galleys with their countless oars moving as one look like an army of centipedes converging on the galleons. The white sails catch the wind, and the Genoese close the distance.

The wind quickens. The galleons pick up speed. They tack and zig and zag, avoiding Baltaoğlu's galleys to head towards the Golden Horn, nimble as egrets, their white sails glaring in the dusk.

Standing at the bow of his galley, Baltaoğlu lifts his battle ax. "Fire. Aim at their sails."

A smoky cloud of burning arrows sinks into the first galleon's sails, setting them ablaze. The second one follows, then the third, and, before long, all four are on fire. The sails burn like torches, lighting the night for all to see, from Mehmed on his hill to the crowded walls of Constantinople.

Mehmed smiles. Good. That's the idea. Constantine and his people must see their hope is unfounded and their resistance vain. The sooner they get it, the sooner this war can be over.

The wind suddenly dies. The galleons, their sails on fire, slow down, then stop dead in the water as Baltaoğlu's galleys surround them. The Ottoman archers unleash another cloud of burning arrows, and the Genoese ships scream their pain. Burning men roll on the decks, struggling to quell the fire that consumes them, wounded scream, dead bodies drop into the water. In the hellish red light, the Genoese captains run from bow to stern, putting out fires and screaming orders that nobody seems to follow. The chaos worsens, while the Ottoman galleys, in perfect formation, close in. Adrift in the sea, the proud sail ships smoke like burning torches. They're easy prey for Baltaoğlu's galleys, whose men get ready to board.

This battle is about to be over.

CHAPTER 99

THE ONE-EYED HERO

S tanding high on the Hill of Maltepe, where he can watch every detail of the battle, Mehmed smiles. "This is about to get good."

Zaganos Paşa agrees. "It's pretty good already. Admiral Baltaoğlu is a great man."

Mehmed nods. He's starving for a victory, and ready to savor every moment. So are his men. Everyone in his camp is watching the naval battle, and so are the Romans, up on their wall.

Baltaoğlu, with two dozen of his galleys, encircle the first galleon. They grab their hooks and their grapples to climb aboard. The other galleys surround the other three like a pack of hungry wolves hunting deer. Three dozen galleys gang against every sail ship. It's almost over, Mehmed thinks, when everything changes in the blink of an eye.

Instead of fighting their attackers like anyone would do, the Genoese throw lines from one galleon to another and tie them together. Bound together, the four ships became a floating fortress. Instead of facing enemy attacks from everywhere, they now only have to protect the outside decks.

Mehmed's soldiers persevere and strive to board them, but it's not easy. Unlike the galleys, whose decks must be low to the water for the oars to reach, the tall galleons are way above. Still, Baltaoğlu's men throw their grapples and hooks on the decks to climb up their ropes, like they always do. Their battle cry shakes the earth.

"Allah-u Akbar. Allah-u Akbar."

But the four ships tied together don't leave them much room to maneuver, and the defenders have less space to protect. Tall and grim, the Genoese sailors stand shoulder to shoulder on the outside decks and fight like angry devils. Their axes cut the Ottoman's lines, their swords slice through flesh and bone, and killer daggers gut the few who make it to the deck.

Mehmed's men fight like men possessed. They brave the Genoese blades like they don't care if they live or die. Wherever one falls, another takes his place, then another. Then ten more.

But bravery just isn't enough. In the low galleys, the Ottomans stand a dozen feet below the galleons' decks. They can't reach the defenders that maul them with lances, arrows, and swords. They try and try again, but to no avail. The air is thick with the agony of the wounded, and the water turns red with the blood of the dead.

Standing in the first galley, Baltaoğlu sees the carnage. He feels the tide turning, so he grabs his axe and throws himself into the thick of the battle. "For Allah! For the empire! For our sultan!" he shouts, grabbing a line to board the nearest galleon. Arrows fly, swords slice, and lances stab at him, but he persists. Heartbeats later, he raises his axe above the Genoese deck. *"Allah-u Akbar. Allah-u Akbar."*

Emboldened, his men follow. Dozens of Ottomans claw their way to the Genoese decks, and the tide of the battle is about to turn again when an arrow sinks into Baltaoğlu's eye. He stumbles and wavers, then falls into the sea with a splash. A dozen men jump to drag him back to the galley.

Mehmed's heart sinks. No matter how many we are, we're not enough, he thinks, just as the wind picks up.

The galleons snap to attention. In a heartbeat, they cut each other loose and sail north, leaving nothing but death and destruction in their wake. Fast as lightning, the Genoese get back to their posts.

Blackened sails spew smoke above the sailors trimming them, and clouds of arrows strike the galleys in their way. Baltaoğlu's oarsmen strive to keep up, but there's no keeping up with the wind. There's nothing left but smoke as the galleons fly into the Golden Horn over the massive chain, lowered to let them pass. Seconds later, the chain is back up.

The battle is over. Mehmed lost again, and his men got to watch.

Even worse, the entire Constantinople watched. Instead of a blistering defeat, Mehmed handed them another glowing victory and covered himself in shame. His blood boils with fury, and his gut twists with worry. "Bring me Baltaoğlu."

He steps into his tent and tries to pray, but can't remember the words. His rage consumes him, robbing him of his senses. Baltaoğlu failed him. Not only did he deprive him of a well-deserved victory, but made him the laughingstock of Constantinople and the entire world. They had a hundred forty ships to the Genoese four, and they lost. How can Mehmed ever look someone in the eye again?

It's Baltaoğlu's fault. He'll crush him. He'll kill him and feed him to the fish, like he promised, since he's the one to blame for what happened.

"We brought him, sultan." It's Zaganos Paşa, the one man he still trusts.

Mehmed takes a deep breath, trying to slow down his heart. He grabs his bejeweled kilij and steps out.

Held up by two men and covered in blood, Baltaoğlu falters. An arrow shaft still sticks out of his right eye.

"You said you'll stop them."

"I failed, my sultan. I'm sorry."

"You were a hundred forty against four. That's thirty-five to one. And you failed."

Baltaoğlu trembles, ready to crumble, and the two men steady him. Mehmed's kilij itches in his hand.

"You're right, my sultan. I failed you. I'm sorry," Baltaoğlu whispers.

"You're a coward. You failed to keep your promise, and for your failure, you deserve to die."

Baltaoğlu hangs his head. Mehmed lifts his kilij, its blade red in the torch light. His blood boils, and his sight blurs as he readies to strike through Baltaoğlu's neck.

The troops stomp their feet and roar. They're glad to see him punished, Mehmed thinks, when Çandarlı Halil Paşa steps forward.

"My sultan, this man is a hero. Nobody could have done more. Killing him would be a mistake." The paşa's eyes are weary, but his voice is strong. The men's roar gets louder.

Mehmed opens his mouth to tell the grand vizier what to do with himself when Zaganos Paşa steps forward.

"My sultan, Admiral Baltaoğlu has always been your faithful servant, and your father's before you. He gave you all he had. Nobody could have done more. Remember that, my sultan."

Mehmed's eyes slide from one to the other, and his fingers tighten around his kilij, itching to kill. One of them, two, or all three. How can his viziers challenge him like that? Even Zaganos Paşa, his most trusted man? He's sick to his stomach with fury when a man steps forward, then another and another, asking for mercy for Baltaoğlu. The whole army roars and clangs their swords to their shields to show their support. They're ready to riot, and Mehmed would better tread lightly.

His wrath sickens him, but he can't help but see that killing Baltaoğlu would be a disaster. Laying the blame on the admiral didn't work, so Mehmed takes a deep breath and readjusts. "Like a faithless coward, you failed me, you failed your men, and you failed the empire. You don't deserve to live. Still, considering your years of service, I won't kill you today. I'll remove every one of your titles, and you'll get a hundred lashes, but I'll let you see tomorrow's light."

Baltaoğlu falls to his knees. "Thank you, my sultan. You are most generous."

Mehmed curls his lip. "Thank your supporters who kept you alive."

That evening, he takes extra care with his ablutions, then prays to

Allah and reads the Quran, but he still feels like a prick. That's not new, but it doesn't feel good.

CHAPTER 100

BETWEEN LOVE AND DEATH

Constantinople parties that night. Oh, how it parties! Hailed as saviors, the Genovese are treated to the best the beleaguered city has to offer. Wine flows like water, and folks who never met hug and kiss like long-lost brothers. The Romans are drunk not from wine, but from the sweet joy of victory. They sing and laugh and dance in the streets, even though little has changed: the city is still under siege, they're still threatened and hungry, and God only knows how much more they can take. They spent weeks under the pummeling of Mehmed's cannons, eating stale bread and sleeping under leaky roofs. They've waited for so long for a sign that God hasn't forgotten them that the Genoese ships will have to do.

Still, there's no food, no wood, and no way to fix your broken home because everything is for the wall. The stones, the bricks, the plaster — it's all for the wall. Even the Grand Palace's roof is leaking. The servants set bowls to catch the drips, but the worn stone floors are still slippery.

That's why Ali keeps her eyes on the ground to avoid the wet spots. Thankfully, her long cloak keeps out most of the rain, and the worn soles of her leather boots hold on to the slippery floor, because she

406

can't afford to get hurt. Dozens of lives depend on her, and even more need her to curb their suffering.

For weeks now, Ali has spent her every hour caring for the sick and the wounded, but they're just too many. Her potions and herbs are almost depleted, and she ran out of the milk of the poppy days ago. She can no longer curb the dying's suffering but by praying with them, wetting their parched lips, and finding them a position of comfort. But she still has her ointments and the skills Smaranda taught her, so she drifts from one wounded to the next to bring them hope and aid, or at least help their death.

No one knows it, of course, since killing people is a sin. God alone can decide how long to let them suffer before allowing them to die. But God has been busy these days. If he saw them, he'd help them way sooner, Ali thinks. He must be busy listening to all the prayers, so Ali does her best to cover for him while he's otherwise engaged.

This jubilant evening is harder than most, since the Genoese paid a heavy toll to get through. Besides the many dead, there are dozens of wounded: burns, arrows, cuts, broken bones, and every other kind of hurt one can imagine.

Down in the throne room, they celebrate their victory and Mehmed's humiliation. They only know that the ships made it through with weapons, soldiers, and supplies, so it's all good. They don't know about the terrified eighteen-year-old choking on his own blood from the arrow in his neck, or about the broken sailor who'll never walk again. He broke his back when he fell from the mast while trimming the burning sails. But down in the throne room, they don't know it, and they don't want to. Knowing the price of victory would poison its sweetness. So they party, while Ali goes from one injured to the next, helping them the best she can.

She's not sorry about pressing a pillow over the eighteen-year-old's face to hasten his horrible slow death, but she can't do that for the broken sailor. He won't die tonight, nor the night after. He may rot in his own piss for years, but that's up to God.

Ali sighs and pulls her cloak closer. Nights are not warm in April, and the rain soaked her to the bone. She kneels by a sailor leaning against the wall. His face is chalk-white, and blood spurts out of the arrow wound in his thigh. He's half gone, but not quite. She cuts off his breeches to expose the arrow shaft. Blood bubbles around it, warm and sticky. The arrow must have hit a vein. It's a terrible wound, and she's not likely to fix it, but she can only try. She grabs a bandage from her bag and ties it upwards of the wound, making it into a tourniquet to stop the bleeding.

"You need help?"

It's dark, and the man is behind her, but she doesn't need to see him to know who he is. His voice is carved into her trembling heart forever. She wants to say no, so he'll leave and she won't need to face him. But this sailor will die unless she stops the bleeding. And she only has two hands.

"I could use some help if you can spare the time."

"What should I do?"

"Can you put your thumb right here? And press like his life depends on it? Because it does."

He kneels by her and gets hold of the thigh, pressing his thumb where she told him, upstream of the arrow. The bleeding stops.

"Good job. Can you hold it?"

"I'll hold it for as long as you need me to."

"Hold on then." She pulls out the arrow. The flesh rips, but not much blood comes out. For now, his pressure stopped the bleeding, but sooner or later, he'll have to let go. Ali gets a wooden spoon from her bag and twists it to tighten the tourniquet as hard as she can. It's not bad, but not as good as his pressure.

"Can you hold it longer?"

"How much longer?"

"Until I tell you to stop."

"Sure."

She nods and moves on to the next wounded, and the next, and the one after that. She does the best she can with her potions and ointments and kind words until she runs out of victims.

She sighs and returns to the man with the wounded thigh, expecting to find him dead and alone, but he's neither. Giustiniani is still there, holding pressure like she told him to.

"Let go."

He lets go and tries to stand, but falls to his side, numb from kneeling forever. The wound is no longer bleeding, and the man fell asleep.

Ali spreads ointment over the wound and bandages it, then covers him with her cloak. She'll return in a couple of hours to loosen the tourniquet.

"Thank you. You may have saved his life. We don't know yet, but he looks good."

"Great. What's next?"

"You should go celebrate. We don't get to do that very often."

"No, we don't. How about we celebrate together, Ana?"

Her heart stops. Nobody spoke her name since the last time he did. She didn't think he'd recognize her — it's dark, and it's been years. But he did.

"I looked for you everywhere. I even sent people to Transylvania, but they couldn't find you. And here you were. Finding you is the best thing that happened to me in ages."

"Why?"

"Why what?"

"Why did you look for me?"

"Oh, Ana. Have you ever been in love?"

"Of course."

He laughs, and his sparkling eyes look at her like she's both precious and funny. "How do you know?"

Ali thinks about Mara, about the blood turning hot in her veins when she went to see her, about the joy of her touch. But that's too long to explain, so she just shrugs.

"Well, I've never been in love before. I loved many women, and I did my best to show them a good time. I was eighteen when my father had me marry my wife, and I did my best to please her, even though I didn't love her. But life isn't about love. It's about responsibility and duty, and doing what's right. Then I met you, staring at me wide-eyed in Eceabat, and my heart flipped. You were dressed as a eunuch, and I thought I had lost it and fell for a man who wasn't even a man.

"I waited for you the whole night. When you came, wet and haggard, with Mehmed's posse on your heels, I knew I had found my woman. We scooped you up and sailed away, but I left you alone for weeks. First, because I couldn't believe my own heart. And second, you needed to heal.

"But there wasn't a day that I didn't think about you. When I finally followed my heart, you learned I was a pirate and left. I had to let you go, even though you broke my heart. But then I wished I hadn't, so I looked for you ever since. And here you are."

His calloused hands touch her cheek, caress her neck, and slide down to her breast. A wave of fire runs through her, and her knees soften as his arms pull her close and his breath tickles her ear.

"Let me love you tonight, Ana. You know we're doomed. We'll do our best, but there's little hope we'll make it. We may not live to see the summer. Will you love me tonight?"

Ali chokes. He's right. They may not make it to the summer. But spring is here. Why not love now?

He holds her close as he takes her to the tiny room in the palace he calls his.

CHAPTER 101
CONSTANTINOPLE
APRIL 21

Spring blooms all around Constantinople. The days are long, hot, and heavy with scents of jasmine and lilac. The fields turned a happy green wherever the fall grains grew heavy with the future bread, and the lambs got big. The nightingales outdo each other with their thrills, and Radu wonders why they call them nightingales if they sing through the day. There's so much beauty that he'd love to sit and watch the world go by and write a poem, but he can't.

He has no time to waste, so he spurs his horse towards Mehmed's vast camp outside Constantinople. He's been riding for two days and two nights, and he's sore. His butt hurts, his eyes burn, and his heart is in turmoil. Oh, how he hopes he's doing the right thing!

He couldn't believe it when he heard it. Nothing but the spiteful words of an angry drunk, he thought at first, so he probed further. The man seemed legit. He's certain, he said, so Radu asked for proof. And he got it. Then, once he knew, he had to choose: pretend he never heard it, or warn Mehmed.

His brain told him Mehmed could take care of himself, and he'd better stay out of it. But his heart said no. He had to tell Mehmed. He had to see him. So he rode to Constantinople like the world was on fire.

But now that he's reached Mehmed's camp, he's no longer so sure. How will Mehmed receive him? And his news?

Too late to worry. He's here; time to get on with it. Afraid he may still change his mind and head back, he spurs his horse towards Mehmed's tall blue tent. Two janissaries he doesn't know guard the entrance.

"I need to see the sultan."

"Who are you?"

"I'm Radu of Wallachia."

"Wait." The guard turns to the tent and shouts. "Radu of Wallachia is here to see you, my sultan."

It feels like years until Mehmed comes out, his cheeks flushed, his clothes a mess. He must have been resting, Radu thinks, shrinking under Mehmed's incredulous eyes.

"Radu?"

"My sultan."

"You're here?"

"I came to speak to you, my sultan."

"About what?"

Mehmed doesn't look pleased to see him, and Radu's throat tightens. He wishes he'd stayed in Edirne, minding his own business, but it's too late. He didn't come all this way for nothing. Be it as it may, he needs to tell him. He glances at the tent.

"It's private, my sultan."

Mehmed whispers something to the guard, then turns away. "Let's walk."

Radu follows him to the edge of the hill. The setting sun turned the Bosporus' waters into blood and gilded the tongues of land where Asia and Europe almost kiss. In the gloaming, the city glows like it's lit from inside.

It's achingly beautiful and thoroughly disquieting, and Radu finally understands Mehmed's obsession with Constantinople. There's no other place like this, and Mehmed ogles it with hate and longing like one would gaze at a cheating lover before turning his troubled eyes to Radu.

"What's up?"

"Çandarlı Halil Paşa betrayed you."

"What?"

"He's been negotiating with Constantinople's megas doux, Loukas Notaras, behind your back."

"How do you know?"

"One of his men told me. He was angry and disgruntled that the grand vizier demoted him last week."

"How do you know it's true? What if he's just trying to take revenge?"

"I saw Çandarlı Paşa's note to Notaras, calling him to meet, under his own seal, with my own eyes."

Mehmed looks away. The sun went down, and the sky is on fire. So is Mehmed, his eyes sick with anger. "Are you sure?"

"I am."

"I will destroy him. I'll tear him apart, limb from limb. His own wives won't be able to recognize him. I will delete his name from history." He trembles with rage, and Radu seeks to slow him down.

"It may be wiser to play him, Mehmed. You could have him feed lies to the Romans, but withhold the things you don't want them to know. You can destroy him after you take the city."

His fists tight, his eyes fierce, Mehmed breathes like he's been running. He finally sighs.

"You're right. I'll have to wait. Thanks for coming to tell me, and thanks for your advice. Will you stay with me?"

"If you want me to."

"I do. I'm in dire need of someone I can trust."

They walk back to the tent, and Mehmed glances at the guard.

"The boy is gone, my sultan."

"Get me Zaganos Paşa."

The blue silk tent is more luxurious than most homes, Radu thinks.

White candles reflect in the silver cups on the low table, and the incense burners fill the air with fragrance. The old prayer rug Radu knows well lies by Mehmed's cot in the corner, which is a mess. Mehmed leans to straighten the sheets, then unrolls a map on the center table.

"You came just in time. I have a plan for tonight that I didn't yet share with anyone. I'll tell you and Zaganos, but I won't tell Çandarlı Paşa. I don't need the Romans to know."

Zaganos Paşa steps in. If he's surprised to see Radu, he doesn't show it. But he already knew, Radu thinks. His spies must have told him when I left Edirne. But why didn't he tell Mehmed?

Mehmed weighs the map open between a cup and his dagger. "Tonight, we take the Golden Horn. Tomorrow morning, our Roman friends will find the Ottoman Fleet in their backyard. That should wake them up."

"How about that chain?" Zaganos asks.

"Good question. See, Radu, Constantinople's eastern side is protected by the Golden Horn, closed to us by a heavy cast-iron chain stretching from their Acropolis to the Genoese colony in Galata. You can get there from here without their permission. That's why the walls on that side are not as strong as the rest. They see no danger there, but we're about to show them. We'll have five dozen ships there tomorrow."

"How?" Radu asks.

"We'll carry them over land. Right here." Mehmed puts his finger on the map. Behind Galata, where the strip of land is less than a mile. "My men cut a trail through the forest to make a path for the boats. It's almost done. Tonight, we drag the boats over and drop them in the Golden Horn."

"I've never heard of anything like this," Zaganos says.

"Neither have I. I hope it can be done," Radu says.

"You'd better, since you'll be in charge," Mehmed says. "You can have all the men you need and any equipment. But nothing should leak to Çandarlı Paşa. Nothing!"

"Tonight? One night?"

"Yes. Otherwise, the secret will come out, and it's over. They'll be waiting to destroy our boats one by one before they touch the water. It must be done tonight."

What the heck did I get myself into? Radu wonders. Two days ago, I was playing my rübap in Edirne, and now I'm about to carry Mehmed's fleet over land and help him take Constantinople. He remembers Mehmed's words: "If one hair of my beard knew what I think, I'd pull it out and set it on fire," and an icy shiver runs down his spine.

CHAPTER 102
A SNEAKY FLEET

This forest must be hundreds of years old, Radu thinks. The pine trees, wider than a grown man, look like they hold up the sky and last forever. But they won't. A freshly cut mile-long trail wide enough for an Ottoman galley is about to reach the Golden Horn.

But the work is still on. First come the woodcutters, sweating buckets as they pull on their saws to cut the trees. As soon as they down a tree, they move on to the next, leaving room for the second team, who cuts off the branches, leaving just the smooth trunks. The next team drags the logs to make a three-foot-wide track, then sets them into place and greases them with tallow to lessen the friction. Right behind them come the boats. They slide over the slippery trail, pulled by heavy oxen and pushed by brawny men.

Radu has seen no one work like this. They drip with sweat, and the veins in their temples pop out like blue worms as they strain against the weight to push the galleys forward inch by inch. The ropes cut into their bleeding hands, but they keep going. Inch after inch, boat after boat slides silently towards the Golden Horn behind the dark Galata colony.

Those Genoese bastards are Christian, of course. They act neutral and suck up to both sides, but they'll betray either when the time is right.

That's why Mehmed had called their leader, Signor Lomelini, to his tent, and put him through his paces. He first offered him wine. "A pleasure to meet you, Signor Lomelini. What a lovely city you got here. Hundreds of years of success and tradition. The world's best merchants, joining the east to the west. All gone. What a pity your city has no future."

Lomelini choked on his wine. "Gone? What do you mean, gone?"

"When we take Constantinople, we'll take Galata too. We want the entire Strait, of course."

"But... you are not at war with Genoa. We are neutral."

"I'd believe it if I was twenty years younger," Mehmed said. He's twenty-one. "But I happen to know that you've been meeting with Giustiniani and the Romans, and you sold them weapons and food. I let that go, since it wasn't much. But it's time you choose sides. Will you stand with Constantinople, which is as good as gone, or protect your city, and give it a chance?"

Lomelini watched Mehmed above his cup. "What chance is that?"

Mehmed sipped on his wine.

"The weather's been lousy these days. Winds and storms and thunder. Your people should pay no attention to the noise coming from the woods. Just trees downed by the winds. Tell your folks to mind their business and keep their mouths shut. If they don't, I can't guarantee that our cannons won't stray from their target. You've been lucky till now, but the gunmen may get confused. A charge or two, dropping on the wrong side of the Golden Horn — by mistake, of course. Wouldn't that be unfortunate? Such a lovely city."

Lomelini left with his tail between his legs. That's why, beyond the many things Radu has to worry about, he doesn't have to worry about Galata's folks talking. They'll be silent as fishes if they don't want to join them at the bottom of the sea.

The first team of woodsmen reaches the shore, and the last log gets laid. That's good, but the moon is already going down. Radu needs to have seventy galleys in that water before sunrise, and he doesn't have one.

"Move. Move faster," he shouts.

The men scowl at him like he's dirt. They worked the whole night, and they're exhausted. They gave all they had, but they're losing the battle with time.

Should I drop the boats in the water, hoping we have enough of them by sunrise to face the Roman Navy? Radu thinks. Or should I wait till tonight, hoping the secret is safe?

By now, everyone in Galata must know something's going on, and people love to gossip. It would only take one woman telling a friend, or one man chatting with a neighbor, and the news will spread like wildfire.

There's no good choice, but it is what it is. They have a couple more hours; the trees are down, and the track is ready.

"Let's go," Radu says, grabbing a rope and pulling along with the others. "Let's do it."

He puts his weight into the rope to pull the ship forward. It slides a few inches, then it gets stuck in the stump of a branch. The men pull even harder. It takes all their strength to move it an inch, but then it gets stuck again, and it's like trying to move a stone wall.

Radu remembers sleighing at home in Wallachia. You needed a slope to gain momentum. So, Radu has the woodcutters shape triangular wooden ramps to slide under the boats to lift the weight off the rails and get them moving. It works like a charm, and the first boat glides like a hot knife through butter. But the next one gets stuck, and then the third, and the next. They need dozens of ramps to slide them all, but, well-greased with tallow, they let the men maintain the momentum, and quicken the process to no end.

It's still dark when the first boat splashes into the Golden Horn, followed by the next, and the next. The men are exhausted but thrilled, and so is Radu. They did something no one had done before: they moved an entire fleet over land.

The sun rises over forty Ottoman galleys rocking in the Golden

Horn. The others follow, one after the other, like baby ducks after their mother.

There'll be a rough awakening in Constantinople. *We did it!* Radu thinks. He's giddy with joy until he remembers they are his fellow Christians. He got so caught up in the challenge he forgot he was working with the Ottomans against his own brethren.

What the heck did he do? And what can he do now?

CHAPTER 103

APRIL 22

After a few lucky days that gave it some much-needed hope, Constantinople is at a standstill this morning. The Genoese ships made it through, bringing food and reinforcements. Their men found Mehmed's Serbian miners, who were secretly undermining the walls, and destroyed them. As for Giustiniani's killing sprees, they spark joy in every Roman heart, and fear in the Ottomans. But the lucky string is over.

The bells started ringing at dawn. From Hagia Sofia to the tiniest chapel, every church in the city rang its bells, screaming: DANGER! DANGER! DANGER!

They haven't yet stopped.

Ion jumps out of bed, throws on some clothes, and blasts through the door. The streets choke with people looking as befuddled as he feels trying to find out what has happened. He follows the others up the stairs to the top of the walls and looks down.

The Golden Horn, their safe harbor, choked with Ottoman galleys. There had to be dozens, since they outnumber the Roman ships three to one. How on earth did they get there? Did the chain fail? And what next?

Ion rushes into the throne room. The council had already gathered, but for once nobody glares at him. They are too busy with their own worries. Even Notaras forgets to hate Ion, consumed with hating Giustiniani.

Ion slips into his seat near Sphrantzes, who looks ten years older than he did last week. He's a good man, Sphrantzes, and loyal to the emperor, but he's a historian, not a warrior. And he's got a family to worry about.

Thankfully, Ion doesn't. He's got no one but Ali, whom he barely ever sees anymore. She leaves before dawn, and she's always late to bed. Some nights she doesn't come at all. They never talk about it, but he knows where she spends her nights, and has no right to complain, even if it scorches him inside. His life has never felt emptier.

The emperor arrives, worn and gray. His weary eyes search for Giustiniani, but the pirate isn't here, and Ion's heart aches knowing who shares his bed.

"Let's get to it," Constantine says, glancing at the door. Giustiniani appears like he's been summoned. He looks like he hasn't slept in weeks, and Ion doesn't want to think about what he's been doing. This is no time for jealousy. They have the empire's survival to worry about.

"Thanks for finally joining us. Kind of you to spare a moment," Notaras says.

Giustiniani ignores him and looks at the emperor. "We are screwed."

Constantine darkens. "You think?"

"The Ottomans penetrated our safest place. We have seventy Ottoman galleys waiting to break us. We need to stop them before they get to do it."

"How?"

"Greek Fire. Let's do it tonight. We load our boats with fire and burn Mehmed's ships before they know what hit them."

"What if we fail?"

"Then it's over. But in the meantime, we may as well enjoy the show."

"I'll do it," Giacomo Coco says. He's Venetian, the captain of one of the sail ships stuck in the Golden Horn after Mehmed's blockade, and a man of courage. He's Giustiniani's rival in all things, like he's meant to be, since he's Venetian and Giustiniani is Genoese. But the weeks of fighting shoulder to shoulder made them into friends.

Giustiniani slaps his back and laughs. "I guess. If we can't find anyone better…"

But Galata's leader, Lomelini, sitting next to Notaras, gives him the evil eye. "Why you?"

"Why not?"

"You're just a guest. We, the Genoese, have a stake in this fight. We want to be part of it."

Giustiniani cuts his eyes to him. If anyone has a stake in this fight, it's him, not the Galata Genoese, who always seems to play both sides. Nobody knows how much to trust them, not even Giustiniani, who'd be embarrassed to admit that he trusts the Venetian more than his compatriot.

Coco frowns. "Suit yourself. Be ready tonight." He stomps out, leaving Lomelini and Notaras grumbling.

"You have a better plan, megas doux?" Giustiniani asks.

"No, but…"

"Speak to me when you do. In the meantime, we'll follow our defender's plan," Constantine says.

"But we can't do it tonight. We need time to prepare."

"Then get moving," Giustiniani says, and leaves without looking back.

Constantine follows, his shoulders hunched under the weight of the empire.

Notaras glares after them, his face a study in spite.

He'd kill Giustiniani if he could, Ion thinks. And, in the battle's chaos, it wouldn't be that hard.

He follows the emperor to see if he can help, even though his hope grows thinner by the moment. This isn't what he signed up for, but whatever will be, will be, and tonight may make or break Constantinople.

They spend the day getting ready. And the same day after, and the day after that, because Lomelini needs more time, even though the secret is harder to keep with every passing hour, and the chances of success keep dwindling.

They take three days to start loading the Greek Fire. The secrecy is so vital that they do it themselves. Constantine takes them to the cells in the dark dungeon where they store it, and hands them each a couple of ordinary brown flasks. But there's nothing ordinary about the Greek Fire, a magic concoction that burns for hours and hours, even in water, and can't be put out. Its recipe is so old and secret nobody knows it anymore, but the Romans saved a few flasks for days like this.

Giustiniani walks gingerly up the steps with a bottle in each arm, carrying them like sleeping twin babies. Sphrantzes follows, then Ion, and even the patriarch, whose old knees wobble as he drags himself up the steep stairs. Ion wonders what would happen if he drops them. But there's no point in thinking about that, so he follows the others to the low gate by the port, where they'll get the flasks into the boats. One by one, they hand them to the Roman captains.

"Don't drop it, or we won't have to worry about the Ottomans anymore," Giustiniani says, handing a flask to one of the captains. The man turns white and cups it between his hands, holding it like it's ready to explode. They all know the Greek Fire is as dangerous as it is powerful, and it doesn't know friends from enemies. Its secret is handling it with care and blowing it into the enemy's face before he blows it into yours.

One after the other, a dozen Roman boats get their loads of Greek Fire and get ready. Mehmed's ships won't know what hit them. Blasting them out of the water will change the odds in this war, and God knows how much the Romans need a break.

An hour after dusk, the fire loaded boats drift towards the chain as if looking for a better spot to anchor. The dark Ottoman galleys seem asleep, so Giacomo Cocco guides his vessel towards one of Mehmed's galleys. Ion holds his breath, watching the silent shadow slip closer and closer to the Ottoman galley. They're just feet away, when a dozen bells start ringing and a hundred torches catch fire.

Heartbeats later, Mehmed's cannons come to life. Gun after gun thunders and spits heavy projectiles, blasting Coco and his Venetians out of the water. The dozen fire-loaded ships burst into unearthly flames that devour them. They turned into massive torches, floating aimlessly across the water, while their crew burn alive. Wounded scream their agony and the onlookers shout their anger while the bells keep ringing. The air is thick with the smoke of burning ships, the smell of gunpowder, and the sickening stench of burning flesh. Seeing the Venetians' terrible agony turns Ion's stomach. The burning men jump into the water one by one, but the Greek Fire is relentless. The entire sea can't put off the flames that eat them alive.

His face frozen in pain, Constantine watches his men burn.

Giustiniani turned dark with rage. "How the hell did they know?" he spits.

"You think they knew?" Constantine asks.

"I know they did. They let them get close, but not close enough to throw the fire, then blew them up. How did they know?"

"Somebody must have talked."

"Precisely. We have a traitor amongst us, and I think I know who that is."

CHAPTER 104

MAY 19

It's a bright day over the Sea of Marmara. Not a cloud mars the blue sky, and the shivering sea sparkles like a million diamonds.

But there's no joy inside the dingy city's walls. After six weeks of harrowing siege, the end is near. They all know it, from Emperor Constantine to the blind beggar soaking the sun on the Hagia Sophia's steps, waiting for a coin or a slice of bread. They're both rare these days, Ali thinks, looking for something to give him.

She gives him the bread and cheese she packed for lunch — she never gets to eat them anyhow — then heads to the castle to see to her wounded. If she's lucky, and the fighting isn't too fierce, she may even get to see Giustiniani. He stops by whenever there's a lull in the action, and they steal a moment in his room when they get a chance. There aren't many, and they're always rushed, but the sweetness of those times makes it worth it. Ali remembers the warmth of his body next to hers, the sweetness of his kiss, and the salty taste of his skin that smells like leather and smoke, and she smiles.

A roar wakes her up from her daydream. Hundreds of people have gathered on the wall, and the church bells start ringing. What now? She rushes up the stairs, and the sight freezes her heart.

The Ottomans are building a bridge over the Golden Horn. Starting from their outpost in Galata, thousands of empty barrels fastened together with iron hooks float towards the city walls. They dance on the waves, as Mehmed's engineers lay planks over them to fashion a bridge wide enough for five men abreast.

The Romans try to take them down, but they're too close for the cannons and too far for the arrows. The archers' cloud of arrows lit with Greek Fire falls short. Most sink in the water, and the few that make it get pulled and thrown into the sea before the bridge catches fire.

Ali's heart sinks. She's always known that Constantinople's end was near. Still, she stayed to help Ion, Constantine, and the wounded. But then Giustiniani came, and she stopped thinking about the future. She lived every day like it was the last, then the next one, and the one after that. But they're running out of tomorrows.

She drags herself to her wounded, but her heart is heavy and her outlook grim.

"Why the long face?" Giustiniani asks when he comes to find her at noon.

Ali's jaw drops. He can't not know! He always knows everything first. "The bridge…"

"Oh. It was bound to happen sooner or later. May as well deal with it now." He grins and puts her arm around her waist. "Come. I'll feed you lunch."

"I'm not hungry."

"Neither am I. Not for food." He grins, his white teeth sparkling in his sun-beaten face, then leans to whisper something in her ear.

Ali listens, but he just nibbles on her earlobe, and Ali's heart quickens, sending fiery blood through her veins and warming her inside. He's right. She's hungry too, just not for food.

Later on, as they lay embraced in his narrow bed, Ali turns to her lover. "What will you do?"

"I'll fight until I can't fight any more."

"And then?"

"I'll probably die. I can't imagine Mehmed will let me live after all this. Especially after refusing his offer."

"What offer?"

"He offered me Lemnos. He doesn't have it yet, but it's just a matter of time."

"In exchange for what?"

"In exchange for leaving Constantinople to fend for itself."

"And you said no?"

"Of course. I promised Constantine I'll see him through."

Ali nests in his arms. She should go back to her wounded, but she'll take another moment. It may be the last.

He traces her temple, then her cheek, then her neck to that hollow above her collarbone he loves to kiss, with a finger softer than a petal. "The question is, what will you do?"

"Me? Whatever everyone else does."

"No, you won't. The Ottomans will take them captive, every one of them but for those they kill, and sell them into slavery. You won't go back there."

He cups her face between his hands and looks into her eyes. His eyes are luminous and warm and smiling like he's not talking about death and slavery. "When they break in, you'll go to the port. You'll find the Genoese Princess, and you'll tell the captain that you are Ana. He'll know what to do."

"What will he do?"

"He'll take you to Chios. That's my island, and that's where I'll go if, by some miracle I make it out alive. We may even sail together, God willing. But if not, you'll go to Chios and he'll take care of you. You will be safe and free."

"I don't want to be safe and free. I want to be with you."

Giustiniani laughs and tightens his arms around her. "You silly girl! Of course, you want to be safe and free. Remember when I asked you to stay with me on the Queen of the Seas? You told me what to do with myself and left me there."

"That was then. This is now."

"Exactly. Then, I was free and nimble. Now, I'm exhausted and committed to saving a city that can't be saved. If I don't make it out of here, at least I'll die happy knowing I kept my word and you're safe and free. Capisce?"

Ali tries to get up, but he won't let her go.

"You're not leaving here until you promise."

"Really?" Her eyes narrow with fury.

Giustiniani bursts into laughter. "You're just the same wild cat who would have killed me with a kitchen knife long ago. Oh, Ana, my love, can't you see there's nothing more important to you than being free? Nothing. Not even me. I want you to have that. Please."

Ali nods, her eyes burning with tears.

He hugs her, then kisses her from her head to her toes, and she forgets about escape, about freedom, and about everything else but the man holding her. Maybe for the last time.

CHAPTER 105

MAY 29

The air throbs with unease as a crimson sun rises over Constantinople on Sunday, May 29th. Dark foreboding shrouded the city like fog, tarnishing its colors and sounds, and hinting at terrible things waiting to happen. It's like God is warning them to get ready, Ion thinks, crossing himself.

The blood-moon lunar eclipse a week ago reminded them of an old prophecy. Saint Constantine, the first emperor, said that "Constantinople should never be lost, until the moon rose darkened when it was at the full, that is lacking the half of it." Whatever that meant, that shook the city to its core.

To give them heart and ward off the evil spirits, the holy priests brought out Virgin Mary's icon and walked it around the city walls. But then a cannon ball fell close, and they dropped it, damaging it beyond repair, conjuring another bad omen. People crossed themselves, and the fear in their hearts grew deeper.

Just two days ago, Hagia Sophia's dome turned red for no reason, looking like it had caught on fire.

"This is God's sign that the city is doomed if we don't surrender," Notaras said, crossing himself.

Giustiniani spat to the side. "The hell it is. It's God's sign that we should get ready. The blooding is about to start. I need more cannons to protect the St. Romanus gate."

"You don't need them. You've got the strongest wall."

"That wall's almost gone. It had so many holes we plugged them with tree branches, and they won't hold against an all-out Ottoman attack. I need cannons to keep them at bay."

"I don't have any to spare. Try again next week."

Giustiniani turned red. Between narrowed lips, his words came out clipped, like he was spitting cherry stones. "The guns aren't yours. They belong to the city. I need them now."

"Well, you can't have them."

"You oily Greek scum!"

Giustiniani leaped forward to punch him, but Constantine stepped between them. "Enough! Our success depends on staying united. Divided, we'll fail! We're standing at the edge of the precipice, and you are fighting? We have no time for this. Notaras, give him the guns."

Notaras glowered and left, his shifty eyes cursing Giustiniani.

That was two days ago. Yesterday, the Ottomans danced to the beat of their drums and cymbals, drunk with joy for the three days of looting Mehmed promised. Perched on their crumbling walls, the Romans watched, frozen with fear. What would happen to their children, to their homes, to them?

Last night, all the Christians in the city held a joint mass. They prayed for Constantinople's children and petitioned God for mercy. The dark-clad Orthodox priests looking like a murder of bearded crows chanted and shook their smoking incense burners around the pope's envoy, red clad Cardinal Isidore. Even the emperor repented for his sins and took communion before inspecting the walls one last time.

Come morning, all hell broke loose. Mehmed's cannons pummeled the walls around the gate of St. Romanus for hours, until they started falling apart. Then he signaled the all-out attack.

Standing in a tower near St Romanus' gate in his borrowed chain-mail, Ion tightens his bow. The air is so thick with dust and gunpowder smoke that it burns his eyes. No matter where you look, the Ottomans are scaling the walls in their assault machines. The sultan's men are everywhere: down at the gates, up on ladders, climbing ropes hanging from grappling hooks. They're like ants, thousands and thousands of them, fighting their way in.

Up on the wall, every able-bodied man in Constantinople struggles to repeal them. Everything is a weapon: missed arrows get returned to sender; hay forks push away ladders heavy with Ottoman soldiers; rocks fallen from the crumbling walls crush the heads and the hands of the foes who made it to the top of the wall. But they're just too many.

First came the bashi-bazouks, the crazy heads, whom Mehmed always sends first. They stormed the walls armed with rawhide whips and fighting irons, battling like devils. Their job is to scare and tire the defenders, and that they did. The Roman's arms hurt from cutting them like hay, and smashing their assault machines into smithereens. But then the second wave arrived. And the third. And the next.

The noise alone is terrifying: the never-ending cannonade, the Ottoman bands beating their drums and their cymbals; the janissaries striking their kilijes against their plated chests and screaming Allah's name at the top of their lungs: *Allah'u'Akbar. Allah'u'Akbar.* The deafening ruckus is just another weapon meant to dishearten the defenders, and it works. Ion's stomach tightens with fear.

The all-out attack came over land and over water. Mehmed's ships brought his men to the shore: eighty biremes lined up like ducks from the Beautiful Gate to the Wooden Gate poured out thousands of soldiers.

Up on the wall with Giustiniani's men, where the fight is the thickest, Ion gets the best view of the fight. Three thousand men defend the St. Romanus gate, more than anywhere else on the wall, but it's not enough. The Ottomans outnumber them ten to one, and they keep coming.

Ion lifts his bow and pulls the string taut. The arrow whirrs and sinks with a thunk in a janissary's red chest. The man gasps and tumbles off the ladder he was climbing, taking two more with him. But that only makes room for more. Ion nocks another arrow and chooses his next target. It's easy. They're so many you couldn't miss them with your eyes closed.

The Genoese fight like men possessed, and so do the Romans. They fight for their lives and the lives of their children, so nothing is too much or too hard. They maim, bleed and kill, and repel attack after attack. Still, the wall gets shorter and weaker by the moment under the relentless assault.

Mounted on his black stallion ahead of St. Romanus Gate, Mehmed himself leads his troops, spurring them to fight. Sitting proud in his shiny silver armor, he shouts orders and gives heart to his men.

Ion readies his bow, aiming for the soft spot under the chin, right above the gorget. He pulls the string taut and gets ready to let go of the arrow when a whiff of smoke gets in his eyes, blinding him. By the time he can see again, Mehmed's gone, but he has another thousand targets. He aims and kills, again and again, though the air's so thick you could cut it with a blade. The sharp fumes of gunpowder mingle with the metallic smell of blood and the stench of opened bellies, twisting his stomach.

He sighs and looks to his right. Constantine, clad in heavy armor with a bird-like helmet, walks from one post to the next, praising the defenders, encouraging the wounded and giving everyone hope.

To Ion's left, Giustiniani fights like a war god. His chest heaves, his broad sword drips with blood, and his voice cracks from screaming praise to his men and threats to the enemy.

"For God and glory! Cut up the bastards! Send them to Allah and his virgins! That leaves more girls for us!"

He roars, lifts his sword to the sky and plunges it over a janissary's head. The blade cuts through the felt hat and the skull and gets stuck between the man's eyes. Giustiniani plants a boot on his chest and pushes him away to liberate his sword. To his left, another janissary lifts his kilij to cut him, but Giustiniani's sword twirls in his hands like it's alive, severing the man's head from his body. He has no time to watch the head roll to the ground as he leaps forward to stab the Ottoman attacking one of his men from behind.

His men follow his lead. They cut and stab and kill, then start over. Bodies pile over bodies on top of the crumbling wall, making it grow.

The Ottoman attack looks like it's slowing down. The sultan's men can't help but lose heart seeing the Genoese fight. Giustiniani leaps towards another janissary. His eyes wide with horror, the man jumps back and tries to run, but the pirate's blade cuts him like he's firewood.

Giustiniani bursts into laughter. It's a powerful, joyous sound that lifts Ion's heart, but it gets cut short. The pirate chokes and wavers, then crumbles to the ground. His horrified men freeze and stare, and it's like the world stopped turning. Watching Giustiniani go down is like watching the moon fall from the sky. Ion saw it with his own eyes, but he can't believe it. That cannot be! Giustiniani is too strong to fall. Even so, he did.

The Genoese rush to him. A culverin's arrow sticks out of his chest, spurting a fountain of blood. The handsome face is white as snow and his breath comes out in red bubbles. His eyes are closed, and his head hangs limp as his men carry him away.

Constantine tries to stop them. He grabs Giustiniani's shoulder and shakes him. "Fight, brother, fight. Don't forsake us in your distress; our city's salvation depends on you. Go back to your post. Where are you going?"

But no one answers. The Genoese avert their eyes and rush away with the pirate. In front of the St. Romanus gate, the drums and the cymbals restart their cadence, and the Ottomans rekindle their attack.

Constantine glances after the Genoese once more, then grabs Giustiniani's sword and lifts its bloody blade above his head. "Let's fight, my brothers. Let's fight for our city, for our empire, for our God. The bravery of our death will make our fame last forever. Death in liberty is sweeter than life in slavery. Let's show the Ottomans what Christians can do." He cuts through the first janissary blocking his way, then leaps to stab the next one, and his broad sword cuts through chainmail like it's cloth. The emperor leaps forward, but his purple boots slip in a pool of blood and he struggles to right himself. A janissary lifts his kilij and lowers it above his head just as Ion's arrow pierces his neck from one side to the other. The man crumbles to the ground as Constantine lifts his sword again to repel the attackers. Heartened by his courage, his men follow.

Just like Giustiniani, Ion thinks. He follows them too, when a sudden pain splits his chest. An enormous weight crushes him and robs him of his breath. He crumbles to the ground, and the world around him turns black. But he's no longer here. He's back in Kronstadt Castle, and a red-haired girl laughs at him. Her ocean-colored eyes smile, and he smiles back.

"Ana…"

CHAPTER 106

CONSTANTINOPLE'S FALL

This is Constantinople's worst day in a thousand years. Despite her defenders' bravery and sacrifice, the City of Gold has fallen. The fight is over, and the indignity has begun, Ali thinks.

Wherever you look, bloodied Ottomans covered in soot roam the streets looking for loot. Drunk with victory, they act like a horde of savages. Worried parents locked up their terrified kids, but it only takes a well-placed heel to break down a door. The city resounds with the wails of the mourning, the screams of the children, and the cries of despondent mothers. They don't pray, since they no longer believe in praying. They prayed and prayed every night and day for the last six weeks and many more before that, and look what good it did to them.

Mehmed gave his men three days to take whatever and whoever they wanted. Anything but the city. That one belongs to him, but all else is free game, so the Ottomans wander from house to house like a clan of hungry hyenas looking for prey. They take whatever they find, then fight over booty under the eyes of the horrified Romans.

"She's mine," a tall Janissary says, clutching a young girl's arm. Her eyes are downcast and her hair the color of butter. She looks no older than twelve.

"In your dreams," the other one says. He's short, dark and angry, and he drags the girl by her other arm as she hangs her head and cries.

Her wrists tied with rope, her mother cries and screams, holding on to her three younger children, but nobody listens.

"No way. I got them first. They're mine."

"You're too greedy. You have the mother, and the other three. That's four already. It's only right that I take the girl."

"But she's worth more than those four put together. Just look at her. She's a beauty, and I bet she's a virgin." He lifts the girl's chin, exposing her tear-stained face.

"Not for long, I bet. She's a paşa's dream."

"For sure. But there's a thousand like her out here. Go get yourself one."

"And thousands of soldiers looking for loot. No, thanks. I'll keep this one."

"You want her for yourself, or just to trade?"

"What difference does it make?"

"I'd like to keep her for myself. There's more to life than money."

The dark man sniffs. "OK then. Take her, and I'll take the rest. But you owe me."

"OK."

The dark man grabs the rope and drags the screaming mother behind him. The tall man keeps the girl. He feels her hair and touches her cheek, but she pulls away like he's hot.

He laughs. "You'll change your mind soon enough," he says, dragging her by the hand to look for more loot.

Ali's heart bleeds for the girl and her family, but there's nothing she can do. That's the fate of losers in war. She kneels by the next wounded soldier, but she's too late to help him. She closes his eyes, crosses herself and says the Lord's prayer over him, then moves to the next.

"Hey, you. What are you doing?" A bloodied janissary glares at her. He helps his wounded comrade sit against the wall, then turns his angry eyes back to Ali.

"Helping the wounded."

"Come here."

She'd rather not, but resisting won't do her any good. She pulls her brown cloak closer to cover her better and steps closer.

"Look at him."

The man is young — but aren't they all? — and paler than winter snow. He must be bleeding somewhere, Ali thinks, and starts looking for the wound but can't find it until he moans, gripping his thigh. The wound isn't gaping, but it's deep and bleeding.

"He didn't look too bad at first, but then he got like this. Can you help him?"

"I'll try. I need some alcohol and some dressings."

The man hands her a flask of Raki. "I have no dressings."

"I'll make do."

"Do so. Take care of him or I'll come back and kill you."

He leaves them to look for loot. Ali rips off the bottom of her chemise and tears it into a long strip, then wraps it tightly around the man's thigh until the skin blanches below it and the bleeding slows down. She cleans the wound with Raki, trying to be gentle, but the man winces. She gives him a sip and rechecks on the bleeding. There's not much, and his cheeks lost their ghastly pallor. She spreads her healing ointment over the ugly wound.

"An arrow?" she asks.

"A lance."

"You're lucky. God willing, you may make it." She tightens the tourniquet further, and he wails. "I'm sorry, but I need to stop the bleeding. We'll release it soon, if you look better. How about some tea?"

"Tea?"

"Willow bark tea. It will lessen the pain."

She lifts his head and gives him a sip. He swallows a little, but most of it pours over his chest.

"That was vile."

Ali wipes his brow as a short bashi-bazouk dragging an old man by a rope stops by their side. The old man shuffles, bent under a heavy rolled carpet.

The bashi-bazouk puts his hand on Ali's shoulder. "She's mine."

Ali's wounded glares at him like he's dirt and grabs his kilij. "Are you out of your mind? Can't you see she's mine?"

The bashi-bazouk glances at the kilij, then makes himself scarce. Ali's mouth goes dry, and her stomach twists. She hasn't forgotten how it felt to be someone's property. Oh, how she wishes she made it to the Genoese Princess!

But she didn't. She got busy with the wounded, and by the time she made it to the port, it was too late. The Ottomans had taken it, and they'd cut the way out for the thousands who tried to embark on the Christian ships. One after the other, the Genoese galleons and the Roman galleys left the Golden Horn loaded with fugitives, but thousands and thousands were left behind.

A crying mother walked into the water to her neck and threw her baby to a departing ship to give him a chance to escape. A dozen hands caught him before he touched the water, and the mother watched him sail away, crying with the sorrow of knowing she'll never see him again. But most didn't make it. Dozens and dozens drowned as they swam to catch the ships fighting their way out of the Ottoman blockade.

Ali sighed and went back to the wall. It was her fault she didn't make it there sooner. She didn't even get to say goodbye to her pirate.

Oh, how she hopes he'll make it! She heard he got wounded, and his men carried him to his boat. She wishes she'd been there to look after him, but she wasn't. Now, she had to make the most of what was left. She looked for Ion and Constantine, but couldn't find them. So she went back to taking care of the wounded, alone again, her heart bleeding for all those she lost.

She wipes her tears with her sleeve, and someone touches her hand.

"What's your name?" the wounded man asks her.

"Ana."

"I'm Omar. Thank you for helping me, Ana. I'll try to return the favor. I'll let you go when you find somewhere safe, but for now, you'll be safest if they think you're mine. Mehmed gave us three days to take whatever we can. After that, it's all his. I'll try to keep you safe for three days, and maybe you can keep me alive."

"Thank you," she says, giving him another sip of tea.

But she wonders what's the point of being alive, and nothing comes to mind.

CHAPTER 107

MAY 30

I t's the second day of looting, and Mehmed's camp is a joyous place today — if you're an Ottoman. After two months of fighting and bitter misery, the reward is finally here. The soldiers returned from the city loaded with all the loot they could carry or burden their captives with. Not one soldier came back without at least a captive, who'll be a slave from now on. The cries of the children and the screams of women being raped all around the camp come through the blue silk of Mehmed's tent like they're happening right inside it, and Radu's brain is on fire.

He's playing chess with Mehmed. He got better at it over the years, but the cries outside distract him terribly. He can't focus on the game while listening to what's happening just feet away.

He moves the white elephant without thinking while listening to a childish voice.

"No, sir. Please, no, sir. Don't!"

"Turn around and bend over."

"No, sir, please..."

A slap, then another, and then silence.

"Check," Mehmed says, moving his vizier.

Another scream, this one of pain instead of fear, high pitched and desperate, and Radu jumps to his feet and darts to the door.

"Don't! Radu, don't!"

Mehmed grabs Radu's kaftan to hold him back. Radu pulls, and they fall to the ground. Mehmed holds on to him, and Radu's fist aches to punch him in the face, but he'd imperil not only his life, but any chance to make things better. He pulls himself together and stands, shaking with anger. His fists clenched, his heart racing, he paces around the tent, panting to calm himself down.

Mehmed stands and takes a deep breath. He pours two cups and offers one to Radu, who shakes his head no. Mehmed drains it and sits.

"You can't do that, Radu. That man is entitled to his catch."

Radu is so furious he stutters. "His catch? This is a human being, remember? A child! Is your man entitled to that?"

"That child, if that's what it is, was unfortunately born to the wrong parents. They stayed with Constantinople until it fell, and are suffering the fate of losers. Allah knows I gave them chance after chance to surrender, the last one just days ago. They refused. We could have saved thousands of lives if they did, and so would they. But they chose not to. Now they have to pay the price."

"But that child had no say in it! Nobody asked him what he wanted."

"Of course not. But we carry the sins of our fathers. He's paying for the sins of his father, like I am, and you are. This is how the world works."

"Why, Mehmed? Why are you letting this happen? Why destroy what's left of this city you wanted forever? Why not show them mercy and kindness, win their hearts, and make your empire safe for the next thousand years?"

"You know why. My men aren't here because they like me, or even to follow the Prophet's hadiths. They came to better their lives, and thousands of them died for that. Those who made it expect their reward. They'll never fight for me again if I deny them. I'd lose their trust, and they may join my foes next time. I can't afford that.

"I promised them their share, and I'll abide by it whether or not I like it. You think I enjoy hearing that kid's screams? I don't. But I must keep my promises. Otherwise, my honor will be sullied, and so will the honor of every sultan after me."

His heart choked with sorrow, Radu shakes his head. "I'm sorry, Mehmed, but I doubt that. I'm not half the statesman you are, but I can't believe that the path to victory is built on raping children." He storms out without looking back. He mounts his horse, wondering where to go, but no place comes to mind. So he just spurs him to walk away. Towards what? He doesn't know. All he knows is he can't watch this anymore.

What should he do? Go back to Edirne, where home is. Or...

Or what? There's nowhere else to go. Vladislav, Father's killer, sits on the Throne of Wallachia. Petru Aron, who killed his Uncle Bogdan, rules Moldova. As for Hunyadi, Father's nemesis, he runs Transylvania and most of Hungary. Vlad's there too, and he's just as likely to kill him as to kiss him. More, in fact.

He remembers Vlad's last message. He got it the morning he left Edirne to join Mehmed, but tried to push it out of his mind. But he no longer can. Vlad's words are burned into his brain.

Buda, 15 March 1453

My dear brother,
I hope my message finds you in good health. It's been a long time
since I last wrote to you, and my situation has changed. I am no
longer a fugitive in Transylvania, running from one place to another
to hide from Hunyadi's wrath. Stefan and I are now his esteemed
guests. We live at his court, waiting for the tide to turn to go back to
our countries and claim our fathers' thrones. How come, you ask?

Good question. Hunyadi's alliance with Vladislav turned sour when the traitor started courting Mehmed. Hunyadi got him that throne, and he'll be the one to help me get him off it, God willing. That's why I'm doing my best to stay in his good graces, hoping to soon head home with an army.

Stefan too seeks his support in toppling his father's killer and taking back Moldova's throne, but Hunyadi is skittish. The Poles are deep to their throat in Moldova's affairs, and he has no desire to irk the king of Poland. Between the Hungarian Diet and his incessant skirmishes with Serbia's despot, he's got enough on his hands. That's why Stefan is looking to join Skanderbeg, the reformed janissary that's giving Mehmed a run for his money in Albania. He hopes to learn his tactics and earn an ally.

You'll be pleased to hear that I found little Mircea, our brother's son. He lives at Hunyadi's court with his mother, and he's the spitting image of his father. I got him a horse and made him a wooden sword. I've been teaching him to ride and fight, even though his mother doesn't like me much; but the kid's a riot and he needs a man to teach him.

That takes me to the purpose of my letter. I know your friend Mehmed is holding Constantinople under siege. Nobody here speaks about anything else. He coveted it forever, and he'll do whatever it takes to get it. Once he does, nothing will stop him from heading west. He'll ravage Moldova and Wallachia before heading into Hungary where Hunyadi might stop him. Or not. But if Constantinople falls, Wallachia and Moldova are doomed, because nobody can stop Mehmed. Nobody but you.

Some here say that you're helping Mehmed take Constantinople. Some even say that you reneged on the faith of our father and converted to Islam, and they call you Radu the Ottoman. But I straightened them out. I told them those are nothing but lies, and no son of my father would abandon his God or fight against his faith. I offered to prove it with my sword, and they went quiet.

But brother, it's God's truth that you are the only one who can put an

*end to Constantinople's ordeal and save our country and maybe
even Christianity, should you choose to. All it takes is a sharp dagger
to his heart while he sleeps or a few drops of poison in his wine. You'd
be long gone by the time anyone reckons it was you, his lifelong
friend. The entire world would hail you as a hero.*

*I know he's more than a friend to you, but if you don't do it, he'll
destroy our country and our faith. Remember what Father told us:
we must stop at nothing to save our country. It's your duty to stop
him, because you're the only one who can.*

*That's all I have to say, my brother. I hope my words find their way
to your heart. Oh, how I'd do it if I could, but he'd never let me get
near him. But you can.*

*Your loving brother in blood and in Christ,
Vlad*

That letter will be etched in Radu's brain forever. When he read it, he thought Vlad was crazy. Not for a second did he consider killing Mehmed. He even came to help him, may God forgive him for this sin and the others. And now Constantinople fell. He lost Mehmed and has no place to go.

He could go to Albania and join Skanderbeg, like Stefan. Or maybe to Genoa or Venice. But after having being Mehmed's friend for all these years, they'll all think he's an Ottoman spy.

He screwed up his life. He abandoned Father's teachings to be with Mehmed, and look what good it did to him.

He sighs and heads west.

CHAPTER 108

MAY 31

li spent the night watching over Omar. Not like she had anywhere else to go anyhow. Their home must be destroyed, like every other home in sight. She'd like to look for Ion, but if she walks away from Omar, one of the Ottomans looking for loot would grab her, no questions asked. She's a young woman, the most valuable of slaves, worth her weight in silver. The beautiful ones are worth their weight in gold, but thank God, that's one problem she doesn't have.

She lies next to Omar and covers them both with her cloak. They sheltered inside one of the Grand Palace's many dilapidated rooms, wide open to the outside after the cannons broke the walls. They watch the stars and listen to the pillage.

"How old are you?" Omar asks.

"Eighteen, I think? I lost count. And you?"

"Twenty-eight. I've been with the janissaries for fifteen years. And all this time, I was sure I was going to make it someday. I was going to get rich. But then I got wounded, and it will be a miracle if I make it. Are you married? Children?"

"No, and no. You?"

"Are you kidding? No time for that while being in the sultan's service." He shivers, and Ali checks his forehead. He's burning, and that's the worst sign there is. You can stop the bleeding if you know what you're doing. You can realign broken bones and pour water down their throats and pray to God they'll make it, but if they get a fever, the end is near. Death smiles upon the burning wounded. They either make it or they don't, and Ali knows of no cure. But there's help, even though she ran out of willow tea.

"Here. Chew this," she says, giving him a piece of willow bark.

His teeth chatter enough to bite through that bark without trying, but it's so awful he spits it out. "What is this? It's disgusting."

"It will make you feel better. Please try! I promise it helps."

He takes it back and chews on it, his face sour with disgust.

"So, you have no kids?" Ali asks, to distract him.

"None that I know of. But who knows?"

"Where are you from? You're devşirme, are you not?"

"Of course. Isn't everybody?"

"How old were you when you were taken?"

"I was nine. The perfect age, they said. They didn't want anyone younger than eight — too much trouble. Nor older than fourteen — too set in their ways."

"Where did you come from?"

Omar chokes and spits out the leftover bark. "This is the evilest thing I ever tasted. I came from Albania. They welcomed me and they said we had some of the best fighters in the world. Have you ever heard about Skanderbeg?"

"Wasn't he a janissary who got to be a paşa, but abandoned the Ottoman Empire and went home to Albania to fight them?"

"Very much."

Omar's voice gets softer and his enunciation less crisp. His thoughts seem to wander as the fever clouds his mind. Once in a while, someone sticks their head in their room to look for loot, but they move on when they see a janissary.

Ali cools his forehead with what's left of her water and checks on the wound. No bleeding, so she loosens the tourniquet to let the blood flow heal it, and pours the rest of her water into his mouth.

But nothing helps. By the morning, Omar no longer makes sense. The wound festered, and he's dying. That's too bad. He looked like a good man, Ali thinks. She props him up to help him breathe better. She sees his dagger and kilij, and wonders if she could handle it if need be. She's never been fond of weapons, but that was then and this is now. A thought comes to her.

He'll die any moment. She may be heartbroken, but she's not yet ready to die. Still, she'd rather die than be taken captive.

She checks that no one's watching, then takes off her clothes. That was the easy part. Next, she undresses him. He's so heavy, she's drenched in sweat by the time she gets him out of his pants and into her dress. It's not a pretty one — she doesn't own pretty dresses — but it's thick and warm.

She can't close it all the way, but who cares? She pulls on his pants and tightens his belt around them, then plops his felt hat on her head, and there she is. A janissary, but for the red hair falling down her shoulders. She'd chop it off with the dagger, but she has no time to waste. The night's almost over, and nobody'll mistake her for a man in broad daylight. She's got to get moving, so she tucks her hair under her collar.

Omar is no longer talking. His eyes are closed, his cheeks burn with fever, and he mumbles words Ali can't understand.

It's now or never. She covers him with her cloak, grabs his weapons and leaves. To where? She doesn't know. Her mouth is parched and her hands shake, but she straightens herself to look bigger and walks like she knows where she's going.

Her pants keep sliding, and the kilij slaps her leg with every step, making her jump. Every scream sets her heart racing, and every wounded slows her down. She'd like to stop and help, but she can't. So she struts on, looking straight ahead, until she hears the screams.

They're two babies, a girl and a boy by the color of their clothes. Frozen with fear, their mother holds them tight as two Ottoman soldiers argue over them.

"I'll take the girl and her mom. You can have the boy."

"Are you crazy? That kid's worth nothing. He's not even three. It will take years until I can sell him to some old paşa."

"That's your problem, isn't it? I was here first. If I let you take anything, it's just out of courtesy."

"Funk your courtesy. I'll take the mother and the boy. You can take the girl. She should be ready before too long."

Their hands on their kilijes, the Ottomans shout at each other, too absorbed in their fight to notice anything else.

Ali walks by the mother and whispers to her. "Follow me. Right now."

The mother stares at her, her huge eyes full of tears. She glances at the Ottomans, then follows, holding her babies close.

Ali wonders where to hide them. The treasury, maybe? It was deep below the Grand Palace, to her left. She glances back to check that the woman is coming. She's falling behind, so Ali stops to wait.

"Give me one. We'll move faster."

The woman hands her the girl and follows her through the broken doors, down worn stairs and along dark corridors nobody knows. But they don't make it far.

"Stop. Who are you?" a janissary asks, coming out of nowhere.

"I'm Omar. And they are mine," Ali says.

The man's eyes narrow. He's suspicious, and for good reason. The woman isn't roped; she follows her freely. And Ali carries a baby. No janissary would do that, and Ali curses her lack of thinking.

"Yours? I don't think so. They're mine now."

He pulls out his kilij, and Ali wishes she had paid more attention to her weapons classes in Kronstadt many years ago.

"Just go," the man says. "There's plenty more where these came from. Leave them to me."

Ali wishes she could, but she can't. She pulls out the kilij. Just holding it feels awkward, and she knows she can't win. Wishing she wasn't so useless, she falls into a fighting position when she realizes she has a sleeping baby in her arms.

"Let me put her down. There's no point in damaging her."

The janissary laughs and lowers his blade while Ali hands the baby to her mother.

"I'll keep him here as long as I can. Take the babies and run," she whispers.

The mother looks into Ali's eyes, and a connection sparks between them. Ali grabs her kilij and turns to the man. She should pray, but she forgot the words. She sighs, getting ready to die, but the janissary bursts with laughter.

"Really! What do have we here? Janissary, my ass! You're a girl!" He comes closer and lifts a hand to touch her. Ali steps back.

The man steps forward, but Ali is ready. She lunges and sinks her kilij into his chest.

The man screams, his eyes wide with surprise. He lifts his blade to the sky then falls it over her, but Ali jumps to the side and the kilij strikes the stone wall instead.

The janissary shouts a curse and lifts his blade once more. Ali leaps back, and he misses again. He screams with rage, aiming his blade at Ali's heart. She jumps aside, but her foot slides and she falls to the ground.

Towering over her like a mountain of fury, he aims his blade to her heart.

It's over. Still better than being a slave, Ali thinks, watching the enraged face come near. He's ready to plunge his sword into her when something hits him in the head. He turns around.

It's the woman. Instead of running, like Ali told her, she put down her babies and threw a rock at the man. She throws another and hits his jaw. He screams and lunges forward. The curved blade sinks into the woman, and she falls like a rag doll.

He pulls the blade out and turns to Ali, who's back on her feet, her sword ready. He lifts his blade, dripping with the woman's blood, to sink it into her. But instead of stepping back, Ali lunges forward and drives her blade into him to the hilt.

His eyes widen, and he cries a blood-curling scream. A fountain of blood spurts out of his mouth as he crumbles at her feet.

CHAPTER 109

SLAVE, AGAIN

Ali drops her kilij and kneels by the woman. Her glazed eyes and ghost-white face tell Ali she doesn't have much left, but her babies don't know it as they crawl over her. The girl nests in her left arm, and the boy in her right, and they pull on her and touch her and speak to her in their baby talk as the woman lies dying. She glances from one to the other, too weak to lift her head and kiss them, then her burning eyes turn to Ali. "Take care of them. They're Leo and Bea. They're one year old."

Ali's eyes burn with tears. "I'll do my best."

She checks on the janissary. He's dead, thank God. She grabs his hat and puts it on, then checks his bag for something useful. Some food would help, but there's none. A bag with gold and coins hangs around his neck, and Ali slips it around hers.

With her teeth, she rips his tunic into two long swaths she ties around her neck to hold the babies. They're heavy, so she can't go far. But where on earth can she go?

There's nowhere to hide, since the city swarms with Ottomans looking for loot. She has no food to soothe two hungry babies, and they won't stay quiet for long. One way or another, she needs to find them food and shelter.

She kneels by the woman, whose frozen eyes look at another world. With trembling fingers, she closes her eyelids and makes the sign of the cross over her, then tries to say the Lords' prayer, but can't remember the words. "Forgive us Father, since we have sinned, and take us into your loving arms to give us peace and succor."

She's pretty sure this is not how it goes, but that's the best she's got. She picks up the boy and puts him in the swath around her neck, then tries to lift the girl, but she won't let go of her mother. She screams like a banshee and holds on to her neck.

A golden chain with a cross hangs around the woman's neck. Ali takes it off the woman and puts it on. The baby lets go of her mother and clings to Ali like a limpet.

Ali struggles to stand. The kids are heavy, and they squirm and scream and pull on her clothes and her hair. She can't go far with them, and she wonders about leaving them here to get them some food. But what if she doesn't make it back? If nobody finds them, they'll die of thirst and hunger. No can do.

She breathes hard as she climbs the steep stairs. The babies grow heavier with each step, and she leans against the wall to rest for a moment before stepping into the street.

It's still dark. Mehmed's soldiers are still roaming, but they're fewer, and they're all burdened with loot. This night was the last, so they've got to be worried about stashing away their catch before dawn rather than going after her.

Ali steps out like she belongs. She takes the street towards the port. With a bit of luck, she may find a fisherman to take them to Galata, and from there, they may find a ship to sail out. She's got enough gold to pay a fisherman, but any of the Ottomans would take her, her gold, and the kids, so she has to be careful.

She shuffles and struggles, since carrying two squirming kids sapped what was left of her strength. But the port is in sight, and she sighs with relief. Almost there.

A dark Ottoman, his face full of glee, cuts her way. "Look at that. Who do we have here? What's your name, girl?"

Ali holds a baby in each arm. She can't even reach her kilij, let alone use it. "Ali," she says.

The man laughs. "Of course. And mine is Sophia. What's your name?"

Ali looks for a way out, but there's none. The babies' mother died for nothing.

"I'm Ali."

CHAPTER 110
THE DUST OF DREAMS.

The three days of looting are finally over, and Mehmed can't wait anymore. He hasn't been so giddy with excitement since he was three and got his first horse. With a wide smile on his face, he mounts Rüzgar and heads into Constantinople. His city.

The second day, when he heard Constantine had disappeared, Mehmed promised a huge reward to whoever found him, dead or alive. He couldn't let Constantine flee to the west and return with an army. He couldn't even allow the rumor that he escaped. That would give the Romans hope, subvert their submission, and threaten his city's future.

Fortunately, they found his mangled remains in the massive pile of bodies near St. Romanus' gate. Constantine's body was so damaged they only recognized him by his purple shoes. Still, they cut off his head and stuck it on a lance on the Augusteum to prove to every Roman that Emperor Constantine was no more. The next day, Mehmed packed it in a precious coffer and sent it to Anatolia, so every Muslim ruler would have proof of his victory.

Jubilant, Mehmed spurs Rüzgar into his city, but his joy is short-lived. Constantinople looks nothing like the city of his dreams. The beauty, the richness, and the splendor are gone, and all that's left of the golden city is a pile of rubble. The Roman roads that lasted for a thousand years didn't make it through the pummeling of the cannons. The Imperial Palace is a ruin, and the buildings are just piles of rubble. The Roman monuments, the charming gardens, the singing fountains — all gone. Hard to believe that this is all that's left from the cradle of a thousand years of civilization.

Mehmed shudders with fury. His Constantinople, the golden city he lusted for, is gone, and this dreadful wasteland is what's left. His fists tighten, and his blood boils with anger.

He takes a deep breath to calm down as he rides towards Hagia Sophia, the Orthodox cathedral he will turn into his greatest mosque. The old church wears the name of his favorite wife. She's now Gülbahar, but she was christened after the Greek goddess of wisdom. That's why he'll let the church keep her name, even though no Christian God will ever be worshipped here again. There is no other God than Allah, and Mehmed's mosque will call the faithful to worship Allah for centuries to come.

He passes by ruin after ruin, all empty. His men took everything of value, so there's nothing left but rubble, dead bodies, swollen and stinking after days in the sun, and a few wounded waiting for God to relieve their suffering. His horse steps over broken weapons, damaged armor and scattered tools that nobody will ever use again, and Mehmed's heart is torn between pride and rage at seeing what's left of his city.

He dismounts in front of Hagia Sophia. The old church is still standing. It withstood the attacks better than most other buildings, and from the street, it seems almost unharmed.

But inside, it's another story. The saints' broken statues lie scattered on the marble floors. The gold and silver vessels are all gone. The precious altar cloth is torn and dirty after the soldiers cleaned their boots with it. A janissary hat covers the carved crucifix, and the altars are upside down to feed Mehmed's men's horses.

The sultan studies the painted saints covering the walls. Their auras glow with gold, and their azure and purple robes steal the light.

Mehmed recognizes a few: the Virgin Mary, her teary eyes glued to her baby; an emaciated Jesus dragging a heavy cross; countless others, frozen in time. Their sad eyes remind Mehmed how much Christians love their icons. They look at them for inspiration, faith, and courage.

But that's not the Muslim way. Human figures distract the faithful from contemplating Allah's will. He lives in their hearts, so they only need to look inside to worship Him. The icons will have to go, Mehmed thinks, and bows deeply to the God in his heart.

"There is no God but Allah and Mohammed is His Prophet," he says.

And, just like that, the Orthodox Cathedral becomes a Muslim Mosque. The muezzin calls to summon the faithful to the afternoon prayer.

Mehmed climbs on the altar and performs his devotions for everyone to see and follow, then turns to Zaganos Paşa. "Get me the megas doux."

Loukas Notaras and his family got caught as they tried to flee. Four guards bring in Notaras and his sons, and they bow deeply.

Mehmed studies them with thoughtful eyes. "Megas doux, let's make something clear. You are responsible for all this destruction, not me. Had you advised your emperor to surrender instead of fighting this hopeless war like a fool, Constantinople would still be alive. And so would be many thousands of my men."

Notaras falls to his knees and touches his forehead to the floor. His two sons follow. "My sultan, I did all I could to stop the war. Everything. I advised the emperor to surrender not once, not twice, but every single day; I held off giving cannons to Giustiniani for as long as I could. I depleted the treasury to prevent Constantine from buying weapons. My sultan, you have no more faithful subject than me. And my sons."

Mehmed glances from him to his sons, and the youngest catches his eye. He's a pretty boy with skin as good as a girl's and smoldering eyes.

"What's your name?"

"Jacob, my sultan."

"How old are you?"

"He's fourteen, my sultan," his father answers.

"Good-looking boy. Tell me, Notaras, how come your emperor didn't listen to you?"

"We... someone on your side said you might still change your mind. And..."

"Was that your old friend Çandarlı Paşa?"

Notaras blanches, sickened by fear, and that's all the answer Mehmed needed. "Don't worry, megas doux. If everything you told me is true, and if you serve me faithfully, like you promised, there's no need to worry. I hope to see you and your sons soon."

He dismisses them with a flick of his hand.

"Get me the grand vizier."

Mehmed's dusty boots clatter on the marble floor as he checks his new mosque. He wonders at the glowing mosaics, just as beautiful today as they were five hundred years ago, before the Ottoman Empire was even born. These walls are older than Mehmed's dynasty, and they're stunning, even though the stained-glass windows's light makes them look like they're bleeding.

It's a shame to destroy them, Mehmed thinks. All that work, and the beauty. What if he had them plastered over to hide them? Who knows? Maybe in five hundred years someone will uncover them for the world to see. The wheel of time never stops turning; those who are up will go down, while the others come up. He remembers an old Persian poem.

"The spider is the gatekeeper in the halls of Khosrau's dome; the owl plays martial music in the palace of Afrasiyab," Mehmed whispers, just as the guards bring in the grand vizier.

Çandarlı Paşa's face is ashen, and his eyes are wide with fear. Mehmed smiles. He's never been happier to see him.

"How good it does my heart to see you, teacher. I've waited years for this moment, when our minds would finally meet. Remember how you taught me to be patient, and had me punished so I won't forget? Well, teacher, rejoice. I did not forget."

Çandarlı Paşa's eyes narrow. He worried about what was coming. Now he knows.

"I had a chat with your old friend Notaras. He told me I can thank you for giving confidence to Constantine to prolong this war beyond all reason, and killing his city and thousands of my soldiers. All thanks to you."

Çandarlı Paşa's steel eyes meet his. "I did my best for the empire. Always. I never wavered and never held back."

"Sure. But which empire? The Roman?"

Blood heats the grand vizier's cheeks. "The Ottoman Empire. I did my best to keep it whole and safe from those who tried to destroy it. You included."

"Well, Candarli Pasa, you managed better than you expected. Now I hold Constantinople, like the old Hadith says: '*Verily, you shall conquer Constantinople. What a wonderful leader will her leader be, and what a wonderful army will that army be!*' It doesn't mention you, grand vizier. The Prophet knew, like I do now, that you'd betray me. You conspired with the filthy Greeks behind my back and tried to stop me, but that's over now. You'll have time to think about your treason and about the things you should have learned from me, while I learned so much from you. And about you." Mehmed turns to Zaganos Paşa. "Take him."

.

CHAPTER III

KARMA

As he sits at the emperor's table, drinking Constantine's best wine from his silver filigreed cup and watching his servants bring platter after platter of deliciousness cooked by the imperial chef, Mehmed should be dizzy with the taste of victory. He finally conquered Constantinople, the city he coveted his whole life. He turned Christianity's holiest church into his mosque. And he got rid of Candarli Pasha, his oldest foe, who awaits his ugly death in some dark dungeon, sweating with fear of what's coming.

Taking Constantinople, his lifelong goal, was neither easy nor cheap. It cost him more money than he can count, and thousands and thousands of lives. But he did it. He did what twenty-three generals before him failed to do, Father included, so he deserves to feel triumphant.

But he doesn't. He feels cheated of the glory, pride, and glory he rightfully deserves. And so alone.

Father is dead. He didn't live to see the son he removed from the throne as unworthy, conquer the city nobody else could.

Mother didn't live to see it, either. Oh, how she would have loved

459

it! She'd have been as proud of his city as she'd been of his son. Maybe more. Because one can have plenty of sons, but there's only one Constantinople. But Mother is gone.

Radu, his best friend and soul mate, is gone. He stormed out in a rage and abandoned him, forsaking his love and friendship, and left Mehmed hollow and lonely.

He drains his cup and asks for more, then glances at the silver platters on the table. There's food for a dozen, but Mehmed isn't hungry for food. He's hungry for companionship, praise, and love. He has nobody to share his victory with, nobody to hold him and love him, and his heart aches with longing.

"Kizlar aga!"

The chief black eunuch appears like a summoned genie.

"Bring me Jacob Notaras."

He sits and drinks cup after cup as he waits for the boy, but the kizlar aga returns alone.

"I'm sorry, my sultan. 'Over my dead body,' Loukas Notaras said. He'd rather lose his head than have his son dishonored. What do you want me to do?"

Mehmed nods. "Fulfill his wish. Bring him first. Then the boy."

A candle later, Loukas Notaras, his elder son and his son-in-law fall to their knees, dropping a heavy bag at Mehmed's feet.

"Mercy, my sultan," Notaras chokes. "This is all I have. My gold, my wife's jewels and my daughter's dowry. All yours. We're your most faithful servants. I beg you to spare our lives."

Mehmed opens the bag. He glances inside and spits to the side. "I can't believe this. You filthy dog! You had all this wealth, and you kept it to yourself instead of supporting your emperor, your homeland, and your brothers in faith? And now you're trying to bribe me to escape the fate you richly deserve. I hope Constantine sees you from his Orthodox heaven. Enemy or not, he was a great man, and he deserved better servants than a slimy snake like you." He turns to kizlar aga. "Take their heads and bring me the boy."

That night, and every night after that, Jacob Notaras warmed Mehmed's bed. And as he held the boy, Mehmed thought of the days, long ago, when he held Radu. He didn't cry, since sultans don't cry. Sultans get revenge.

CHAPTER 112

SOARING

Trapped inside a rainbow of colors twisting faster and faster, sucking him in, Ion struggles to grab on to something to stop. But there's no stopping this vortex that swallowed him whole. His stomach twists and leaps, and he gets dizzy. He tries to take a deep breath, but he can't. He opens his eyes. Nothing but darkness.

"Is this big enough?" someone asks.

"Not even close. Get moving, you lazy Greeks. We don't have all day. This whole damned city is choked with dead bodies that need burying before they fester."

"Why don't you grab a shovel, then?" the first man asks, but the crack of a whip cuts him off.

"Shut up and dig."

For a while, there's nothing but the harsh sound of shovels cutting through dirt. Ion tries to sit up, but can't. Something heavy keeps him down, pinning his arms to his sides and crushing him. Whatever it is, it's so heavy it's hard to breathe and impossible to move, other than wiggling his fingers.

Where the heck am I?

"There now. That should be big enough for this pile. Throw them in," the whip-man says.

A shuffle of steps, then the sound of something getting dragged, then a *plop*. The same, again and again, until the weight crushing Ion down seems to lighten. Even better, he can see. Not that he likes it. He's lying in a pile of corpses that a couple of gravediggers buried in a massive grave.

They grab the body next to him by his arms and legs and shuffle to the edge of the grave, drop him in and return for the next. A woman this time, by the long hair covering her face. They drop her in and come back for another.

Ion's heart quickens. They're about to bury him alive. For a second, he wonders if he's really alive, but he's got to be. He sees the sky, and Hagia Sophia's shining dome in the distance. He hears the seagulls' mournful cries and smells the salt in the warm breeze, though nothing can cover the stench of death imbuing his clothes and his soul. He's alive, all right. This isn't heaven, and it's not hot enough to be hell.

Should he tell them he's not dead?

He glances at the janissary with the whip. He may not kill him, but he'll take him captive and have him dig graves with the others, and Ion has no time for that. He has to find Ana, alive or dead.

They drag the last man off his chest. He's next. It's time to do or die, and Smaranda's words, spoken years ago, ring inside his mind: "You, Ion, have this magic power inside you. You've been wise not to use it. But someday, when something will matter to you more than your oath, more than your secret, and even more than your life, it will still be there. When that time comes, you'll be glad you're a *zmeu*."

That time has come. Ion takes a deep breath and unchains his rage. He's kept it locked in a corner of his mind for years, ever since he killed his father, the *zmeu*. Torn by terrible guilt, he swore to never, ever, let himself go again.

And he didn't. Through all his time in Kronstadt, when the Saxons treated him like dirt, then through his slavery in Edirne, and even here, in Constantinople, with that venomous snake Notaras, he kept himself in check. Because he knew that losing control meant breaking his oath and killing.

But if there ever was a time to let it rip, it's now.

A wave of rage courses through his veins like Greek Fire. His heart swells as it fills with the fiery blood of the dragon. His breath torches the inside of his chest, and a whiff of smoke escapes his mouth as the tremendous power inside him grows too big to hold in.

The gravediggers grab his arms to drag him to the grave with the others, but they scream and let go as soon as they touch him to stare at their blistered hands. The whip cracks, but they come no closer. They're more frightened of Ion than the whip.

The janissary turns to him, and his eyes widen in horror. He lifts the whip to lash him, but Ion's breath sets it on fire.

He jumps to his feet and somersaults. The magic power spreads throughout his body, from the top of his head to the tip of his toes. His skin blisters and chars, thickening into a cast-iron scaly crust. The fire coursing through his veins melts his bones, lengthening them, and pulls him into a shape that's not human. A long spiky tail thicker than a tree trunk sprouts out of his backside, twitching like an angry cat's.

His nails burn to black and harden into dagger-like claws, and his hair burns off into charred spikes. His eyes blur, and the world around him disappears. Nothing's left but the green flame that consumes him. His lungs fill with fire, swell and burst, splitting his chest. His shoulder blades slip out and melt into dark wings that take a life of their own. Ion's world smells like smoke and destruction.

He's no longer human, and he's petrified. He opens his mouth to shout his fear, but no word comes out. Just a terrible roar, and a river of flames scorching everything in sight.

What the heck did I do? And what do I do now?

His wings flap. His long lizard's body is so massive they couldn't possibly lift him up, but they do. They're spiked and leathery, much like a bat's, and stretch for twenty feet on each side. They harness the wind and lift him up like he's a feather. One more flap, two, three, and he's so high the men on the ground look like children's toys.

A cluster of fluffy clouds rush to meet him, and Ion plunges into them like he used to plunge in fresh snow as a child. The white steam tickles his nose and he sneezes, bursting out a crop of flames. The clouds melt into rain, and he laughs.

He flies above the clouds, diving deeper and deeper into the blue sky hugging him, and soaks the sun's golden heat that gives him strength. Every heartbeat sends more power into his body, and every beat of his wings brings him closer to the sun. Could I reach it, he wonders? But he notices the view and forgets. Far below, the deep-blue Sea of Marmara, looking like a beaver on the run, sparkles like it's studded with diamonds. The long, slim ribbon of the Bosporus ties it to the dark Black Sea, shaped like a camel's hump. And, right below, Hagia Sofia's golden dome mirrors the sun.

Ion never thought flying could be so much fun. He plunges to the ground until he's ready to crash into the dirt, then sweeps up, twisting and twirling. He chases his twenty-foot-long tail like a kitten, and scratches his chin on the long spike at its end. He turns on his back and loops, faster and faster, until the sky and the sea blend into one. Oh, how much fun this is!

Then he remembers he has no time to play. He must find Ana.

CHAPTER 113
THE FATE OF LOSERS

The merciless sun burned the grass into hay and baked the dirt into a packed crust that splinters to dust under the hooves and the feet. The saddest caravan there ever was has left Constantinople two days ago, heading west. They're the Ottomans' prisoners on their way to Edirne. There, the lucky ones will get ransomed, and the unlucky ones sold — if they make it that far.

The men died in battle, so most prisoners are women and children. Their faces are ashen, their clothes torn, and their hearts hopeless. They lost their city, their home, and their freedom, and many lost everyone they held dear.

They're not all Byzantine. Some are Burgunds, Jews, and even a few Genoese and Venetians, who missed the last ships sailing to safety. But they will get ransomed and go home. Unlike Constantinople's citizens, who no longer have homes or kin. Their life as free folk is over.

It's been years, but Ali didn't forget the slave market. She and her friends stood naked for the customers to measure and bid on. But then, she only had herself to worry about. Now she has Bea and Leo, and truth be told, the twins are more than she can handle.

They're heavy and squirmy. Even worse, they're so hungry they haven't stopped crying for two days. Ali tried everything — she rocked them, sang to them, gave them water — but nothing helped. They needed milk.

"Go ahead and feed them," the guard said, when they stopped for the night.

"I... have nothing," Ali said.

The guard frowned and stared at her bosom. "How come?"

"I... ran dry," Ali lied. What else was she to say? *They're not mine; they belong to some woman that I killed a janissary for?*

The guard scratched his head and talked to the others. They shrugged.

"Does anybody have some milk for these babies?" they asked. But nobody did. And if they did, they kept it for their own. That's why, two days later, Ali and the babies got to the end of their rope.

The kids are pale and drawn and hoarse with crying, and Ali is about to lose her mind. She goes to the guard. "They need milk. They'll die if they don't get it."

The Ottoman rolls his eyes. "What do you want me to do? Make it out of thin air?"

Ali points at a tiny house off the road. "Maybe they have a cow? Or a goat?"

The guard sighs. "OK. Let's go."

The old farmer measures them with worried eyes. The last thing he needs is a janissary on his doorstep. But he has a cow, and thank God, he has milk.

Their bellies finally full, the babies fall asleep. Ali picks them up and heads to the door. The farmer turns to the guard. "Listen," he says, "how much do you want for the boy?"

Ali's heart freezes.

The guard's shrewd eyes narrow. "Who wants to know?"

"I do. My wife and I lost three boys in their first year of life. She hasn't been heavy with child ever since, and we're growing old. We need someone to help around the farm and look after us in our old age. That boy looks healthy and strong. I don't have much to give you, but it will be more than you'll get if he dies on the road. You've got weeks to go to Edirne, and nothing to feed them. Why don't you leave him here? Nobody will know, and I'll give you a silver ducat."

"One ducat? Are you crazy? For a handsome, healthy boy like this? No way. I need at least five."

The farmer sighs. "One ducat. That's all I've got. Remember, he'll be worth nothing if he's dead."

The guard softens. "You know what? I really like you, my man. And this handsome kid deserves to go to a good home that will treat him like their own son. I'll take two."

The man shakes his head. "I really can't. I have to buy seed and fix the roof before the winter. I can't…"

"You know what? I'll make you an offer you can't refuse. Give me two ducats and I'll throw in the girl. Just look at that blonde hair and blue eyes! She'll grow up a beauty! In ten years, you can sell her or marry her yourself to make you more sons. In the meantime, she'll help around the house, and keep the boy company. What do you say?"

The farmer scratches his head and looks at the girl. "OK."

He puts two coins in the guard's hand, and the man slips them inside his sleeve.

"Good luck, my man." He turns to Ali and reaches for the babies. "Put them down and let's go."

CHAPTER 114

GOING HOME

Ali clutches the kids to her chest.

"Go where?"

"Where? Where do you think? Back to the caravan. Get moving."

"But the babies..."

"The babies stay here. You should be grateful to this good man for taking them. He'll look after them like they're his own, instead of some filthy paşa using them for things you don't want to think about. Get moving now."

Ali glares. "I'm not going anywhere without my babies."

"They're no longer your babies, they're his. Now, for the last time, get moving."

"No."

The first slap snaps her head to the side. The second one throws her to the ground.

The guard reaps the screaming kids from her arms and hands them to the farmer.

"Get up and get moving, woman."

Ali shakes her head.

The guard grabs her hair and drags her out the door. He lifts the lash. "Walk, I said."

Ali doesn't.

The first lash twists around her back like a venomous snake, sending a wave of pain throughout her body. The second catches her belly, and the third curls around her throat.

The guard grabs her hair and drags her towards the caravan. The other janissaries see him struggling and head back to help.

His twisted face dark with anger, the Ottoman shouts: "Get moving, woman, or, as Allah is my witness, I'll kill you right here and now. I don't care how much you're worth. You're not worth squat to me if you don't behave. Move."

Ali hears the truth in his words. He'll kill her here and now if she doesn't get moving. And there's nothing she can do but die. And that won't help the babies.

But she's so tired. Tired of losing those she loves, from Father to Giustiniani. And now these babies she promised to protect with her life. She's tired of being alone. And she's so tired of fighting. Maybe dying isn't that bad. She might go to Heaven and find Father. But most likely not.

But if she goes to Hell, like she deserves for her sins, she's pretty sure she'll find Giustiniani. He wasn't Heaven material either. Unless Catholics have their own Hell where they don't mix with the Orthodox, they're bound to roast over hot coals together.

The thought makes her smile. She curls with her knees to her chest, waiting for the janissary to butcher her.

But he's not looking at her; he's staring at the sky. His eyes grow wide, and his face blanches with fear. He screams something she doesn't understand and grabs his bow.

Ali looks up. The endless blue sky has two suns.

A golden form flies towards them like the wind. Its scales mirror the sun, and its wings shadow the earth. Whatever it is, it's enormous, fast, and frightening. Heartbeats later, it's right above them, lazily flapping his leathery wings and blowing black smoke through his nose. That's when it dawns on her.

It's a *zmeu*! a Romanian dragon, Ali thinks, staring at him in wonder. She's never seen one, but she knows about them from Father's bedtime stories. "A *zmeu* is so powerful, my dear, that nothing can stand in its way. Other than Prince Charming, of course, who always ends up with the girl," Father said, glancing at Mother. "Serves him right."

"Are they bad?" Ana had asked.

"Some are good, and some bad, like everyone else. But people like to think they are bad, just because they're different."

The *zmeu* opens his massive spiked muzzle, which is red-hot inside. A roar shakes the earth, and a river of flames erupts from his throat, scorching everything in sight.

The janissary lifts his bow and aims, but before he lets the arrow go, the flames engulf him and torch him alive. He screams in agony, but seconds later, he's nothing but ash.

The scorching heats Ali's cheeks. Her hands shake, and her heart pummels, struggling to break out of her chest. She knows she should be terrified, but she's not, even when the *zmeu* roars again and spews another wave of fire to the janissaries shooting their arquebuses at him.

The zmeu folds his wings and lands by Ali's side. His spiky head turns to her, his amber eyes smile, and his heart speaks straight into hers.

Come on, Ana. Let's go.

"Ion? Is that you?"

Who else?

And just like that, it all makes sense. Why he was always hot to the touch. Why he healed so quickly. The secret she felt in his heart, but could never read.

"I thought I'd lost you."

She struggles to her feet and stumbles towards him. He crouches to the ground, inviting her to mount him, but he's as big as a barn, and his hot scales are slippery and hard as rocks. No way can she climb on his back without breaking her neck.

He curls his thick long tail at her feet. She mounts it and holds on for dear life as he lifts and drops her on his neck. She settles and grabs on to the six-foot spikes on his shoulders.

Are you ready?

"I am."

Let's go then.

An arrow whizzes past Ali's ear, missing her by inches. Another strikes a golden scale by her thigh and slides to the ground.

The *zmeu* rears, roars, and stretches his wings. Heartbeats later, he rides the wind, high above the scorched plains, leaving the caravan behind them. From up there, the green trees, the brown fields, and the blue rivers look like they're painted on a parchment map, and Ali smiles. She always loved maps.

"Where are we going?" she asks.

"We're going home."

THE END

To find out what happened to Vlad, Radu, Mehmed, and our other heroes, read **Wrath of the Impaler**, Book 4 in The Curse of the Dracula Brothers series.

To learn more about the Draculas' history, read **Throne of Thorns**, the series' prequel.

AFTERWORD

Thank you for reading Song of Swords. If you enjoyed it, please take a minute to **leave a review** and tell a friend. That will help other readers like you discover this book, and I'd really appreciate it.

To find out what happened to Vlad, Radu, Mehmed, and our other heroes, read **Wrath of the Impaler**, Book 4 in **The Curse of the Dracula Brothers series**.

You may also enjoy **Throne of Thorns**, the prequel novella of the series.

RR Jones

ABOUT THIS BOOK

This entire series only exists because of George R.R. Martin's Game of Thrones. Reading it made me itch to write my own GOT, set in my birthplace, Romania, whose history is just as gripping and wild.

But I wasn't ready to write a whole saga spanning countries, decades, and dozens of characters, so I started writing what I knew: the ER. I wrote **OVERDOSE, A Medical Thriller,** as Rada Jones MD. That turned into a whole series and inspired another: **K-9 Heroes** featuring a cast of heroic bomb dogs in the Afghan war. They're quite a roller-coaster, but they all end well.

When the urge to write my Romanian GOT returned, I started the Curse of the Dracula Brothers series.

Radu, Vlad, Ștefan, and Mehmed are real historical figures you can find in history books. So are the sites. I read about them, researched them on line, and went to most of them to do them justice. I smelled Constantinople's flowers, ate the Transylvanian food, and drank the Wallachian wine. I even partook of the hammam and petted the cats. Somebody had to, after all.

The magical characters are drawn from the Romanian folklore. The *zmeu* - the Romanian version of a dragon, the *vârcolac* - werewolf - and *Baba Cloanța* live in our legends. And they may still roam Transylvania's dark forests to this day.

ABOUT THE AUTHOR

RR Jones was born in Transylvania, ten miles from Dracula's Castle. Growing up between communists and vampires taught her that humans are fickle, but you can always trust dogs and books. That's why she read every book she could get, including the phone book (too many characters, not enough action), and adopted every stray she found, from dogs to frogs.

After joining her American husband, she spent years studying medicine and working in the ER, but she still speaks like Dracula's cousin.

RR Jones, her husband, and their dog Guinness live in a tiny cabin in the woods whenever they aren't traveling to faraway places. She spends her days writing, hiking, and day-dreaming about her imaginary friends.

facebook.com/RRJonesBooks

instagram.com/RadaJonesMD

bookbub.com/profile/rada-jones